TALES FROM THE LYON'S DEN

STORIES FROM THE
FOUR HORSEMEN UNIVERSE

Edited by
Chris Kennedy and Mark Wandrey

D1596296

Seventh Seal Press
Virginia Beach, VA

Chris Kennedy/Seventh Seal Press
2052 Bierce Dr., Virginia Beach, VA 23454
http://chriskennedypublishing.com/

Publisher's Note: This is a work of fiction. Names, characters, places, and incidents are a product of the author's imagination. Locales and public names are sometimes used for atmospheric purposes. Any resemblance to actual people, living or dead, or to businesses, companies, events, institutions, or locales is completely coincidental.

Tales from the Lyon's Den/Chris Kennedy. -- 1st ed.
ISBN 978-1948485623

This book is dedicated to all the men and women who have given their lives defending our freedom. This book is for you.

Preface by Chris Kennedy

This book was born in a different place than the rest of the Four Horsemen Universe—this one was born in the Facebook 4HU Merc Guild (https://www.facebook.com/groups/536506813392912/). It's a group for fans of the 4HU (come take a look, if you'd like). It had been about six months since the last anthology, and a number of authors wanted to know when the next anthology was coming out, *because they wanted to write a story in the 4HU, too!*

And that's the thing with the 4HU—the bigger it grows, the more people want in. I think this is for two reasons. First, it's just darn fun. Who doesn't like squashing bugs in a giant mecha or becoming the preeminent assassin in the galaxy? I do, or I wouldn't write it. Second—and more importantly—the universe is big enough for everyone. With hundreds—even thousands—of races, you can introduce just about anything you can dream up (even dinosaurs!), but with only 37 merc races (38 if the war ever ends, and the Humans can get the SalSha certified), everyone is grounded in the same battlespace. It's big enough for everyone...yet small enough for readers to appreciate new stories that are just darn good.

And that's what Mark and I have tried to bring you with this book, and the one which will follow it ("Luck is Not a Factor.") Darn good stories. Just like the first trilogy of anthologies, we have an all-star cast of authors, plus a number of authors you haven't heard of...yet. When we said we wanted to do another anthology, the response was overwhelming. I only wanted one volume, but was forced to do two to get all of the great stories in...and both of them will *still* be over 150,000 words. Because we had that many stories that were just that darn good.

Like its predecessors, "Tales from the Lyon's Den" takes on various aspects of the universe, giving you additional insight into a galaxy where people will do almost anything for a fistful of credits. Not everyone wants to kill aliens, and, in a galaxy this big, you don't have to—there are numerous ways to make a few credits. Nigel Shirazi, however, would disagree. It's fun and profitable—all at once—to kill aliens and get paid. We've got some stories of that for you, too.

So strap into your CASPer or buckle on your armor, and let's go make some credits, shall we?

Chris Kennedy
Virginia Beach, VA

Contents

* * * * *

The Devil in the Pit
by Mark Wandrey

Part 1

"This is a merc pit, get out!"

Jim Cartwright didn't know what race he was speaking to, only that he needed to get inside before the bidding stopped. Looking like a furry, upright turtle, the alien wasn't half Jim's height, but it acted like it was twice as tall as the Human.

"I'm a merc," Jim said, the pendant he wore around his neck translating his speech into Veetanho. He'd taken to using that language because no one outside of Karma station had the script for English programmed into their translators.

"Excrement," was the simple reply. The alien put its little arms against the side of its shell and stared at Jim with its beady black-on-black eyes.

Jim was used to this. Just two years after the first mercs ventured out from Earth, less than 20 merc companies were working contracts, mostly around their home planet. When he left two months earlier on the 3rd contract Cartwright's Cavaliers had accepted, rumor had it colonization efforts were beginning on a couple of planets. He looked forward to maybe seeing one of them in the future.

He had developed a way of dealing with characters like this turtle thing. Jim handed it a computer chip. The alien took the chip, eyes narrowing as it examined the logo of the Galactic Mercenary Guild on one side. Power, Service, Profit was written in a triangle, and the design included a sword, a laser rifle, and a red diamond. Jim thought he'd like to get his hands on some of those red diamonds. Next to F11, the ultra-rare isotope of fluorine which made fusion power possible, red diamonds were the most valuable resource in the galaxy.

Taking a small slate, a thin, mostly plastic computer that was common in the Union, from a pouch glued to its shell, the alien inserted the chip and read the information. "Human," it said with some difficulty. "A new merc race?" Its eyes grew wide in amazement. "There have been no new merc races in my lifetime or my grandsire's lifetime!"

"Well," Jim said and spread his arms wide, "feast your eyes on the next big thing." The alien's eyes narrowed. It pulled the chip from its slate and shoved it at Jim as though it were a sword.

"Here you go, big thing. Good luck inside." Jim took the chip and moved around the alien and into the merc pit.

The first time he negotiated a contract, the merc guild came to him. One hundred Human merc companies took contracts of all kinds throughout the galaxy. Only four of those companies came home. His Cartwright's Cavaliers, recently formed from the small civilian military contracting firm he used to run, was one of those. They were a diverse bunch, but they'd managed to agree to work together for PR purposes. The four companies were instantly multi-billionaires, and they labeled themselves "The Four Horsemen."

The second and third time, Jim travelled with his company to the Karma system and Peepo's Pit to find contracts. After completing the second contract, he had enough money to buy an old, small cruiser he had converted to serve their purposes. The ship had given them the mobility and versatility they needed to take the contract they'd just completed. Mobility was a two-edged sword. They were a long, long way from home.

Chromo's Merc Pit was located in the system of T'Viendre, the second world in the system. Jim's copy of the GalNet, the Union's version of the *Encyclopedia Galactica*, didn't say much about the world except that it was frequented by mercs. It was in the Jesc arm of the galaxy. Jesc was composed of the two arms trailward of Earth's Tolo arm. Each arm was divided into three primary regions: close to the core, the center, and the extreme outer rim. T'Viendre Two was in the Crapti region, in the outer rim of Jesc, somewhere around 30,000 light years from Earth.

"It's no surprise they don't know what a Human is," Jim said as he looked around. Peepo's Pit reminded him of an OTB, or an off-track betting parlor, back on Earth. There were places to eat and drink along with numerous kiosks where you could place bets. In a pit, the kiosks displayed available, underway, and completed contracts. This pit had a harder, grittier edge to it. None of the information displayed was in English, so he took out his slate, aimed one of its cameras at a kiosk, and activated the built in translator.

The screen displayed lots of alien contracts on alien worlds. He smiled when he saw Cartwright's Cavaliers scroll by with the notation that the last contract was satisfactorily completed. Three contracts, three successes. And the other horsemen were doing as well or better. He wondered about the companies formed since the Alpha Contracts. How were they doing?

Jim looked around until he found a kiosk displaying contract offerings, then took a seat nearby. There were a variety of chairs available, tailored for each of the different species. He found one that didn't make him feel like he was perching on a fence rail. "Wish I'd brought Ted," he mumbled. His XO, Ted Oxnard, was on their ship, *Traveler*, still in orbit. They'd decided bringing down a big group of Humans could be inflammatory in a region that had never heard of Humans. At the very least, it would draw undue attention.

He used his slate's recording feature to log the long lists of contracts scrolling up the screen. When the data began repeating, he set the slate in front of him and initiated the translation routine. He still marveled at the computing power of the slates. In 2025, just before the first alien ship arrived, it would have taken an incredibly powerful computer to perform text capture translation on the fly. In fact, since the languages were so disparate, it might have taken a supercomputer. His slate now did the job, and he knew from experience, it used a small fraction of its computing power to do so. Scientists on Earth said the tablets operated on a hybrid electronic/optic/quantum processor. The processing and storage power of the simple consumer slates outshone that of the best Earth-made supercomputers. The computers aboard *Traveler* were many times more powerful.

After two hours of scanning contracts, he sent a slew of them via radio to Ted to get his opinion.

"I'll go over them with Alex and get back to you ASAP." Alex Pinot was the Cavaliers' computer expert. A former US Air Force Combat Controller, he was more than brilliant and had recently begun studying merc law, which was proving invaluable.

"Tell him to pay special attention to anything heading toward home," Jim reminded his XO. "I'd rather not have to flush the F11 out here, in the middle of nowhere."

"Roger that," Ted said and signed off.

Jim looked up from the slate and around the bar. Many of the aliens wore some sort of clothing, though none were covered from head to toe like he was. The world was pretty cold by his standards, so he had on artic gear and his signature blue beret.

He recognized a few of the races. A pair of MinSha were on the far side of the pit, leaning over a series of slates, in quiet conversation. There wasn't a Human who wouldn't recognize the praying mantis-like race. He wondered how his friend Kuru Shirazi was faring. It seemed the man's only interest was killing MinSha, which didn't strike Jim as wise or overly profitable.

Jim went back to his game of *Guess that Race* to pass the time. He recognized a big, wolf-like Besquith sitting by himself near the bar. However, the huge dinosaur-looking thing with the flattened head was a mystery. And was that a fucking rabbit with tentacles on its head?! And what he thought was an artfully designed table turned out to be a five-foot wide crab. *These are all merc races,* he thought. *So fucking many!*

A bipedal Bengal tiger pushed past his table, and Jim did a double take. It was only a little over 5-feet tall, but it was massively built, just like an Earth tiger. Three more walked closely behind as they wove among the tables toward an obvious goal—the MinSha.

"This looks interesting," he said to himself.

When the tigers were about 20 feet from their objective, one of the MinSha turned to face them. As they had multifaceted eyes, it was impossible to tell exactly what the MinSha was looking at.

"You cheated us!" one of the tigers yelled at the MinSha and pointed a clawed finger.

"Pushtal fool," the MinSha replied, making a dismissive gesture with his barbed arm. "You are lucky we didn't destroy your pathetic ship and watch you die in vacuum." The pit had grown completely quiet as everyone observed the encounter with as much interest as Jim did.

"We offer honest trade; you only give lies!" one of the other Pushtal said. Jim made a note on his slate. The Human mercs were sharing data on alien races on the Aethernet back home. This encounter appeared to be useful intel.

"No one can trust a MinSha!" one of the other Pushtal bellowed.

"You started the vendetta," the MinSha replied.

"And we finished it," the other MinSha said. The aliens looked at each other and gave a very Human nod of approval. "I would tell you to go home, mammal, but you no longer have a home." The two MinSha chittered happily.

The lead Pushtal started to say something else, but his three companions were done with the discussion. In an instant they produced pistols and began firing.

"Oh fuck!" Jim yelled and dove under the table.

At first, there were just a few shots and a long pause. Jim wondered if the Pushtal had taken out the MinSha and that was the end. He peeked around the corner of his table. The MinSha had flipped their table, and the pause was so they could ready their weapons for a counter attack. The Pushtal were moving closer as the pit's numerous patrons ran, slithered, and hopped for cover. One of them rose to its full height to try and spot the MinSha, only to have a well-placed laser punch through its head. Then the gunfire erupted again.

Jim fell back, using the large metal column supporting the kiosk as a shield. He looked around, trying to find an escape route. MinSha fire passed overhead, and answering laser and ballistic gunfire began to flash in from the sides. It seemed the squabble between the group of Pushtal and MinSha was evolving into a serious bruhaha.

With a growl of frustration, Jim released the retention holster and pulled out his sidearm, a somewhat venerable H&K USP in .45 ACP. There was a new company on Earth called Ctech which was researching alien technology, hoping to develop and produce an upscale handgun more suitable to merc use, however he'd only seen prototypes. Jim only had so many credits to use for tech development, and just then, most of it was being spent on personal armor and some promising research by a Japanese firm. He checked that the chamber was loaded and palmed the gun.

Peepo would *never* have tolerated an outright firefight in her pit. Jim was stunned that Chromo, whoever that was, hadn't weighed in with a squad of armored Oogar to crack heads or something.

A laser *ziiinged* as it burned a hole through the plastic tabletop of his hiding spot, and Jim pulled back farther. A second later, a large cockroach skittered toward the fight, two vicious-looking, curved blades in its hands. *Trying to stop it or joining in?* Jim wondered, then decided it didn't really matter.

Deciding he'd better GTFO, Jim holstered his pistol and rolled onto his hands and knees. He waited for a brief lull in the action, and, crouching low, he ran toward a cabinet which might provide some concealment. He doubted it would count as cover. The instant he reached it, a projectile took a chunk of out the cabinet's corner, and someone in the room opened up with a *big*, fully automatic weapon. Jim crouched with his back against the cabinet, his breathing hard and his eyes wide, just as his communicator beeped.

"Go," he said.

"I think we found a good contract…" Ted started, then paused.

"Is that gunfire?" An explosion made Jim's body jerk and his ears pop. He snarled a curse and dug out his ear protection, thinking himself a fool for not doing so when the shooting started.

"Yeah," Jim answered.

"Damn, Colonel!" Alex said.

"What the fuck did you get yourself into, boss?"

"I don't know, actually." Another explosion boomed. It had to be grenades.

"I'm getting First Platoon into a dropship, and we're coming down to extract you."

"Negative," Jim said. "Prep the team but do not, I repeat, do not come down." He looked around, noting the exits, observing the flow of aliens leaving, and evaluating his chances. "I need to get out of here before it's safe for you to come. The starport will shit a brick if you bring that thing down here." It looked like as many aliens were coming in as were leaving. *Swell. What the fuck have I gotten myself into?*

"I don't agree," Ted said, "but you're down there, and I'm not."

"I need to hang up and get out of this cluster fuck," Jim said. "Monitor the frequency. Out." He cut the channel before his old friend could complain, then moved.

A minute later he'd only made it 10 feet closer to the exit. The pit was a maelstrom of gun and laser fire. One wall was ablaze, the bar had been demolished by several grenades that were tossed over it, and dozens of alien bodies littered the floor. "It's like a bad B-rated movie," he said as he prepared to move again.

The door he planned to head for was suddenly blocked by a group of figures. They looked like Veetanho, only they were shorter and more squat. Jim had seen their kind before. They weren't Veetanho, they were Aposa. The Aposa weren't the tactical geniuses the Veetanho were. They were savage fighters with short lifespans and little to no regard for their personal survival.

The Aposa didn't come in carefully, they entered in a rush. They only wore minimal armor and harnesses to hold weapons, of which they had a shocking variety. The first two were blown away before they could cross the threshold, their small bodies crashing to the floor. Before their corpses settled, several more vaulted over them and began firing small machine guns into the room. *So much for that exit,* Jim thought.

A round tore through the pedestal he was hiding behind, proving that it was concealment, not cover. Luckily, it hit him square in the chest, in his armor. He grunted and ducked lower. *Ouch,* he thought as he felt the impact. His armor had held. *I gotta get out of here!*

Jim desperately scanned the exits, but all were held by various pissed-off aliens busily spraying Chromo's Merc Pit with deadly fire. Then he noticed a door he hadn't seen before slide open. He wasn't sure it was an exit, but he didn't care. Nobody else seemed to notice it, so he got up, keeping as low as he could, and ran for his life.

Laser and bullet fire flew all around him. "Shiiiiiit!" he yelled as he ran, diving for the doorway at the last second. He felt the sting as a laser beam cut along his left leg as he flew through the door, crashed into something hard and sent it flying.

"Careful, you idiot!" the thing he'd collided with yelled.

Jim got to his knees, drew his pistol and turned toward the door, but another being was already sliding it closed. He pointed the gun at the alien. It screamed when it saw him and raised its hands to cover its reptilian face.

"No shoot!" it cried.

Not a merc, Jim thought and swept around the room with his gun. The furry turtle he'd encountered earlier was just getting back on its feet. Despite a non-expressive face, it still managed to look indignant about being knocked over. "You again?"

"Of course," it said, "this is my pit!"

"You're Chromo?" Jim asked. The alien nodded. "Your pit is getting the shit shot out of it."

"The vendetta between the Pushtal and the MinSha is bitter. I tried to stop the cats from coming in, but they rushed past before I could summon assistance."

"Well call it now!" Jim said, gesturing at the sound of the pitched battle on the other side of the door.

The alien took out a communicator and looked at it. "I have tried," it admitted, "but my security team is not responding. I do not know where all these combatants came from."

"It's a setup," Jim said. "They're using your pit to go after someone."

"You are crazy, Human. Why would they do that?"

"Judging by your lax security? I'd have to say because you're gullible." While Chromo spluttered, Jim looked around. The room was about 20 feet on a side. It held two desks, several chairs, a couple of safes, and a computer stack. Three other aliens were in the room: two reptilian elSha like the one at the door and a 7-foot tall, burly humanoid with four arms and a thick head. He was pretty sure it was a Lumar. They might be a merc race, but they weren't known to be overly bright. This one had been tending bar before the fight began.

As Jim looked around, he spotted a single door. "Where does that go?" he asked the flummoxed alien. It said something in its native language that Jim's pendant translated as bathroom. *That's no help,* he thought as several more explosions sounded from the main pit. He'd gotten away from that, but now he was cornered.

Jim looked at Chromo who was standing by one of the desks, casting his beady eyes this way and that in near panic. "Where are your guns?" Jim asked.

"Guns? I have no guns," the alien said.

"What?" Jim queried. "What kind of merc race doesn't keep guns around?"

"The T'suko are not mercs," it said indignantly. "We make money with our brains, not our brawn!"

"Figures," Jim said disgustedly. *That explained the pathetic security.* Every pit he'd been to was run by mercs, usually retired, like Peepo. When you dealt with mercs your whole life, you gained the instincts you needed to run a pit and to be prepared for…shit to happen.

"I bought this pit a few months ago," Chromo said. "I saw opportunity!"

"Yeah, an opportunity to get your ass shot off." Jim wondered if he'd pissed off the wrong people, or if someone saw this soft target as an opportunity to level the playing field. He pushed past one of the nearly apoplectic elSha to listen at the door. The gunfire seemed to have fallen off. He reached into a pouch on his belt and took out a micro drone. He only had one, so he considered for a moment, whether this was the right time to use it.

"You must help me, Human," Chromo said.

"Shut up and let me think," Jim snapped.

"You cannot address me like that—"

Jim pointed his H&K USP at the pit owner's head and got instant silence. "That's better," he said. "Are these the door controls?" he asked, looking at the closest elSha and pointing to a control panel. It just stared at the wall. "Hey!" Jim snapped, and the alien's eyes jerked toward him. "I asked, are these the door's controls?"

"Y-yes," the alien replied.

Jim examined them for a minute, but they were not labeled in a script he could read, and he didn't have time to screw with his slate's translator. "Show me how to open it, but only a couple of inches."

"Open the door?" the elSha squeaked. "You are insane; they will kill us."

"Only if there's a merc this small out there," Jim said and held the micro drone out in the palm of his hand. The elSha looked at it, uncomprehending.

"What are you going to do?" Chromo asked.

"Get out of here alive," Jim said, *if I can.*

"You will take me with you."

"Are you ordering me again?" Jim asked. Chromo spluttered. "I am Colonel Cartwright, owner of Cartwright's Cavaliers. That might not mean much to you, but considering what you have to work with…" He gestured around the room. The Lumar was sitting in a chair, tapping away on a slate, apparently playing a game.

"Fine, I wish to hire you."

Jim almost laughed, then stopped. Merc Guild law included some special rules concerning commanders on contracts. They provided a little more protection from indiscriminate slaughter. It wasn't much, but it was better than nothing. He took out his slate and set it to record. "Twenty thousand credits," Jim said. "Verbal control, 2-hour duration, personal protection."

"Twenty thousand credits?" Chromo spluttered. "Ridiculous!"

"Fine," Jim said, "save your own ass," and he moved to put away the slate.

"Wait!" Chromo snapped. "Ten thousand."

"Fifteen thousand and a twenty-five percent combat bonus."

Chromo made a face, then nodded.

"Verbal agreement required," Jim said.

"Fine, yes, agreed. Fifteen thousand and twenty-five percent combat bonus."

Jim grinned. "Accepted." Since combat was pretty much guaranteed, 18,750 credits would be just fine, assuming he lived. "Now, tell your lizard to show me how to operate the god-damned door!"

"Askul," Chromo said, "show the Human how to operate it."

"It will get us killed!" the elSha complained.

"It is a merc."

"That?" the elSha asked. "It is softer than I am."

"Don't judge a book by its cover," Jim suggested. Both aliens looked at him in confusion. Jim sighed. "I'm tougher than I look."

"Just do it," Chromo ordered. The elSha did as instructed.

Jim used the controls to slowly inch the door open less than a handspan, then tossed the little drone through the hole. The gap allowed a curl of smoke to come in, along with the sounds of multiple alien languages, cries of pain, and curses. Most of the weapons fire was now lasers, and that explained why Jim couldn't hear it anymore. Lasers were much quieter than other weapons.

The drone disappeared into the smoky pit, and Jim closed the door. Putting his full-sized slate away in its sheath on his belt, Jim turned to the little one on his wrist. It was like a smart phone back home, though a million times more powerful. It didn't have as much power as a full-sized slate, but it linked with his bigger one. It was quite versatile and more useable in combat situations.

The drone was already paired with the wrist slate, so he brought it online. In the pit, the little drone unfolded its tiny ducted fans. The machine could operate in any orientation, the fans running in both directions to provide lift. Inaudible over the din of battle, it rose a few inches above the debris-cluttered floor. Jim used hand gestures to guide the diminutive machine, and the wrist slate projected a small Tri-V in the air in front of him. He'd read about the implants some of the aliens had in their brains, how they could operate things with their minds, and he wondered if it was worth it. The problem was, the tech hadn't been adapted for humans, and he didn't feel like being a guinea pig.

The inside of the pit looked like a charnel house, with body parts everywhere. A low whistle escaped his lips as he surveyed the situation. He switched the drone's camera to a mixture of infrared and ultraviolet, and the air was suddenly crisscrossed with dancing lights. A laser battle of epic proportions was raging.

The drone skimmed over a smoldering Pushtal corpse, then what appeared to be half a MinSha. He paused when he saw it was the upper half, and the alien was still shooting a laser pistol. *Talk about hard to kill,* he thought. After a moment, he guided the drone onward.

"I don't understand the purpose of this," Chromo said.

"It's called reconnaissance," Jim explained. He glanced at the alien who was watching him. "If we rush out there, we're dead. Does *that* make sense?"

"When you put it that way..." Chromo replied.

Jim continued slowly sweeping the room. At one point, he inadvertently flew the drone a few inches from the head of an Aposo that responded by spinning and firing its laser pistol crazily in all directions. "Jumpy things," Jim said as he slid the drone behind the bar for cover.

He popped it back up after a few seconds and scanned the exits. Aliens of various races were using them for concealment, and they popped up and fired weapons from time to time. It was more like a classic free-for-all than a battle. WTF what going on? Then he saw something.

"Hey," he said, "is that an escape hatch behind the bar?"

"Yes, but what good does that do us?"

Jim looked over the desk, then pointed at the Lumar. "How strong are they?"

"I very strong," the Lumar said without looking up from his game.

"I have an idea."

* * *

Part 2

The combatants in Chromo's Merc Pit were split into two distinct groups: those trapped inside, fighting for their lives, and those outside trying to get in and kill them. Those at each of the three entrances wouldn't have minded killing any of those at the other entrances either. It was a strange sort of tag-team death match with very few rules.

Nobody noticed when the office door slowly slid open and something moved out, into the pit. One of the two surviving Push-tals was the first to notice, and he did a double take as a huge desk came out, top first. The alien merc cocked his head in confusion. Who would carry a desk into the middle of a firefight? The desk moved directly and quickly toward the bar. Unfortunately, while he was pondering what the moving furniture meant, a surviving MinSha that had taken cover on the far side of the bar shot him dead.

Jim risked a quick peek around the desk just as the Pushtal met his fate. The bar was a few feet away, and he knew the surprise of a moving desk would quickly end. "Go!" he yelled.

The Lumar accelerated. Jim had been shocked when the four-armed alien lifted the desk with little more than a grunt. He was further amazed by how easily the Lumar carried it. And he was stunned when the huge alien accelerated into a loping run. Chromo and Jim rushed to stay close to the Lumar as it crashed into the bar.

The plan had been to flip the desk and create a ramp for them to scramble over and behind the bar. The Lumar apparently hadn't listened too closely to the planning session. It slammed the desk into the bar with a thunderous crash, temporarily stopping its forward momentum. Jim and Chromo crashed into the desk and the Lumar, then the bar collapsed, and the entire conglomeration flipped over the top.

"Shit!" Jim yelled as he cartwheeled through the air. "Shit, shit, shit, *ooof!*"

In an instant he was part of a pile of bodies. Unfortunately, Jim ended up at the bottom of the pile. It took him a second to sort out what had happened and to ascertain that he wasn't full of holes after the crazy run, collision, and flip. "You all okay?" he asked the others. One of the elSha looked more squashed than Jim, but it nodded. The Lumar gave a rather surprising thumbs up, making Jim wonder where he'd learned that move. "Great. Where's the hatch, Chromo?"

"There," the alien pit owner said and pointed. Quite a lot of debris had piled up behind the mostly ruined bar.

Lasers slashed at the bar as Jim moved to clear some of the debris, looking for the hatch. When he turned over a large piece of the shattered bar, Jim spotted something that had been underneath. "What the hell?" he wondered aloud. It looked like a huge house cat with black fur! Only house cats didn't wear belts or bandoliers with little pouches or delicate golden chains with pendants around their necks. He crouched down, felt for a pulse, and found it. The being's fur was incredibly soft.

The Cartwrights had always been dog people when they had pets. However, his cousin Jennifer who lived in Topeka was decidedly a cat person. In fact, you could probably, rightfully, call her a crazy cat lady. She had at least 20 of them, and they were all beasts. Jim remembered how he'd felt having a cat sitting in his lap, purring, when he'd visited with his family one summer. This one was much larger than those house cats, but it was still the same sort of being.

"What are you waiting for?" Chromo asked as he cringed against the bar. A burst of gunfire made him duck even lower, if that was possible.

"There's an injured alien here," Jim explained.

"Who cares?" Chromo screamed. "Get it out of the way. Who is paying you, anyway?"

Both of the elSha were hiding as well, their independent eyes glancing at the alien Jim found, obviously not terribly interested. The Lumar, though, knelt next to Jim to examine it.

"I know that being," he said, the English from Jim's translator a stark contrast to the alien's words which sounded like grinding rocks and rasping wood.

"What is it?" Jim asked.

"I no not remember the name," the Lumar said, shaking his thick head sadly. "But I do remember they are...dangerous."

"Dangerous?" Jim asked. He looked at the helpless cat that was obviously injured when the bar was demolished by the Lumar and his huge desk. "How can an oversized pussycat be dangerous?" The Lumar shrugged, an interesting action for a being with four arms, and Jim grunted. He wasn't going to let someone kill it, he decided. The alien had taken refuge there when the fight started, that much was obvious. No matter what shenanigans brought this sort of insanity to Chromo's pit, the cat was an unfortunate casualty. He gently picked it up and slung it over his shoulder. It didn't weigh more than 20 pounds. He pointed at the rest of the debris. "Can you clear this away?"

"Yes," the Lumar said, and started hurling large chunks of wood, plaster, and metal over the bar. Someone must have thought it was a counter attack, because the shooting suddenly slackened. Jim nodded in appreciation. It only took the huge alien a couple of moments to reveal the trapdoor. It had been covered by a false floor which was now torn to pieces, revealing the simple, digital lock that secured the heavy, metal hatch.

"About time," Chromo snapped and pushed past the Lumar to tap in a code. The lock beeped once, and the door retracted into the floor with a disturbing grinding noise. "It hasn't been maintained in quite some time," he admitted, then dropped into the hole. Considering the diameter of his shell, it was a remarkably close fit. Jim guessed it was custom made for him. The two elSha didn't wait for an invitation and shot down the hole right behind him.

"Can you fit?" Jim asked the Lumar as he watched for intrusions over the bar.

"I flexible," the Lumar said, beginning to wiggle into the hole face first.

Jim watched slack-jawed as the Lumar squirmed in, somehow slipping his four-armed, barrel-chested physique through the hatch. He guessed the alien's shoulders weren't constructed like Humans'. It only made sense, he thought. Once he got past his chest, he fell through easily. His hips were considerably narrower. "Impressive," Jim said.

Just then a huge purple snout looked over the bar, right at Jim. He shot the Oogar in the face. The .45 caliber slug grazed the side of the alien's head, leaving a disturbingly small gouge of red meat and a trickle of blood behind.

"Argh!" the Oogar bellowed and grabbed for Jim who jumped into the dark hole.

Jim bent his knees and prayed it wasn't very deep. It wasn't. He hit in less than a second, landing on top of the Lumar who grunted at the impact. "Sorry," Jim said, and rolled to one side, trying to protect the cat. "Clear the door. An Oogar is up there!" A 5-foot-high tunnel ran in one direction. Lights illuminated the tunnel every 10 feet or so, and he could just see the retreating forms of Chromo and his two elSha.

The Lumar crouched in the gloom of the tunnel, looking at Jim without comprehension.

"An Oogar up there!" Jim said and pointed. The concept registered in the Lumar's eyes just as a huge purple paw reached down and wrapped around its neck.

"Gack!" the Lumar squawked as he was hauled back up.

"Fuck!" Jim yelled, drawing his USP and trying to aim at the Oogar. The Lumar blocked the entire hole. It gave a strangled scream as the Oogar tried to pull it through the hole. Jim heard a ripping sound, and the Lumar's body fell backward, spraying bright red blood. Jim cried out and lunged down the tunnel as the purple paw returned, dripping with Lumar blood, and searched for more prey.

It was not really possible to run in the tunnel, which was about a foot shorter than he was. It didn't help that Jim was scared half to death, bruised and sore from the whole ordeal, and had a fucking 20-pound housecat over one shoulder. The visage he'd just seen, though, helped push him to speeds he hadn't thought himself was capable of. That the Oogar couldn't pursue them down into the tunnel never entered his mind.

He caught up with the other three as they reached another coded door, and Chromo was punching in the access code. The door slid aside. Jim dropped into a crouch, reloading his USP and pointing it down the tunnel. He was breathing hard and shaking from the exertion, but he sensed there was no one in the tunnel behind them, so he slowly backed inside. He didn't relax until the door slid closed again.

Jim rolled the cat off his shoulder and rose to his full height. The space they entered looked like some sort of storage room, though it was empty and mostly full of dust. It might have been part of the pit long ago. They'd come at least 50 yards, and he was sure nobody from the pit would search this far. They were clear, and he'd just made about twenty-thousand credits. The click of someone releasing a weapon's safety caused him to freeze.

"Excellent job, Human," Chromo said as Jim looked at him. The merc pit owner was pointing a very lethal-looking pistol at him. "Lower your weapon."

"I thought T'suko weren't mercs," Jim said as he lowered his gun.

"We're not mercs, but we're not stupid, either." Chromo gestured to the elSha. One accessed a computer installed in the wall, and another came over and took Jim's gun. The little reptile was twitchy as hell, but he took the weapon.

"Now what?"

"Now, I wait for the battle to play itself out, then I go pick up the pieces and the profits!"

"Profits?" Jim asked. "What kind of profits can there be in having your pit shot to pieces?"

"You Humans aren't very smart," Chromo said, his mouth bending into a toothless smile. "Why do you think so many found enemies in there?" Jim shrugged. "Because I told them they'd be there, and they paid me for the information! I bought the pit, though I was almost broke and had no stock, for a steal. There are lots of desperate beings in this backwater hellhole, and lots of mercs have enemies here."

"And you put them together on purpose," Jim said. Chromo nodded. "You planned to be in the middle of that?"

"No," Chromo admitted, "something went wrong with the timing. It wasn't supposed to happen for another hour, minimum." The alien gestured at Jim with his pistol. "You were both a complication and a blessing. You got me out of there."

"For a fee," Jim reminded him.

"Yeah, about that fee," Chromo said, his grin widening.

Motherfucker, Jim thought.

"Scanners show all clear," the elSha at the computer said.

"Well," Chromo said and raised his gun, "that about completes our business."

The alien was too far away. Jim gritted his teeth and waited for the shot. Then the lights went out. He didn't hesitate. He dove to the side an instant before Chromo spat a curse and a shot boomed out. As quietly as possible, Jim bent over and drew the little pistol he kept in a leg pocket of his uniform pants. The ME380 was a .380 caliber semi-automatic from Magnum Research called the Micro Eagle. It was a present from an Israeli merc, received in exchange for advice about setting up the first Jewish merc unit. He didn't know how useful it would be against the seemingly thick-skinned and shelled T'suko, but it was better than nothing.

He heard a gasp of pain and something hit the floor with a wet thud. Jim tried to track the sound, but Chromo yelled something and fired blindly. The muzzle blasts were deafening in the small room, but the flashes from the firearm marked his position perfectly. Jim raised the Micro Eagle and aimed, but something warm and furry pushed his hand down.

"No," a voice purred in his ear.

"Wha...?" Jim started to ask, but the hand was gone.

Chromo fired several more times, then let out a startled yelp before something that sounded like a shell hitting the floor reverberated through the room. There was one more little scream, then silence returned.

What the fuck just happened? Jim silently wondered as he clutched the pistol and tried to penetrate the dark with his senses. When the lights came on, he yelled and spun around, gun out, searching for a target. There were none.

One elSha was by the computer, where he'd last seen it. A tiny knife protruded from its neck, and it looked very dead. The other one was just a few feet from Jim, lying on its back, staring at the roof. Another tiny knife stuck out of its chest. Its ribcage still rose and fell, though slower and slower, so Jim guessed it would be dead soon. Chromo was on his behind, his back propped against a wall. The cat stood to one side and held a knife to Chromo's throat. The T'suko looked at the cat in horror.

"Why are you doing this?" Chromo asked.

"It is my job," the alien purred and smiled.

"I will pay you."

"I have already been paid, Chromo. The Pushtal clan, Kzall, sends their regards."

"But—" Chromo never got to finish his question because the feline slit his neck. With a bright spray of pink blood and a look of surprise, the former pit owner and devious betrayer fell over sideways.

The feline alien turned its head and looked at Jim in a very cat-like manner, a tiny smile on its face. Jim's gun wasn't pointed at the alien, but it was close. They were maybe 15 feet apart. The feline looked at Jim's gun, then at him, and cocked its head.

"Now what?" Jim asked.

"Welcome to our negotiation," the alien said, quickly wiping its little knife clean on the dead Chromo.

"What are you?" Jim asked.

"That isn't important," the alien said. "What *is* important is your role in all of this." It gestured at the three dead aliens. "My job was to dispose of this entire operation. I've been working on that for quite some time. I figured it was taken care of when I changed the meeting times Chromo arranged. I hadn't factored you into that plan. A Human, so far out here and so soon after you arrived on the galactic stage. You are indeed a tenacious species."

"You're an assassin?" Jim asked.

"That's an over-simplification. My contract was for all the associates of that," the alien said, gesturing toward the quite dead Chromo. "You mentioned payment, so that means you were an employee. Therefore, I have to take care of you, too."

"Chromo refused payment and was about to kill me," Jim said, "so I wasn't really employed anymore."

"Point in your favor," the feline said, eyes glittering.

"I also saved you in there," Jim added. Who do you think carried you out of the pit?"

"I was never in any danger. After you fouled my plan, I was partially caught in a grenade explosion. While not injured, I spotted your breakout with the Lumar and decided to place myself in a convenient location for your arrival." Again its eyes twinkled, perhaps in amusement. "My plan was to kill all of you there, then escape. Your *saving* me was a surprise, so I simply played along and allowed you to proceed. It let me gather more information."

Jim swallowed. "You took a chance that I wouldn't kill you."

"I doubt you could have."

"You couldn't be sure about that," Jim said. The slight smile returned. "In fact, I believe you owe me."

The alien regarded him for a very long moment, long enough for Jim to wonder just how fast it was. He couldn't see in the dark, but he suspected the alien could. Finally, it spoke again.

"Humans are going to make things very interesting," it said and sheathed the dagger in its bandolier. Jim took a deep breath and slowly dropped the pistol into his pocket. Not quickly enough to alarm Jim, the alien went around the space and retrieved its weapons. Twice it stopped to rub a cloth over something, then it went to the computer and inserted a chip. A second later the computer's plastic body shattered, and the alien removed the chip. "I believe we will have more business with your kind, in time."

"You stopped me from shooting Chromo," Jim said. "Why?"

"It wasn't the right thing to do."

Jim narrowed his eyes and grunted. "I don't understand."

"No, I don't expect you do." The alien came closer, took an item from a pouch, and held it out to him. Jim took the offering, a small coin, about 2 inches across. It was simple with an alien symbol he didn't recognize on one side, and a stylized paw print on the other. He looked at it, then up at the alien with a quizzical expression. "It is called a favor token. You have done a good deed for me, and this may allow my people to do one for you some day."

"May allow?" Jim asked, even more confused.

"If it is meant to be," the alien said and bowed its head slightly.

"My name is Jim Cartwright," he said. "I'm the commander of Cartwright's Cavaliers. May I ask yours?"

"I am Meeru of the Whispering Fear clan. It is good to make your acquaintance, Jim Cartwright. This concludes our negotiation." The alien bowed its head, then faded into a slight shadow until it was gone.

"Holy fucking shit," Jim said, shaking his head. "Did I just save a ghost?" There was no answer.

* * *

"You gotta be fucking with me," Ted said after another sip of his beer. Peepo's Pit was bustling, the same as always, and Jim was drinking his customary Coke. His senior officers were looking at him with a mixture of amazement and doubt in their eyes.

"Not at all," Jim said. As proof, he reached into a pocket, took out the favor token and set it on the table. "I checked the GalNet and didn't find anything. But when I hooked up my translator to a slate and ran the log, it showed a translation from a Depik. The GalNet says they are a feline race, not Union members, and are to be avoided."

"Why didn't you share that detail before now?" Ted asked. "Shit, boss, that was six months ago."

"Because I wanted to be as far from that Depik as possible, before I told the story." He looked down at the token, then picked it up and put it in his pocket. "I have a feeling I made a deal with the devil, himself."

"Who knew the devil was a cat?" Alex asked with a smirk on his face.

"Who indeed?" Jim replied. "Who indeed?"

#####

A Job to Do
by Quincy J. Allen

Part 1—The Lyon's Den

P rivate Max Boudreaux stood at the south end of a dusty strip mall that would have been demolished decades earlier except for the last, open establishment. Boudreaux wiped his brow and, for the first time since his freshman year at the Academy, felt nervous—at least a little.

The heat and humidity of Houston's infamous August climate pressed into him, but unlike most, he was at home in soupy climates. They reminded him of the South Louisiana swamps where he and generations of Cajun ancestors had made their homes.

"The Lyon's Den," he said under his breath and smiled. He removed his short-brimmed cover and ran a hand across the high-and-tight buzz-cut he'd had since fifth grade. A sense of awe filled him as he stood there. Though most sentients didn't know it existed, the Den was *legendary* among those who even thought about becoming a merc. And he was about to go inside to meet his new fireteam leader. Aside from a name, Corporal Killian, Boudreaux knew nothing about the man. He fingered the fresh Hawk insignia stitched onto the front pocket of his camo jacket, feeling the poly-film bulge of his orders beneath, tangible proof that his hard work and sacrifices had been worth it.

All he'd ever wanted was to be was a merc. He'd scored in the 95th percentile on his VOWS and excelled in his training—mental, physical, technical, and tactical. As a junior, he'd heard about Hu's Hawks, created two years before he joined the academy, and as their reputation grew, he'd decided that was where he wanted to find a home, make his riches, and create a legend of his own. With the Hawks as his goal, he'd graduated at the top of his class with a specialty in reconnaissance operations.

"Boudreaux?" a woman's deep voice called out behind him, interrupting his dreams of glory and a mercenary company of his own someday.

He turned and found three privates in black and burgundy camo fatigues identical to his own walking toward him from the dusty shuttle-pad that lay a klick away. Each wore the distinct Hawks' patch, a red diamond barely containing the shape of a black hawk about to capture prey. The Chinese characters in the upper-left quadrant read 'Eternal Vigilance and Sacrifice.' Boudreaux glanced at the names embroidered on their pockets and realized they were the other members of his new fireteam.

Keenes was a thick, curly-locked redhead who towered over Boudreaux's nearly two meters. The bigger man had an easy smile, sharp, brown eyes crinkled with laugh lines, and a furrowed brow that suggested the massive private was quick to both laughter and rage.

Fujimoto stood twenty cents shorter than Boudreaux, and her hair had been buzzed around the sides and back, leaving a shock of longer hair drooping down around her bright green eyes in a manicured bob. She carried herself like a fighter—every move reminded him of a wild panther—and her fatigues looked loose over a frame he suspected didn't have an ounce of fat.

Mopantomobogo, the woman who had called out, stood eye-to-eye with Boudreaux, and her ebony skin seemed to absorb all the light around her. Her hair had been cut to within a couple mills of her shining skin, and her dark eyes hinted at both strength and intelligence. A slow smile split her face, shining like a half-moon cutting across a midnight sky.

He picked up just a hint of Central Africa in her low-timbered accent as she greeted him in Mandarin, her hand outstretched. "You got the same cryptic message, yes?" she asked fluently in the same language. The Hawks spoke to each other in Mandarin, and a knowledge of the language was a requisite for joining the mercenary company.

"Yes," Boudreaux replied, replacing his cover and shaking Mopantomobogo's hand. "*Lyon's Den. 15:30 hours. Eat first,*" he quoted. "Fireteam Cooper?" he asked. All of Hu's fireteams were named after hawks from around the world, including the Cooper's Hawk from North America. The three privates before him nodded as Keenes and Fujimoto exchanged handshakes with Boudreaux.

"It's twenty-four after," Fujimoto said, not looking at a chronometer.

She probably has pinplants, Boudreaux thought.

"Let's move," Mopantomobogo ordered, sounding as if she took to command easily.

Without another word, Boudreaux turned, and they walked through the deserted mall as the sun did its best to scorch them into slag right there on the pavement. They immediately stepped into an easy cadence, their boots clomping out a steady rhythm as they scanned the boarded-up storefronts one-by-one. Finally, near the south end of the mall, they stopped before the second door from the last. The dingy, time-weathered pane of what appeared to be real glass, not modern Polyclear, looked centuries old. Plastered across the inside was a field of faded, blue paper with the faint, golden outline of a rampant lion.

"This is it," Boudreaux said, remembering all the tales he'd heard about the Den. He caught the anxiousness in his voice and cleared his throat. Turning, he realized the other three privates were just as anxious as he was. "Into the Lyon's Den," he quipped with a grin, eliciting an easy chuckle from the others. The four privates turned away from the door and stared into the stark glare of sunshine reflecting off the permacrete. Years of training and muscle memory pulled at all of them, and they stood at ease with their hands behind their backs, as if they were in formation. It was automatic, and it pleased him that they all already seemed to be on the same page. He couldn't tell if the others were holding their breaths, but he sure as hell was. If the people inside didn't like the looks of them, they wouldn't be let in. Those were the rules. And if they didn't pass this first test, they'd probably lose their asses when Killian caught up with them on the shuttle to Shanghai and Hu's HQ just outside the megacity.

A loud *Click!* filled the air, and that sound was all they needed.

"That's it," Mopantomobogo barked in Mandarin. "Thirty seconds. *Move!*"

They turned like they were on a parade ground and yanked off their covers as Boudreaux grabbed the latch. With only a moment's hesitation and a flash of doubt, he pulled the door open and stepped inside, his comrades on his heels. They marched down a dark hall-way, rounded a curve, and found themselves staring at two, towering, four-armed Lumar sporting a pair of heavy laser pistols on their hips and big-bore assault rifles slung over their shoulders. The rifles were so large, Boudreaux figured most Humans could use the things as vehicle-mounted auto cannons.

In perfect Earth-Standard, the larger of the two said, "Welcome to the Lyon's Den." His voice was a low rumble that reminded Bou-dreaux of a rock crusher. "You know the rules?"

"Yes," the four privates barked in perfect unison. Both Lumar bared their teeth in what the privates hoped were smiles. The aliens stepped aside, and one of them pulled open a blue curtain, exposing the Lyon's Den.

The room was cavernous, with a massive octagonal bar in the center like a fixed fortification of dark, polished wood and steel. Every surface had enough stains, gouges, and scorch marks to tell a thousand heroic tales, most of them *tall*. Massive Tri-V screens plas-tered the walls around the bar, broadcasting a mixture of galaxy-wide sports, news from the core worlds, and a long list of available merce-nary contracts that promised riches and glory. To the right stood a bank of two-meter tanks full of gasses and liquids glowing like rain-bows, each one holding a different precious atmo for the off-world mercs who wanted a taste or smell of their home world.

"Fireteam Cooper!" a man shouted in Mandarin, his voice easily carrying over the music. The four privates turned toward a round table set in the far, back corner, well away from the kitchen doors. "Front and center!" he barked.

They marched over to his table, where they found four empty seats. Four shot glasses full of a dark liquid sat in front of each seat;

the stuff looked more like motor oil than any libation. The man who wore black and burgundy fatigues with the Hawk insignia on the front pocket and the double-slash rank of Corporal on his right sleeve stood slowly. His eyes took in every detail of the four privates before him, his lips pressed together in a grim line. The name on his fatigues read KILLIAN.

He was under two meters tall, about halfway between Boudreaux's and Fujimoto's heights. A heavy musculature filled his fatigues, making him appear almost as wide as he was tall. The only word that came to Boudreaux's mind was *tank*.

"I'm Corporal Hank "Bitchy" Killian," he said with an emphasis on "Bitchy" and paused, watching each private's face.

He wants to see if we laugh at his nickname, Boudreaux thought, and fought the urge to do just that.

"Let's get one thing straight. I don't care what it says on that piece of poly-film you have in a pocket somewhere. You aren't in the Hawks…."

Boudreaux's face registered surprise, and he figured the others' faces did too.

"*Yet.*" Killian added. He waited a few seconds, letting that sink in, then he sat down. "Now, take a seat," he ordered.

They did.

"The reason the four of you are sitting in those chairs, and I'm sitting in this one, is because all of Fireteam Cooper was wiped out on a shitty, little jungle world called Kuason. Let that sink in. A whole fireteam was wiped out in the blink of an eye, for nothing more than money, and it happens all the time. All of you are expendable. *I'm* expendable. Every member of Hu's Hawks is expendable when we're on a mission."

Boudreaux gulped. This wasn't quite the pep-talk he'd been expecting.

"We are *all* expendable—even old man Hu—for one reason," Killian continued, "and one reason *only:* the mission *requires* it. I don't care who you are or where you came from. I don't care about what you've done or what you think you can do. All I care about is getting the job done. And if that means I have to drop all of us into a meat grinder to make it happen, that's the drill." He paused, as if he were mulling over his own words. "Does anyone have a problem with that?"

All four privates said in unison: "No, Corporal."

Killian nodded.

"As of today, I'm starting a new tradition." He nodded at the viscous drink in front of him. "I want to raise a glass with the men and women under my command *before* our next insertion and before the MAC rounds start flying. I learned Rule Number One the hard way: mercs don't always get a second chance to toast each other, toast their heroes, or toast the ones who aren't with us anymore. That ends *today*. I'm going to tell you a story." He paused, thinking for a moment. "Well, two, actually, about how I got my callsign, how I got promoted, and how none of it was pretty, but all of it was glorious. And when I'm done, you'll either drink with me and become part of Fireteam Cooper, or you'll walk out that door and never look back."

Part 2—Reliak IV

We huddled at the bottom of a deep crater, hidden in shadow, awaiting orders. The funny thing about standing in zero atmo is that your suit sounds different. You hear more of the inside than you do when the air is thick outside the layers of armor that protect you from death. Our Mk 7 CASPers, covered with gray, tan, and white digi-patterns, blended well with the surface of the planet we'd landed on several hours earlier.

"You have point, Killian," Sergeant Yeo ordered over the company-wide comm frequency. As always, her voice was icy and emotionless, but there always seemed to be an edge in it when she addressed me. "Take a heading of two-seven-five at 10 kph through those canyons. The Veetanho are in that labyrinth, somewhere, and so is our payday. The rest of Fireteam Shikra will slot in behind you at twenty meters. Do a full sensor sweep. Be sure to check your targets. We're looking for a Depik advisor that will probably be in an EV suit. We need it alive, not blown in half or freeze-dried in vacuum. If we lose comms, launch flares each minute you are engaged with the enemy."

"Roger that," I replied, then swapped to the Shikra frequency. "Jesus Christ," I grumbled "Shikra takes point, and the *heat*, yet again."

The rest of my fireteam chuckled, then Corporal Hsiu said, "You're the one who told everybody you were the best. We should all be bitching about that big mouth of yours and how it keeps putting us in the shit. So, shut your mouth and do your job." Hsiu's reply was light-hearted, but there was a certain edge to it that I couldn't miss. Hsiu had been running Fireteam Shikra for a year and took me under his wing the day I arrived three months earlier. We'd become fast friends, spending hours talking rocket-ball stats and drinking bourbon until the wee hours whenever we had down time.

Hsiu also did his best to get between Yeo and me whenever she was up my ass about something.

"I swear, she has it in for me," I groaned.

"She doesn't work that way, *Private*," Hsiu said easily. "And if you pushed your ego out of the way for half a second, that might just sink in through that thick skull of yours."

"Yeah, yeah," I said, then climbed out of the asteroid crater and headed toward the canyon. A pale blue sun, about twice the size of Sol, sat about forty-five degrees above the horizon and shone on my back, casting a dark shadow in front of me across the dusty surface of Reliak IV. "This thick skull is the only thing between you and a few squads-worth of VeeTee lasers."

"It surely is," Hsiu said with a laugh. "Just watch yourself. You're fast in that Mk 7, but a laser will bore through it quickly, and with no atmo, we *might* have just enough time to hear you scream."

"Hey, it's *me*," I bragged. "Besides, these laser shields are pretty durable." I hefted the shield attached to my left arm and extended my right to activate the heavy-duty spring-blade all Hu mercs were equipped with. Hu basic training included a regular regimen with what was essentially close-combat sword and board—Kung-Fu style—and I was very, very good at it.

Hsiu sighed heavily. "Chang, Kilgore, Pardeaux, you know the drill. Slot in behind Mr. Hot Shot and do it like we did in training. I'll slot in behind you at twenty meters, and we'll see what there is to see."

"Affirmative," we all said in unison.

Reliak IV's surface was similar to that of Earth's moon, but that's where the similarity ended. It was thirty percent larger than Earth, with roughly the same gravity but a slower rotation. It had been a living world about a billion years ago, but something ripped away its atmosphere, leaving a barren, airless surface with all the details of a Terra-type world, minus the oceans.

The ground sloped away from me, descending into a warren of canyons that reminded me of Goblin Hills, Utah, back home. I had no idea what made it look that way, but close quarters and lean LOS was about the worst sort of terrain a mostly recon company could mix it up in. High-magnification optics and 25mm, shoulder-mounted MACs were our preferred tools.

This contract was different, though. We were after some Depik advisor who had managed to piss off a Besquith high roller with deep pockets and a real hard-on for whatever was in the fur-baby's head. We'd tracked it and a small Veetanho company it hired for protection to Reliak IV, and all we cared about was bringing it back alive.

"Making my run," I said into the general comm.

"Fireteam Levant," Yeo said. "Shikra is in motion. Begin your pass from the south and meet up at grid Delta Six-Niner via the pre-scribed route. Gabar and Doria, come in from the north. Engage all enemy at will and check your targets for the Depik. Anyone who kills our bounty will pay the tab."

"What a bitch," I grumbled into the fireteam's comm.

"What was that, *Private?*" Hsiu asked.

"Nothing at all, Corporal," I replied.

I swapped over to an isolated, low-band frequency used by only two people in the entire company. "Andropov?" I called.

Yuri Andropov, a heavy-suit driver on Fireteam Doria, had been my first and only roommate at the Academy. We came up together and sought a slot in the Hawks together. We'd had each other's backs in more barroom scraps than I could count, and when it came to close-quarters combat, he was the only guy who ever gave me a run for my money. We both excelled at recon tactics and tech, so we applied, and we got our orders within about ten minutes of each other.

"Here, Comrade," he said with that familiar trace of Mother Russia.

"You'll never guess who's on point...*again*."

He chuckled. "No surprise there, my friend," he said sympathetically. "Even if Yeo didn't have it in for you, you're the best man for the job. This shit show will be in-fighting the whole way. *I* would have sent you in there."

"Shit," I muttered. "Just watch yourself, you hear? And if I come scrambling out of these canyons, try and keep them off my ass with that big bore of yours, would you?"

"Count on it," he said. The comm was quiet for a few seconds, and then he added, "And be careful. I hear these VeeTees can be wicked smart. Keep an eye out for traps and red halibut."

"Herring, man. It's red herring. And copy that," I said as I entered the canyons.

As the rocky ledges rose higher, I took a deep breath and put on my game face. Through my pinplants, I ran another sys-check as I flexed my shoulders and neck, loosening them up. To the CASPers behind me, it must have looked like I was flapping my arms. Onboard systems came back nominal, so I stepped up my pace, jogging at a comfortable 10 kph. As I rounded each corner, I angled the laser shield to deflect any incoming fire. The strategy was to take any volleys head-on, let the shield do its job, and charge enemy positions of four or less. For more than that, or barricaded positions, I would fall back to wait for support from my fireteam and indirect fire.

The narrow alley of stone curved like a sidewinder, headed in a roughly westerly direction. There were side passages and forks along my path, but my HUD laid out a nav-point course to where the sensors had detected power emanations of a sizable VeeTee contingent focused around grid Delta Six-Niner. The plan was to come at them from three sides and drive them toward a wide, open plain about seven klicks away, where Colonel Hu and the rest of the Hawks were set up along a ridgeline, MACs ready.

We were up against a smaller company with heavy weapons operated by the Veetanho, a species renowned for their deadly tactics. They were chess players who lived for outwitting their opponents. The Hawks were something else: hunters. Unfortunately, in canyons like this, where MAC snipers wouldn't have LOS, it was probably going to be a slug-fest down in the dirt.

At least the playing field will be relatively level, I thought. It was a shitty deal, though.

"This isn't what I trained for, god-dammit," I said into the fireteam comm.

"Quit your bitching, would you?" Hsiu groaned. "This is the job, and you're the best one for it."

"I know, I know," I said, sounding a bit whinier than I would ever admit.

It was five klicks to Delta Six-Niner via my winding route. I slowed as I rounded each corner and picked up the pace in the straights. If they had seismic detectors—a strong probability—they'd know I was coming. I just had to hope the shield kept me in one piece long enough to close in on them.

I'd covered two clicks and rounded a bend when my sensors lit up like Chinese New Year. Four units spread out behind large boulders across a sixty-meter opening in the canyon glowed red on my HUD just as their first volley came in. Two laser blasts hit my shield and deflected to my left at a shallow angle, one went by my head at about a decimeter, and the fourth grazed my shoulder, tearing a furrow in the plating. An alarm sounded at the impact, and my training kicked in.

"Contact!" I shouted. I leaned forward, dashing for the canyon wall, and accelerated to full speed. "This is Shikra Unit Four, I repeat, contact!" The big advantages of Hu's modified Mk 7s were weight, agility, and speed. We couldn't take near as much punishment as a standard Mk 7, but we were more mobile than just about any opponent we encountered. We were like ninja's up against Medieval Knights. Activating the jumpjets through my pinplant interface, I leapt five meters, keeping the shield between me and the VeeTees. I ran a half-dozen steps across the vertical rock face of the canyon, leapt outward, and hit the jumpjets. I sailed over the wide opening, closing the distance to the enemy positions at 50 kph. All four of their barrels rose to track me, and they let loose two more volleys, all missing my feet by meters.

From my angle, I confirmed there were only four armored VeeTees, their pointed helms and heavy limbs easy to identify. Checking my trajectory, I hit the jumpjets one more time and crossed their line of fire. I twisted hard as I came in, rotating my feet over my head, around, and beneath me to land on the extreme right side of their line. The VeeTees were now lined up so only one of them could fire at me at a time.

The one in front aimed its rifle at me, but I brought my shield down hard on it, prompting a shower of sparks as the weapon went dead. I slammed the VeeTee's arm sideways and came in hard with the extended blade, jamming it into the notch between its helmet and left shoulder.

Metal rang on metal, but then I felt the blade penetrate.

"Sorry, buddy," I said and yanked the blade free. Atmosphere blasted from its respirator in a fountain of gas and crystals. I wrapped my arms around the VeeTee, and with the shield covering its back, stepped backward, dragging it with me. I had about five meters of space behind me, but that was more than enough.

Glancing to my right, I saw the rest of Fireteam Shikra step out into the open, their shoulder MACs lowered. All three CASPers shuddered at the same time, firing together. A kilogram of depleted uranium, accelerated to Mach 6, slammed into each of the remaining VeeTee units.

I leaned sideways, peeking around the VeeTee suit in my arms, and watched all three enemies blossom with fire from the impacts to head and torso before falling backward and hitting the dusty ground.

"Four enemy units down," Hsiu said into the general comm. "At grid Alfa Four-Seven. We're…" The ground shook violently beneath our feet, cutting him off. One, two, three detonations reverberated in rapid succession. "Command, are you reading explosions?" The walls of the narrow canyon just beyond the enemy position erupted. The force sent us all sailing back the way we came as rocks and debris hammered against our armor.

I slid across the dusty ground as a long series of explosions continued to quake through our suits. My HUD jittered and static blared in my ears for a few seconds, then the system came back on line.

"—ders check in." It was Yeo's voice, urgent but icy calm. "I repeat, fireteam leaders check in."

"Gimmie a status, GO-NO-GO by the numbers!" Hsiu ordered through the fireteam comm. We all reflexively ran a sys-check.

"Shikra Two, GO," Chang groaned, grunting as his CASPer rose to its feet directly in front of me.

"Shikra Three, NO GO," Kilgore added. "Limited mobility and MAC off-line."

"Shikra Four, GO," Pardeaux said. "Ready to rock and roll."

My sys-check came back nominal. "Shikra Five, GO," I growled as I got my feet under me and looked at the damage around us.

The narrow gap along our intended route had completely collapsed.

"Kilgore, limp back to the crater and stand by," Hsiu said into the fireteam comm, then he swapped to the command comm. "Shikra One reporting in. Four CASPers operational and one damaged but marginally mobile. Our path to Delta Six-Niner is blocked. I'm sending Unit Two back to the crater at Grid Alfa Seventeen for EVAC. Shikra can either go back the way we came or over the top. What are your orders?"

"Standby, Shikra," Yeo said urgently. "Collating options. It's hotter to the north and south."

"Roger that," he said.

"Well that sucked," I said into the fireteam comm. "What the fuck just happened?"

"I suspect the VeeTees just shut a bunch of doors," Chang said, his frustration coming through loud and clear.

"And maybe buried a few of our friends," Pardeaux chimed in.

"Shit," I barked. "If we have to hump it across the top, we're gonna be sitting ducks."

"Stow that," Hsiu ordered. "If it's the top, it's the top. We spread out, deploy shields, and take them head-on. At least our MACs and those on the ridge will give us some advantage. Our shields will give us plenty of time to spot them and turn those VeeTee units into Swiss cheese."

A full minute passed as we waited for orders from Yeo or Command.

"May day!" a woman shouted over the general comm. "Doria Two reporting! The corporal is down, and we're taking heavy fire! Half of Gabar is buried in a landslide. The rest are supporting our position from cover. We have the package but are about to be overrun. Some of them got behind us, and we're bracketed."

"What is your position, Doria Two?" Yeo asked, her voice calm, icy. The woman never lost her cool.

"Grid Charlie Eight-Niner!" the woman shouted. "Andropov, lay down some suppressing fire with that LMG. Get those fuckers off us and buy us some time!"

"Roger that," Adropov said as the comms filled with the reverberation of machine gun fire coming through his chassis. Then it cut off.

"Command?" Yeo asked. "Do you have LOS on Grid Charlie Eight-Niner?"

"Negative. There's a low ridge between us and them. It's not more than a ripple in the topography, but it's enough. I doubt that's a coincidence, though. They didn't take the bait we set. They squeezed north rather than being pushed west. You're on your own unless you get everyone on this side of that ripple."

"Copy that. Will improvise." There was a pause of about fifteen seconds, then Yeo's voice came over the general comm. "Doria Two, this is Yeo. We can't get to you in time, but Shikra has a bead on you from heading zero-six-zero at about two klicks with a clear line and an open expanse between you. I need you to take Gabar, the remaining Doria units, and the package. Make a run for Alfa Four-Seven. Cooper, take your remaining active units and set up at Charlie Seven. I think you have a rise there. We can all tear them apart when they pop their heads up to track the package. Sorry, Doria Two, but you'll have to be the bait to get them out in the open. Jump to the top and high-tail it. I repeat, make a run for Alfa Four-Seven."

There was a pause. The comms opened and closed once to the sound of breathing, as if she'd started to say something, then stopped, then again, to the sound of two MAC rounds fired in short succession.

Seconds later, Gabar Four said, "Are you sure? Our asses are going to be awfully exposed up there."

"Confirmed. I know you know what that means. Rest assured, we won't miss."

"Affirmative," the reply came, quiet and resolved.

"Call out ten seconds before you start your run. And remember, you've *got* to protect that package. See you on the other side, Bai."

"Roger that." There was a long pause, and then she added, "Raise one for me, Jiang. You know the drill."

"I surely do."

"Command?" Yeo said.

"Go ahead." It was Colonel Hu's voice.

"I need a rocket barrage dropped on grid Charlie Eight-Eight on my mark. Fire everything and drop it right on that mark. Saturate that area and the area south of it. *Nothing* goes north. I want to drive those VeeTees out of the canyons."

"Copy that," he said. There was worry in his voice. "We'll melt the tubes. Everything goes on Charlie Eight-Eight."

A few moments later, the private frequency with Andropov chirped. "Killian?"

"Yeah?" I replied.

"Thanks for everything, my friend," he said, his voice low and full of fear.

"What?"

"There's no way we'll make this run in one piece," he said. "Tell my parents what we did here, will you?"

"What are you talking about?" I asked. It was my turn to feel the fear. "Just run your asses off, and we'll cover you. We got this!"

"Sure you do, buddy," he said quietly, and then the comm cut off.

"Starting our run in ten …nine …" Doria Two started counting down.

"Command," Yeo said. "Fire at will. Fire for effect. Cooper and Shikra, hit the rims and line up on grid Charlie Eight-Eight. You see a VeeTee unit, you put a hole in it."

"Copy that," Hsiu and the other fireteam leader said together.

"You heard the sergeant," Hsiu said into the fireteam comm. "Hit the ledge! MOVE!"

There was no more time for talk. All I could think about was Andropov and how exposed his ass was about to be. We hit our jumpjets, rising fifteen meters to the top, and lowered our shoulder-mount MACs. The grid appeared in my HUD, and the four of us spread out five meters apart, sighting in on the enemy position.

The white trail of rockets appeared a handful of klicks off to the west, dozens of them in wave after wave, coming from the distant ridge line and arcing in toward grid Charlie Eight-Eight.

"GO! GO! GO!" Doria Two shouted. What remained of Fireteams Doria and Gabar shot into the air, jumpjets flaring, looking as if they'd been fired out of canons. They arced up, over, and then down to land about a hundred meters from where they'd emerged, all of them moving in a dead run.

There were six left, and they took up a phalanx formation, with Doria Two at the point leading them. I zoomed my optics in to see her racing forward at 50 kph, a trussed and squirming Depik held in her left arm, and her shield swapped to her right arm, protecting it. Two units trailed behind her at five meters, practically side by side. They'd swapped their shields as well, covering the unit on their right. Behind them ran the remaining three CASPers, also holding out their shields to cover the unit on their right. In one motion, the five units behind Doria Two reached for their waists, yanked grenades, and hurled them blindly toward Charlie Eight-Eight.

The grenades went off, raising plumes of rock and soil, and then a line of five VeeTees rose over the ledge, opening up at the phalanx. Orange chem-lasers skittered across the plain, scoring several hits as my targeting system danced over them. The instant I heard a lock-on tone, I quickly fired three MAC rounds. The VeeTees fired another volley, then four of the VeeTees staggered backward as the energy of our rounds penetrated their armor. The fifth VeeTee fired another volley and took out the leg of a trailing Doria CASPer, knocking it down and sending it sliding across the earth in a gout of soil, atmo venting from the bottom of its chassis. Its momentum carried it over the edge of a canyon where it disappeared.

"Goodbye, my friend," Yuri gasped over our comm, then went silent.

My heart broke.

The VeeTee that had killed Yuri stepped backward and disappeared into the canyon it had come from.

That's when Hu's rocket barrage hit Charlie Eight-Eight. The ground erupted in high explosive detonations, sending rocks and debris sailing into the air and creating a curtain of smoke along the enemy position.

"Move it, Bai!" Yeo shouted into the comm.

The remaining five CASPers moved forward, putting on an amazing burst of speed, leaping over canyons as they tore across the surface.

A dozen VeeTee troopers rose out of the smoke enveloping Charlie Eight-Eight, their lasers tearing up the earth around the fleeing units. Another CASPer went down, and another. Then we returned fire.

It was the worst kind of slug-fest.

Fireteam Cooper laid into the southern line of VeeTees hard, and the nearest alien blew apart like it had been full of explosives. Shikra hammered the center of the VeeTee line, blowing legs off and putting holes in torsos. Another CASPer went down, leaving Doria Two, one of the units behind her, and one behind that.

"Shikra, move to meet Doria Two!" It was the only time I'd ever heard desperation in Yeo's voice. "Fire on the move!" she shouted into the comms. "Cooper, lay down suppressing fire! All weapons!"

Fireteam Shikra moved as one, striding across the plain at full speed. We emptied our MACs, all of us running out of ammo as we closed in on the last three retreating CASPers. Four VeeTees remained, pouring laser fire across the field. I pulled my heavy laser pistol and emptied that, too.

"Cooper is empty." I recognized the voice of Corporal Stallings, the fireteam leader. "All MACs are depleted, and our sidearms won't get the job done."

"Shit," I barked into the comms.

"Fall back and reload each other," Yeo ordered. "And pray, while you're at it."

A VeeTee went down just as the remaining enemy units brought down the rear CASPer and the one directly behind Doria Two. Atmo vented from both. Doria Two leapt, hitting her jumpjets and thrusting in a low arc, heading straight for us. We all fired at the remaining VeeTees, bringing down another, but not before Doria Two took a hit that spun her. She pulled the Depik close to her chest and managed to rotate her body so that it was on top of her, and then she hit the ground, sliding across the surface and coming to a stop five-hundred meters short of us. We ran in hard, waiting for the last three VeeTees to start shooting at us. As I watched, waiting for the sound of venting atmosphere, a wound from a MAC round blossomed on a VeeTee's chest, and then another's.

"Got you covered," Kilgore said. I checked the grid and realized he had come up out of the canyons halfway between the crater and where we'd found the first VeeTee squad. "Get the package."

The last VeeTee unit disappeared into the canyons, obviously preferring to be the last VeeTee alive than the last one killed.

Fireteam Shikra made it to Doria Two and the Depik in a matter of seconds. The alien was still clutched in her arms, wriggling. We surrounded the damn thing, staring down at it, and it glared back at us through its purplish faceplate. I fought the urge to reach out, grab the faceplate, and squeeze it until it shattered. The Hawks would lose a ton of credits but getting drummed out of the mercenary guild might just be worth it.

Before I could make the wrong decision, Yeo stepped up beside me and wrapped a couple more body restraints around the feline alien.

"Command," she said into the general comm, "I suspect the VeeTees will pull out now that we have the package and they've taken such heavy losses. I'm requesting a mop up and EVAC. Let's collect our people and equipment and get the hell off this rock."

"Acknowledged," Colonel Hu said. "Dropships inbound. I'll come down with the three fireteams from the ridge and lend a hand."

"Roger that," Yeo said as she picked up the Depik and stared into its face. "You'd better be worth it," she said.

* * *

The mop-up took us hours.

There were seven dead, three injured, and more CASPer junk than anyone wanted to think about. The *only* things we had going for us were that we'd gotten the Depik safely into custody and the VeeTees had apparently given up on their payday.

Aside from orders given by Hu and the staff sergeants, the only person who said anything was me. I wasn't silent about how the mission went, or about losing my friend. I bitched about the whole thing non-stop until we were on the dropships, heading back to our tender. Fireteam Shikra and Sergeant Yeo were on our ship, along with the bodies and the wreckage, which spurred me on. Fortunately,

Hsiu had isolated my comms so that only he could listen in. He was kind and courteous, letting me blow off steam, until I started in on Yeo's command ability. That's when he gave me my callsign.

"Command," Hsiu said into the general comm, interrupting my next tirade, "this is Corporal Hsiu. I think I finally have an appropriate callsign for Shikra Five."

"Go ahead, Shikra Leader," came Hu's curious reply.

"I'm officially designating Shikra Five, 'Bitchy.'"

Hu chortled once, then got ahold of himself, cutting his laughter off with a feigned cough. "Roger that, Shikra Leader. Shikra Five is designated, 'Bitchy.'"

I spotted the slight, tell-tale shifting and squirming of my fireteam laughing inside their suits, but they all had the decency not to broadcast their laughter over the comms. Yeo's suit didn't move a millimeter.

I snapped.

"Go fuck yourself, Hsiu," I shouted. "Yeo doesn't care about her people. And what's worse, she's a coward, barking orders from the rear—"

Hsiu moved so fast I didn't know I'd crossed the line until he came out of his seat, grabbed my suit, and slammed me against the bulkhead, the point of his blade filling my HUD.

"Shut your fucking mouth, Killian!" he growled. "You don't have the slightest idea what you're talking about." The point of the blade didn't waver. "I tolerate a lot from you, because you're damn good at what you do, but you say anything like that again, and I'll kill you. You think you're the only person who's lost a friend? Bai, Doria Two, was like a sister to Yeo. Corporal Stallings in Cooper lost his little brother in that phalanx, and Bai Zhāng was Bao Zhāng's older brother. You know, Bao from Fireteam Cooper." He finally lowered the blade and let go of me. "We all lose people, Killian. That's the job, and if you can't hack it, get out. Now…Suck. It. Up!"

Part 3—The Downside of Contracts

All four privates were silent as they stared at Corporal Killian. In turn, he eyed each of us, his mouth pressed into a grim line.

Boudreaux had to admit, all he'd ever heard about the Hawks was how much ass they kicked. They really were a legend at the Academy and throughout the Mercenary Guild. They'd been in the top ninety-seventh percentile of successful missions since Hu took their first contract.

"Fortune and glory," Killian finally said. "That's why you're here, why you joined Hu's Hawks. But it isn't all money and high-fives. Not by a long shot. I hated Yeo after Reliak IV. And my relationship with Hsiu was strained, at best. But I couldn't get his words out of my head. I still can't. Sometimes I wake up with that speech ringing in my ears. I'll be honest, I was ready to quit. Unfortunately, I'd signed a twelve-month contract with the Hawks. That stuck me with Yeo and what I privately referred to as her "shit show." To get out, my only options were dying in battle, fragging her on the field, or paying a serious fine and losing my merc license for breaking the Hu contract. Shitty options all around."

Killian took a deep breath and leaned back in his chair, dragging a hand over his head like he was trying to dislodge memories, pull them out of his skull.

"Part of my problem," he continued, "was that I graduated at the top of my class and figured I knew it all." He looked at us and smiled. "Sound familiar? I'd been a natural pick for Hu's Hawks, like the four of you, but I was so full of myself, I figured the rules didn't apply. That's the reason I'd always been in Yeo's crosshairs. And why Hsiu covered for me. They both needed to take me down a notch without breaking me."

Leaning forward again, he said, "I told you that story, so I could tell you this one." He took a deep breath and let it out slowly. "After everyone healed and Hu replenished the fireteams, we shipped out for my fifth real mission, Kuason, a pure recon contract on a jungle world against an unknown enemy. It was the perfect sort of gig for the Hawks, so Hu took it and assigned one platoon to complete the reconnaissance. Yeo's platoon was going back into action, but with Fireteam Fiji temporarily replacing Doria, which was full of raw recruits. The mission was to get in, gather data on a race called the Thelosi, tag one of their landing craft with a beacon, and get out. It didn't go like we planned."

Part 4—Kuason

We entered Kuason's atmosphere in LAHVs (Low Altitude High Velocity aircraft). They're sleek, near-silent, needle-shaped aircraft with variable-swept-wing configurations. Capable of near-supersonic speeds in any atmosphere greater than half of Terra's, they were exceptional insertion craft for the Hawks. We dropped like javelins, burning our way through the atmo and leaving thin white plumes.

The planet was a hot, humid jungle world with several shallow oceans, millions of creeks and rivulets, a shit-ton of rain, and enough flora and fauna to drive any naturalist to the heights of ecstasy. Its atmosphere was also close enough to Terra's that we could breathe without equipment.

"At least we won't have to worry about decompression this time," I said as the LAHV shook around me. Already suited up, Fire-team Shikra and Sergeant Yeo sat in a single line on one side of the narrow compartment. Our equipment was at the back of the LAHV, tied down but ready for action.

"That's better," Hsiu replied, sounding like he was talking to a kid. "Keep finding that silver lining, and I may just change your callsign to 'Sunny.'" He laughed at his own joke.

I sighed, bit my tongue, and pulled up a map on my HUD as our LHAV free-fell into the atmosphere two thousand klicks north of the objective. I memorized the route we intended to take, marking several geographical features discovered as we orbited the planet. I assumed everyone else was doing the same thing, since nobody said a word. The whole company had been quiet since Reliak IV. The heavy losses there had really put a choke-hold on our spirits.

The LHAV wings finally swung out, and we endured ninety seconds of high-G turns as the pilot leveled us out at about a thousand feet. We felt him drop even lower and endured the rise and fall of nap-of-the-earth flight for a couple of hours as he hugged the treetops covering the rippled terrain of Kuason before touching down on the leeward side of a low mountain.

The whole platoon spent half a day setting up a comm post at the top of the mountain, then we mounted our Dragonflies. Capable of lifting Hawk's Mk 7 CASPers, Dragonflies are still my favorite bit of equipment utilized by the company. A cross between motorcycles and four-fan drones, they make the perfect vehicles for recon squads. In hover mode, the four lift fans form an X beneath the chassis and operate like a helicopter. In fast flight, however, the fans swing into a single line, two fore and two aft, and can hit speeds of 200 kph.

Twenty Dragonflies sailed and darted through the boles of 130-meter trees that looked a lot like Terran redwoods, but had peeling bark that rained down on us in a constant drizzle. We raced above the lower canopy that rose about 15 meters above the sun-starved ground beneath us. There were whoops and cheers as most of the platoon indulged themselves in flying through the trees like they were teenagers at an amusement park.

"Okay, children," Yeo said in an easy tone, "fun time is over." We were eight klicks out from our objective. She goosed the throttle and shot out ahead of us. "Level out, tighten up into fireteams, and go comm-silent. Stallings, Fireteam Cooper gets tracker duty. Intel puts that landing craft on the far side of their position. Sweep west and radio in only if you succeed or engage the enemy."

"Roger that," Stallings replied. Without another word, Fireteam Cooper rose a few meters then swept off to our right, quickly disappearing into the trees.

"Gabar goes left, Fiji right," Yeo ordered. "Flank at 200 meters and pace us all the way in. Shikra and I will set down one klick out, just like we discussed." She rose a few meters and decelerated, dropping her Dragonfly right between me and Hsiu. "Everyone remember that this is recon. We want to gather as much intel on these Thelosi as we can, then head out without any firefights breaking out. No Human has seen one of these things before. They're not indigenous, and we don't know what brought them to Kuason."

Suddenly, something began eating at me. "Hsiu," I said on a private channel. "Does any of this seem odd to you?" When we'd had the mission briefing aboard our tender, it seemed like just another recon mission. But when Yeo laid it all out like she did, I got some serious jitters. We were practically flying blind.

"Don't start," he replied with a bit of an edge. Hsiu and I were cool, but he'd put a clamp on my bitching.

"I'm not," I replied. "I swear." I took a deep breath and tried to ease the worry in my voice. "I just have a bad feeling about this one, like we're heading into another shit show."

"You're just gun shy after Reliak IV," he said in an easier tone. "This should be an easy ride. Sneak in, scan some freakies, and head home for what I'm told is one hell of a payday."

"I don't know, man." I said. "Maybe I'm still stinging from Reliak, but this isn't that, or not all of it."

Yeo's voice cut in on our channel—what I *thought* was a private channel. "You're not wrong," she said. "I've got the same feeling, Killian, but orders are orders."

I didn't know what to say, and I didn't know if I was more surprised to hear Yeo agree with me, or that she'd been listening in on a private channel.

"We're Hawks," she added, "and we have a job to do."

Yeo spoke again, but on the general comm. "Everyone, listen up. I want you all to be extra careful on this one. I know we don't have as much intel as we would like, but that's the deal. I want *everyone* going home today. Full sensor sweeps and Level Five safety protocols. Nobody works alone except Stallings, who has to recon that lander. And if I call 'bug out,' you drop what you're doing and hightail it to the CP. Now move out!" she said. Without another word, she nosed her Dragonfly toward the ground, aiming for a hole in the lower canopy wide enough for two Dragonflies side-by-side.

I started to ease back, giving Hsiu and Yeo lead, but Hsiu dropped back hard and slotted in behind me. Two-by-two, the six of us dropped down into darkness.

My HUD automatically adjusted, turning the dark into a sharp, green-tinted fairyland full of deep colors, dancing insects the size of dinner plates, and glowing shafts of light that brightened the forest around us every fifty meters or so. Yeo drifted left and right, swerving around trees like we were on a slalom track. I paced her turn for turn, anticipating every path she took. I have to admit, she was good.

We reached the designated coordinates and set down in a whirl of dancing leaves and bark. Most of it was soaked, and our landing struts sank into the soft forest floor several inches. We cut our engines, dismounted, and checked our weapons. We'd swapped the high-profile, shoulder-mount MACs for another Hawk special: recon packs full of specialized sensor tech and a networking protocol.

"Dropping the grid," Yeo said. Our HUDs instantly lit up with a grid superimposed on the terrain around us. The map placed our starting position into the default Alfa Three-Six which put our objective at or near Bravo Two-Five, about a kilometer distant. Friendlies appeared on the map as green dots, and enemies would be red.

"Pardeaux," Hsiu said, "launch the hawk."

"Copy that," he replied.

He released a drone about fifteen centimeters across, made mostly of a clear polymer from his pack. The translucent device floated silently into the air on six small fans, quickly disappearing through the canopy. We couldn't see them, but the other fireteams would be doing the same thing when they reached their positions.

A half-minute later, the CASPers in the network linked together, tying the individual sensors into a single, real-time battlefield image shared and broadcast to the comm emplacement we'd set up back on the mountain. We called it the Hawk-Net, and everything we encountered would be recorded so that, even if we didn't make it, the intel *would*. Hu didn't like to miss paydays. We could toggle between our standard HUDs and whatever was in front of us in any position illuminated by the network.

"That's it," Yeo said. "Everybody start your sweeps."

Fireteam Shikra spread out in pairs ten meters apart. Oddly, Yeo partnered with me. We moved in toward Bravo Two-Five. The specialized actuators in our suits' legs, coupled with the damp litter of the forest, made our approach remarkably quiet, despite the fact that five half-ton CASPers were taking a stroll through the woods.

Stallings pulled ahead of Fireteam Cooper and launched a drone similar to the hawks but equipped with a tracker. Proper placement required LOS on the target to determine the best place to put it. The general rule was to place it between the engines and sensor arrays as closely as you could. Engines could drown out the signal, and sensor arrays had a better chance at detecting transmissions. Stallings was our resident expert on the things, so he usually got the duty.

We all held our breath as we watched Stalling's green dot sneak across the map and finally pause. A minute later, our network picked up the tracker, five-by-five, placing it squarely at Bravo Two-Seven. The first part of the mission was complete. However, we still needed to gather data on the Thelosi.

The plan was to scan at least one of the aliens, gather some medical data if possible, and observe their behavior. We scanned as we walked, using a variety of protocols including IR, ultra-high frequency SONAR, thermal imaging, and magnetic resonance imaging.

Despite that, we never saw what hit us.

* * *

"Contact! We've got unkno—" The signal cut off, replaced by a high-pitched screech that filled the comms across the entire bandwidth. We all flinched when the shrieking hit our ears, and we shut down our comm systems. The voice belonged to Stallings, but with our comms down, we couldn't communicate with Fireteam Cooper or each other.

Yeo stepped in front of me, held up her fist, unslung her rifle, and went down on one knee.

For a moment, my HUD showed an alarm, indicating enemy units, and then the alarm faded. It flickered again, on-off. Checking the map, I saw a whole platoon laid out in four patches of green dots, then two of Cooper's fireteam's dots went dead. I looked for red dots anywhere on the map. At first I didn't see anything, then I picked up just the faintest flicker of red here and there. A red dot would start to form, then fade. Most of them focused around Bravo Two-Five, but some of them appeared in the forest around us... *all* around us.

"What the fuck?" I growled.

I switched my HUD to the Hawk-Net, scanning for any sign of enemy movement. Here and there, I thought I saw faint shadows, black on gray, shifting through the forest. I yanked my pistol clear with my right hand and extended the spring blade on my left arm. I turned, scanning the forest around me.

That's when something slammed into my right shoulder, accompanied by the '*ratatatatat*' of high-cyclic weapons fire. I staggered sideways from the impact and reflexively went with the force and rolled down to a prone position. My sensors picked up a weapon about three meters off the ground next to the bole of a tree. I raised the pistol and fired. The forest lit up as two laser blasts hit something clinging to the tree. I couldn't see it clearly. It was mostly a shadow falling across a backdrop of shadows, but I knew something hit the ground and the hot-red glow of a rifle was not far from it.

"They're fucking ghosts!" I shouted, and then the forest lit up with laser fire lancing out from each of the hawk positions. We'd all been engaged by these things. Another flicker of red emerged from behind a tree. I fired twice, forcing the shadow to disappear behind the bole.

Something grabbed my leg, and I staggered. I instantly pointed my pistol at whatever it was. It was Yeo, clinging to my leg. One of hers had been blown off.

She rolled slowly onto her back and held up a grenade.

It was all the go-ahead I needed. I tried to grab the grenade with my left arm and realized it was out of commission. Holstering the pistol, I grabbed the grenade, activated it, and threw it just past where the enemy still hid. The second the grenade hit the ground, I spotted a shadow rushing sideways, away from the ordnance. Grabbing my pistol, I emptied it as the thing ran. It was small, no more than a meter and a half tall, and *fast*. My last round hit its midsection, and it went down flailing.

I dropped to the ground just as the grenade went off, lighting up the forest with a bright flash of white light. Shrapnel zipped by and pinged off my armor. Yeo held up another grenade, so I holstered my pistol, grabbed and actuated the grenade, and threw it at the next flicker of red I saw on the HUD.

Grenades started popping all around our perimeter. The rest of the platoon had figured it out.

Yeo tapped my leg, and I looked down. She gave the sign to fall back and pulled both grenades off my belt. Clipping them to hers, she picked up her rifle and struggled to a sitting position. Then she thumbed backward toward where the Dragonflies were.

It took me a second to figure out what she wanted, but finally, it sank in. She wanted me to drag her out, and she would provide covering fire. Her leg was a wreck. Blood seeped out from the chassis of her CASPer and had formed a pool where she sat. I realized she probably wasn't going to make it. In that instant, it occurred to me that I could just leave her there. The comms were down, and she was bleeding out. All my troubles in Hu's Hawks would be solved if I made it home, and she didn't.

Nobody would ever know.

Epilogue—The Lyon's Den

Boudreaux sat there, appalled. He glanced to his left and right. Mopantomobogo didn't look appalled, she looked disgusted. Keenes looked surprised, and Fujimoto's face was a blank slate.

Killian smiled.

Boudreaux couldn't tell if it was triumph, humor, or madness.

Why would the corporal tell such a story? There were rules, weren't there? Sure, everyone hears stories of people fragging their commanders, but Killian hadn't done that. He'd just let her bleed out. He said she was going to die anyway. But there were rules.

"Now you need to decide if you're gonna drink with me or not." Killian said.

Killian raised the first shot glass and toasted the four privates in front of him. "Who's with me?"

None of them moved. They sat there, staring at Killian, wrestling with who they were as mercs and Human beings.

Just as Killian had done on Kuason.

Killian laughed.

It started as a quiet chuckle and grew into a belly-laugh. He had a bizarre twinkle in his eyes, which seemed to be focused on something behind the four privates.

"What's the matter?" a woman's voice piped up behind them. It was a quiet voice, firm and bordering on icy. "Don't you want to drink with your new fireteam leader?"

The four privates turned to see a small, wiry woman of Chinese descent. She wore Hawk fatigues, had a Lieutenant's insignia on her collar and a Hawk patch on her breast pocket. "YEO" was stitched above the company insignia. She had the telltale, angular lines and bulges of an advanced prosthetic beneath her left pant leg.

"I told you they'd pass," Killian said.

The four privates turned, staring at Killian wide-eyed.

"But I thought you…" Boudreaux stammered. "You said…" He couldn't get the words out.

"Said what?" Killian asked, a shocked expression on his face. "That I let my commander bleed out on some alien world because of a personal grudge?" Killian shook his head. "Tsk-tsk-tsk," he admonished. "What sort of gaping asshole would do such a thing?"

"I...we..." Boudreaux stuttered.

Mopantomobogo started laughing, a deep, throaty laugh that lit up her entire face. Fujimoto's smile was slim, but her eyes danced with delight. Keenes leaned back in his chair and chuckled.

"You assumed," Killian went on. He leaned back and put his hands behind his back. "This is the Lyon's Den. You can't believe *anything* you hear in the Lyon's Den."

Yeo spoke up again. "Wrap this up, Killian. We're pulling out. I want you and any rookie who decides to step up back at the spaceport in forty-five minutes."

Killian stood and saluted her. "Yes, ma'am!" he said. She started to turn, but stopped when he said, "I still don't like you, you know."

This time, it was her turn to smile. She winked, then proceeded out through the curtain at the entrance.

"Here's the deal," Killian said. His smile was gone, replaced with deadly earnestness. "If you down these shots with me, you agree to be a Hawk, with everything that goes along with it. You are expendable. I am expendable. Yeo and every other member of Hu's Hawks are expendable, but *only* for the mission. That's the deal. You drink; you're in, plain and simple."

He pointed to the first shot glass. "This one is for Yuri Andropov, my best friend, who will never raise a glass again." He downed the first shot, and the four privates followed suit, gasping as the dark viscous mixture hit their throats and burned like gasoline.

He pointed to the second. "This one is for Fireteam Cooper, who gave everything they had on Kuason for the mission and the five of us." Five shots went up and five went down, followed by more gasping.

He pointed to the third. "This one is for Sergeant Yeo, who gave a hell of a lot more than she wanted to and taught me more about being a merc than I ever learned at the Academy." He downed his shot and watched as Keenes and Fujimoto struggled before joining the other two in the painful act of swallowing.

Killian locked eyes with them, one at a time. "I swear to you, here and now, that I'd die to save any one of you. I also swear that I'll send any one of us to the wolves if the mission requires it. That is my solemn oath to you. And if you drink this last shot, you're swearing the same oath to me. Am I understood?"

"Yes, Corporal!" they shouted in unison.

Killian lifted his last Cignus, light refracting off the inky blob and waited.

The four privates lifted their glasses.

"Hu's Hawks," Killian said.

"HU'S HAWKS!" they shouted, then all five members of Fireteam Cooper downed their shots and slammed their glasses on the table.

# # # # #

For the Honor of the Flag
by Doug Dandridge

C ade McGowan woke as usual from his nightmare, one word on his lips: Sabrina. His daughter had been bright and beautiful, with a future ahead of her. He had been off-world when she was kidnapped and killed. The mercenary had never forgiven himself. Alcohol, drugs, and a near psychotic break had ruined his life before he got himself under control—or as under control as he was capable.

The project waited for him, and he was putting all his spare time into it. Some people thought him crazy, but as long as the authorities didn't think so and didn't pull his license, let them think he was crazy. As long as he didn't tell anyone about the nightmares and the voices, they wouldn't think him the kind of crazy to pull his weapons permit.

The ex-mercenary patted the hard armor of the CASPer unit as he looked it over, standing where the second car would have gone in his garage if he needed one. As a confirmed bachelor, one was all he needed, which gave him the room to work on the powered armor.

I still wish I had gotten some cash from the company when they went under, thought the ex-merc. He had served in Gerowski's Fusiliers for over a decade, much of it in this suit of armor. It wasn't the most advanced version of CASPer. Hell, it hadn't been when he first got the armor. Nonetheless, it was still capable, or would be when he finished switching out the electronics. The parts weren't cheap, but he made good money and had nothing else on which to spend it.

Shame the Fusiliers went out of business, thought the private investigator. He wasn't there when they did, having already retired to Earth to see to his family. His wife had divorced him, blaming him for not being there for his daughter. He had blamed himself as well and found solace in a bottle and a pipe.

He walked up the stairs to his apartment. It wasn't a large space, just three rooms. It was expensive, and floor space had nothing to do with the cost. The view of Chicago through the huge picture window in the living room was the reason.

Cade missed his former life but couldn't bring himself to go back. Earth made much of its interstellar exchange from the companies, but the units were treated as revenue generators and nothing else. Contracts could be lucrative, but most companies operated on a small margin, what with the cost of equipment. A couple of bad contracts or heavy losses in a fight could be a ticket to bankruptcy. The Fusiliers had enjoyed exceptional luck with their contracts. However, a battle that had taken out three quarters of its mercenaries, including Colonel Gerowski, had spelled the end, and Cade wasn't willing to go through the hoops of joining another company.

Cade banished the thoughts of the past and connected to his comm. It was time to live in the present, and, hopefully, he had another job waiting.

"Mr. McGowan," said the man on the Tri-V. "I heard you were the best. If so, you're what I need."

Flatterer, thought the PI with a laugh. He knew he was good. An over ninety percent success rate gave him a reputation. Unlike most PIs, he did more than try to get the dirt on unfaithful spouses. His sense of adventure led him to take cases that gave him an adrenaline rush that lifted him from his dead emotions—locating missing persons, solving unsolved cases the police had given up on, things like that. It often brought him into very dark territory, and he had been threatened by people of power, both legal and illegal. After losing his family, threats didn't frighten him.

"I'm Gustav Schmidt. My sister is missing. We haven't heard from her in almost a week, and my parents are frantic."

The name sounded familiar. Cade did a quick search through his pinplant and had the man pegged. Schmidt electronics, based out of Germany, was one of the largest companies of its kind in the Solar System. Someone could ask for a huge ransom from them, if that was the motive.

"Connect," said Cade, waiting a moment.

The face on the Tri-V was one he recognized. It wouldn't be to most of Earth, but he had been dealing with the industry while trying to get what he needed for his CASPer.

"Mr. McGowan. Thank you for returning my call."

"Where was your sister when she went missing?" asked Cade, getting right down to business.

"In your city," said the man in a low voice. "Dagmar was studying quantum electronics at the University of Chicago."

Cade whistled. He himself was no dummy, but to study in that field took true genius since U of C had the best program on the planet. He looked at the face on the Tri-V. He could see money reflected there—perfect blond hair cut over perfect skin, blue eyes that might or might not have been natural. Those eyes were used to looking down at others, but now they simply looked scared.

"Where was she the last time she was seen?" asked the PI, pulling up a map of the University of Chicago and its environs.

"Her friends said she was at a place called *Obsession*."

Cade frowned. He knew of the place, although it was not one he frequented. It was an upscale nightclub near the campus, catering to students with money. At U of C, that meant just about all of them. On the surface, it seemed like a legit club, but the detective had heard rumors about the place and its underworld connections. The list of people who had gone missing at the club was long and growing. The police hadn't found anything shady about the place, but enough money in the right hands would make their cooperation a sure thing.

"Send me all the information you have on your sister, and I request a retainer of ten thousand credits. My fee is a thousand a day, plus expenses."

He didn't always charge that much. If people who were barely making ends meet called and seemed as if they had nowhere else to go, he might do it pro bono. For others who had money, like these, he would charge what the market would bear.

"Fine, fine. When will we hear back from you?"

"I can't give you a timetable, Mr. Schmidt. What I can tell you is I will be right on this case. Rest assured I will be concentrating on nothing else. I would appreciate it if you didn't call on an hourly basis. In return, I will call your number every morning to give you a report."

"Do you think you will be able to find her?"

"I think so," said Cade, feeling no such thing. Missing persons cases normally didn't turn out well. Whether it was some vagrant grabbing them for rape and murder, or someone who needed a pretty girl for prostitution, most missing people just disappeared off the face of the earth—but he would try. From the expression on the industrialist's face, the man didn't think he would get his sister back. That he had to try was a given. Cade was sure he wasn't the only avenue the family was pursuing. As long as those other assets didn't interfere with him, he didn't care.

Better get to it, he thought, taking a seat behind his desk to go over what Schmidt had sent him.

Dagmar Schmidt was truly an outstanding woman. Physically, she was a knockout. She had a perfect face—the kind that showed the genetics of the owner and was not a product of biosculpting—with a light dusting of freckles across her nose and deep blue eyes looking out at the world, all framed by silky blond hair. The pictures of her in a swimsuit showed a compact athletic body, the kind that reminded Cade of Sabrina. She was an athlete, a world-class soccer player, and was on the team at U of C.

Her mind was just as wonderful, with high genius IQ, a master of not just electronics and sciences, but a prodigy at music and art. She was a young lady, seventeen as of last month, who had a bright future ahead of her—even if she hadn't come from wealth.

Sabrina, he thought again. Dagmar was so much like her, yet unlike. Cade closed his eyes tightly and banished his daughter from his mind. This was not his daughter, no matter how much she reminded Cade of her. Still, it lent a new sense of urgency to the case, as if in saving Dagmar, he could also rescue the daughter he had failed to save. With that thought, he got back to business.

What had happened to her? He read deeper and saw she liked to have a good time. Drinking, dancing, even light drug use was not anything horrible, but the wrong people could take advantage of that.

After looking over her dossier, he pulled up information on Obsession. There was an extensive history there with many complaints, some court cases, and no findings. That was suspicious. Even a legitimate operation would get into some trouble now and then. There were always findings and some judgements against. The fact that Obsession had none screamed mob.

Mr. Taganaki, thought Cade with a frown as he saw the listed owner of the club. Taganaki had definite, though unproven, Yakuza connections. That sent a chill down the detective's spine—not for himself, but if the young lady had fallen into their hands, her bright future had turned very dark. The good news was that the Yakuza weren't about to waste such a jewel. She would most likely be funneled into a local prostitution ring, one that catered to high rollers. After she had become worn from overuse, she would be shipped to Asia, where girls like her were in great demand.

"Lt. Warshawski, CPD," said Cade into his system. It took time for the connection, and he used the time to look up Dagmar Schmidt in the local news. There was only one notice placed by her family in all of the newscasts, along with an offered reward. Other than that, he saw nothing.

"Cade," said the dark-skinned man on the Tri-V. "What rock have you been hiding under?"

"Good to see you too, Lieutenant," said Cade, a smile stretching his face. Warshawski was also a former mercenary, though luck didn't make for a long career. One hard battle and two amputations later, he was in the police academy. Artificial legs allowed him to walk and run, but as Cade well knew, the pain never left. "Work keeps taking me south. Not that I missed the bitch of a winter Chi-town throws us."

"Lucky bastard. I think you still owe me a beer from your last case."

"Let's set a date and time, then."

"I'm sure you didn't call me to reminisce. What can I do for you?"

"I got a call from Gustav Schmidt."

The eyes of the detective widened, and Cade knew he had struck a chord.

"Dagmar Schmidt?"

"That's the one. Gustav complained he couldn't get any help from your department."

"You know the rules about missing persons," said Warshawski, shaking his head. "When he called, she had only been missing a couple of days. You know how many young kids go out on a binge for a few days?"

"It's been more than a couple of days, Ernie. So, what gives?"

"We're swamped with missing person's cases," answered Warshawski, looking down.

"Bullshit, Ernie. There are missing person's cases and VIP missing person's cases. Dagmar Schmidt is definitely VIP."

"I can't talk about this on a link," he replied, looking down again, then up into Cade's eyes. "Meet me at our old spot tomorrow for lunch. I'll see what I can find out."

The link died, killed from the other end. Ernie had looked scared at the end, and Cade could only think of one thing that could scare a cop in this city. His own suspicions had just been reinforced.

Nothing more I'm going to get from the police, for now, he thought, checking the time and making a plan. Obsession wouldn't open until late afternoon and wouldn't be rocking until much later. Still, he was making a thousand credits a day, and he felt obligated to do something.

Might as well go visit the university, he decided, going into his bedroom to prepare himself. He didn't think he had ever been to that institution, the most famous in the region. It was about time he rectified that lack.

* * *

"I'm not sure I should be discussing this matter with you, Mr. McGowan," said Dean Margaret Townsend.

Cade was sure the office had been designed with intimidating visitors in mind. The desk was more than the administrator needed, with an expanse of carpet leading from the door. While it might frighten an undergraduate called to the mat, it did nothing for him.

"If you check your system, you'll see that Dagmar's parents sent a release, along with a court order."

"I've seen the release. The court order is from Berlin, so I'm not sure it carries much weight."

"Oh, come on, Dean Townsend. That's a world government court, and their decisions are legally binding all over the planet."

"Maybe we should appeal to the local court," said the scowling woman, shrugging her shoulders.

"And while you do that the life of a young woman is in danger. Aren't you responsible for her safety while she's a student here?"

"We do have some responsibility, Mr. McGowan. But do you really think we have that kind of control over our students? They are considered adults, free to do as they will on their own time."

Cade glared into the woman's eyes. He couldn't understand why she was obstructing him. If he had been in her shoes, he would have been bending over backward to help.

"I guess I could go to the papers and give them a story about how you are denying the validity of a court order," he said, flashing a cold smile.

"And we will sue."

"Very good. I have the Schmidt's paying my expenses. I'm sure they wouldn't mind paying for the best attorney they could find."

Townsend closed her eyes and let out a breath. Cade could tell she was rattled. Pressure was being applied by someone who didn't want a successful conclusion to this case, and here he was, applying pressure from the other side. *Time to apply some more pressure.*

"Perhaps if I got another court order," he said, smiling. "One allowing me to have a look at your personal accounts."

Townsend sat up straight in her seat, her eyes darting right and left in panic. Cade knew he had her. She had received a payment from some party she would prefer not to make public. She tapped on some keys, then withdrew a small data disc, handing it over.

"Here. Everything I have on Dagmar. And you didn't get it from me."

"If it has what I need, you won't have to deal with me again. But I need something else—the names of Dagmar's friends."

The dean sighed, then shrugged. She pulled out another data chip.

"Thank you, Dean Townsend," he said, standing. "And one last caution for you. I have friends who know I came here—friends from my days as a mercenary. If anything happens to me, they will be visiting you."

"Is that a threat?" asked the woman, eyes wide.

"Yes. I think it is."

Cade walked from the office, his back to the woman. He wasn't sure what would come from his final interaction with the academic, but it was sure to stir up something.

* * *

"That was the last time I saw her, Mr. McGowan," said the cute coed sitting on the couch. The girl next to her nodded, a concerned look on her face.

The apartment was larger than Cade's, with more luxurious furnishings. Cade had found that Dagmar's parents had rented the apartment, and the roommates had been given a free ride. Both girls had seemed bothered when he came calling, and he wondered how much that had to do with the thought that the meal ticket might have disappeared.

That's unfair, he thought. These were Dagmar's classmates as well as roommates. They took the same classes, went to the same parties. Of course, there was some real concern there.

"Any changes in behavior before that night?"

The two girls looked at each other for a moment. Heidi Walsh, a freshman from California, was the cute redhead, while Daisy Bush was a much plainer brunette from England. Heidi nodded, and Daisy spoke.

"We think she had made contact with some really bad people," said Daisy in her cultured British accent. "We think she had been taking drugs. She started missing classes and couldn't wait for the evening so she could go out and party. The night she disappeared, she was hanging with the people who worried us. She went to the bathroom and never came back."

"What clubs did she frequent?"

"Obsession—the club on the edge of campus. That's the only place she's wanted to go for the last couple of weeks. Heidi and I suggested some other places, but she told us she was going where she wanted to, and we could go hang out wherever we wanted."

"We're really worried, Mr. McGowan," said Heidi, looking at Daisy. "Disappearing like this isn't like Dagmar. Until recently, she never missed a class. She studied at least a couple of hours every night—until she stopped studying. The look in her eyes wasn't normal."

"Who were the people she was hanging with?"

"I don't have names, sir," said Daisy, looking down at the floor. "I can tell you that they were all Asians. Not that we have anything against Asians, but Dagmar was much more likely to hang around Europeans or people of European descent."

"What kind of Asians?"

"Japanese," said Heidi. "Mostly young men, with a few older guys. They sent chills down my spine, the way they looked at women. They surrounded themselves with girls—White, Black, Latino—but not a single Asian. It's like they were trying to gather a harem. The same girls were there every night, mostly. A few would go missing every night, replaced by some new ones."

"Did you talk with any of the men?"

"One asked to buy me a drink," said Heidi, who Cade thought met the requirements of these people. "I refused and never bought another drink at the club."

Smart girl. "Why did you go back?"

"Because Dagmar kept going," cried Daisy, closing her eyes and blinking back tears. "We wanted to protect her, but we couldn't."

Cade left the apartment feeling an overwhelming rage. All of these good kids had bright futures—like his daughter. They were the kind who would benefit the world once they finished their studies, but evil men wanted them for something else. At least, they wanted the beauties like Dagmar and Heidi. He decided it was time to visit Obsession.

* * *

Obsession was a couple of blocks off the campus, in the basement of a large skyscraper office building. Like a score of clubs in the neighborhood, it was intended to separate students from their parents' money. Like a hundred other clubs around town, it was designed to reduce the inhibitions of its patrons—it was just a little higher class.

The doorman was a mountain of muscle who looked like he had inherited his build from a genetics lab. He decided who could enter and who couldn't, and Cade was wondering what he would do if he were refused. He could leave and come back, or try to argue. There was no way he was going to fight that guy unarmed, and the City of Chicago frowned on people gunning down citizens.

"Aren't you a little old for our establishment?" asked the doorman, looking down at Cade from his seven-foot height.

"I like them young, if you know what I mean," he told the doorman, holding out a thousand-credit chip in his palm where the bouncer could get a good look at it without making it seem too obvious.

"Enjoy your evening, sir," said the man, palming the chip.

Cade walked in, sure that the doorman would be telling someone upstairs that he was someone to watch.

There had been no noise outside, but the wave of sound hit him as soon as he walked through the entry hall and into the club. A high-tech sonic shield kept the cacophony inside, making sure there were no complaints from neighbors. Music surrounded him, as if he were centered in the sound system, and moved with him. Thousands of voices almost overwhelmed the music, but not quite, which was another testament to the sound system.

Over a thousand young people inhabited the central room of the club. Holographic images played everywhere, some of low enough quality that they were not difficult to dismiss, others so real it was frightening. Dragons danced in the air, below a ceiling a hundred feet up. Or was that another holographic simulation? The dance floor was hopping with men and women moving to the music that vibrated the air. Watching closely, Cade saw some dancers move through the images of others—more holographs.

The odor of sweat filled the air, along with the scent of alcohol and the latest fad in inhalable drugs. A number of doors sat against the lower walls, entries to private party rooms, while stairs wound upward to balconies where worn out revelers could sit with drinks and people watch.

Cade worked his way around the dance floor to the bar. It was crowded with people trying to get drinks—all but one area to the left, where a dozen or so Japanese men stood. They had a look about them that was very familiar to the mercenary—hard men, with eyes devoid of feeling. He caught a glimpse of the hands of a couple and noted the missing finger joints.

Yakuza, he thought. From what he had heard, this place was owned by the Japanese mob. Organized crime was still a thing on Earth, and probably always would be. Many of the older crime organizations had gone under. The Mafia and the Cartels had been destroyed. However, the Asian gangs, the Tongs of China and the Yakuza of Japan, had embraced technology, developing their skills hacking into government systems to cruise along like money vacuuming sharks.

"What will it be, sir?" asked the bartender when Cade was finally able to get to the bar.

"Scotch, rocks," he ordered. As much as he wanted to, he was determined to not drink too much. In fact, he wouldn't take more than a couple of sips of anything this place served. He had even ingested some slow-release Quick Sober before leaving his car to be sure that nothing given to him would take him out of his game.

As soon as the drink came, he grabbed the bartender by the forearm. The man looked at him with hostility.

"Take your hand off my arm, sir," said the bartender in a quiet voice. "If I say the word, you will be out of here."

"I just have a question," said Cade, holding out a holo disc and activating it. The image of Dagmar Schmidt appeared, looking as real as life. "Seen this girl?"

"Sure," said the man, eyes narrowing as he studied the figure. "She used to come in here. Haven't seen her in quite a while, though."

Cade took a sip of his drink and closed his other hand over the disk, terminating the holo.

"Her friends say she used to hang out here with some older Japanese men. Men like those." Cade looked down the bar, noting that a couple of the men were now staring at him.

"A word of advice, friend," said the bartender, leaning forward and speaking in a low voice. Despite the blare of noise around him, the man was understandable, a tribute to the system of the club. "Don't stick your nose into the business of those gentlemen. You won't like what happens when you do."

"What will happen if I do?" said Cade, pulling out the false police ID he carried and flashing it quickly in the man's face.

"That shit won't protect you with these people. Even if it's legit."

"Any trouble here?" asked a soft voice. Cade turned to find himself looking into the eyes of one of the Japanese men. They were cold eyes, like those of a shark taking a bite out of its prey.

A pair of his friends were walking up, moving with grace and economy of motion that told the PI these people were trained. He wasn't sure in what method, but it had to be some fighting style. Cade wouldn't have wanted to fight them on the street. Give him a CASPer, and he was sure he would destroy them. He would give himself a good chance with his sidearm, but not here and now.

"No trouble," he replied, flashing a smile. "I'm just looking for a girl."

"We might have one for you," said a second man, shutting up as the first man turned a glare his way.

"What my partner was saying, was that we can provide female company for the discerning gentleman as soon as you pass our background check."

Meaning they want to make sure I'm not the police, and that I have the money to pay their price.

"I'm looking for a young girl. Athletic, blond with blue eyes. Just something that turns me on."

"Why not a nice Asian girl?"

"I have a thing for blond, blue-eyed Europeans. It just turns me on."

"You don't like Asians. Are you a racist?"

Cade didn't like the way this was going. It seemed like they were trying to provoke him. He was determined to not play their game. As long as he remained calm and didn't escalate, he was sure they wouldn't do anything in front of witnesses.

"I'm with the police," he finally said, confident that he wasn't going to get what he wanted by playing the John. "I'm looking for a girl who used to come here. Every night, from what I heard."

Cade opened his palm and activated the holo disk, showing the men the image of Dagmar.

"Are you kidding me?" said one of the Japanese men, looking around. "You see how many people come here. It's like this every night. So many pretty girls, it will make your head spin."

"Her friends say that she disappeared here."

"So she wandered out of the club. Fell victim to a street hood. Happens all the time. Our people are told to watch out for anyone too drunk. We cut them off, but there's nothing else we can do."

There was no proof that anything else happened, was there? "Thank you for your cooperation," he said, knowing that was all he would get from these people. Nonetheless, he decided to play one more hand.

"What relation are you to Mr. Taganaki? And what is your position in the Yakuza?"

The look on the elder man's face turned cold, while that on the other man scrunched up in rage.

"I think it is time for you to leave," said the older man. "And don't come back."

A couple of the younger men came over and bracketed the detective. When he didn't move quickly enough, one reached out and grabbed his shoulder in a vise-like grip. Cade was sure they didn't want to make a scene in the club, though if it came down to it, a little bit of creative holo work could cover up anything that happened to him. He turned to leave, then spun around when one of the young thugs pushed him in the back.

"Watch it," growled Cade, turning and pointing a finger in the man's face.

What he got in return was a cold smile and a fast-moving hand that grabbed his finger and twisted it. Cade cried out in pain, afraid that he was going to walk out with a broken finger, if not more. A shouted word in Japanese from the older Yakuza, and his assaulter let go.

Cade let the pair of thugs lead him out, noticing they weren't heading for the main entrance, wondering if they were going to do something to him they wouldn't want the police to know about. The weight of the small slug thrower in his pants pocket was a comfort, though he wasn't sure he could draw it in time to help against these two flanking him. Still, he had his hand on it, which gave him a chance to get off a shot.

The alley they had led him into was dark and narrow. Cade held his pistol in his hand, waiting for the thugs to make their move. He breathed out a sigh of relief as their move was comprised of them turning and going back through the door, slamming it with a hard bang.

Obviously, they didn't want anything to happen to him in the club. Now that he was off their property, he was fair game. While he was a hard and dirty fighter, he didn't think he could handle the Yakuza. Even one would have training and abilities beyond him. If it came to a firefight, he liked his odds, or he would have if he had any kind of real weapon. Combat vets seemed to do better in firefights than those who had only shot on the range or, in the case of the thugs, shot unarmed people down as they begged for their lives. Even so, the ten-millimeter slug thrower was not his first choice.

The detective walked back to his parking place, his eyes scanning, and his breathing shallow. He started when he heard approaching footsteps, only to relax when a young couple stumbled into view. An Asian man shared his elevator up, and Cade kept waiting for the guy to make a move. It didn't happen, and he was relieved when he reached his car, letting himself into the cab and pulling a laser pistol from the glove compartment.

The weapon was not strictly legal in Chicago, at least not for civilians, but his PI license gave him the clout to purchase such a weapon. He doubted the Yakuza would have much of a problem getting weapons as good or better.

Letting the car pilot itself home, Cade thought about what he had learned—not enough, at least for a court of law.

* * *

Cade's phone rang. "They're holding the girl in the sub-basement of the Taganaki mansion, up in the Heights." Cade knew the area, where old money still lived in the city. The hoods had been able to buy the mansion, probably by making an offer the owner couldn't refuse.

"Who are you?" asked Cade, not wondering too hard why there was no Tri-V accompanying the call. It seemed likely this man, if man it was, didn't want to be identified.

"You don't need to know that. What you need to know is the mob kidnapped her, like you thought. They made a mistake, not realizing who she was. Now they have a problem on their hands. In a couple of days, they will make that problem go away, so you need to move fast."

"Do you have some proof?"

"Don't believe me?"

Cade wasn't sure he did, but what the person was saying made sense. Fact, Dagmar had disappeared from the club. Another fact, her family had not been contacted about a ransom, which would have come if the kidnappers had known who she was from the start. They hadn't, and it still hadn't come when they had time to find out who they had. Thus, it wasn't coming.

"The police and judge will need proof."

"Then I guess you're not going to have the law on your side," said the voice. "Look," he continued, his voice lower. "I feel like a shit for my part in this. I don't want anything happening to that kid, but I also don't want to put my hide on the line. So, you've been given the information, and I'm out of here."

Cade immediately contacted his friend in the department, hoping for better than he was sure he was going to get.

"We're going to need more than that, Cade," replied Warshawski to his question. "There's no way the department is going to raid that house without hard evidence, and no judge is going to give us a court order based on an anonymous report. If it doesn't pan out? Well, you should know that careers have ended up in the crapper for less."

"We're talking about a young girl here," said Cade, the image of Sabrina in his mind. *I'm losing it*, he thought. It wasn't Sabrina. It was someone else's child, and not his responsibility.

"I know how you feel, but my hands are tied. Get me something else, something solid, and I might be able to move on it." The cop looked into his eyes through the Tri-V. "And don't do anything stupid, you dumb Irishman."

The Tri-V died, and the PI knew he wasn't going to get any help from the law. The clock was ticking. From what his informant had said, when the alarm went off, Dagmar would be gone without a trace.

That's not going to happen, he thought, again thinking of Sabrina. But how was he going to prevent it? He couldn't do it by himself, and he didn't have a company to back him. However, he did have something that could turn him into a one-man army, didn't he?

* * *

"You can't park here," growled the angry cop, her eyes glaring.

"I'll only be a minute," said Cade, getting out of his seat and into the body of the moving van, sliding the door closed behind him.

"Hey!" yelled the cop, hitting the side of the van. "Move this damn thing, now."

Or what? thought the detective, climbing into the CASPer. *Your bosses in the Yakuza might withhold a payment?*

Cade used the equipment to power up the mecha, then strapped himself into it. It was a tight fit in the cockpit in the best of times. Since he would have to dismount for part of the mission, he wore a protective armor suit that made it an even tighter fit. Add to that, he was sharing the cockpit with weapons, so there was no room to move. He never would have fit in a newer model.

The detective plugged in his haptic leads, engaged his pinplants, and pulled up some small Tri-V screens. A quick check showed everything was functional. *Thank you, Gustav,* he thought. The industrialist had come through with electronics that were a perfect fit. It was more than Cade could have bought with a year's earnings.

Here goes. A command started the loading hatch to pivot out and down, forming a ramp. The cop yelled out, heading for the back, and then yelped in panic as she saw what emerged.

"We have a situation here!" the officer yelled into her comm, pulling a laser pistol.

Cade doubted the police weapon had the power to penetrate. However, he wasn't willing to take the chance that she might sever a hydraulic or electronic run. As she leveled the pistol, Cade took a step toward her, swinging an arm with a folded laser shield and smacking her away. The cop flew through the air to hit a car. She slid down, her face scrunched up in pain.

That was yet another charge he would face if he survived. Since the odds were against that, he wasn't about to worry. He had enough on his mind.

Taking a step to the left, he faced the mansion. The gate was closed, and a few men stood guard outside. They were gesturing and yelling into comms, one pulling a weapon from under his jacket. Cade couldn't blame them for being in a near panic. A working suit of powered armor was not something seen every day on the streets of Chicago. In fact, it was something almost never seen, unless the police were deploying a heavy SWAT unit.

The detective visualized the movement of the suit in his mind, and the images fed into it through the haptic leads. It was also reading the movements of his muscles, the trained motions of an experienced operator. Starting with a couple of steps, he moved into a jog. The laser shields unfolded on the arms, and the autocannon on the shoulders started to rotate onto the target acquired by the operator.

The Yakuza pistols were slug throwers. If that was all he had to face, this mission was going to be cake. As they started firing, and the rounds bounced from the hard armor, he knew that wasn't going to be all he faced.

The CASPer arm reached out and grabbed one of the gate guards, jerking back and throwing the man into the air. The Yakuza screamed as he flew ten feet up and twenty feet away to land on a walkway with a loud crunch of breaking bones. The second gate guard flew into the fence to slide to the ground with a slack face and body.

Cade grabbed one side of the gate, jerking it away with the groaning of tearing metal. Tossing it out onto the street, he strode into the mansion compound, the sensors of the suit sampling the environment and feeding it into his brain. The air was alive with electronic emissions: sensors, comms, possibly weapons systems warming up. Voices were shouting, most in Japanese, which the suit computer dutifully translated. He looked out through the sensors, seeing a multitude of people that were prioritized as targets.

There were a number of laser rifles in the hands of people coming out of the mansion, while several windows were outlined and zoomed to show Yakuza with heavy weapons in their hands. All looked to be military grade, and totally illegal in just about any jurisdiction on Earth.

Cade raised the arms and unfolded the laser shields just in time to catch some beams before they hit the body of the suit. Sparks flew as metal vapor spurted into the air. Given time, they would get through the shields or start getting hits on the suit itself. Cade was not about to give them the time.

The magnetic accelerator cannons, or MACs, on the shoulders pivoted to a target. The one on the right spit out a round, cracking through the air as it flew at hypersonic speed into the first target, a man raising a laser rifle to his shoulder. The round hit dead center, the kinetic energy tearing the man in half.

The detective pivoted the weapons onto one of the windows while rifle beams were intercepted by the laser shields. This time, he fired both weapons, and the rounds went through the window. An armed thug and another Yakuza were eliminated.

The CASPer ran forward, picking out and engaging targets. Trained soldiers would have known how to engage the powered armor, but these men were not trained soldiers. They were thugs, used to terrorizing people who didn't know how to fight back. They stood out in the open as if they were fighting helpless victims, making themselves easy targets. In less than a minute, the battle for the front yard was over. Almost twenty Yakuza were reduced to shredded torsos and severed limbs. There were seven holes in the facade of the building, including the five widened openings of windows.

So far, so good, thought Cade, jumping toward the entrance, bursting through the heavy wooden door and sending a shower of splinters through the entry hall. A Japanese woman cried out as a long splinter penetrated her abdomen, sending a wave of guilt through Cade until he saw the laser pistol in her hand.

Cade brought up the schematic of the house. From what he had been told, Dagmar was being held in a sub-basement. The ceiling of the basement and the stairway leading down to it were high enough to fit the ten-foot-tall suit. However, he would have to dismount to get into the sub-basement. He needed to hurry, since the Yakuza were likely to start seeing her as a detriment and a witness and consider getting rid of her.

A man came down the stairway with a rocket launcher on his shoulder, swinging it toward Cade. The CASPer fired at the same instant the thug launched his rocket. The shell got there first, blasting the man into fragments that showered over the steps. The rocket hit an instant later on one of his laser shields. The explosion shredded the shield and damaged the hydraulics of the arm underneath. A quick diagnostic check showed the arm was still functional, though not a hundred percent, and the shield was mostly gone.

Cade fired a half-dozen rounds at the top of the stairway, hoping that would dissuade anyone who was trying to summon the courage to come down and face him. A scream at the top brought a smile to Cade's face. The more he killed, the less he had to worry about others coming up behind him when he went down to the basement. With that in mind, he fired another half dozen rounds, this time through the ceiling into the rooms above. That done, he pushed through the house, heading for the rear and the basement. Two more well-dressed thugs got in his way. He made sure they would never get in anyone's way again.

Here we go, he thought as he saw the heavy steel door the schematic said blocked the way to the stairs down. Holding forward the damaged left arm, he activated the built-in laser and started to burn his way through. It took longer than he wanted.

I'm coming Sabrina, he thought, his mind no longer in complete touch with reality. He hadn't been able to save his little girl and refused to fail in the rescue this time. Stepping onto the stairs, he started down, the floor rocking under the weight of his mecha.

A heavy beam weapon fired on him as soon as he stepped into the main room of the basement. The gunner must have been rattled, seeing the large machine coming at him, and the beam struck low to the left, sheering into the machine and damaging the leg joint. It froze up for a moment before moving with a screech of metal, and the hydraulic warning light came on. Cade didn't let the Yakuza correct his mistake. Instead, he sent three rounds into that area of the room, killing the gunner and his assistant, spreading their blood over the walls and ceiling.

Cade turned the CASPer around, feeling the wobble in the leg, looking with alarm on the warning schematic that showed it would soon fail. Voices came from above. The sensors of the suit picked up movement. It looked like a number of people were gathered up there, getting ready to rush down.

"You shouldn't be here, sir," said a voice translated by the suit.

"Whoever that is downstairs has invaded my house and killed my people," said a rough voice that Cade took to be that of Mr. Urishu Taganaki, the leader of the Midwest North American Family. "I will see his head taken."

Or not, thought Cade, checking his loadout and grunting with satisfaction. Both MACs swiveled onto the stairs, moving up to the top, while he waited for the first of the thugs to show. Three came into sight in a rush, lasers firing. One struck the CASPer and splashed alloy from the lower torso. All were wearing body armor that would have protected them from civilian slug throwers. The MACs sent their rounds into the men, blasting through the armor and bodies, shattering them. He continued firing, sending a dozen rounds to the top of the stairwell and into the room beyond the door he had demolished. Cries and screams came over the microphones.

"The bastard killed the boss," called out one voice. Cade smiled. No matter what else happened, he had taken out one evil bastard. That the man would be replaced in a day didn't mean anything. He had cut off a head of the hydra.

Maybe you should be more concerned with yourselves, thought the former mercenary, his sensors showing him more heat signatures getting near the stairs, some almost blotted out by the hotter blurs of fires his shots had started upstairs. The thugs weren't soldiers, or if some had been, they weren't acting like it now. They were bunching up, making a good target for the cannon rounds—rookie mistake, one that was beaten out of most real fighting men in basic training.

As soon as the heat signatures had gathered close enough to indicate that they were going to charge down the steps, he took aim with the cannon. Four came down the steps, trying to avoid the new gaps in the wood while trying to fire. Their beams lanced out into the basement, hitting walls, ceiling, and floor—seemingly everything but the mecha.

The CASPer pumped six rounds into the men, killing three instantly, leaving one to fall with shattered legs down the stairs to land at the bottom. Cade continued firing another six rounds, again through the landing above and the room beyond. More cries and screams let him know that he had hit a concentration, while the heat signatures falling to the floor gave visual reinforcement.

The system of the suit was running a constant scan of comm frequencies, anything that was broadcast. He had caught some Japanese, translated for him, with men talking about the intruder. Now, he caught one short phrase—*German girl*.

"We can't let that bastard get to her," came a command. "If you see her, I want her dead. Understood?"

"If he comes down here, I'll make sure she doesn't leave alive," said another voice.

Down there, thought Cade, breathing out a sigh of relief. His information was correct. He just needed to get to her before the guy in the sub-basement killed her. Yeah, that was all.

The system locked onto another transmission, one he had been hoping to hear.

"We're in position, Lieutenant," came a voice over the police emergency net. "But I'm not sure we have jurisdiction to go in there."

"Dammit, there's a battle going on in there," came the voice of Detective Lieutenant Ernie Warshawski. "We don't need no flippin' court order to enter the premises when it's obvious a crime is ongoing."

"But, what about Mr. Taganaki?"

Afraid you're going to piss off your cash cow, thought Cade with a laugh. He knew some of these cops were being paid off, but surely the Yakuza weren't paying off all of them.

"I don't give a shit about that crook. Move onto the premises and lock down the outside of the house. SWAT will be here in a few minutes. We'll let them go in. That's what they're paid for."

Time to go, thought Cade, opening the cockpit of the mecha and unbuckling his straps. He disconnected his leads, climbed out, then reached back to pull out the other equipment he had brought. It took a moment to place the web gear on his body and click the buckles closed, then sling the power pack over his back. Holding the heavy laser in both hands, he turned toward the door the schematic told him led to the downward stairs. He set the mecha for automatic operation, tracking and firing on anything that moved above. He only hoped it wasn't the police.

I'm coming, Sabrina, he thought. Cade closed his eyes as the painful thought entered his mind. It wasn't Sabrina. His daughter was dead, gone. He hadn't been here when she needed him most. This was another girl, simply a client. Nothing to him, but the most important thing in the universe right now.

The door was locked, of course. He burned through the lock in a couple seconds, kicking the door in as soon as the last piece of molten mechanism fell out. A laser struck the doorframe a moment after the door swung in. Cade ducked down, slowing his breath, calming himself. He was probably charging to his death—not an easy decision, and one that many people couldn't make. There was no time for thinking, so he jumped up and ran down the stairs, taking three at a time.

The laser reached out again, hitting the stone wall and burning into it. A glob of molten rock landed on Cade's left shoulder. He cried out, then dove forward into a roll, aiming for a couch that was sitting in the middle of the floor a couple of yards from the bottom of the steps. The Yakuza burned holes in the couch—any one of which would have burned through Cade if he had been in line with them.

"Help!" yelled out a voice faint from distance, or from another chamber. "Whoever you are, help me!"

"Shut up, girl, or I'll come in there and kill you now."

The thug gave Cade two pieces of information: first, that Dagmar was still alive; second, that her executioner was not with her. The schematic in his head showed three other chambers. One was another large room, and the others were the size and shape of cells. If she was in the cells, she was safe enough for now. She wouldn't be if he let the thug get to her.

Another beam hit the couch, burning through inches from Cade's face. The heat of the miss burned like a flame. It gave Cade a good idea of where the Yakuza was, and that he was probably on a knee.

The mecha fired up above, letting loose another barrage at the people trying to reach him. While it was in operation, he was safe enough from that avenue of approach, which left the primary obstacle to his front.

Cade gathered his legs under him, his heart beating in fear, his mouth dry. He really didn't want to do this. In an instant, he could be dead. Then again, he might be dead if he didn't act, burned down cowering behind a piece of furniture, acting like all the other victims these people killed. That thought brought on the killing rage. His heart was still beating hard, his mouth was still dry, but his muscles were now adrenaline-fueled.

The PI jumped up from behind the couch, sweeping his laser in an arc that covered all the possibilities for the location of the Yakuza. The thug shot him first, his beam striking Cade in the right leg, cutting through it and dropping him back to the floor—but not before Cade's beam swept through the thug at chest level, leaving two unequal pieces to fall over.

Cade gritted his teeth, holding back the scream that threatened to burst from his lungs. His leg hurt like fire. Fortunately, it wasn't bleeding, cauterized by the heat of the beam that had amputated the leg just above the knee. If he screamed, the Yakuza might believe him injured and redouble their attempts to reach the basement.

Crawling to the door was hard, but he had to rescue his little girl. Putting his back against a piece of furniture, he took aim at the locking mechanism.

"Get away from the door, baby. Daddy will have you free in a moment."

"Daddy?"

It's not Sabrina, thought the rational part of his mind. The guilty part still thought it was his daughter he had come to rescue. *It doesn't matter,* thought the most coherent part of his mind as he triggered the beam and burned through the lock.

"The door is hot, baby. Be careful."

The woman who came through the door looked so much like he remembered his daughter—beautiful beyond belief, the dream of any young man, enough to make any worried father proud.

It isn't her, he thought, the differences penetrating his fogged brain.

The young lady knelt beside him, wide eyes looking at his missing leg, then wandering to the thug he had sliced in half. She looked back at him, and Cade noted that her pupils were constricted. She was probably drugged.

"Who are you?" she asked in a soft voice. "Who's Sabrina?"

"Sabrina's my daughter," said Cade, reaching up and taking one of her delicate hands in his.

"I'm sorry, but there was no Sabrina here."

"I know. She died a long time ago."

The eyes of the girl reflected her confusion. "I'm Dagmar. I'm so sorry about your daughter, but thank you for coming for me."

"Not that it did you any good," said a harsh voice from behind. Dagmar looked that way, her eyes growing wide.

"I don't know what you were thinking, Gaijin. You wrecked our house, killed Mr. Taganaki, and took out most of our soldiers. Coming for this piece of ass? And all you've accomplished is the death of you both. Now drop that weapon to your side and slide it away."

Cade didn't see where he had a choice. The man had the drop on him. He dropped the weapon and pushed it away. It slid maybe a foot, not that far, but enough to satisfy the Yakuza.

The man stepped into sight, the middle-aged gentleman from Obsession. He held a military grade laser pistol in his hand, pointed at Cade.

"I knew I should have ordered you killed after you left the club," said the man, a frown on his face. "My associates thought we could wait and see what you did. Well, we waited, and most of my associates are dead."

"Too bad I didn't get all of you," said Cade, grimacing from his leg pain. "Go ahead and kill me, but you don't have to kill the girl."

"Ah, yes. The girl. Dagmar Schmidt. When we picked her up, we thought we had just added another whore to our stable. Exquisite, I will admit, and one that some of our customers would pay a fortune to be the first in. We had no idea who she was, only another naive student from U of C. Then we found out who her family was, and that produced a dilemma."

"You had kidnapped the scion of a wealthy family, one that might be able to hurt you if something happened to her. And you couldn't let her go."

The Yakuza smiled. "Smart man. We were shocked when we found out who she was. Her family has connections with the world government military—connections that could come down on even a family like ours. So we couldn't let her go, not knowing what she did about us. If we gave her back to her family, we chanced them still taking action against us."

"So instead you kept her, and they hired me to find her."

The face of the man twisted up in rage, and he aimed the pistol at Cade's head, then lowered it. "We didn't think the investigator they hired would be a madman, or that he would have access to military grade weaponry."

"No. Only scumbags like you people should have access to military weapons."

"I will tell you what is going to happen here," said the Yakuza. "I am Mr. Taganaki's nephew, now the Mr. Taganaki of this family, by the way. And, of course, you will die. I would prefer that your death come slowly, but Chicago's finest are demanding entrance to the house, and they are not about to take no for an answer. Normally, we could stall them, but a warzone and scene of mass murder allows them to enter without a court order. So you will be killed, shot down while invading our house. This young lady will also die, though in her case, I will drop the body in the vat of molecular acid we keep for ridding ourselves of inconvenient things."

"Why kill her? She's an innocent. Use some mind wipe drugs on her and release her downtown."

"No!" cried Dagmar. "Not that."

Cade could understand her feelings. She would forget her entire life, everything she had learned and achieved. However, death would also do that, and living meant she would still have a life ahead of her.

"No, you've already inconvenienced us too much. So say good-bye to your knight."

The man turned the weapon on Dagmar, taking aim at her head.

The image of Sabrina flashed before Cade's eyes. He couldn't have come this far, just to lose her again. Cade's hand darted under the equipment vest, touching the butt of a small slug thrower that he carried as a backup. Taganaki must have seen the motion out of the corner of his eye and turned, swinging his weapon around to aim at Cade.

Dagmar made her move. Despite the drugs and the fear, she allowed her body to fall into the patterns that had been trained into her. She took a step forward and slammed a hand into the neck of the man, following with a backhand to his face as he tried to turn. Cade had his pistol out by then, aiming at the Yakuza, trying to raise the point of aim to the head and finding he didn't have the strength. Pulling the trigger, he sent a shot into the back of the man, horrified the see the flattened slug fall to the floor.

Taganaki slapped Dagmar with an open hand, then turned to aim at Cade. He started to push the firing stud when his head exploded into steaming brains and pieces of bone.

"Cade. Are you okay?"

Lieutenant Warshawski stepped into view, laser pistol in hand.

"I'm much better now," said Cade with a smile as the image of the cop faded into blackness.

* * *

"I think he's with us again," said a familiar voice as Cade opened his eyes. Warshawski sat in a chair by his bed, a beautiful vision in the chair beside the grizzled detective.

"What happens now?" asked Cade, croaking out the words from a bone-dry mouth.

"Well, Taganaki's lawyers are screaming for your blood, and the DA wants to nail your ass to the wall. I don't think there's a crime on the books they aren't thinking of charging you with."

"So, prison." He knew that would be the end. The Yakuza would make sure that his first day in prison was his last.

"Not prison," said Dagmar, smiling. "In thanks for your services, the world government handed down a pardon, and my family has a job offer for you."

"Job offer?"

"We have some concerns off planet which could use a security supervisor, and Detective Warshawski has told us there are many contracts that have been taken out on you. My family is concerned for my safety as well. So, I will be studying on Mars. And you? You can have the position of security chief on our Ceres manufacturing facility."

Back off planet, thought Cade, smiling. He had thought he would never leave Earth again, but getting out of this hellhole sounded like the best thing that could happen to him.

# # # # #

Lucky

by James P. Chandler

1. Day One

A growing mound of poker chips on the brightly lit table drew a crowd into the shadows around the three players. A couple of security personnel stood close by to discourage gawkers from disturbing the game. Modeled after those on Earth, the local casino was Nolan Kantner's favorite spot on the planet Loosenshoor. The Lotar were notoriously xenophobic but had found kindred spirits in Humans when it came to recreation. They had even imported cards to allow for a proper game of poker.

Nolan ignored the gawkers but relished the glare of Soolunoo Hootushou. His Lotar opponent watched him over the cards he held in his secondary hands, his shoulders slouched forward, his primary hands under the table. The merchant's close-set eyes narrowed, and his round mouth pinched in a short, thin line.

Nolan had fleeced the guy all night after starting with only a few hundred credits. In the few hands he lost, he refused to bet enough for Hoot to win back his losses. Hoot had run out of chips, again, after matching the last bet. Nolan tried hard not to underestimate the guy, but it was hard to be intimidated by someone who looked like a beanbag Christmas tree.

"Oh my, oh my, oh my," Nolan's pinplants translated Santinger Kah's words. It was exceedingly rare to see one of the famously nervous Zuparti without a contingent of bodyguards. It was a testament to how safe he felt among the Lotar and Humans. Kah only played for his amusement since the entire pot would barely register on his accounts. Nolan couldn't complain; Zuparti weren't suited for poker, and his losses doubled the take. "He's out of chips again, Lucky."

"I noticed." Nolan smiled at Kah. "And don't call me Lucky."

"Isn't that what your friends call you?" Kah asked.

"Yes, but Dad says it's bad luck to call a gambler lucky."

"How odd," Kah said.

"Your move, Hoot. Raise or call?" Nolan asked. The thumping in his chest threatened to drown out the noise around them.

Hootushou's dark, monochrome eyes flickered from the pot to Nolan's neat stack of chips. He pulled out a Universal Account Access Card, often called a "yack," and handed it to the dealer with a comment that was too quiet for Nolan's pinplants to translate.

"I'm sorry," the dealer responded, "I cannot approve a loan against this collateral on behalf of the casino. Of course, the casino has a strict policy against the direct purchase of assets. You may find a third-party lender…"

"May I put the asset, itself, in the pot?"

"Only if the other players agree," the dealer responded after a thoughtful pause, "but the house will still need its cut." A murmur passed through the growing audience. "I believe you will need Merchant Guild approval before transferring such an asset."

"What is the asset?" Kah asked. "As the planetary representative for the Merchant Guild, I certainly have authority to approve such a transaction."

"Merchant Hootushou," the dealer explained, "wishes to put his manufactory into the pot to raise the current bet. Are you willing to allow him to do so?"

Nolan stood up straighter. The manufactory had to be worth hundreds of millions of credits, possibly billions.

Kah fidgeted more than usual as he pulled a small slate from his harness and tapped its surface for several seconds. "I have approved the contingent transfer of ownership of Manufactory GBX49881 for this game. Also, as a participant, I agree Hootushoo may bet the manufactory."

The dealer turned to Nolan. "Do you agree?"

"I'm not sure I can match the bet," Nolan said, watching Kah. Zuparti really weren't suited for poker. "I don't object, in principle, but what would I do with a manufactory that doesn't work?"

Lotar speech came from sounds produced through a complex system of tubes connected to breathing vents, similar to fish gills, on both sides of their necks. They could generate a vast range of tones but could not shape them into words as did Humans and most other species. Instead, they conveyed meaning through pitch, duration, timbre, harmonic chords, and other sound characteristics.

Hootushou squawked at Nolan like an abused harmonica, and Nolan's pinplants crackled with static, failing to translate the sounds. "The only reason it doesn't work," Hootushou insisted, "is because your friends locked the computers!"

"I have no idea what you're talking about."

The merchant stood abruptly and leaned over the table, supporting himself on the three-fingered fists of his primary arms and shouting like bagpipes being trampled by a goat. He waved his cards in his secondary hands but managed not to expose them. The other games around them went silent.

"The [crackle, crackle] you don't. Your little pranks have cost me millions."

"Just because you bought some relic you don't know how to use..."

"You [crackle, crackle] dare to [crackle, crackle]. You worthless [crackle, crackle]."

"If you don't calm down, I'm not going to agree—"

"[crackle, crackle]." The merchant's tone suddenly increased in pitch. Nolan winced and wiggled a finger in his ear.

"Fine," Nolan relented, waiving the Lotar back to his seat. "I'll accept the bet, if you agree that all the chips I have left will be enough to match."

"[crackle]. And you'll release the computers for my engineers."

"I still don't know what you're talking about."

"[crackle, crackle] mercenary [screech]."

"Fine. If I lose, I will ask Mutt and Jeff to help, but no promises."

"[crackle], Human."

"Shall we proceed?" the dealer asked politely as Hootushou settled back into his seat.

The dealer pulled out a square tablet not much larger than one of the chips on the table. He tapped the surface and touched Hootushou's yack to the mini-slate, then placed it with the pot.

"There," Hoot said, taking his yack back from the dealer. "I raise you one manufacturing company."

Nolan leaned forward, pushed the remainder of his chips into the pot, and nodded at the dealer to indicate he was calling.

Hootushou turned over his cards, a strong full house, 10s and Aces. A smile crossed the Lotar's whistle-shaped mouth, and the Human and Lotar spectators "oohed." Kah turned over his cards. Nothing. They were all the same color, but nothing else matched.

Nolan checked his hand again, and his heart beat even faster. He set his cards down and looked at the dealer for confirmation.

"Straight flush. Mercenary Kantner wins the hand."

2. Two Weeks Earlier—Evening

Nolan leaned on the bar and stared down at the two fingers of scotch in his glass. He twisted the glass between his thumb and forefinger.

"There you are, Lucky," Nolan heard behind him. Grady patted his left shoulder and sat next to him. "Mizz Honey said I'd find you here." Grady was the kind of friend everyone should have—loyal, forgiving, and a little bit reckless. Standing just over two meters tall, with biceps the size of rugby balls, his casual pat was going to leave a mark.

"Don't call me that," Nolan said quietly and downed the scotch.

"Oh, come on. It's not that bad." Grady shook him and smiled. "This place is great. Booze, cigars, gambling, gravity that won't crush you, atmosphere that won't poison you, and locals that actually like Humans. They don't seem to like many other species. Heck, if you don't look too closely at the clients, this could be Vegas." He waved an arm around the casino bar.

"You act like we're on vacation." Nolan motioned for the bartender to refill his glass.

"Why not?" Grady laughed. "The Colonel apologized for stranding us here. She said she'd make arrangements to get us home or, at least, to Karma."

"She what?"

"She apologized. Said she thought Hoot would extend the contract and ended up overspending on equipment and stuff," Grady explained.

"Sam said it was her fault?" Nolan asked, incredulous.

"Yeah. She expected Hoot to keep us on. He seemed to like us."

Nolan nodded thoughtfully as he looked into the fresh pour of scotch. That was not how he remembered it.

"Did she say why Hoot didn't extend the contract?"

"Didn't seem to know." Grady shrugged and sipped his beer.

"Was she mad?"

"Nah, just disappointed."

"How many of us are stranded?"

"You, me, the twins, Remf, and a couple others."

Nolan turned when someone tapped his shoulder, and he found Mutt and Jeff sitting on two stools to his left. Mutt was a Jeha, a shoulder-height centipede analogue, and Jeff was an elSha, a little reptilian about half the height of the Jeha. The unlikely companions had worked for the Honey Badgers since before Nolan signed on. They were genius engineers, but rumor had it the Badgers was the only unit in the Union that would hire them since they were borderline insane.

They seemed like nice fellas to Nolan, and the nicknames were too obvious not to stick.

"Old Hoot's gonna regret this," Grady said, raising his glass.

Nolan looked at Grady, then at the engineers.

"What'd you do?"

"Just a little encryption," Mutt said.

"I thought we decided no more pranks," Nolan said, looking from Mutt to Jeff and back. "We don't want to put him out of business."

"But he's a jerk, and we're bored," Jeff said.

"Really bored," Mutt affirmed, nodding decisively.

"You're only bored if you're boring," Grady said, nudging Nolan with an elbow.

"A bored mind is a terrible thing to waste," Nolan countered with a shrug and a grin.

"I want to see the thing work," Mutt said. "Took two months to decompress that hidden data, and we still can't find the language on the GalNet so we can translate the file names. We think they're manufacturing designs, but we don't know what for. It could be stuff we've never seen before."

"Only one way to find out," Jeff said, his eyes bright. "Turn it on and watch it go."

"Your big plan is to plug it in and see what it makes?" Nolan asked.

"We need to give it raw materials to work with," Jeff said, nodding.

"I don't think they need to be raw, scrap should work," Mutt said. Jeff nodded.

"What could possibly go wrong?" Nolan deadpanned.

"I wonder what Hoot would do if we moved it," Grady said.

"That's a really bad idea," Nolan said.

"It just needs power," Mutt offered. "It breaks down into twelve four-meter by fifteen-meter units. But the fusion plant is critically low on F11. It will only work for a few minutes, not long enough for disassembly."

"External power," Grady offered.

"We should stop talking about this, and you should buy me another drink," Nolan said.

"Very possible," Mutt said and looked at Jeff, "maybe a transport shuttle or one of those big ground haulers?"

"I'm pretty sure I could find a hauler to borrow." Grady said.

"Should be easy," Jeff said. "We know the power runs."

"Horrible idea," Nolan said, distracted, fingering a spot of moisture on the bar.

3. Day Two

Just like in Vegas, the casino comped Nolan a large suite in its hotel. And just like in Vegas, they pretended it was generosity, though the house's cut from the game would pay for the room for a few decades. Nolan had invited all the remaining Badgers to join him. The party had started before noon and lasted well into the night. Some of the casualties were still sprawled around the suite in various stages of consciousness.

As noon approached, Nolan sat in a stuffed armchair resting his feet on a table, his slate on his lap. He kept checking his yack to see that he was the proud owner of Hootushou Manufacturing and 6.8 million galactic credits. He had not realized the pot was that big.

A knock on the door broke the silence. Nolan set aside his slate and picked his to way to the suite's double doors. Outside stood a man of average height wearing a coverall uniform common among Human mercenaries. He was clean shaven and fit, a walking recruiting poster.

"Yes?" Nolan asked quietly, opening the door far enough for the man to see the other mercs.

"Good morning. I'm looking for Hootushou Manufacturing."

"Nolan Kantner," he held out his hand, "new owner as of about 28 hours ago."

"Mike Gibson," the man said as they shook, "Antonelli's Armadillos. Reporting for duty." He refrained from saluting.

"Let me guess," Nolan said, "you're here to take over the garrison contract for the Honey Badgers."

"You betchya. You don't seem excited to see me."

"I wasn't aware there was a mercenary contract, though I guess I should have expected it."

"We're here, all the way from Karma."

Nolan had met hundreds of Mike Gibsons during his years as a mercenary, men who never suffered from a lack of imagination in the same way turnips never missed having legs. They thrived on certainty and routine, always happiest building the boxes outside of which others tried to think.

"How much is the contract?"

"Ten million credits. Two platoons, backed by two tanks and four CASPers, for one year."

"Damn good contract," Nolan said.

"Twenty percent combat bonus, too."

"Ouch. I would never agree to more than five." Nolan shook his head.

"Good thing our contract is with the company, not you."

"You're probably right," Nolan said thoughtfully. "Have you already received a deposit?"

"I did," Gibson nodded sharply.

"I guess you work for me, but I don't have the funds to pay you."

"Then, we may have a very big problem," Gibson said tightly.

"I'll figure something out," Nolan assured him with a smile. "Where are you staying?"

"At the starport. They won't let us land at the site."

"Well, this isn't some frontier world," Nolan said. "I'll send someone to show you where you need to be as soon as I can."

"You'd better figure this out quickly," Gibson said. "I may be patient on watch, but I'm not when it comes to getting paid."

Nolan closed the door, shaking his head, as Gibson turned away. His visit wasn't unexpected, but ten mil for a garrison contract was steep and far more capital than he had.

He was returning to his seat when Grady came in, slamming the door behind him. Heads raised around the room, and some of the sleepers sat up to look at them.

"What's with Captain Generic?" Grady asked.

"Badgers' replacement."

"Here already? That was quick."

"What'd you get?" Nolan asked as he sat back down, and the other mercenaries sat up to listen.

"Another company from Earth took a contract with Theen Seemisroo, Hoot's big rival."

"Which outfit?" Nolan asked.

"The Knights Templar," Grady sneered.

"Never heard of 'em. Wannabe Horsemen?"

"Not those guys." Grady shook his head. "They were a drug gang out of South America before First Contact. Haven't changed much. They have face tatts and everything. Bigger guns and better drugs, too. They were chartered after the Alpha Contracts, when we were short on mercs."

"Bad news?" Nolan asked.

"Real bad. Smash and grab. They go in behind big fights and snatch up whatever gear they can, not always under contract. Rumor says they kill survivors."

"I guess we leave before they get here," Nolan said.

"Only if we leave tomorrow. They're scheduled any day."

"Frak, that'll be cutting it close."

"By my count, that's one too many shoes dropping," Grady said.

"In the Galactic Union, the other guy sometimes has more than two feet."

"Fair point."

"Hey, Remf," Nolan nodded at the junior comms operator lying on one of the couches. He was around the same age as Nolan, but his boyish face made him appear much younger. He was good people, earnest and reliable. He also got distracted easily and never got a joke the first time around.

"My name's Jared, why do you keep calling me that?"

"Term of affection," Grady answered firmly.

"You think you could cozy up to that guy who works at the Planetary Authority?" Nolan asked.

"It's a she, and she hates you."

"No, she doesn't," Nolan waved away the tech's concern, "she just owes me money. See if you can get her to watch for this other merc company. We need an early warning."

"Sure, I'll track her down." Jared stood, patted his pockets, ran his hand through his hair, and left the suite. Nolan walked over and picked up the tech's boots and equipment belt from the floor and held them out patiently. Seconds later, Jared came back and took his gear from Nolan with a nod of thanks.

4. Day Three—Early

"Good to have you with us, Seetleshee," Nolan said to their Lotar driver as the rented aircar descended toward a dusty landing spot. Driving most vehicles on Lotar required four arms, making the engineer a necessary addition. "Good thing Gibson made me realize you guys work for me now."

"It's better to work for you than against you." Seetleshee whistled. "And it's nice to know whose side those guys are on." He gestured at the twins crowding next to Grady in the rear. "Mostly sure, anyway."

"Heh," Grady said. "It's much easier than trying to drive ourselves, wouldn't you say, Lucky?"

"That was pretty awkward. For some more than others as I recall. Hey, didn't you say we should never talk about that?" Nolan twisted around and gave his friend a scandalized look.

"Yeah, let's keep that between us," Grady said, his eyes wide.

"Oh, there was definitely something between us…"

"Lucky…" Grady warned.

"I mean, if you need to talk about it, I'm here for you—"

"Never mind. Never happened."

"Just trying to help, Buddy—"

"Never. Happened." Grady released his flight harness. "Look, they're settling in nicely," Grady said.

Nolan turned back to look out the windshield, chuckling to himself. He could see the Armadillos' units positioned around the facility. Mercenaries swarmed the area, some patrolled the perimeter while others prepared fixed defenses. From this side of the facility, he could only see two CASPers and one tank.

Nolan and Grady exited together and approached the perimeter. Mutt and Jeff followed closely behind with Seetleshee. Mike Gibson walked out to meet them, armed and armored.

"You set up pretty quickly," Nolan said to the mercenary.

"Some of us are professionals," Gibson said coldly.

"We won't be very long," Nolan said. "We just need to run some checks on the computer and begin getting ready for transport."

Nolan took a step forward, but Gibson held up a hand to stop him.

"Not so fast, Lucky," Gibson sneered. "You can do what you need to as soon as you show me proof you can pay the contract."

"Hey," Grady said and squared his shoulders. Nolan held out an arm to keep him back.

"Don't call me that," Nolan said. "What the hell are you talking about?"

"Simple calculation. As long as we protect the manufactory from attack, we're fulfilling the contract. Doesn't mean I have to let you in."

"You can't be serious," Nolan argued. "Protecting the asset is useless if I can't get to it. How am I supposed to make money with it?"

"Nice try, but you just said you want to move it." Gibson looked smug, his hand resting casually on the grip of the laser rifle he cradled.

"How the hell am I supposed to pay you? I either have to use it or sell it."

"Not my problem," Gibson shrugged. "Get a loan?"

"Who's gonna lend me money on a manufactory that's not producing?"

"What part of 'not my problem' was unclear to you, Boss?" Gibson leaned forward, all pretense of friendliness gone. "Listen, Lucky, I came out here for a contract. You know what'll happen if I take this to the Guild? They'll make you pay the contract in full plus legal, and you won't be able to work as a merc until it's paid."

"That's not my name," Nolan said and shook his head. "How about this? Let my engineers run a quick diagnostic. I'll see what I can do about the money."

"Good plan," Gibson nodded, puffing out his chest a little more. "As soon as you show me proof you can pay, your engineers can do what they want. Letter of credit, bond, escrow account, whatever. I'm flexible."

"This is blackmail," Grady growled, clenching his fists. Gibson looked at him and adjusted his rifle.

"You're in breach of your contract," Nolan pointed at Gibson's face.

"You can bring that up with the Guild."

Grady leaned forward, and Nolan held his arm out to stop him again. "I'll be back," Nolan told him. "Come on," he said to his group. "I guess I need to round up some cash." Nolan led them back to the aircar, and they lifted off seconds later.

"He has no idea," Seetleshee said, incredulous. "You're much more fun to work for than Hoot."

5. Two Months Earlier

A sharp clanging brought Nolan to full alertness. He looked around his gunner nest atop the manufactory, instantly triggering the targeting protocols on the HUD of his combat helmet. He was positioned behind a tri-barrel laser cannon and scanning his kill zone before he realized the comms were clear of warnings. It wasn't an attack.

The clanging came from below, so Nolan left the nest and walked to the side of the roof. He left the rifle in place, but automatically checked his sidearm. He leaned over the edge and saw Seetleshee, one of the client's engineers, hitting the front wall with the biggest wrench he had ever seen. Curious, he climbed down the ladder fixed to the side wall, sliding most of the way.

Around the corner, he found Seetleshee still hammering away, his primary arms swinging with power while his secondary arms remained folded across his chest. He looked like an angry parent.

"You okay there, Seetle?" Nolan asked.

The Lotar turned and lifted the wrench as if to hit Nolan with it.

"Whoa!" Nolan cried and held up his hands to calm the engineer.

"You're right," Seetleshee lowered the wrench, "it's not your fault this time."

"I don't know what you're talking about," Nolan assured him. "What did the manufactory do to you?"

"It lied."

"Umm," Nolan responded. "I'm not quite sure I understand."

The surface of the manufactory was tan with patches of red and green, like a half-painted hot-rod. The wall was smooth, with no visible doors or access panels, though Nolan knew there were ways to access the interior. Nolan looked closer at the side Seetleshee had been hitting. He couldn't see a scratch.

"Is this armor?" Nolan asked, lightly touching the wall. "Why would a manufactory need armor?"

Seetleshee cocked his head to the side and examined the wall closely, his engineer's curiosity overriding his anger. He felt the wall with a secondary hand. After a moment, he raised the wrench and struck again. Nolan was surprised there was no echo or vibration, just a dull clang.

Seetleshee whistled exactly the way a surprised Human would. "Remarkable," he said.

A door opened in the side, appearing like magic from the seamless panel. Mutt leaned out, his centipede-like body curving around the edge of the opening. Jeff scampered out from behind and waved a hand at them.

"What are you two doing here?" Seetleshee asked.

"Trying to help," Mutt said. "It's still not working."

"I know," hissed Seetleshee. "We reassembled it exactly according to the instructions, but I keep getting fault codes. When I check the fault, nothing's wrong. And when I check the computer again, the first fault is cleared, even though I did nothing, but there's a new code. I check that one, and the same thing happens." The engineer's tirade sounded like dueling kazoos. "It's as if the computer is playing a game with me."

"Weird. We removed all the puzzles and games," Jeff said.

"At least you're not pretending you didn't put them there."

"I have no idea what he's talking about," Mutt said.

Seetleshee hit the wall with the wrench, and Mutt started. Then he stroked the wall and examined it, distracted again. The twins joined him for a closer look. Mutt pulled a device from a pouch on his belt and ran it over the wall.

"It doesn't recognize the material," Mutt said, surprised.

"Of course not," Jeff insisted. "I told you, the computer shows it has a stealth mode, which means the exterior must be something we're not familiar with."

"I don't have faith in a computer that plays games," Seetleshee responded.

"A stealth mode?" Nolan asked. "For a manufactory?"

"Hard to believe, but it makes sense if you have powerful enemies and want to hide what you're making or where," Jeff said.

"So, Seetle, help me understand," Nolan said. "Hoot bought this from somebody. They sent it here, but you don't know how to operate it. Now it's playing games with you? And it has a stealth mode?"

"Not quite," Seetleshee said. "One of our exploratory vessels found it. It was on a planet that has been mined until there wasn't anything valuable left. If any civilization ever lived there, it died long ago, and there's almost no trace left. Jeff claims the manufactory has a stealth mode, but I haven't seen it. We're pretty sure we can operate it if those faults would stop popping up."

"How'd they find it?" Jeff asked.

"Accident," Seetleshee explained. "There was a navigational error. They were forced to land to fix the ship. There weren't many safe places to land, and they landed near it. No idea who made it."

"It's actually salvage, then," Nolan said, slowly stroking his finger across his bottom lip. "You sure you can make it work?"

"Almost certain," Mutt answered. "It's ancient tech but may be more advanced than most Union tech."

"Not really sure," added Jeff. "We need to explore more."

"Pretty sure," countered Mutt.

"More time," Jeff said.

"Little more time."

"You probably shouldn't be helping without the boss's permission," Nolan said.

"I think you've helped enough," Seetleshee said.

"You think we should stop?" Mutt sounded perplexed at the idea.

"No," admitted Seetleshee, "you've helped as much as you've hurt. Might as well keep going."

Mutt and Jeff looked at each other. Jeff gave him a thumbs-up, then both engineers disappeared back into the manufactory.

"[Squawk], what did I just do, Lucky?" Seetleshee moaned.

"Better to have them on your side. What could go wrong?" Nolan shrugged. "And don't call me Lucky."

6. Day Three—Late

"This is the Planetary Authority of the Loosenshoor system to Maki freighter, *Galactic Harvest*. What is the nature of your business on

Loosenshoor?"

"This is the Maki freighter *Galactic Harvest* to Planetary Authority. Our purpose is to deliver the Human mercenary company The Knights Templar to the planet's surface. They have a valid mercenary contract."

Soolshoon, the Lotar operator, looked over her shoulder at Jared and nodded. Jared could only hear her side of the conversation, but he could guess what the operator on the freighter said. "Just like we planned," he whispered, giving her a thumbs-up. Soolshoon nodded, then shook with laughter as an idea struck. She looked at Jared and winked.

"Maki freighter *Galactic Harvest*," she said. Jared fought back laughter at her slow speech. "You are required to transmit a copy of the mercenary contract for verification, before we can grant you permission to land."

The Maki captain responded with a request for clarification and a protest of the demand.

"I regret the inconvenience," Soolshoon replied, "but we are an extremely peaceful planet. All mercenary activity must be verified before we can allow ships to land. We require a copy of the contract so we can confirm its validity with the Guild representative before granting permission to land."

Jared waited impatiently as Soolshoon listened.

"No, you may not begin your approach to the planet until your business is verified."

Another pause.

"I understand you will expend additional fuel to slow down, but that is Loosenshoor policy."

Jared smiled and nodded, imagining the captain's irritation.

"Ah, yes. I have received the transmission with the contract. Now, please hold your position until contacted. We will verify the contract with the Mercenary Guild office. Thank you for your cooperation."

"That was great, Soolshoon," Jared told her, patting her on her back. "Give me a copy of the contract, and I'll take it to the Merc Guild rep."

Soolshoon looked at him quizzically and whistled. "Seriously?" came the translation.

7. Day Four—Early

A sharp rap on the door of the hotel suite silenced everyone in the room, including the two Lotar meeting with Nolan at a round table near the full-length window.

Nolan nodded to his guests and went to open the door. Santinger Kah and Hootushoo stood in the hall, both grinning in their own ways.

"Good morning, Lucky," Hoot said brightly. The Lotar sounded like a saxophone with a broken reed.

"Don't call me that," Nolan replied automatically, inviting them into the suite. "What are you so chipper about this morning? I thought you'd be looking for work."

"I see your party was successful," said Kah, looking around at the mercs littering the suite.

"Some duties need to be taken seriously," Nolan deadpanned.

Houtushou walked in, looking around, his body language exuding an air of ownership that translated easily. His pompousness was spoiled when he did a comical double-take upon seeing the two Lotar sitting at the table. Nolan knew Soolshoon was considered extremely attractive.

"What are you doing here?" Hootushou asked Seetleshee.

"Lucky owns the company," the engineer responded. "I work for him now."

Nolan shrugged at Hootushou with a half-smile.

"I guess that would be accurate," Kah mused aloud.

"What brings you here, Hoot?" Nolan asked.

Hootushoo laughed like a honking goose, then looked at Nolan politely, expectantly, as he sat in Nolan's preferred chair.

"Oh, you came to gloat." Nolan folded his arms across his chest. "I knew something was up. Kah's got the worst poker face in the galaxy. The only question is why?"

"I told you why, Lucky. Payback, my friend."

"I have no idea what you're talking about."

"When I learned Seemisroo had hired another Earth company to take the unit from me, it seemed fair to drop the problem on your shoulders."

"You want it back? I might be in the mood to sell."

"Why would I invest in a manufactory that doesn't work and will likely be taken by force any day? Why would any legitimate buyer be interested?"

"You don't think the Armadillos are good enough to hold off the Knights?" Nolan moved to stand closer to Hoot.

"Doesn't matter. There's no value in the expense if the unit doesn't work."

"Would you buy it back if you were confident it would work?" Nolan stroked his chin.

"I would be happy to pay you 50,000 credits for the unit," Hootushou said, gesturing with his secondary hands. "That was the amount of your matching bet. I can also arrange for transport for you and the remaining Honey Badgers from here to Karma. That will be at your personal expense, of course."

Nolan shook his head slowly as the pieces fell into place. "Which would cost me the low, low price of around six million credits, I'm sure," Nolan concluded.

"Transporting such small cargo is very expensive," Hootushou said.

"I'm not sure if I should be pissed or impressed."

"I like you, Lucky. You amuse me." Hootushou stood up. "But I didn't succeed by being simple. Your pranks may be amusing, but they've cost me much."

"I still don't know what you're talking about."

"You keep telling yourself that, Lucky." Hoot's tone became serious, his patience spent. "You will pay a steep price for your games."

"One billion credits," Nolan interrupted.

"What's that?"

"My price. I'll sell you the manufactory for one billion credits."

"I don't think you—"

"Oh, I understand. You're offering me the chance to end up either penniless on Karma or buried in debt and unable to work as a mercenary or run the manufactory."

"You could die in the fighting." Hoot twisted the metaphorical knife. "What do you say…Lucky?"

Nolan opened the door with a smile and gestured to the corridor. "Two billion credits."

Nolan felt a familiar hand rest on his shoulder as he closed the door behind Hootushou and Kah.

"You sure, Lucky?" Grady asked softly. "We could get work on Karma, maybe even hook up with the Badgers again. It wouldn't be bad. Easy come, easy go, and all that. You don't have to prove anything to them."

"I have my reasons," Nolan replied.

8. Two Weeks Earlier—Morning

"You rang, Boss?" Nolan asked as he stepped into the Armored Personnel Carrier the company used as a mobile office.

"I did," Samantha Honey said, leaning back against her desk. Just past 40 years old, she was a striking woman. Tall and athletic, she was beautiful in a natural, authentic fashion—no cosmetics or surgical corrections for this colonel. She kept her dark hair short for convenience, and it framed a fine-featured face highlighted by light blue eyes. Nolan had idolized her since she'd hired him right out of high school seven years earlier.

His ready compliment died on his lips when he saw the cold look on her face.

"Am I in trouble?" Nolan stood up straighter, trying to ignore the hollow space growing in his stomach.

"I understand you enjoyed this contract," she said, tapping her foot. "A nice, quiet six months of garrison work, no combat, no danger. Just the way you like 'em."

"Umm—"

"Don't interrupt." She held up a finger. "I've deposited your last paycheck into your account."

"Wait, you can't—"

"Shut up," she said, smiling casually and crossing her ankles. "I just finished closing out the contract with Hootushou. Not only is he not extending, he's back-charging me almost a million credits for the pranks you and your minions played, keeping the manufactory from going online. He included every cost he could justify as well as lost opportunity and other penalties. It's perfectly legal; it's all in the contract."

"I'm—"

"Still not a good time to talk," she warned. "Not only will I see almost no profit, it's gonna take some serious ass-kissing to get a new contract if anyone contacts Hoot for a reference. On top of that, I had to cancel our transport plans home and find a cheaper alternative. There's not enough room for everyone with all the equipment. That means I have to leave some of you knuckleheads here until I can figure out something else, and possibly until I get a new contract." She shook her head, her eyes boring into him.

"I just figured nobody would attack a manufactory that didn't work."

"Which means less work and less danger for you. But, to me, that translates to back charges and no combat bonus," she said. She moved close to him, and he arched his neck to look up at her. He breathed deeply to catch her scent. "Maybe, just this once, you should have thought about how your decisions might impact someone else." She looked down into his eyes with a sad smile and stroked his cheek with a long finger. "Such a waste of a pretty face. Give me a call if you ever decide to grow up."

9. Day Four—Late

"This is the Maki freighter *Galactic Harvest* to Loosenshoor Planetary Authority requesting permission to approach. What's taking so long?"

Soolshoon waited several seconds before answering. Jared stood behind her impatiently.

"Maki Freighter *Galactic Harvest*," she said into the transmitter, slowly with a brief pause between each word, "we have verified your mercenary contract. However, your manifest is troubling. It appears you intend to use dropships to attack your target, here, on Loosenshoor. Is that correct?"

There was a lengthy pause before the freighter responded.

"Planetary Authority, this is the captain of *Galactic Harvest*. My clients refuse to release any details about their action plans. They assert the right to confidentiality in their business operations under the rules of the Mercenary Guild."

"*Galactic Harvest*, this is Planetary Authority," Soolshoon intoned slowly, "your clients' desire for confidentially must certainly be respected. However, this is a peaceful, civilized planet, and the contract provided appears to call for an attack on a target in a heavily populated urban center. We cannot allow an attack by means of dropships due to the risk of harm to civilians and infrastructure. If any dropships exit the hold of the freighter, *Galactic Harvest*, without express landing permission and instructions, they will be summarily destroyed by Planetary Defense. Is this understood, *Galactic Harvest*?"

"What options do my clients have?"

"They may land their dropships at the starport and unload their personnel and equipment there like a civilized species."

Jared fought back laughter.

"However," Soolshoon continued before the freighter could respond, "since your clients' dropships are considered armored attack vehicles, there is a tax of 75,000 galactic credits for landing each dropship."

Soolshoon leaned back in her chair. After a pause, the captain responded briefly before a Human replaced him. He spoke at length protesting the tax, but Soolshoon simply ignored him. She looked over her shoulder at Jared and smiled. "My translator doesn't seem to know what this Human is saying."

"Probably speaking Spanish," Jared whispered.

Soolshoon waited another few minutes until the representative for The Knights Templar finished speaking. "We understand this may pose an inconvenience," she consoled, "but this is not some backwater mining planet. The tax is security for any damage you may cause with heavy weapons. If you are unwilling to pay the tax, you will need to land the freighter, itself, and unload your personnel and equipment. But, the tax will apply to each piece of heavy armor you wish to unload." She paused at an urgent gesture from Jared, who quickly whispered in her hear. "That would include paying the tax for each of your Combat Assault System, Personal units. I understand they are called CASPers."

"LAND THE FREIGHTER???"

Jared rushed out of the room, into the hall, laughing so hard he had to hold his stomach.

"Very well," Soolshoon continued speaking slowly, fighting off her own laugher, "Maki freighter *Galactic Harvest* is granted permission to land on Pad 3 Alpha. That is our largest pad and the farthest from the terminal. Just follow the beacon."

"Wait," the Maki captain yelled, "I didn't ask to—"

"I'm sorry, Captain, I have given you your landing instructions. Please make it clear to your clients that they may not unload any armored vehicles or 'CASPers' without paying the armor tax. You must have valid proof of payment ready to present to planetary officials upon request."

"I won't have enough fuel to take off again…"

"I'm sorry, Captain, I must turn my attention to others. Your transit time will be twelve hours, local. Do not deviate from your course and be sure to calibrate your chronometers. Good day."

When he returned, Jared found Soolshoon rolling on the floor laughing. It sounded much like the flutes and clarinets were arguing.

"Tell Lucky," Jared's pinplants translated through the laughter, "twelve hours."

10. Day Five—Early

Nolan arrived at the Armadillos' encampment at mid-morning. Grady and Jeff came along, and one of the Hootushou engineers drove the aircar. Nolan had ditched his coveralls for a business suit he commissioned through hotel services. The bowtie surprised him almost as much as the cowboy hat, but he decided to go with it. At least the boots and hat made him feel a little taller.

They left the engineer with the aircar, engines idling, and approached the perimeter formed by the mercenaries.

"I hope you have good news for me, Kantner," Gibson said when he came out to greet them.

"I didn't come to see you, Mr. Gibson," Nolan assured him. "We're here to meet someone."

"Who are you meeting?"

Nolan shrugged and checked his jeweled wristwatch, another new addition. Imported from Earth, it was useless for tracking time on Loosenshoor, but it sure caught the eye.

A moment later, they heard another aircar approach from the city. This one was long and sleek and painted glossy black. It reminded Nolan of a limousine, which was probably the intent. It settled on the deck gently. Nothing happened for a few seconds after the engines were cut as the small cloud of dust raised by its landing cleared. A Lotar driver exited the front, moving slowly and stately, and opened the rear door. Another Lotar stepped out. He was taller than Gibson and waddled more than most of his species as he walked over to join them.

"Nolan Kantner?" he asked.

"Theen Seemisroo, I presume," Nolan responded with his best salesman smile and held out his hand.

"Why have you asked me here? I was given the impression it was very important." Even through translation, he sounded entitled.

"It *is* very important," Nolan assured him. "As the new owner of Hootushou Manufacturing Company, I have a business proposition for you."

"I thought that story was just a rumor." The Lotar's laugh sounded like an orgasmic saxophone. "I never thought Hootushou would be that stupid."

"I would never disparage the intellect of someone who just made me wealthy, but I understand your disbelief." Nolan smiled a little more brightly.

"So what is this proposal?" Seemisroo asked, clearly in better spirits.

"Simple." Nolan gestured behind him past the mercenary perimeter. "I would like to sell you my company's only asset. I have no plans to relocate to Loosenshoor. It makes no sense for me to keep it."

"Mr. Kantner," said the Lotar, shifting into negotiating mode, "I happen to know quite a lot about this asset, including the fact that it has never been operated."

"That's why I brought my engineer along," Nolan gestured to Jeff, who waved to the Lotar. "He's here to show you that the unit functions perfectly well, despite rumors to the contrary."

"If you can demonstrate that it works, I would consider purchasing it, if the price is right, of course."

"Of course," Nolan almost shouted. "I will sell it to you for the exceptionally reasonable price of one billion galactic credits."

Seemisroo smiled with his tiny mouth and squinted his too-close eyes, amused. "I think you can do better than that, Mr. Kantner. After all, I've already hired a team of Human mercenaries to take the unit for myself. Why would I pay more than the cost of hiring the mercenaries?"

"You what?" Gibson interrupted.

"Stay out of this," Grady said to the mercenary.

"You certainly make a fair point, honored Seemisroo. But, have you considered the cost if your mercenaries fail? That's the cost of uncertainty. By purchasing the unit outright, you avoid that cost altogether."

"Or I could just hire better mercenaries," Seemisroo offered.

"Exactly," Nolan said brightly. "A simple buy-out would avoid that extra expense."

"You make a good argument, Human," Seemisroo nodded, very like a Human, himself. "But, I could hire many mercenaries for a billion credits.

"More importantly," Seemisroo held up all four hands, "we are getting ahead of ourselves. You need to demonstrate that the unit works."

"You're right. Let's proceed. Jeff," he turned to the elSha and gestured toward the mercenary perimeter, "let's show the good man this thing will work."

Jeff looked at Nolan, his eyes wide, and started wringing his hands nervously. "Lucky, I—"

"We don't have to make anything right now. We just need to show him we control the unit," Nolan said, nodding encouragement and repeating his gesture.

Jeff turned and walked toward the mercenaries.

"Not so fast, lizard," Gibson said, stepping in front of the engineer. "Not until I see proof we'll get paid."

"Seriously?" Nolan squared off with the taller man. "This again? You've got to be kidding! If I can sell the thing, obviously, I'll have the money to pay you."

"I haven't agreed to purchase it yet," Seemisroo said. "However, if he can demonstrate that it works, I am prepared to pay 20 million for it. I assure you, the price is well within my means."

"Twenty million?" Nolan said, shocked. "Are you joking?"

"A purchase only makes sense if—"

The scream of an aircar racing in for a risky landing not far from Seemisroo's vehicle interrupted them. Dust and gravel scattered dangerously. Nolan grabbed his hat, and several of the mercenaries on the perimeter leveled their guns at the new arrival.

Before the engines stopped or the dust settled, the gull-wing doors popped open. Hootushou and Santinger Kah hopped out and rushed over to where Nolan stood with the others.

"What's going on here?" Hootushou yelled, his voice moving into penny-whistle range.

"What do you mean? I'm in the middle of a negotiation," Nolan snapped back, gesturing at Seemisroo.

"You cannot sell to him," Hootushou said.

"I can sell to whomever I want. You passed on your chance."

"Not at the price he will offer you," Kah responded.

"I'll take—"

"You don't understand, Lucky," Kah held out his hands in a calming gesture.

Nolan glanced at Grady, who checked his slate. Nolan bit back a sigh at the almost imperceptible shake of the big man's head.

"...will never approve a sale made at gun point. This is not altruism, mind you, they simply cannot allow competitors to employ such extortion tactics to forcibly lower prices. The Mercenary Guild will also object to such tactics."

"You mean my mercenaries," Nolan gestured to Gibson, "will have to fight his mercenaries if we can't agree on a price the Merchant Guild agrees with?"

Kah nodded and shrugged, wringing his hands apologetically, almost exactly as Jeff had. Hoot nodded.

"It makes perfect sense…" Kah said.

"If you're not the one getting shot at," Grady interrupted.

The discussion quickly devolved. Nolan complained about fairness, while Kah defended the Merchants' Guild. Hootushou blamed Nolan. Nolan quickly pulled Gibson into the argument. Hootushou and Seemisroo were soon shouting at each other, and it sounded like a jazz orchestra warming up.

The sound of more aircars approaching abruptly silenced the argument. Six aircars arrived almost as fast as Hootushou's had. They were large, multi-passenger vehicles often used by Lotar families. They landed ungracefully near the other aircars, and the doors opened and a couple dozen Humans poured out. They wore combat armor and carried modern small arms.

The instant they saw the perimeter of mercenaries, the newcomers formed into groups and readied their weapons. The Armadillos dropped behind cover and raised their weapons, ready to defend.

"Whoa! What the hell?" Nolan cried out and held up his hands to the newcomers.

One of the newcomers shouted an order Nolan did not understand and strode forward. The rest lowered their weapons but continued to scan around them for threats.

The man who approached stood only a few centimeters taller than Nolan and was whipcord thin even in his combat armor. He opened the face plate of his helmet to reveal a permanent scowl accented by tattoos.

"I'm looking for someone named Seemisoot," he said with a heavy Spanish accent.

Nolan looked at the Lotar as he came forward. Then he looked at Grady, who gave him the tiniest of nods. Jeff was nowhere in sight.

"I am Theen Seemisroo," the Lotar acknowledged.

"Francisco Ortega," the man held out his hand. "I command this unit of The Knights Templar mercenary company from Earth. Your assistant told us we could find you here."

"It is good you are here," Seemisroo said, uncertainly. "However, the contract specifically called for heavy assault armor, preferably what you Humans call Combat Assault Systems, Personal, the friendly ghosts. I don't see any with you."

"There was a problem with Planetary Authority," Ortega said tightly. "An issue that was not covered by the contract."

"I'm not complaining," Nolan said. "I don't think you want to take on the Armadillos without armor."

Ortega sneered at him, but quickly sobered as he looked at the armor and defenses the Armadillos had in place. All four CASPers were conspicuous.

"Now you really can't sell to him, Lucky," Hootushou said smugly, "at least not for any price he would pay."

"Don't call me that. What do you mean?"

"If you sell too cheaply or abandon the asset," Kah explained, "the Knights will say the Armadillos were on the losing side of the dispute and, based on that, claim salvage rights against any equipment used by them."

"Really?" Nolan looked at the Zuparti, who nodded in affirmation.

Ortega smiled at Nolan coldly. Nolan looked at Gibson, who stared at him, his eyes just as cold.

"Lucky," Grady said and walked over to whisper in Nolan's ear.

"He can't get his own ride?" Nolan asked his friend.

"He wants to talk first. You can discuss terms on the way back."

142 | KENNEDY & WANDREY

"If his money's good, it's worth the inconvenience," Nolan said with a tired shrug.

"Gentlemen," he addressed everyone gathered. "I have another buyer interested in the unit. I need to pick him up from the starport. I may be able to convince him to secure payment for the Armadillos, so we can demonstrate that the unit works. You can wait here for a couple of hours until I get back or go about your business."

"Gibson," Nolan said, turning toward him, "since you won't let me have access, I don't expect you to allow anyone else access." Nolan waited for the other man's nod. "It might also be best to hold the Knights here, so they can't get their armor. Keep your enemies closer and all that."

"Can't disagree with that logic," Gibson said.

"Will you let my engineer in so he can get started while I'm gone?"

"If you can show me proof of payment. Remember, if I need to shoot one of these lowlifes, we get our combat bonus."

"I'll take him with me."

Nolan took his leave and walked slowly over to the aircar with Grady at his side. It took all his self-control not to run. They found Jeff in the aircar, ready to leave. As the aircar lifted and raced away, Grady looked out the window and chuckled.

"Am I dreaming or did the infamous Knights Templar just show up for a battle in a bunch of mini-vans?"

Jeff laughed maniacally, and Nolan chuckled along with Grady and the driver.

"Did you disable their flyers?" Nolan asked Jeff. The engineer laughed harder.

On Mike Gibson's order, the Armadillos, backed by all four CASPers, surrounded the Knights, gathering them in a circle and disarming them.

"I don't understand why you didn't bring the armor called for in the contract," Seemisroo said to Ortega as they watched, helplessly.

"It was the tax, man," Ortega snapped. "The armor tax. I don't have enough cash to pay it. Everything is stuck at the starport. I came to you to get the money or to get you to grease the wheels or something."

"What armor tax? I've never heard of such a thing." Seemisroo said.

Mike Gibson found the two arguing as he approached to disarm Ortega.

"We didn't pay an armor tax," he told them with a shrug. "I guess it could have been taken care of already."

"They said they'd blow us out of space if we tried to drop the armor without paying the tax," Ortega explained.

"Wait a minute," Gibson said, turning to the other Lotar. "You're Hootushou, right?" The Lotar nodded. "You're the one who originally posted our contract and paid the deposit?" Again, the Lotar nodded. "Did you pay some type of armor tax so we could bring the tanks and CASPers?"

"No," Hootushou answered. "I'm not aware of any such tax."

"Looks like someone pulled one over on you." Gibson smirked at Ortega, holding out his hand for the laser carbine. Ortega fumed as he handed it over.

"Do we need to wait for Lucky to return?" Hootushou asked the Zuparti. "I'm not sure why we're out here."

"I'm not familiar with that phrase," Kah said, turning to Gibson. "What does it mean to 'pull one over'?"

"He was tricked, made to believe something that wasn't true."

"You think Lucky tricked him?"

"Wait," said Gibson, turning to Hootushou. "What do you mean you're not sure why we're out here? We're here guarding the manufactory." He pointed toward the perimeter.

"That's not the manufactory," Hootushou said, confused. "That's just a badly-painted warehouse."

They looked at each other then looked toward the spot where Lucky's aircar had vanished in the distance. Gibson laid his head back in disbelief and moaned as the situation clarified.

"That means," the Zuparti said through growing laughter, "you're in breach of contract. You protected the wrong place when the opposing force arrived." He shook uncontrollably as he pointed at the commander of the Knights.

"But, this is where the guide Lucky sent said we needed to be," Gibson said confused.

"Yes," Kah agreed, "you need to be here instead of at the manufactory while Lucky gets it ready for transport. Did the guide ever say that building was the manufactory?"

"Well, he…," Gibson concentrated, "I don't think he did." Gibson's shoulders slumped. "He just said, 'here we are,' and I assumed he meant…"

"It doesn't really matter," Hootushou said bitterly, "he has no way of moving the unit off planet. There are no freighters in system large enough for it, even if he found a way to disassemble it without power. We can stop him from moving the unit to orbit. I do not know if that will save your contract."

"Madre de dios…" Ortega spat and kicked the ground. Gibson watched the other mercenary as he spewed a string of Spanish curses, words and phrases he had never heard growing up in south Texas.

"What?" Gibson asked when the tirade finally slowed down.

"There is a freighter," Ortega said, forlorn. "They made us land the Maki freighter we came in on. Our armor and dropships are still on board."

"You landed a freighter?" the Zuparti asked, shocked.

"It's not a big freighter, but it's big enough and half empty. If Lucky has enough money for fuel to get the thing back into space, the Maki captain will probably take him anywhere cheaply."

"Fuel isn't a problem." Hoot said, with a moan worthy of a sad accordion. "The company has credit with several fuel companies. Even without capital, he has access to enough fuel."

11. Day Five—Late

Nolan settled into the launch couch and strapped in. Grady handed him a cigar, a brand he had grown fond of while on Loosenshoor.

"Loading is almost complete, Lucky," the Maki captain said, stopping on his way through the passenger cabin. He handed Nolan a slate. "We could barely squeeze those twelve containers into the hold with the dropships and other cargo. Should we unload those?"

"Oh, no," Lucky said, "I'm keeping those as salvage." He grinned at Grady.

"Some of the Lotar engineers have asked to come along. They say they work for you, and you need them to help set up the manufactory on Earth." The captain gave him a conspiratorial wink. "I think they also want to see what you'll do next."

Nolan looked at Grady, who shrugged, amused.

"No problem. Add them to the registry," Nolan said, smelling the cigar. "And don't call me Lucky."

12. Day Six

Soolunoo Hootushou looked up from his slate as the door opened, and Santinger Kah stepped into the office. Without a word, Kah pulled a device from a pouch on his belt and activated it. He slowly walked about the office waving the device over every wall and surface. When the device found nothing, he nodded in satisfaction.

"I had it swept last night, but I appreciate the caution," Hootushou said as Kah took a seat across the desk.

"You were right," Kah said, as he placed a metal disk on the desk, a large red diamond sparkling in its center. "He and his friends worked their way out of the situation. He never gave up and didn't resort to violence."

"I told you these Humans are smarter than everyone claims. They could be allies." He picked up the disk, toying with it.

"Do you think the Veetanho will suspect anything?"

"I don't know," Hootushou said, placing the disk in a drawer. "I doubt Lucky will give us up. I hope they get that thing to Earth and unlock its secrets."

"So," Kah said with a grin, "what's our next wager?"

13. Day 13

Nolan checked his watch, now set to Greenwich Mean Time. Transition to Karma was only a few minutes away. He looked at his cards, then around the table. The games were less interesting since everyone refused to play for anything valuable, but it passed the time.

"Go fish," he said.

Seetleshee and Soolshoon giggled every time he said it. Nolan loved Seetleshee's enthusiasm, but Soolshoon had proven to be clever and endlessly devious. She fit right in.

"Transition in 3, 2…" the captain announced over the intercom.

The sensation of being unmade came and went as they transitioned from hyperspace to normal space. Those around the table shook it off.

"Lucky, we have a big problem," the captain said through his pinplants.

"Excuse me, guys," Nolan said. He set his cards down and made his way to the flight deck.

"What's happening?" he asked, looking around the monitors at the Karma system, the home away from home for mercenaries.

"There's a fleet guarding the transit point." He pointed to a display that meant nothing to Nolan. "There's an arrest order from the Union through the Mercenary Guild. We're instructed to turn over any Human mercenaries along with their equipment."

"That can't be right," Nolan said.

"What do we do, Lucky?" the Captain said.

"First thing we do is stop calling me Lucky."

# # # # #

Shit Day
by Marisa Wolf

Tamir Alcuin was having a bad day. The sort of bad day that not only makes you wish you hadn't gotten out of bed that morning, but also that your parents had never met, exchanged biological matter, and allowed you to make it out into the world.

The point is, it was a shit day.

Tamir, a bounty hunter often employed by the Peacemakers Guild, had had her fair share of shit days. Humans didn't have much of a presence outside the Mercenary Guild—not much of one there, either, but that grew every day. In the hallowed halls of the Peacemakers, Humans were...allowed. She could still take whatever bounty she could get her hands on, but the days of preferred assignments and getting tapped by a Peacemaker had dwindled.

So she'd taken a shit bounty, on a shit planet, on a shit individual. Unsurprisingly, it had all gone to shit.

Hanging upside down in a cave kind of shit.

If only her mother hadn't been such a good dancer, and her father had just kept walking on by.

"I told you, I'm here on behalf of the—"

"Human, if you say Peacemaker one more time, I'm going to eat one of your livers."

"I only have one liver," she said, twitching on her line to turn and see the speaker. The thin rope binding her tightened with each abortive motion, pressing her clothing so deeply into her skin it might as well have fused into one. Her shoulders pulled past the point of pain, and her eyes were heavy with the weight of her blood trying to rush out of them. The words continued out of her all the same. "So you wouldn't have dessert. You have to know there's a bounty on you. You *ate* half a dozen ElSha young."

"I ate their livers, human. They have more. They should have survived."

"I don't think you understand livers—or surviving. Just let me down, and we'll talk this out." She twisted her hips, grateful the bindings ended at her shoulders so she couldn't choke herself. The motion turned her back around just in time to get a face full of long, black fur, and the odor of spoiled meat and buttered popcorn slapped right up her nose.

The Sirra'Kan stared down at her. Tamir's fallen torch cast enough light in the cave gloom to reflect eerie green off his predator eyes.

"Go find a mad tiger," they'd said. "It'll be easy. You know Hunters. You've gone into the homes of the deadliest almost-felines in the galaxy, an entire planet of assassins that even the Veetanho step carefully around. What's one crazy anti-empire alien holed up on a nothing little rock planet?"

"Nobody likes humans." He had a nice voice. It was low and soft and entirely reasonable—like a grandfather after a lifetime of cigars, mellow and rich. This was not the tone she would have expected from a six-foot cat covered in old blood and urine.

"Sure," she agreed, trying to pinch her nostrils shut. "But a bounty is a bounty. If it's not me, it'll be someone."

He leaned in, smelling her knees, then squatted to take a deep breath of her midsection. She recoiled, the instinctive rejection enough movement to turn her like meat on a spit. Without straightening, he reached above her ankles to steady the rope, and the nearness of his unfamiliar felinoid features and fetid breath made acid writhe out from her stomach and down her throat. Tamir fought back her gag reflex as he continued his examination—no need to provoke him with teeth that close to her more necessary organs. After another deep breath, he snorted hot, heavy air out in a rush that was almost, but entirely unlike, a hunter's chuff and shoved her back so hard she went spinning.

Flash of cave wall. Flash of pile of rocks. Flash of Sirra'Kan eyeing her like a slab of meat in a gyro restaurant. Flash of the darker hole of the cave entrance, where a much more innocent Tamir had stalked through only hours ago. Flash of cave wall. Flash of the vomit spewing from her mouth as some of it burned its way up her abused nose. Flash of the Sirra'Kan either interested or disgusted or both—who could tell, because he was utterly insane.

He reached out to spin her again as she slowed, and she caught a glimpse of a figure across the way. Tamir couldn't focus on what it was before three things happened in rapid succession.

She spun away, faster than before. Blinding light flooded the cave. She blacked out and saw nothing at all.

* * *

A whole-body cramp had Tamir sitting up before her eyes fully opened. Her mouth tasted like carrion and her head pounded, but she could move every limb—and feel every screaming nerve. Blinking, she tried to focus in the dim lighting to determine her surroundings and distract herself from the burning of abused muscles regaining all their feeling at once.

"Whoa! Hey, it's ok. You're safe."

"Am I?" She forced the tension away, as her body was only too happy to lock up again. When she squinted to focus, her head throbbed in answer. The combination of all the different pain outputs and uncertainty roughened her voice. "Who're you?"

"Not a cave monster trying to eat you." The voice, male and warm, didn't come closer. She determined which shadow was his—either a rough blob or a humanoid in a chair. His voice sounded natural, not through a translation box, so she figured humanoid.

"Congratulations on that. So you are…?" She angled to see him better, taking inventory. Besides the fiery protests of muscles unkinking, everything seemed in one piece. The rope had been thin enough to cut despite her clothing, and her ankles especially burned. As she worked her jaw, she felt the ache from the back of her neck stretch up around her skull from the angle she'd held her head while upside down. Either her hair or her mouth radiated the smell of death and vomit, and she endeavored to ignore both. The Sirra'Kan had taken her holster but not the small bag she kept strapped under her jacket. She was fairly sure she could wrangle enough body parts to defend herself if male-voice attacked, but the longer she could put that off, the better.

"Elias Burnell."

"I'm running out of snappy comebacks, Elias." Inch by careful inch, she scooted her legs to the edge of the surface holding her and oriented her body toward his voice. Every bit of her protested, and she ignored that too.

"Ah! Sorry." He did something to bring the lights up slowly, and her eyes tried to shrivel into her skull. The throbbing in her head became a stabbing pain, and she fought back a surge of bile. There was nothing left in her to vomit, but it was enough of a struggle she almost missed his next words. She closed her eyes and focused hard.

"I'm a miner," he said. "We're on contract here, and I've been mapping some of the cave system, testing for ores. There are bitey things here that don't like the light, so we all carry flash bangs. I used one to knock out that Sirra'Kan and drag you out of there."

From not enough information to too much, she processed it and cracked her eyes back open again, finding the light less offensive. Elias was human, leaning toward her from a normal chair, and she was on a normal cot. They were in his quarters, perhaps? She would have been sorry to have gotten vomit and probably a bit of blood on his bed if she had any idea who he was or where they were.

There were a few mining collaboratives on this rock. However, there was nothing approximating a government she'd had to check in with, so she hadn't spent much time investigating them. Instead, she'd focused on tracking down the baby-eating Sirra'Kan before he got bored, found some other den, and she had to start the hunt over again. She hadn't noticed a crew of Humans on the docket, but she supposed it made sense given how narrow the margins were out here. Few of the major mining concerns would bother with such an out-of-the-way prospect.

"Did you know there was a monster in your caves, or just bitey things?" She studied him, categorizing. Elias was roughly her age, tall but shorter than the Sirra'Kan, fighting shape but not gratuitously muscled, attractive but more bashful than her usual taste.

"Ah…no. We get weird shadows, and everyone's got a story— but it's just talk. It's enough to keep us on our toes on new rocks. I saw you moving through one of our connection points." He ducked his head away from her, rubbing the back of his neck. "I know all the Humans here, so I was curious who you were. But before I could catch up, I heard a roar and…it took me a little while to figure out what had happened and what to do about it." Dull color creeped up his throat and shaded his cheeks.

"So then you went against a Sirra'Kan?" She stared at him, not bothering to hide her disbelief.

"I mean…what was I supposed to do? I knew you were there. I couldn't un-know it, and I couldn't leave you there."

A smile crept into the corners of her mouth, and she shoved it back down. He'd thought she was cute, followed her, got surprised by a legitimate monster in the caverns he thought he knew, and then had taken a bit to get his courage up and a plan together. The fact that he *had* gotten his courage up made all the rest of it irrelevant. She'd worked with a few bounty hunters who would have done a whole lot less and told a whole lot bolder of a tale after her bones had been picked clean.

Brave *and* a good guy—she liked that.

Shit. Not the time, on a job and covered in vomit and who knew what else.

"That's a helluva introduction, Elias Burnell, miner. I owe you all you can drink and maybe a ticket off this rock. Thank you. And now—" She interrupted herself with a hiss. The attempt to get her legs the rest of the way off the cot knocked her breath out before the shooting pain across her midsection registered. Pulled muscle? Tweaked rib? Didn't matter. Stubbornness kept her moving through the betrayal of her body, and Tamir stood. She wavered, but held onto her balance enough to remain upright. "Now, I need to get back to work."

"Uh, yeah. You're wobbling, and that big cat is definitely awake by now. I got us a cart and as far across the caverns as I could, but there's no telling where he is." Elias glanced over his shoulder, as though saying it would cause the door to explode inward and reveal a snarling galactic predator in its place.

"He smells like roadkill in Houston in the middle of July, so I'm pretty sure I can find him." She reached to adjust her necklace and froze, staring at his cupped hand. "What do you have there?" She focused so hard on him her body forgot to tremble or sway.

"Your necklace? Right, sorry. It got caught when I pulled you into the cart. I put it in my pocket and took it back out so I wouldn't forget to give it to you." He opened his hand, revealing the soft gleam of perfect metal attached to a small, round pendant.

Tamir leaped across the space between them, her legs not realizing they should protest until after she'd snatched her necklace away from him. She crushed it until she could feel the token's simple design etching itself on her skin, then stepped back from him.

She'd once considered embedding a magnet in her chest to ensure the necklace stayed on her body. That had seemed overkill at the time, but now she reconsidered. If she had lost it, chasing down some half-credit crazypants on a disregarded rock…Tamir held herself rock still and studied him. Her locked muscles complained, but

Tamir ignored them. How lucky was it that he'd been there and chosen to charge into a Sirra'Kan's temporary lair, take its prey, and run away with her?

Luck, or something entirely different? Someone trying to use her to get close to a powerful Depik clan? Gain her trust and steal her token? Follow her connections back to the Peacemakers and…and…what?

No. Her closest relationships on Khatash were gone, because Hunters didn't live nearly long enough. No one but her could convincingly use that token and live. In the grand scheme of things— even in the small scheme of things—she was of little consequence and not worth hunting to the ass end of nowhere. She glared at the surprised miner, unable to figure out any ulterior motive that made sense.

"What *is* that?" Elias stared up at her, hand still open mid-air, held out toward her. "You were hung upside down for hours and then crammed passed out in a mining cart, and you just moved like…like—"

"This," Tamir said in the most level of tones, "is mine. If the wrong being found you in possession of this without a proper explanation, you'd be halfway to dead in a heartbeat and wishing the rest would come faster."

"I didn't realize you were so attached to your jewelry."

"Adorable." Despite his attempt at charming levity, she let ice creep into her tone and looked over his head toward the door. "What direction are we from where you found me? I'll come back to pay my debt, but I have work to do." He sat up straighter to catch her eye, and then stood when it didn't work.

"Setting aside the forty other questions I have—who are you, and what is your job? Why would you go back to a Sirra'Kan that was, in case you forgot, going to *eat* you?"

"Tamir Alcuin." She considered giving him a mocking bow, knew her legs would not support it, and shrugged instead. "Working to secure a bounty on behalf of the Peacemakers."

"You work for the Peacemakers?" At Tamir's 'more-or-less' gesture, he leaned back and whistled. "The Peacemakers are after a Sirra'Kan?"

"This one's been eating babies of various species across multiple systems. Plus, he's probably an embarrassment to all the Sirra'Kan who aren't insane." Tamir focused back on the miner's face to keep from thinking about how lovely a return to unconsciousness would be, just for a little while. A small, velvety nap would make everything better.

"So your job is to hunt down a crazy, giant, baby-eating predator and drag it back for payment."

"Yep."

"Your job sucks."

"Sure." With everything aching and her brain slamming itself against the inside of her skull, Tamir thought he might have a point. Her VOWS had given evidence that she had the temperament for violence and following orders and courting danger on alien shores, but the killing of aliens just to get paid hadn't been her thing. She'd had a few offers from smaller merc units and went logistics for a few tours, enjoying the puzzle and hectic action of it all. With a few paychecks under her belt, she chose freelance, picking up smaller bounties and then slightly-larger bounties. It didn't take long to confirm she preferred bag and tag to shoot and die.

That had gone incredibly well for her for a handful of decades. The last few years, though, had been much less fun. She'd lost some friends, lost some missions, lost some connections, and now a loony Sirra'Kan had gotten the drop on her on a dusty rock halfway to nowhere.

"Uh...Tamir?"

"What?" She took a step back from him, loosening her death grip on her token and slipping the necklace back where it belonged. The fact that she'd almost lost it made her wince, and she held her hand over the now-invisible lump under her shirt.

"You spaced out on me there for a minute. You all right? Seeing spots?" He crossed the small room to close the distance between them, peering into one of her eyes and then the other.

"I'm fine." She took her hand from her shirt to ward him back. "You're right, my job sucks. And it's mine, so again—which direction takes me back to the cave you found me in? I should be able to track him from there."

"How about—just a suggestion—we get you at least a shower first?" He held his hands up before she could snap at him. "You're stalking a predator, and I bet he has a better nose than us, right?"

She nodded, unwilling to agree out loud.

"Yeah, you're gorgeous, so don't get me wrong. But you...you're kind of gross right now. I can smell you, so the Sirra'Kan..."

"I get it. I get it. Point me to the cleaning unit."

She spot cleaned her clothes as best she could and rinsed everything. Thankfully, her tactical gear was made to clean up from the worst of viscera and bodily goos. The shower might have been more enjoyable if everything didn't sting, ache, burn, or otherwise reject the warmth of the water, but she was fairly certain she got all the dried vomit scrubbed away.

"All right, caretaker Burnell. Care to point me the right way now?"

"I'll walk you. I should get back to work before I get too far behind on quota, and my assigned mapping is back that way. It's not all saving beautiful women from tigers, you know. I gotta dig stuff up too to get paid."

"I hope you're a better miner than you are a flirter," Tamir said, her tone so dry they both knew his attempt at charm was working.

* * *

"I'm coming with you."

"You are obviously not." Tamir pointed at the cart. "Get back in that, go back to work, and I'll find you when I'm done."

"How could I let you just go in there on your own?" Elias did not go back to the cart and, instead, took several steps closer to her.

"I'm armed—"

"He took your gun—"

"I'm *still* armed, and I took some of your flash bangs."

"You...?" Bewildered, he studied her body to find where they were hidden. Her jacket revealed no tell-tale bulges of a weaponized variety.

"I already transferred credits to you. I'm armed; I'm trained; and it's my job."

"Again, your job sucks."

"I'm not disagreeing with you, Elias. But it's mine, and I gotta do it to get paid. I like getting paid, and I like the idea of a rogue Sirra'Kan *not* eating any more species' young. So I'm going to go do my job, and you are going to go do yours." She still pointed toward the cart, which might have been a useless gesture, but one she had decided to stick with until he listened.

"You need backup." He was smart enough not to step any closer, but she frowned at him all the same.

"I never have." Technically, Tamir didn't lie. She hadn't *needed* backup, even *then*, but who in their right mind turned down teaming up on a ferocious predator with the ability to be invisible and a love of wholesale slaughter? Especially when that sweetly-sociopathic Hunter used her to train other Hunters? Some of the best years of her life.

Her throat closed tightly around the sudden rise of grief, and her still-unsteady stomach roiled at the familiar sadness. She couldn't think about that right now. She had to dissuade this overly-eager miner from proving himself to her. As though pulling her ass out of a Sirra'Kan's jaws—almost literally—hadn't done that well enough.

"And you're not who I would pick to start, *if* backup were needed." Her tone sharpened on that addition. She could imagine how Flame would have—Tamir swallowed hard against the knot of loss and cut the thought short, frowning at Elias all the harder.

"I get it. You don't need help. You're super tough and great at your shitty job. But that Sirra'Kan got the drop on you already, and—"

"And he won't do it twice. Thanks for the reminder. You saved my life, but I won't need your help again. Now go, before you get gutted, and I have to cry over your intestines."

"Because you care?" Confidence brought a saunter to his step as he moved closer.

"Because intestines smell really, really bad. Come on, Burnell. Don't walk right into it. How about this," she dropped her voice and leaned in closer to him. "You go back up to the turnoff and wait with the cart. You hear something coming, and I don't yell clear, throw the flash bangs and run. Maybe blow up the cart to buy yourself some time."

Tamir didn't wait for his answer, turning on her heel and marching down the tunnel.

* * *

Three hours later, she pressed her back against the long curve of cool cave wall and wondered if he were still waiting somewhere far above her. The Sirra'Kan had left various markings that made tracking him both possible and immensely frustrating. Piss, shit, claw marks, refuse, and what looked suspiciously like a Human jawbone littered the depths of the tunnels. This bounty had no care to be hidden, and also had chosen to cross and re-cross his own path so often there was no telling where it started or ended. The freshness of Sirra'Kan markings, she now had cause to know, was debatable when your species' noses could only differentiate 'good,' 'bad,' and 'oh, gods and all that is good, that feels like acid in my nose hairs.' Sirra'Kan waste was of the latter variety, regardless of how recently it had left the Sirra'Kan body.

When even a Hunter couldn't teach you the subtleties of scat differentiation, you followed the path as best you could and took all the corners slowly.

Tamir had just let herself consider how it were possible Elias and his crew hadn't noticed either the revolting smell or the giant cat-alien in their tunnels when a scraping noise ahead brought her full attention back to the matter at hand.

"Don't stop now, little human. You're getting so close."

"I'm a fully-adult human," Tamir called back, wishing she could determine the direction of the sound. "Not your favorite meal."

"You all taste the same. Come around the corner, little bounty hunter. I'm ready."

Tamir had made a lot of mistakes that day, but this was not going to be one of them. She scanned the ceiling and, not for the first time, wished she still had a friend who scaled bare walls as easily as breathing.

"Would it help if I told you I lost my liver in an accident? I'd be really boring for you to eat."

"No, you misunderstand. I'm ready to be brought in, face your Peacemakers, defeat them in battle, and crack their bones."

"They don't all have bones. What changed? I asked you to come in earlier, and you spun me like a space station."

"You were upside down, in no position of power." The voice maintained its calm richness, and its distance. "I'd already knocked you out and tied you up. You managed to escape, and now I've reconsidered. And this moon bores me."

"It's a planet." Tamir touched her necklace then slid her hand into the pouch in her jacket. The bounty paid significantly more for alive than dead. However, she had recordings of his unrepentant admissions, and a confession was enough to finagle a bonus. His being dead might even be considered a win for the sane Sirra'Kan— both empire-bound and not—the ones who didn't go on murdering-and-eating sprees across galactic arms.

Just because she preferred bag and tag didn't mean that straight killing didn't have its own appeal in certain settings. She couldn't have had a Depik for an almost-partner off and on for a decade and a half and not appreciate the power of that final call.

Nonetheless, bringing him in alive would rebuild her credibility in certain halls of the Peacemakers. She'd be more likely to be in favor again, get tapped for the better jobs.

Her hand closed on the familiar, streamlined handle of a small weapon she shouldn't have. With her first grin in months, she lowered a shoulder, dropped into a roll, and fetched up on the other side of the stony corridor just as a giant furred arm tore through the air above her.

Damn Sirra'Kan had been throwing his voice.

She steadied her arm and fired three neat shots, two in the chest and one in the head. The Sirra'Kan's claws were still grasping as he fell, surprised. His ears pivoted toward her, pointed in a silent question he never got to ask.

Depik and Sirra'Kan were nothing alike, but something about the dimming of his large eyes caught her gut in a way she didn't like.

Less money this way and less glory, but fuck it. Her job sucked anyway.

She fired once more to be sure, and then tucked away the Depik laser that neither Hunters nor Humans knew she had. She wasn't even sure if any non-Hunter knew such a weapon existed. It was a bit of overkill when the Sirra'Kan wasn't even wearing body armor. But he'd taken her gun, and she missed Flame. The Sirra'Kan wouldn't tell anybody. She grinned again and went about the messy job of preparing what she needed for transport. If luck held, her sense of smell would give up before she was done.

* * *

"**D**o you like mining?"

Elias flew out of the cart with a flash bang in each hand, eyes wild, hair mussed. He'd overdosed on his own adrenaline and fallen asleep, and it was one of the cutest things she'd ever seen.

"Do I—are you—is *that*?!" He blinked so fast it made him stutter, and she had to bite her cheek to keep from laughing.

"Do you like mining? Yes, I'm fine. Yes, this is a Sirra'Kan head. I put it in a sack, but there's still something…head-like about it, right? Probably, you can smell it. My nose packed it in a couple of hours ago."

Staggering back against the cart, Elias tried to catch his breath and composure. Both seemed far out of his reach. Tamir let him take his time, putting the head-in-a-bag on the ground and running through a few subtle stretches.

"You've been gone for hours." His tone had steadied, but accusation lined his face.

"Sure. And I'm back now! You waited."

"I waited."

They stared at each other.

"After the third hour, I opened GalNet."

"Oh, you have a pinplant, huh? That's bold." She let the smile crack through and gave him a once-over.

"I think I figured out what's on your necklace."

Her smile dropped, and she picked up her bag again. "Oh?"

"Why didn't you use it? If it is what I think it is?"

"Using a Hunter's favor token for a shit job like this…" She cast about for a proper comparison and laughed at the uselessness of it. "It's like nuking a planet from orbit and bringing the merc guild down on you because you didn't like the color of their clouds—just a waste of a good orbital bombardment."

"So it is…" He trailed off, eyes fixed at her chest. She was pretty sure he was looking for the token. "They are real?"

"Gonna assume you're talking about the Depik, Burnell, and yes. They are. So…you like mining?"

"Um." He blinked at her, shook his head, and blinked once more as he shrugged. "Yes?"

"Like, really like it? You're good at it, and you like it?"

"Yeah. I don't like working for the shit operations that fund us off Earth, but—"

"Good." Tamir swung the bag a little, contemplated doing a fun joke with the head, and decided that would make her look as crazy as the Sirra'Kan had been. "I've got some money to invest, and I'm of a mind to change occupations."

Elias boggled at her as though she were as crazy as the Sirra'Kan after all, and she wished she'd done the bit with the head despite her better judgement. Might as well earn that reaction.

"I mean, we could get a drink first. I owe you about a hundred, and I guess I should know more than that you're brave and stupid enough to go into a tiger's den for me before you even really met me…"

His mouth snapped shut. He stopped gaping in order to smile instead as he realized it was a real offer, and also her asking him out on a date. Elias shook himself, tucked the flash bangs back into the cart, and offered her his arm. Then, remembering she had an armful of large, smelly, and vaguely-dripping head, he swept into a bow instead.

"I could use a drink. And maybe a story of what went on down in that cave?"

* * *

"**A**t least, that's how my parents always told it, and who am I to doubt?" Ziva leaned back in her chair and grinned, spinning an old coin on the table between her and her four squad mates.

"Bullshit, Alcuin. I don't buy it. No Humans worked for the Peacemakers before Francis. And no way your mama took down a Sirra-fucking'Kan on her own."

"Another beer, please." Ziva shrugged, unphased by Aaren's doubt, and knocked back the rest of her drink. "You asked, bud. Why I'm not rattled by shit days like this last fucking tour? That's why."

"You ever put your hands on that token?" Lug glanced over his shoulder at the glass case displayed with the best liquors above the bar.

"My mama's still alive. Hell, no! She doesn't let us touch it." Her new beer, frosted exactly as she liked it, slid home in front of her, and she took a healthy swig.

"So she took down a Sirra'Kan." Lifting his glass in toast, Lug tilted his head, inviting more explanation.

"Turns out you learn a lot, running with a Depik." Ziva's smile was all challenge, and they'd all seen too much of that look in the field to push it. "Imagine what we could do if we all got those moves."

"You got trained by a Depik?" Aaren asked, still doubtful, even as he leaned forward for the answer.

"C'mon, Ran. You've seen me in the shit. Do I move like I was trained by assassins?"

"You move ok." Drea leered and tipped her smoking drink toward the rest.

"My mama did more than ok—faced down a Tortantula once, too."

"Oh, for fuck's sake." Aaren gave up, believing the rock-solid conviction in her tone despite himself. "Fine, your old-ass mama is a badass old-ass mama. What's that gotta do with your keeping clear when we're in the shit?"

"Figure, if my mom can meet the love of her life on the day everything goes wrong and my dad can charge a tiger to prove himself to her, I can deal with whatever bullshit each day brings." Ziva sat forward to clink her glass with his. "Someone make that into a snappy motto for me, yeah?"

# # # # #

The Charge of the
Heavy Brigade
by Chris Kennedy

"Pssssst. Over here!"

Colonel Dan Walker pulled his hand back from the door to Peepo's Pit and looked around. It sounded like the voice had come from the alley next door, but there was no one there. As walking into alleys was a good way to get separated from your money, and possibly your life, Walker decided to pretend the lisping voice was a figment of his imagination and turned back to the door.

"Over here!" the voice called again, and Walker whipped his head around, his hands on his pistols. This time he was sure he had heard the voice. Once again, though, the voice had no source.

"Up here!" the voice called, and Walker tilted his gaze upward. An enormous muzzle and one eye gazed down at him from about 12 feet above; he'd been looking too low. The mouth was full of large, razor-sharp teeth that any great white shark would have been proud to call its own. Walker's jaw dropped open—the only thing he could equate the image to was a picture he had seen in his childhood. A Tyrannosaurus Rex.

"Me?" Walker asked. No other words came to mind as his jaw fell open again.

The enormous head nodded to him as the eye made contact. "Yes, you," the creature said. "Come here, please. Quickly, before someone sees you."

Walker felt himself drawn along, unable to break contact with the mesmerizing gaze of the enormous eye. After a couple of steps toward the alley, he looked away and shook his head. What the hell was he doing? Another few steps, and he'd be lunch for the monster. He shook his head again to clear it and drew his pistols, laser in the left, old-time projectile thrower in the right. "What do you want?" Walker asked, keeping his eyes on the creature's chest. Neither of his pistols—nor both together—was going to put the monster down quickly, but he wasn't going to go out without a fight.

Unless the monster swallowed him whole.

"I want to talk to you about an opportunity," the creature said. "You were going into Peepo's for a job, yes? I can't be seen in there, though. Even if I could fit through the doorway. Please come into the alley."

"Yes, I was looking for a job," Walker replied, "but I'm not coming within striking distance. If you want to talk, you're going to have to back the fuck up…like, way, way back."

The creature vanished around the corner as it withdrew, and Walker approached the alley, walking toward its center so he could get a good look at what he was getting himself into.

Shit. The behemoth *was* a Tyrannosaurus Rex, and it was in the alley next to Peepo's.

"Further back," Walker said, motioning with his pistols. He didn't want to be anywhere near its massive 5-foot-long jaws. On closer inspection, it might not completely eat him in one bite, but he doubted it would take more than two. And he definitely did not want to find out.

The creature obliged, walking backward, until its enormous tail swept over two refuse bins, sending waste scattering in a cacophonous clatter. The creature shut its eyes and appeared to wince. "Is this far enough?" it asked when it opened its eyes again. "This is supposed to be a *secret* meeting."

"Yeah, I guess," Walker said. He got a better view of the creature as it turned somewhat to avoid the bins; it was nearly 35 feet long from its snout to the tip of its tail, and it stood 15 feet high in its normal pose. It looked like a sprinter, with strong thighs, and it had a long, powerful tail. There was no way he was going to outrun it.

There was also no way he was going to out-shoot it. He put his pistols away. Now that he'd had a little time to process the fact that he was talking to a no-shit Tyrannosaurus Rex, he realized how little effect his pistols would have on the beast. Even the explosive-tipped bullets in the slug-thrower wouldn't stop the creature before it ate him. He was at the creature's mercy. "What do you want?"

"My name is Pep'Sop," the monster said. "We need your help."

* * *

The creature led Walker through a maze of back allies to a large warehouse. During the walk, Walker queried the GalNet with his pinplants and identified the monster's race—the Zhuch. They lived on a backwater planet at the end of the Jesc arm. Despite their ferocious appearance, they were listed as intelligent but cowardly. In order to live as a civilization, they had given up their carnivorous ways, and practiced a life of peace and serenity.

And, apparently, the only reason they hadn't been conquered was because the planet didn't have any resources any of the other races particularly wanted…a fact that wasn't lost on someone whose job required payment for services rendered.

Walker entered the warehouse to find two other Zhuch waiting for them. The aliens were looking around as if they expected to be attacked at any moment. Their actions caused Walker to check behind him as he approached.

"I found a mercenary," Pep'Sop said. "This one has experience with killing MinSha."

"Were you followed?" one of the others asked.

"No," Walker replied. "We weren't followed."

"Good," the same one replied. "I am Kee'Top." The alien indicated the third Zhuch. "This is Tip'Rop. We are glad you came. We are…inexperienced with mercenaries, but we need some now."

"You need mercenaries? What for?" Walker asked. The giant aliens continued looking around, and it really set him on edge.

"We need help," Kee'Top replied. "The MinSha have taken our children."

"The MinSha?" Walker asked. "You mean the entire race of MinSha, or just some of them?"

"Just some of them. A platoon is holding our children, and we need help getting them back."

"Do you know how many MinSha are holding them?"

"Yes," Kee'Top replied. "There are 20 of them holding our children. I believe you would call that a platoon."

"A platoon? That's it? Why don't you just attack them and eat them, or something?"

"Oh, we are not meat eaters," Pep'Sop replied. "We gave that up a long time ago—many centuries, in fact. We found we were too territorial as meat eaters. We also gave up fighting, to the point that we no longer know how. That is why we need you to come fight for us."

"Before we discuss whether or not I will take the job, I'd like to know why they are holding your children."

"I can answer that," Tip'Rop said, "since it was my company that caused this." He nodded several times, then continued, "We have long been a very poor society, without many natural resources. I decided to try mining deeper than anyone has ever gone before in search of valuable minerals. After several attempts, we recovered a silvery metal unlike anything we'd ever seen. When people started getting sick around it, we realized it was radioactive. We tested it and found it to be what you call Californium. Apparently, this does not occur naturally very often, and when word of it got out, the MinSha arrived to take it from us. We know they are contracted by some company, but do not understand why they would do such a thing."

"So, a platoon of MinSha is holding your children in order to take the Californium from you?"

"That is correct. They also say they'll kill them if we don't continue to mine it for them...and we haven't been able to find any more since the first strike. They also said if we try to get help, they'll kill our children."

"As it turns out, we can help," Walker replied. "My company, the Roughnecks, was nearly wiped out by a group of MinSha on our last contract. I've done some recruiting, though, and have put together a platoon of my own. With CASPers and surprise on our side, we ought to be able to take care of the MinSha pretty easily and rescue your children."

"Really?" Kee'Top asked. "I thought the Roughnecks employed a battalion of CASPers. We were looking to hire two companies for this job. You think one platoon will be enough?"

"I'm positive," Walker replied. "I've got enough weapons for a battalion, but CASPers have been hard to find lately. I'll see how many more I can get before we leave, but one platoon of CASPers ought to be enough, especially if we can surprise them."

"Okay…" The alien didn't seem convinced.

"Really," Walker confirmed. "We've got this. The only issue is that we're going to need some jump juice for our CASPers. Although I was able to find enough suits for a platoon—not the best, but they're serviceable—at least a quarter of them are out of jump juice."

"Jump juice?" the alien asked. "Nothing could be easier—we can get that for you; in fact, we can make as much of that available as you need. Our only problem will be sneaking you onto the planet. One of the MinSha is watching our ship, and another is at the main spaceport on our planet."

"Do you have a plan for that?"

"Yes," Kee'Top replied. "If you can go outside the station, we can sneak you into one of the holds on the ship that is currently empty, then we can get you off the ship when the MinSha at the spaceport isn't looking. We have a plan for both of these things."

"That sounds good," Walker replied. "We can get into the specifics of how that will work later. First, let's talk terms…"

* * *

"Colonel, what do you want me to do with all this gear?" Staff Sergeant Ramirez asked, waving a hand at the piles of weapons in the warehouse.

"Mount as much as you can on the CASPers we have," Walker replied.

"Sure thing, sir," Ramirez replied. "A lot of the suits won't be very mobile, though, if I do that. About half of them are scout models that aren't built to carry a lot of armament for a long time." He shrugged. "And, even if we do that, there are still going to be a lot of extra weapons."

"We can always take the extra weapons off the scout suits once we get there. As to the rest of them, we'll have to carry them along with us."

"Seriously, sir?"

"Let me put it this way," Walker said. "If we leave the weapons here, on Karma, in an unguarded warehouse, how many do you suppose will still be here when we get back?"

"Roger that, sir. We'll carry them with us. I'll see what I can do to rig up something to help with that."

* * *

"Colonel, sir?" Corporal Harmon said over the comm. "I think you're going to want to see this."

Walker looked up from the map stuck on the cave wall. The transport and insertion onto the planet had gone as smoothly as possible—they had snuck into the hold of the ship from the outside and had snuck off the ship when the MinSha at the spaceport had gone to inspect another transport that had arrived at the same time. From

176 | KENNEDY & WANDREY

there, Pep'Sop had led them, at night, across several miles of fields to the base of a mountain range and into a large cave complex. After another day of travel, they had reached the other side of the mountains through a set of caverns and connecting tubes big enough for the Zhuchs to get through, so moving the CASPers hadn't been a problem.

The Zhuchs had even set up fueling stations for the CASPers like they had promised, and they had assured Walker they had the jump juice his suits required waiting in the final cave. Everything had gone almost too well; he'd even been able to find another squad's worth of suits before he left, so they would outnumber the MinSha by 50 percent. Upon reaching the end of the caves, Walker had sent his scout, Corporal Harmon, to reconnoiter the area outside, while he discussed the final assault plans with Pep'Sop and Kee'Top.

"I'm coming," Walker commed. He switched to his speakers. "Stay here," he told the Zhuchs. "I'll be right back."

Walker left the cave and jogged over to the scout who was standing at the base of the hill between the cave complex and the town that supported the mining facility. "What is it, Corporal?"

"My math might not be so good," Harmon said, pointing in the direction of the town, "but that ain't no platoon."

Walker climbed the hill, then crawled to the top and gazed down into the village, several miles south along the mountain chain. The corporal was right; there was at least a company of MinSha moving around or in defensive positions around it. "Damn it," Walker said softly under his breath.

He went back to the cave.

"What the hell?" he asked as soon as he saw Pep'Sop. "You said a platoon of MinSha were guarding the children. There is at least a *company* of MinSha surrounding the town!"

"I think there are two companies guarding the town," Pep'Sop replied.

"What!? You said there was a platoon!"

"No," Pep'Sop replied, ponderously shaking his giant head. "I said there was a platoon guarding the children. There are two companies guarding the town. You never asked me about other forces in the area."

"And you didn't think you should tell me about them?!" Walker exclaimed.

"I don't know anything about fighting," the Zhuch replied. "I assumed that if they had a platoon guarding the children, you'd know there were other forces guarding the town they are being held in."

"You assumed pretty damn wrongly," replied Lieutenant Christopher Hayes, the platoon's XO. He turned to Walker. "This is where we leave, right? You don't plan on continuing this contract do you?"

"I don't know yet," Walker replied. "It will depend on whether or not we can get in close." He turned back to the Zhuch. "I don't suppose these tunnels run under the town or anything like that, so we could sneak up on them?"

"No, the tunnels we dug actually run to the north. If you went down them, you'd be further from town."

"Wonderful," Lieutenant Hayes said. "This day just keeps getting better and better."

Walker shook his head. *What else could go wrong?* He looked at the map again and considered. With enough jump juice, they could launch themselves from the mountains and fly into town. "We could jump over them. If we fly in high, they wouldn't be able to target us as easily." He pointed to a spot on the map. "We've got three squads of CASPers; we can jump off that mountain, snatch the kids, and hit them from behind." He looked around the cave. "Where's the jump juice you promised?"

"It's over here," Pep'Sop said, leading them to a stack of barrels. There were a number of pitchers sitting on top of them. Taking one, Pep'Sop put it under one of the barrel's spigots and turned the tap on. When he had filled it, he filled up two more, then turned and handed one pitcher each to Walker and Hayes.

"What is this?" Walker asked.

"This is jump juice," Pep'Sop replied. "I didn't think you Humans would have heard of it."

"You've got to be fucking kidding me," Hayes said. "*This* is your jump juice?"

Pep'Sop nodded. "Yes. It is made from the finest jump berries. Personally, it is not my favorite to get drunk on, as it makes me quite groggy the morning after, but if that's what you Humans drink before battle, I will join you. "

"Oh, fuck," Hayes said. "How the hell do I get out of this unit?"

Walker sighed. "Look at it this way," he said to Hayes. "At least I held out for payment in rare Earth elements. They originally offered to pay us in jump juice when I said it was valuable to us. Can you imagine going home with several thousand barrels of the stuff?"

"You're not going to go forward with the assault, are you?" Hayes asked. "We need more jump juice to have any chance of taking back their children."

"Yes, we're going forward with the attack; however, we're obviously going to need a new plan."

Hayes' jaw dropped as Walker turned back to Pep'Sop. "The buildings in the town looked like they were made of metal plating. Can you get any more of that?"

"Yes," Pep'Sop replied. "We were expanding the town, so there should be some close by."

"Good," Walker said, nodding. "How many of your people can you assemble here quickly?"

* * *

"So that's the plan," Walker said to the assembled group of nearly 100 Zhuchs.

"No, no, no, no, no," one of the Zhuchs in the front row said. Most of the Zhuchs Walker could see appeared to echo his sentiments. "We can't do that. *I* can't do that. I'm not a fighter."

"Yes, you can," Walker replied. "Evolution designed you to be the perfect killing machines. All you have to do is run forward, holding the big sheet of metal in front of you, and when we get there, throw it into the defenders and eat them."

"Eat them?" several Zhuchs asked. "Gross!"

"No, no, no, no, no," replied the first Zhuch. "We can't do that. Eat a live being? That is unacceptable in our religion."

"Okay, don't eat them, then. How about biting them in half? Is your religion okay with that?"

"No, sadly, it isn't," Pep'Sop replied. "We don't kill living beings."

"Well, what the hell do you eat?" Hayes asked.

"A nice vegetable we grow on farms nearby," Pep'Sop replied. "It can be cooked in a variety of ways. Baked, it has a very spicy flavor, while boiled—"

"I don't give a shit what it tastes like!" Hayes yelled. "Are you seriously telling me you can't—no, that you *won't*—help us, even if it means we may not get your children back?"

"We can't intentionally hurt other beings," Pep'Sop said. "That is how they captured our children in the first place."

"Well that's just—"

"That's enough!" Walker yelled, silencing Hayes. He turned to Pep'Sop. "Okay, you can't kill the MinSha. That's what you hired us for, and I know *we* don't have any problems killing them, right, boys and girls?"

A chorus of replies came from the assembled CASPer drivers behind him. Most were fairly bloodthirsty, including one woman who yelled something about eating MinSha hearts for breakfast. Not all the Zhuchs had translation devices, but the ones who did turned green and looked decidedly uncomfortable.

"So, you don't need us?" Pep'Sop asked, sidling away from the CASPer pilots.

"Yes, we need you," Walker said. "The entire assault *depends* on you. In fact, if you don't help us, there is no way we can do this. We will instead go back to Karma and let the guild decide who is in breach of contract—you for not giving us all the required info, or us for not being stupid enough to throw our lives away for a lost cause."

"But you are mercenaries, and we can pay!"

"Mercenaries only make money by successfully completing contracts, not by getting killed unnecessarily. And, without your support, that is exactly what we'd be doing." Walker glared at Pep'Sop, who flinched away. "So, what's it going to be?" Walker continued. "Are you going to help, or are we going to leave?"

Pep'Sop looked away from Walker, unable to meet his gaze, and toward the assembled Zhuchs for support. All of them looked nervous, although Walker couldn't tell whether that was because of losing their children or having to do something they found inimical.

"I want my kids back!" a voice from the back of the cavern yelled. It was followed by several others, scattered throughout the group, and the Zhuchs appeared to steel themselves to the unpleasant task at hand.

Pep'Sop turned back to Walker after watching the group for several seconds. "What do we have to do?"

* * *

"So who's going to lead the T-Rex charge?" Hayes asked as they filed back toward the smaller cavern that held their CASPers and gear.

"I am," Walker replied. "You're going to take a platoon and rescue the kids while I take Third Squad and create a diversion to get the attention of the MinSha defending the town."

"You are? You think that a squad of CASPers will be enough to keep these chicken-shit T-Rex pretenders heading into combat? Smart money says they'll turn and run from the first laser bolt that comes in their general direction."

"I'm hoping their feelings for their children are stronger than their fear of combat."

"Hope isn't much of an operational plan. Do you seriously think their feelings are stronger than their fears?"

"I can't say for sure. If they're not, we're screwed, and your platoon will have to pull back immediately, or you'll be overrun."

"Why don't you let me lead the T-Rex unit?" the XO asked. "You're too valuable to the unit. Besides, who's going to signal the retreat if you're dead?"

"Nope," Walker said, squaring his shoulders. "Ain't gonna happen. I'm leading the T-Rexes. Maybe I can say something that will put some steel in their rubber spines. You can look at it as the charge of the heavy brigade. Maybe someone will make up a poem about it someday."

"You know the historical charge of the Light Brigade was a loss, right? Most of them were killed, and the rest were forced to retreat."

"I've got heavier forces, though," Walker said. "Can you imagine being on the receiving end of a hundred-Zhuch charge?" He winked. "Besides, when am I ever going to get the chance to go charging into battle riding a T-Rex again?"

"With all due respect, sir, I still think this sounds stupid."

"You're right," Walker said, and Hayes looked up in surprise. "We've got extra weapons. We should arm the T-Rexes, too."

* * *

"This still seems like killing to me," one of the Zhuchs said several days later as the tech finished strapping a railgun onto it.

"I've run the odds," Walker said, "and you have less than a one percent chance of actually hitting anything with the weapon at a full run."

"If that's the case," the Zhuch said, "why do I have to carry and fire it? It's *heavy!*"

"Because if we get several of you firing at the MinSha, it will help keep their heads down," Walker replied. "The fewer enemy that are firing at me, the less likely I am to be hit, and the more I like it. Also, as you are a much larger target than I am; I would think you'd like them to keep their heads down, too."

"Why can't we all just carry metal plates?" another Zhuch asked. "We could all carry metal plates and charge at them. That would be distracting."

"Yes, it would be distracting, but not as distracting as having people shooting at them," Walker said. "Trust me on this. Besides, if no one is shooting at them, the MinSha can take their time aiming at areas of your anatomy that are exposed. We want to make sure that as few people as possible get hurt. If we have a lot of people firing on the MinSha, fewer of our people will get hit."

"How many of our people will be hit?" a third Zhuch asked. "No one said anything about that! I don't want to be shot."

"I can't tell you how many people will be shot," Walker said. "It will depend a lot on how well you do your jobs. Hopefully, very few." It seemed odd to use the term, "people," with a race of beings that looked like giant, carnivorous dinosaurs, but sometimes the galaxy was weird that way.

After dealing with several other, similar whines, Walker left his men to deal with the Zhuchs and went to find Lieutenant Hayes, who had just started his CASPer but hadn't shut the canopy yet.

"We're about to head out to our positions," Lieutenant Hayes said.

"You'll probably need to use some of your jump juice on the way there," Walker noted. "The mountains are steep. Make sure you save enough to jump into town."

"Thanks, mom, I will," Hayes replied, his lips curling in a sarcastic smile. After a moment, the smile slipped away. "Sure I can't talk you out of this, sir?"

"Positive." Walker looked toward the cave entrance. It was still dark, but wouldn't be for much longer. "You'd better get going. We can't let them see you getting into position. Their eyes are supposed to be on me." Hayes nodded, and Walker added, "Save the kids."

"You got it, boss." The canopy started down, and Hayes moved toward the rest of the CASPers on his team before it sealed.

Walker nodded once then went and manned up his own CASPer. He arrived at the main cavern and found the Zhuchs milling about. A new scent was in the air, and Walker was pretty sure it was some sort of fear pheromone, because the aliens were all acting skittish. Seeing that the rest of the squad had already mounted, he walked to the mounting block that had been assembled so the CASPers could get on the backs of the Zhuchs with a minimum of damage to both. Pep'Sop was waiting for him, wearing the saddle they had jury-rigged.

"Are you ready for this?" Walker asked.

"Not really, no," the Zhuch replied, standing several paces from the mounting block.

"Are you going to get closer so I can climb aboard?"

"I'm trying, but I don't know that I can," Pep'Sop replied. "I don't think I can do this. I just can't kill anyone."

"Is that what everyone is worried about?"

The Zhuch nodded.

Walker sighed and opened his canopy. "Can I have your attention?" he yelled. When most of the Zhuchs ignored him, he turned his speakers up to maximum and shouted, "Shut up!"

That got their attention, and they all quieted and turned toward him. "I was just talking to Pep'Sop," Walker said at a more tolerable volume, "and he said he was worried about having to kill the MinSha. He said he didn't think he could do it. Is that what's bothering everyone?"

His question was greeted with a number of shouts and displays of affirmation.

"I understand," Walker said. "In fact, I understand more than you might think. There was a time I was very much like you are right now. I didn't know if I could kill." Many of the Zhuchs looked startled at his admission. "It's true," he added. "I killed someone, and I didn't think I could do it again. I didn't want to kill *anyone*, ever again, no matter what the circumstances. I think that's pretty much what you're feeling, right?"

Once again, he received a round of affirmation. "What did you do?" one of the Zhuchs called out.

"I did what you're doing now," Walker replied. "I avoided killing. I refused to kill—no, I wasn't *able* to kill, even someone who desperately needed killing. But there came a day when two people were going to kill an innocent young girl, who had done nothing wrong; she simply had the misfortune of being the daughter of someone important, and the two people were trying to use her to get what they wanted. Even if they got it, though, I knew they were going to kill her. I could see it in their eyes. When it came down to it, I found out that I could kill in order to save a child, and I killed them both.

"Your position is very similar—your children are being held, even though they've done nothing wrong, and the MinSha are going to kill them. If they say they are going to do something, trust me, they will. They *will* kill your children. Now, we're going to do our best to get your children back, but we need your help. We need you to help us distract the MinSha guarding the town, so the rest of my men can rescue the children; if you don't help us, then we will fail, and your children will die. Is that what you want?"

"No!" many members of the crowd yelled back.

"That's not what I want, either. I want to save your children. But if we don't distract the MinSha, your children *will* die. So we're going to attack the town, and you're going to have to carry us. What happens when we get there? I don't know. Some of you may find you have the will to kill, after all, and may want to join in and help us kill the enemy who would kill your kids. Maybe you won't, and that's all right. Throw down your shields and run. If you can, feel free to throw the shields at the MinSha and distract them a little so *we* can kill them. Or stomp on them as you run by. Eight tons of Zhuch will do a lot of damage to their exoskeletons, I imagine." He smiled, and several of the Zhuchs chuckled at the idea, but then sobered when they realized what it meant—killing the enemy mercs.

"I don't care what you do when we get there—whether you fight or flee—but you have to get us there so we have the opportunity to do our jobs. Can you do that? Can you be brave enough to carry us to the enemy—to charge across the field?"

A few Zhuchs replied, "Yeah," and, "I think so."

Louder, Walker said, "Can you get us there?"

"Yes!" more of the Zhuchs replied.

Walker turned his speakers up even more and yelled, "I said, can you get us there?"

This time, there was thunderous agreement. Walker turned to Pep'Sop. "Now get over here, so we can get this done."

Pep'Sop stepped over to the block, and Walker got on his back. There was a handle to hold onto but no reins. The Humans hadn't added them because they didn't think they'd be needed with sentient mounts, although Walker was beginning to have his doubts about that. Spurs would probably have been a good idea, too.

"Follow me!" Walker called, and he nudged Pep'Sop in the direction of the cavern exit.

Staff Sergeant Ramirez sat on a Zhuch at the doorway and was organizing the troops to follow him. They had split the 98 Zhuchs into two groups—shield bearers and weapons users—who would work in pairs. A shield bearer would carry a large, 12-foot-square piece of metal, which would serve as protection for the Zhuch carrying it as well as one of the weapons carriers who held either a modified CASPer MAC or laser rifle.

Every fifth weapons carrier also had a CASPer on its back. Walker hoped the mercs would be able to keep the Zhuchs headed in the right direction, although Walker had his doubts about that, too. If they could at least get the mercs close, his men might have a chance. If the Zhuchs all ran away, though, Walker and his squad were probably going to be slaughtered.

Walker led the skirmish line along the back side of the hills that separated them from the town. When the entire line was in place, he indicated that Pep'Sop should climb the hill. The rest of the line followed, although he could see some of the Zhuchs lagged behind, and the line lost a bit of its cohesion.

"Are you ready for this?" Walker asked, sensing Pep'Sop's continued reluctance.

"Was your story true?" Pep'Sop asked. "Did you really kill those people to save the child?"

"I did," Walker said. "What I didn't tell you was that those two people were my mother and father."

"You killed your mother and father to protect an innocent child?"

"Yeah," Walker replied. "They weren't good people, and they really were going to kill the girl." He paused a second, remembering, as they reached the top of the hill and looked down into the town. It didn't take long before the MinSha saw them and started scurrying about.

"I'm going to save your kids," Walker said, "and I'm prepared to kill these mercenaries who would use your children as leverage against you. I don't need you to kill anyone—we'll do that—but I need you to get me there. I can't do this without you. Can I count on you to get me there?"

The Zhuch squared its shoulders and stood taller, looking even more like a T-Rex. "Yes, Walker, I will get you to the town. I don't know what I will do then, but that much I can do."

"Good," Walker replied, raising his rifle so everyone down the line could see it. "Then let's be about this." He dropped the rifle down to his side, and the line started forward at a walk, picking up speed as it headed down the hill. As they hit the valley floor below them, the Zhuchs switched from a jog to a canter, then, as they started taking fire, to a run.

Into the valley of death rode the brave 11 Roughnecks.

* * *

As Lieutenant Christopher Hayes watched the line of T-Rexes assemble, he finally understood the plan. Walker *wanted* them to be seen by the MinSha. Even if you knew the giant Zhuchs were nothing more than oversized, scaredy-reptiles, as the MinSha commander, you still had to honor the threat...and 100 of the enormous creatures, lining up in a frontal assault was just that—a huge threat. The creatures turned to face the town and paused for a few seconds, then turned the massive pieces of metal they were holding toward the MinSha, presenting—what looked to him—like a nearly impenetrable wall. Hayes had a second to wonder if the MinSha would—or could—shit themselves, then, with a massive cloud of dust, the wave of T-Rexes charged down the hill and raced toward the town. He was deliriously happy not to be on the receiving end of that charge.

"That's our cue, boys and girls," he announced over the platoon's comm channel. "First Squad, attack!"

With a blast of flame, Hayes jumped off the cliff and ignited his jumpjets, not thinking about what would have happened if they'd failed. Five seconds later, Second Squad launched. Using his enhanced vision, Hayes had a brief moment to see that all of the movement in the town seemed to be toward the front line. *This may work, after all,* he thought, then his attention was on the target.

It was easy to find the building where the MinSha were keeping the youngsters; it was the largest building on the south end of town—the side away from the charge. A square at least 100 meters on a side, it stuck up over 30 meters. In less than a minute, First Squad was coming down toward the roof, and his laser slashed a large "X" into it under his point of impact as members of Second Squad flashed past and landed on the street.

The "X" complete, he cut his jets and slammed into the roof, bursting into the building in a spray of debris, along with the rest of First Squad. He triggered his jets again as he saw he was coming down on a group of young Zhuchs, who were fleeing the falling pieces of ceiling. A MinSha pointed a laser at one of his troopers, and he fired his MAC. The round went through the MinSha's un-armored thorax in a gout of blood, and the alien was thrown to the side.

A laser flashed past him, and he cut his jets again, dropping the last five meters to the floor. He bent his knees to absorb the blow, then threw himself forward, spinning to find the MinSha who fired on him. The alien merc was hiding behind a giant machine, and Hayes didn't have a shot at him. Sergeant Hearne did, though, and killed the alien from the other side.

Hayes triggered his jumpjets for a second to get a better view of the factory floor and killed another MinSha who'd been about to shoot some of the fleeing children. He shook his head; *the MinSha really were going to kill the kids.*

He had just decided the battle inside the factory was in hand when his jumpjets cut off—out of jump juice—and he dropped back to the floor.

"Report!" he ordered, after he regained his balance.

"First Squad has one man down," Sergeant Hearne reported. "The MinSha are all down, and we're starting to round up the children."

"Good," Hayes replied. "Give me a count of the children when you can." He called up the squad's status on one of his Tri-V displays. The legs of Private Marker's suit showed red. He was down, but probably not out.

"Second Squad has two men down, including one dead," Sergeant Brand added. "We caught a squad of MinSha returning. They aren't going anywhere now. Entrances are secure, and we're setting up defenses."

An explosion punctuated his words. Walker had authorized dropping the nearby buildings if needed to make fortifications; apparently Second Squad had deemed it necessary.

"Lieutenant Hayes," Sergeant Hearne called. "Looks like we got all the children. Three of them were hurt by falling debris when we busted through the roof, and one was shot by one of the MinSha, but none of their wounds are life threatening. The medic's looking at them and is giving me a thumbs-up."

"Got it," Hayes replied. He smiled, his first one in several days. With the children in hand, all they needed to do was hold. And they were very good at holding.

* * *

*T*his must be what it feels like to be in a blender, Walker decided as the Zhuchs charged across the intervening territory toward the MinSha. Not only did the T-Rex analogues pound the ground *hard* as they ran, they also had a side-to-side motion that made him queasy the longer it went on.

Half the Zhuchs carried big sheets of steel. Unlike their terrestrial analogues, their arms were a little longer and far stronger; the sheets of metal were big enough to protect the Zhuch carrying them, as well as the ones to their right who tried to fire at the MinSha as they ran toward the enemy. Most of the shots didn't hit the metallic cover provided by their shield bearers…but some did. Walker winced as a Zhuch with a MAC hit the shield protecting him, and it was torn from the hands of the Zhuch holding it. The creature slowed, unsure whether to go back and get it or keep running, now unprotected, toward the enemy.

"Keep going!" Walker yelled as the nearby Zhuchs slowed, bowing the line.

"Keep going!" Walker transmitted over the radio. "Hold the line!" His troopers repeated the commands to the Zhuchs they were riding, and the charge continued.

Walker tried to ignore the queasy feeling in his stomach by focusing on the enemy and firing at them as they poked their heads up from cover. It got easier to ignore the sensations in his stomach when the MinSha began returning fire.

The volume of fire they were receiving continued to intensify, and the Zhuchs holding the shields began to stumble as rounds impacted them. "Keep firing!" he yelled at the Zhuchs to both sides of him who had stopped and were trying their best to hide behind the shields nearest them. Seeing that was a common response down the line, he repeated it to his troopers who yelled at the ones near them. As the return fire from the Zhuchs increased, the amount of incoming fire slackened, although not as much as he would have liked. The MinSha were professionals, after all.

Walker picked off a MinSha who stood in place too long, trying to target a Zhuch, and he had a moment of sympathy for the ancient horsemen who had to fire from the back of a steed. Even with gyro-stabilized weapons and a targeting computer, it was *hard*. He couldn't imagine trying to do it with a handheld bow and arrows.

Several Zhuchs dropped out of the charge. Walker couldn't tell if it was because they'd been hit or couldn't keep up, but the line convulsed with each of their departures, returning, more or less, to a line afterward, then contracting as his troopers tried to slide over to fill in the gaps.

Walker hit another MinSha, and it dropped, missing part of its head. Then his shield bearer dropped with a scream. There had been a laser flash. Walker knew the Zhuch had been hit.

Pep'Sop slowed, dropping out of line.

"Keep going!" Walker urged.

"Without our shield?" Pep'Sop asked. "We'll be killed!"

"Screw this!" Walker shouted. He could see more and more of the Zhuchs looking back at them, and the charge was slowing. "If you're too much of a baby to protect your own children, I'll do it myself!"

Pushing off, he jumped out of the makeshift saddle and hit the ground running. Unfortunately, he misjudged it a little, and without his jumpjets, he couldn't recover in time. He fell on his side and rolled twice, slammed around inside his restraints. He shook his head as the motion ceased, got back to his feet, and began running toward the town.

It was hard to run and shoot at the same time, but that was at least something he'd practiced, and something his suit was built for, and he picked off another MinSha as he raced after the line with only half a mile to go. The Zhuch carrying one of his troopers went down, but the CASPer was back up and running within seconds.

Walker let loose with a battle scream as he rejoined the line with a quarter mile to go, which was picked up by his troopers and then the Zhuchs, turning the charge into an avalanche of sight and sound. He could see several of the MinSha abandoning their positions as the wave of metal and flesh rolled ever closer.

Then Walker was upon them, and he snapped out his arm blade for close-quarters work. He batted up a MinSha's rifle with his MAC while slicing off the enemy's head with the blade.

He could see peripherally that some of the Zhuchs had stopped, while others had kept running through town, but he didn't have time to worry about them. A round impacted the right side of his suit, spinning him around, and he dove to the ground as another round passed. He turned the dive into a roll and came up firing. Two MAC rounds hit the enemy merc, blasting it backward.

"Watch out!" he heard Pep'Sop yell, which was followed by a loud *chomp!*

Walker spun to find Pep'Sop standing over the lower half of a MinSha, which fell to the ground. Pep'Sop spit out the upper half of the enemy soldier and shuddered, then started crying. Walker didn't have time for crying—there's no crying in frontal assaults—and killed another MinSha who was trying to line up a shot on one of his troopers.

Within another minute, it was over, and the remaining MinSha surrendered. Walker strode through the remains of their lines and looked at the devastation; the MinSha had died in several ways, and he couldn't tell which was the most horrific. He'd seen the aliens after being hit with MAC or laser fire before, and, although disgusting, it no longer bothered him. After the wave of Zhuchs had come through, though, that was the least of it.

Some Zhuchs had dropped their steel shields on the MinSha, and a number of them had squashed or cut pieces off the defenders. Other Zhuchs had fled, stomping on the MinSha as they passed. Eight tons of dinosaur was enough to make the aliens explode, painting the nearby buildings in surreal, abstract patterns of blue. Then there were the unlucky few MinSha who had shot Zhuchs at close range and had triggered fight responses in them. While the Zhuchs had practiced peace and tranquility for hundreds of years, thousands of years of carnivore evolution lay underneath that, and the response had been horrific as the Zhuchs had bitten most of those MinSha in half.

Many had instantly been ashamed of themselves, but that didn't help the MinSha whose body parts lay around town where they'd been spat out.

But, they'd won, and the children had been recovered, with very little loss of life to the Zhuchs. They'd had eight wounded in the assault and three killed—as well as two Roughnecks—but the Zhuchs had shown they could rise to the challenge, and most of the survivors were looking at each other with a newfound sense of respect.

Walker went over to where Pep'Sop and several other Zhuchs were reliving their experiences. "Thanks for saving my life," Walker said.

"I didn't want to kill him," the Zhuch replied, "but it was either do something I found morally reprehensible or allow him to kill you—someone who risked his life to save our children. It was shame that drove me to follow you when our shield bearer went down, and shame that made me attack him. It wasn't something I wanted to do…but it was an act that was necessary."

"I understand," Walker replied. "Even though killing is part of our business, most people don't like it. Sometimes, though, it's necessary to protect the ones you love or to fix the wrongs being done to others."

"I understand that now," Pep'Sop said, "and I only have one question."

"What's that?"

"How do you get the taste of MinSha out of your mouth?"

# # # # #

The Bottom Line
by Michael J. Allen

The smaller of the two Houston enforcement officers opened the door to Stag Pit Barbeque and stepped out of my way. Neither of the armed and armored men had said much since I picked them up. Tension stiffened both Martin's and Blank's stances, their eyes on the Humvee marked with two bloody H's on the ears of a four-tusked war elephant. Not surprisingly, they let me enter the lion's den first.

What's their problem? I'm not expecting them to gun down a bunch of mercs.

Both officers were only there to serve as official witnesses. They'd only fight in the highly unlikely event that Hannibal's Hammers decided to sacrifice its licenses just to kill the messenger.

"Still sure you want to do this?" Blank asked.

I rolled my eyes and stepped into the dimly lit restaurant. The vague silhouette of a hostess delayed my charge. Any attempt to blink away the gloom revealed it as one of the dive's permanent features.

"Can I help you?"

Inhaling to speak resulted in my choking on thick smoke. "Isn't smoking illegal in a public establishment?"

She pointed. A sign warned patrons the kitchen's open fire grill produced smoke. I knew tobacco when I smelled it, but I wasn't with the Health Department. Like those heroes that had taken down Hoffa and Capone, I faced far more important, so-called untouchable criminals.

I presented my UAAC, flipping it over to display my badge. "Ronald Gerard, Internal Revenue Service. I need to see Commander Quall of Hannibal's Hammers."

Her eyes flicked toward the dining area. She moistened her lips with her studded tongue. "I should...I'll get Dutch."

"Get anyone you like, *after* you show me to Commander Quall."

Every inch of her body language suggested she was a moment away from flight. My pulse quickened. She wasn't my prey, but she feared my badge for personal reasons, or she knew the merc company's sins.

Maybe this place helps launder merc money.

I seized her arm as she moved. "I don't think so. Gentlemen, find Commander Quall."

The two officers slid by us into the dining area, splitting to either side to orbit the room and scan faces. The hostess' focus traded off between watching me and the dining room.

"What are you so worried about? Guilty of something?" I asked.

Her color fled. "What? No. I haven't done anything. I mean, I pay my taxes, even on cash tips."

Of course she does.

I drew a slate and held it out. "Thumb to the slate and speak your full name, for the record."

"What? Why?"

Martin appeared before I could answer. "He's in a private room. Most of their company is in there."

If he thought a bunch of mercs were going to stop me from performing my duty, he knew nothing about the type of men who *really* protected Earth. "Lead the way."

An older man, muscles long gone to seed, stopped us. "What's going on here?"

He didn't look like merc stock and certainly wasn't a kid on lookout. "You the owner?"

"Yeah. Dutch."

Running interference for these crooks?

"Martin, keep him here a moment." I ignored Dutch's protests and marched toward the private room. My tread wasn't heavy enough to make a sound appropriate for the kind of doom I intended to bring to Hannibal's Hammers. I'd root them out and, with that victory, move on to bigger, better prey.

My entrance didn't register against the vulgar excess and debauchery. Hannibal's Hammers laughed and ate with a gusto that left food and drink slopped across the floor while people not a mile away were starving to death.

Enjoy it while you can, bastards.

I scanned the crowd. My pinplant link allowed me to upload each face into the secure law enforcement Aethernet, updating my case files and providing me vital statistics on each. I stopped on a beefy man in his late forties who required no facial recognition. Commander Nicolas Quall hadn't missed a night's sleep worrying about his next meal in quite some time.

Quall noticed me first, eyes locking onto me from opposites sides of a hawkish nose. He whispered to an attractive woman with a blond pixie cut. She turned. Chin-length bangs swung aside, ruining the illusion of beauty by exposing a half-melted face.

Quall shifted his weight to rise, but I closed the distance before he could. It delighted me to loom over the bastard as I presented my badge. "Ronald Gerard, IRS."

Anger flashed so hot in the woman's eyes she could've melted her ruined face. Her sudden expression change triggered my memory. Lucinda Kalae, Quall's executive officer, tensed, and reaction spread through the surrounding mercs like a wave.

Silence fell over the room as if it had been plunged into the vacuum of space.

"Who the hell are you?" A bear of a man stood up, looming over me, his hands loose near his holstered sidearms. I opened my mouth to repeat my credentials, but he cut in. "Do you have any idea what you're interrupting?"

I let disgust color my voice. "The gluttonous excesses that brought down Rome?"

The bear snarled at me. "We're feasting the dead."

"Based on your casualty reports, you must eat like this a lot."

Chairs scraped away from tables as mercs rose.

"First Sergeant, Hammers, as you were." Quall rose, reversing our respective positions and looking down at me. "What can I do for you, Mister Gerard?"

I handed over a slate. "You are hereby served notice of your class seven audit."

Quall glanced at Kalae and mouthed, "Seven?"

"All access, full asset accounting." She gave him a sly look. "You know, a Grendel."

Quall's expression flickered uncertainly for a moment. "Fine. I've been served, now if you'll excuse us. We're celebrating our dead—"

"—and a huge damned payday!" A nearby merc laughed, slapping his neighbor on the back.

"Shut up, Brooks."

Kalae's hand on my shoulder made me jump, evoking laughter from the mercs. Her firm grip softened but didn't leave my neck. The beautiful side of her face smiled at me. "A contract already filed with your office and fully paid. Since you'll be working mostly with me throughout this audit, how about we set up our first meeting while I escort you out? Maybe we can meet at my place later."

Several mercs listed in my files as squad leaders suppressed their lewd comments.

"This is a Level *Seven* audit. Bottom line, I won't be leaving, and I'll require a senior officer or NCO in my presence and at my disposal at all times." I took a step toward her and slid out from under her grip. "Commander, duty requires I caution you regarding the various bribery classifications defined in IRS regulations and their penalties."

Quall bracketed me against his XO. "How long do you expect this audit to run?"

We stepped into the main restaurant before I noticed they had herded me. "Full course, Commander, until I've reviewed all books, equipment—on world and off, documentation, and interviewed all personnel in your employ, man, woman or alien."

Quall stiffened. "We do not employ aliens."

"So you say." I allowed myself a smile. "We will see, won't we?"

Dutch made his way over. "Commander? What is this all about?"

"We're being audited, Dutch. Nothing for you to worry about," Quall said.

Dutch glowered at me. "Why are you auditing Hannibal's Hammers?"

"Inconsistencies in the mercenary community as a whole and filings made by Hannibal's Hammers."

"What inconsistencies are you talking about?" Kalae asked.

"I am not at liberty to discuss the specifics that red-flagged Hannibal's Hammers," I said.

Kalae scowled. "All right, what about the others?"

"Surely, you're aware Cartwright's Cavaliers was rendered insolvent and yet, not a year later, fielded two platoons for a garrison contract. You might not know they purchased their ship, *Bucephalus,* back from the Hussars for next to nothing in an obvious boondoggle to avoid paying capital gains taxes." I stared into Quall's eyes. "So-called trusts and museums used to hide resources, and evidence of, dare I say, financial fraud are cropping up everywhere these days."

Quall and Kalae shared a significant look that proclaimed them guilty.

"The IRS isn't alone in suspecting merc companies of avoiding their financial obligations. I understand the Cartographer's Guild called for payment in full of all the Hussar's debt."

"Taxes from mercenary contracts are the source of most of Earth's income," Dutch said.

"Exactly why it is absolutely essential to the whole of Earth's populace that the IRS and our sister agencies ensure every mercenary company helps by paying its full share."

* * *

Quall slammed a fist into his office's window frame. "And then the little shit actually suggested that we *fake* casualties."

Kalae took a long draw on her cigar, making sure Quall was actually taking a breath, before answering. "What was his reasoning? Death benefits to the families can't be taxed at the same rate as income?"

"That and that every casualty allows us to write off CASPers, dropships, or other equipment to lower our taxable income." Quall gritted his teeth, glowered out the window at the IRS auditor, and watched as First Sergeant Radley assembled their earthbound personnel for slate scan. Quall adjusted the pitch of his voice into a decent imitation of the self-important auditor. "'You cannot possibly go through men at the rate you're reporting.'"

"Did you explain to him that our specialty is frontal assault?" Kalae asked.

"Yeah, and he blew it off. 'If you really went through *that* many men, you wouldn't be able to keep refilling your ranks.'"

Kalae snorted. "Wasn't he the one complaining about the number of desperate, hungry people on Earth? Sure, we accept high-risk contracts, but we expect a commensurate payout."

"I tried explaining that to him." Quall flopped into his seat. "He can't seem to grasp the fact that people are willing to risk death for the kinds of payouts we get."

Kalae massaged the bridge of her nose. "You know, if he digs deeply enough—"

"And this guy will." Quall snorted. "Gerard actually *believes* he's the hero, and we're villains."

"What're you going to do? Grendels?"

"I don't think we've got any choice. He won't take a bribe," Quall said. "Either we turn him, or we've got trouble."

"We could kill him and bribe the next one," Kalae said.

Quall shook his head. "No, that's tantamount to paying a ransom. Grendels did it for Dad. It'll probably work again. What were Gerard's VOWS?"

"Eight ninety, barely too low. He got the nanite treatment, though, in addition to his pinplants."

"The plot thickens." Quall chuckled. "Anyone in his family with the companies?"

Kalae smiled.

"That makes things very clear. Make the call while I distract our little wannabe."

* * *

Despite being a somewhat smaller merc company, Hannibal's Hammers owned property near the Houston startown. I'd already scanned all the Earth-based workers First Sergeant Radley brought me. The merc company's inventory system was sketchy enough to allow for miscounts, so I had teams from a local office tag each piece of equipment and all the weaponry down to ordnance.

While they completed the grunt work, Radley showed me the company's green mercs, training in CASPers on a large section of former tarmac.

"You just let new mercs waddle around in CASPers?" I asked.

Radley responded with a sharp, short, "No."

I gestured at a CASPer as it bungled a short jump, twisted and toppled, sliding sideways across the ground until the pilot or, more likely, his instructor doused the jets.

Radley glared, not answering the question I had clearly implied.

"Maybe the best thing would be for you to see our training methods first hand." The sound of Quall's voice caused me to turn around. He smirked. "First Sergeant, have Mister Gerard fitted for a haptic suit, then take him through VR while we get him set up for trooper training."

Radley leered at me. "You got it, boss."

As much as I looked forward to bringing Hannibal's Hammers down and setting my sights on an even bigger merc company, maybe even one of the Four Horseman, the opportunity to pilot a CASPer took my breath away. The idea set my heart racing almost as fast as it had when I waited for my VOWS score. I slid my fingers into my pocket reaching for a challenge coin long worried clean of the logo of the merc company that'd given it to me.

One of Quall's armorers fitted me for a suit in a bay of CASPers docked in their maintenance harnesses. I stared at the big Mk 7 battle machines while he worked. It was part of my audit, not a bribe, I repeatedly reminded myself. Once fitted, Radley escorted me to another warehouse. Several of the ugliest Mk 7 CASPers I'd ever seen hung from robotic arms as if they were in toddler swings.

"Repurposed for training. They don't look like much, but they function inside."

"Written off as destroyed or reallocated?"

"You'd have to ask the boss."

Radley led me past the swings into a side bay and a wave of overly aggressive air conditioning. We passed rows of round simulator pods bigger than some hotel rooms I'd stayed in and so old they resembled metal invasion pods from awful, old Sci-Fi movies. Thick wire trunks rose from each into a rat's maze of cabling. Young troopers were visible through door-length plexi fogged by age. One merc jerked his gun to one side, an angry grimace visible beneath his VR visor.

"Boss said to run you through." Radley pointed toward the back room. "VR suits are back there. Change, and we'll get you started."

The old VR suits were basically cast off haptic suits. *Why run me through training? Was it a stall tactic to distract me while they moved evidence?*

"Move it, greenhorn."

I jumped and had both legs in the generic haptic suit before I remembered I didn't work for Radley. The silky, metallic suit fit well. My hands shook as I fastened it tight and coiled the cable mess I'd made with my inexpert suiting-up skills.

Radley waited just outside the locker room. He gave me a once over and grunted, obviously unhappy that I had managed without a babysitter. We entered an empty VR pod together. He walked me through connecting the cables, locked me into the full-body support chair that would help simulate motion, and then turned me loose.

The tutorial covered most of what I would have suspected, but unlike when I jacked into the Aethernet VR through my pinplants, the realism of the simulation felt plastic and obviously fake. It walked me through the virtual interior of a CASPer. I keyed the exit sequence after finishing a rudimentary CASPer control scenario, unplugged my suit and popped my head outside.

Radley reclined in a rolling office chair. He glanced up from his slate. "Yeah?"

"This sim is pretty low quality. Is there any way to jack in with my pinplants?" I asked.

"Thought you wanted to train like everybody else."

"Surely some of your trainees have pinplants."

He nodded, a smirk of approval on his face. "True enough. Some of them even learn better that way."

He rejoined me in the pod once he'd fetched an extra set of cables. I went through the control scenario again. The resolution wasn't much better, even with the data pumping directly into my brain, but it was more immersive. In an egregious lack of common sense, being jacked into a CASPer, real or virtual, with pinplants didn't help me move the armor. It added pinlinked targeting options, better control access, and some other computer-related functions, but I still had to move *my* legs to move the CASPer's legs. The mind-bogglingly dull training tutorials were comprehensive. By the time I finished, I felt capable of piloting a CASPer in most situations if not actual combat.

Radley's voice entered the sim. "Doing pretty good, Gerard. Let's get you through virtual fire training. Then you should take a break, and I don't know, inventory something."

I'd put up with the boring tutorials, and while the thought of a virtual firing range was intriguing, I wanted to try something fun. It wasn't like I'd have the opportunity in the future. "Is fire training the last of the virtual training your troopers get?"

He hesitated. "No. Troopers get a few combat sims before moving to the swings."

"Didn't commander Quall say I was to go through the full training?"

Again, Radley hesitated. "I suppose, but I don't see—"

"If you want to prove your casualty numbers aren't from inferior training, I want to see it all."

"Look, if you were really going through trooper training, you'd run sims one week, swings the next, then CASPers."

"I think we can afford a full day's sim training. I'm not perfect, but I'm getting this."

"Yeah, I guess. If you insist."

"I do."

I heard laughter, but it wasn't from Radley. "Loading you into fire training. Pay attention if you want to do well in the drop sim."

Fire training was a whole lot easier with pinlinked access to the targeting system. My time training at Glencoe and practicing in our Atlanta office firing range didn't hurt either. My score wasn't perfect, but I was happy with the results. As soon as I finished training, Radley opened the pod door. "All right, Gerard—"

"Do I need to change simulators?"

"No, but you've been jacked in and exerting yourself for quite a while. I ain't having you blame Hannibal's Hammers when you fall out, so you're taking a break for chow, fluids, and the head."

I wanted to argue because I really wanted to drive a CASPer. I'd wanted to be a merc since I was old enough to listen to my dad and uncles tell war stories. There were VR simulators of course, but they weren't genuine training sims. Maybe I'd find out there wasn't a difference, but I wanted to see for myself.

Radley took me to a dining area. A group of new troopers clustered toward the center bragging about their simulator scores. Quall's older mercs immediately started ragging on the younger mercs' ratings. Hazing in military companies was a tradition that probably went back further than there were records.

"That's bullshit, Urchin. I was watching your sims. You were about as graceful as a blind, three-legged foal."

I couldn't help laughing at the image.

"You weren't much better when you started, Brooks."

Brooks gave the other old merc a hard look. "Shut it, Card."

Brooks turned toward me. "Urchin's sim wasn't the only one I saw...not that watching you was really interesting, *accountant*. You didn't even bother to run a combat sim before you gave up."

I bristled and opened my mouth, but Radley dropped a tray on the table in front of me and shoved me into a seat. "Cool it, Brooks. I pulled Gerard. He would've kept right on going, probably until he passed out. Wish the rest of you trained that hard."

It took a bit of effort not to leave my mouth hanging open like the rest of the mercs. Radley was a hard bastard who was probably dirty enough to spend the rest of his life paying fines and penalties, but after coming to my defense, I knew I'd feel sorry about ruining him. Bottom line, it didn't matter how I felt about him. I had a job to do.

A job I'm shirking for the chance to play in their training simulator.

Brooks recovered first. "Bullshit. You're covering for the pansy desk jockey."

Radley darkened. "When have I ever covered for anyone?"

"Sure as hell never covered for me," another merc said.

"You're so sorry, even a mother couldn't love you, Spade."

Spade laughed, but there was something in his eyes that promised Brooks payback. Radley slammed a bottle of water against the table, shaking my tray and reminding me I needed to eat and drink.

"If you aren't on duty, Brooks, why don't you clear out while you can still walk?"

"Hell, no, Radley. I want to see the I-R-S man get his A-S-S kicked. What's he running anyway? Some milk run? We got a garrison sim now?"

210 | KENNEDY & WANDREY

"HALD." Radley's one word shut everyone up. Murmurs started a few moments later, and I'm pretty sure Union credit chips passed back and forth, their small red diamonds glinting in the dim LED ceiling lights.

I pulled up HALD with my pinplants and nearly dropped a forkful of some brown protein. High Altitude, Low Deployment airdrops were usually reserved for contested worlds. Nausea and excitement warred for dominance, until I reminded myself that it was only VR and the anti-air fire would be simulated.

* * *

The fairings broke off my CASPer, reverting my controls to ground assault mode ten miles above the surface of the poorly rendered planet. The four white-hot fairings joined other decoys tumbling around my simulated squad, presenting ground batteries with enough targets to minimize casualties. The heads-up display on the interior shell of my CASPer showed me off target, requiring me to use what I'd learned in tutorial mode to adjust my flight path. My pinplants did the math and suggested course corrections.

Easy enough.

While my pinplants could calculate jumpjet angles and duration, I had to do everything else manually using the suit's controls. I fired the jets, sending the CASPer into a wild tumble like an out of control balloon. Had I been in a real suit, I'd probably have passed out from the resulting gravities. The VR tried to make me "feel" the fall with slight, intermittent suit pressure and rapidly moving images. I did end up a bit nauseous right before I slammed into the ground—Game Over.

I reset the sim.

Splat.

Again.

Crunch.

The seventh time, I impaled the CASPer on a tree trunk.

The fourteenth, I left its severed legs smashed along a ravine ridge.

On the thirty-fourth, I landed intact and was promptly shot by a striped felinoid alien's laser rifle during my celebration. A quick GalNet check listed feline merc races, along with their weaknesses and preferred tactics. My killer wasn't a Depik assassin; I'd seen it slaughter me. Although the coloration didn't match exactly, my killer resembled a Pushtal closely enough to add disgrace to my death. I'd been killed by a member of a failed merc race reduced to piracy.

Three Wile E. Coyote imitations later, I landed safely, ducked low in the thick rainforest foliage and scanned my surroundings. The alien that had killed me on my first successful landing had worn camouflage. Hannibal's Hammers' CASPers were painted base grey with twin, bloody H's on them. Camera scans didn't identify any combatants. I shifted to Infrared. The sweltering jungle almost blinded me. UV proved better, but not enough.

My HUD displayed the distance and direction to my objective. I took a moment to orient myself before extending a blade from one of the CASPer's arms. I raised it, intent on hacking my way forward through the dense foliage but stopped.

If I move through this mess, cutting my own path, it's going to slow me down, leave a clear trail, and probably get me shot in the back. I'd seen troopers practice bounding during one of the inventory counts. Scanning the dense jungle eliminated bounding from my options. My skill in the

CASPer was not sufficient to move through that many obstacles at such a quick pace, and huge flying robots didn't sound very stealthy.

I did a slow, methodical search in an outward spiral and hit pay dirt, finding a game trail. The game in question wasn't CASPer-sized but moving along the path would limit the trail I left behind. Moving as stealthily as big, metal, battle armor can, I followed the path toward my objective. The CASPer's filtration system kept jungle scents from my nose, but the speakers picked up a symphony of environmental noises like those on the background track of any jungle video.

I was so intent on following my HUD and the path that the sudden silence almost escaped me. I dropped to a crouch as the first shot burned over my suit. I rolled toward a large tree for cover, fouling the roll recovery I'd learned in the tutorial and slamming crotch first into the tree, one leg on either side.

Supremely glad the suit had taken that hit rather than me, I scrambled behind cover and unfolded the reflective shield on my right arm. Another shot slammed into the shoulder plates of my left arm, turning my health indicators amber. My reticles followed my gaze, fine-tuned by my pinplants. The second alien fired again, attempting to distract me from the first's stalking advance. I nailed them both with an arm-mounted, magnetic accelerator cannon, MAC, and resisted the urge to pantomime blowing smoke from the barrel. I confirmed both were dead. Several shots had removed the first one's head. The second one had a big hole in its light chest armor.

I stared down at the simulated aliens. Up close, the details weren't there. They didn't look real enough to trigger killer's remorse.

The path turned out to be a mixed blessing. Due to lazy programming, paired aliens ambushed me three more times. The four assaults occurred at almost identical intervals, forewarning me of the fifth just before I reached my objective. A shot from behind a tree bole took out the closer alien. I edged around the opposite side for a clean headshot at the other.

My suit jerked.

I could see nothing but the salt and snow of signal static.

The full-body support chair stood me up. I lifted my visor, blinking at a disapproving Radley.

"Never take your enemy's tactics for granted," he growled.

I wanted to kick myself. Bottom line, between a relatively safe HALD and predictable enemies, the sim's programmer had led me by the nose to a very valuable lesson without the hard price tag of actual death: never drop your guard.

I nodded. "You're right. I walked right into that."

He chuckled. "You aren't the first. Chow's almost ready in the galley, if you've had enough for today."

The perfectionist in me wanted to go back inside and do the whole thing again until I beat it, but I was beginning to feel the hours of exertion. I could probably reach the hotel, shower, and eat heated-up leftovers, but the effort sounded like too much.

Maybe if I got some food here.

"Yeah, sounds good. All right if I shower first?"

Radley laughed. "You'd better, or they're likely to do the cleaning for you. That won't be fun, no matter how kinky you are."

Applause welcomed me to the galley. Some seemed halfhearted and a smattering was sarcastic. Brooks stood, gesturing at a meal

214 | KENNEDY & WANDREY

waiting at his table. "Got to give it to you, pencil neck. You don't give up, no matter how many times you go splat."

"Brooks is right," Radley said.

I shook merc hands until I reached my seat, then sat and drank half a bottle of water before answering. "In my job you have to keep digging until you find what you're looking for."

"Pity you didn't manage your VOWS," Urchin said. "You might've made a decent merc."

I froze, bottle almost to my lips. No one had brought up my VOWS since the last time my father decided to reinforce his disappointment in me.

It's insulting enough that neither he nor my uncle vouched for me with their company. I set down the bottle to keep from dousing myself by squeezing it tighter. *But, they refused to believe the truth about that proctor.*

"Mister Gerard?" Radley asked.

I shook off the anger. It didn't matter. You only got to take VOWS once. I'd never be a merc, but I could still make a difference to the poor people of Earth. I stood, unwilling to be distracted by the friendliness of the tax-evading criminals trying to subtly manipulate me and keep me from finding out the truth. "Guess I'm not hungry after all. If you'll excuse me?"

"Swings tomorrow?" Radley asked.

"No. There's a lot to do before we launch for Karma."

Several mercs looked at each other, but Radley knew their upcoming garrison mission wouldn't stop the audit, assuming I didn't find something to keep them on planet before their launch.

* * *

Results from another auditor awaited me when I woke, proving out much of what I'd expected. A museum trust devoted to Hannibal's Hammers had purchased extensive display equipment from Quall at rates far below salvage. Vid-capture images showed that the so-called replicas were in far better shape than any of the training CASPers.

I sent Nicola a message thanking her and encouraged further digging. Poor business acumen and foolish practices weren't against any government law, but if we could substantiate a pattern of actions meant to defraud the government, we'd have Hannibal's Hammers.

Kalae escorted me back to the swing room. Unlike Radley who didn't care how long I stared as the CASPers jerked cadre troopers back and forth, Kalae seemed restless.

Jumpy, maybe? It certainly appeared as though she would rather be somewhere else.

"Look, Gerard. If you're just going to stare, can we schedule this for another time? I've got a deployment that needs attention."

"Why are you escorting me today instead of Radley?"

"The First Sergeant has mercs to train."

"You don't involve yourself in that training?"

She rolled her eyes. Her voice hardened. "I do when I can. Right now, someone has to stay with you while you stare like a homesick puppy."

Part of me did want to take the swings for a spin. The more advanced simulation no doubt offered troopers firsthand experience without risking damage to functional CASPers. Quall's overly generous offer to run me through the full training had fueled my dreams. I'd awoken eager to continue but equally convinced that Quall was trying to keep me in the training hanger. The reasons I'd chosen to do my thinking near the swings, beyond the air-conditioning holding off the brutal Texas heat, had nothing to do with continued self-indulgence and everything to do with Nicola's report.

The museum-owned cast offs were better than the equipment the trainees used. If they were simply intact shells with gutted interiors, what kept Quall's mechanics from relocating components from the more modular Mk 7s to make them field ready? I turned my back to the swings and met Kalae's eyes. "I need to interview your mechanics."

"They're busy."

"Are you denying me access, Miss Kalae?"

"No, but they're getting ready for deployment."

"If that's the problem, I'll make a call and ground your company."

Kalae's attitude shifted dramatically. "Do you have any idea what that would cost us in reputation and income, not to mention our lost contract retainer?"

"After what I saw the other night, I doubt any of you will starve." I glanced down and saw her shaking fists held tightly against her thighs. "Now, are you going to escort me or am I making a call?"

"Fine."

* * *

"Look." The lead mechanic ran a hand behind his head, soiling his dark blond curls. "We fix what they bring us and report the results. If the boss or XO decides they're unfit for battle, it's none of our business."

"They're selling so-called repaired units for less than scrap rates," I said. "What does that say about your skill, Mister Giles?"

Giles clenched his jaw for a fraction of a second. "I guess I'm shit at my job and lucky they haven't gotten rid of me yet. Can I go? Are we done?"

"No."

"Look, I can slap some paint and bondo on any old CASPer and make it look brand new. Hell, I can probably rig it to march, salute, and maybe even shoot, but that doesn't mean I'd trust it to protect one of our mercs from a real hit in combat."

Radley replaced Kalae after the first hour of questioning. His dark expression was back, but he didn't seem on the edge of putting a bullet through me. Kalae's attitude had convinced me I was onto something. After my next interview, cooperation from Quall's mechanics ground to a halt. They all answered my questions the same way, claiming incompetence and ignorance.

Giles must've spoken with his team while I interviewed his second.

* * *

After three more days of interviews, digging, and inventory scrutiny, the powers that be decided we didn't have enough to justify grounding Hannibal's Hammers. Radley saw me up to their old cruiser, *Codicia,* and I strapped into a seat in my quarters for transition into hyperspace. The restraints were too tight, but they kept me from further making a fool of myself in zero gravity.

I couldn't see what was going on. Other than ship-wide announcements on the 1MC, all I knew was that *Codicia* and the small cross-section of ships at Earth's stargate were poised to transition into hyperspace in fifteen seconds. Someone counted down. My heart rate increased in anticipation. My palms were sweaty. I was leaving my home system, alone, among a potentially hostile group of lying, cheating mercenaries.

It hadn't been much of a problem to leverage additional IRS manpower on Earth. The evidence I'd presented along with my working case theory had been enough for my boss to encourage others to accompany me, but no one was willing to assist with the audit once it left the planet.

Killing me would only doom Hannibal's Hammers and bring to light the conspiracy perpetrated by the mercenary companies at the expense of Earth's people. I didn't have a death wish. I didn't want Hannibal's Hammers to jettison me into space, but my father had beaten into me the importance of defending people. I hadn't made it into mercenary service, but I could protect Earth's people when others couldn't. *I might never be anything but a failure to my family, but starving children will have me to thank when their bellies are filled courtesy of the money these companies are holding back.*

Nausea hit me. I reached for the bag Radley had left that I'd tucked away as unnecessary. I was too late; I made a mess of my quarters.

Despite my attempt to clean up after myself, knowledge of my mishap spread through the crew. Apparently only one other newbie had lost his lunch. I buried myself in the audit. Using every one of the unrestricted movement hours available, I tagged and inventoried all the shipboard equipment and any brought aboard in orbit. With restricted access keeping me from interviewing the ship's crew, I completed all my work in the first few days of the 170-hour hyperspace transition period. I rechecked spaces at random to ensure no one snuck anything by me, visibly irritating Radley.

I was poring over my reports in the galley when a chorus of greetings made me cringe. "Upchuck Urchin!"

Urchin's ears burned red as he collected his meal with feigned indifference. He stopped beside me. "All right if I sit here? I don't want to interrupt anything important, and I'm not trying to spy. It's just—"

"Misery loves company?" I asked.

"Hey, look, Urchin and the accountant are going to make babies together!" Brooks said.

I keyed off my slate and gestured toward the opposite seat. Urchin sat, hooking a leg out of habit from lower gravity seating. I didn't want the company, but I'd been going over and over my reports, and while I knew the smoking gun was there, I couldn't find it. "I need a break anyway."

"Someone said your family were mercs?" Urchin asked.

"Yeah."

"Not interested?"

I sighed, folded my hands on the slate and looked into his young, earnest eyes. "I only got an eight ninety on my VOWS. My family wouldn't vouch for me with a merc academy or sponsor me into cadre training with their company."

"That's rough." Urchin took a big bite.

The old wound acted up, and I tightened my fists. "It was all because of some sl—girl."

Urchin grinned. "Blow your VOWS screwing all night?"

"We had a really public fight over, well, it doesn't matter now." My voice was full of resentment. "Bottom line, it got out of hand. She got expelled the week before VOWS."

Urchin frowned.

"Her uncle proctored my test."

It took a moment, then understanding registered on Urchin's face.

I nodded at the table. "He couldn't fail me. No one would've believed it with my earlier PT scores, but he tweaked my numbers just enough."

"Eight ninety," Urchin shook his head. "Just enough to keep you on the outside. Wasn't that a pretty big risk on his part?"

"I'm far from stupid, but it was no secret I sucked at exams. I suppose if he'd estimated wrong I could've scored over nine hundred, but that's not how it worked out."

"That why you hate the rest of us?" Urchin asked.

I met his gaze. "I don't hate mercs. I hate people who use their positions to cheat the rest of us. Bottom line, I'm pretty sure Hannibal's Hammers and other companies are cheating Earth's people out of credits that could be used to feed them."

"I'm too new to say one way or another, but I don't think anyone here would line their pockets at Earth's expense."

"We'll see."

Urchin went back to eating, a thoughtful expression in his distant gaze. I left him to his thoughts. I'd realized the depth of humanity's treacherous nature when I was about his age. Being the one to show him the snakes made me feel guilty, so I rose to return to my quarters.

"Hey," Urchin grabbed my arm. "We're doing CASPer training a bit later. Didn't the boss give you carte blanch to train with us?"

I hesitated. "Yeah."

Urchin shrugged. "CASPer training or paperwork? I know what I'd choose."

* * *

Urchin, whose name was David Rutherford, turned out to be a pretty nice kid who'd lost his parents early. He seemed almost a natural in a CASPer. Radley didn't say a word about my training with the other green mercs, and it filled the time while I continued to mentally review the reports, searching for my smoking gun. As we approached the end of our hyperspace travel, training ceased, and I was sidelined for emergence preparations.

Radley strapped me in and wordlessly handed me two bags before departing for his duty station. Kalae's voice came over the ship-wide intercom, "Set Condition One throughout the ship. Emergence in five minutes."

Why set Condition One going into someplace safe like Karma?

Emergence made me dizzy, but I only used one bag.

The crew wasn't allowed shore leave during our short turnaround at Karma. I did a quick inventory of their limited holdings and almost empty storage warehouse. I would have liked more time to search for evidence of reportedly deceased mercs living on false UAACs, but Radley made it clear they'd leave without me.

Our next hyperspace jump gave me more than enough time to audit everything and everyone that had come aboard on Karma, including several huge crates that now filled Cargo Bay Four. Scans verified they contained raw materials.

"They're for building a standard garrison HQ planetside," Radley said.

Something about his claim was off. It would come to me.

Radley and Urchin included me in a bit more training, but I bowed out as the end of the second hyperspace leg neared, and I was no closer to a solution. Quall and Kalae had tolerated more questions, but I didn't manage to shake loose any secrets.

Radley strapped me in once more and handed me two bags. "This time be ready and don't soil yourself."

I didn't respond to him or his laughter, but I did prepare one of the barf bags. We began emergence, and when the count dropped beneath thirty seconds, I placed the bag over my mouth. The emergence effect hit me, nauseating me and making me dizzier than any of the previous transitions.

Rough transition…may-mayb—

* * *

I awoke from unconsciousness to blaring alarms and the acrid scent of burning insulation. Smoke filled my room. My pulse shot from lethargic to pounding in an instant.

I broke free from my restraints and opened my door. The corridor was in shambles, but the smoke wasn't nearly as heavy. Radley appeared like a monster out of the mist and slapped a respirator on me.

"What's going on?" I asked.

He answered in bullet blurts as he dragged me down the corridor to a ladder leading off the gravity decks. "Emerged straight into an interdiction. They jumped us before our sensors were back online."

Interdiction? Was someone trying to take over the contract system? Why?

A loud explosion sounded behind us, and Radley knocked into me, bouncing me off a bulkhead. He helped me scramble into the ship's core corridors and pushed me toward the nearest aftward handholds.

"Where are we going?"

In answer, an announcement blared over the 1MC. "All personnel, abandon ship. Repeat, abandon ship."

"I thought the shuttles were forward."

"They were." Radley shoved me aft. "Get moving."

Even *I* thought the panic in my voice was poorly hidden. "The shuttles are gone? How are we getting off then?"

"We still have the dropships."

"Won't they attack the dropships?"

"Yeah." Radley shoved me through a door. Others from his squad scrambled into CASPers locked into the dropship's cradles. Radley pushed me in through an open side door. I grabbed the restraints on a jump seat and started to strap in.

"No," Radley snapped. He jerked me from the seat and shoved my haptic suit into my hands. "If a CASPer doesn't break free and smash you, high G maneuvers will snap your neck like a chicken's. Change!"

I stared at the suit, then glanced at a few nearby CASPers with their clamshell access doors gaping open.

"Change!" Radley demanded.

A young woman shouted down from the cockpit. "Hurry up down there. *Codicia* isn't going to give us cover much longer. We need to launch soon."

Lieutenant Tellane had boarded at Karma which was bad luck for the attractive redhead.

"Soon as I get him jacked in."

Radley picked me up and dumped me feet first into an open CASPer. I tried to help, but he snatched the cables and shoved them into place. He handed me the pinlink cables and slapped the controls, ducking out just as the CASPer's cockpit doors closed.

Despite my familiarity with connecting pinlinks to my pinplants, my shaking hands made the process difficult. The dropship lurched, and though muffled by the CASPer's hull, a vast explosion told me we had escaped just in time.

Pinlinks and implants finally mated.

"—erard. Gerard, report! Are you online yet?"

"I-I'm here." I noticed he had linked me into the command channel, probably to keep me from saying something that interfered with the squad's orders.

"Power up and double check your systems, this is a hot combat drop."

"Please tell me this isn't a HALD."

"Not unless you survive their blowing the dropship away around you," Radley said.

Squeezing thumb and pinky together powered on the system. I ran through the checks like the tutorial had instructed, noticing how breathtakingly vivid the Tri-V projections along the interior of the Mk 7 hull were compared to the sims.

Thank God I had that chance.

The power flickered off as I felt a huge sideways jerk and a lot of gravities. Whatever was going on left a giant standing on my chest. I fought for breath and mostly lost. Then gravity eased off, and I was able to fill my lungs, keeping me from blacking out. An explosion rocked the dropship.

Very unfeminine and very redheaded cursing preceded Tellane's announcement. "We're hit. Prepare to drop."

I searched the Tri-V for our altitude, then remembered my pinplants. We were just below ten miles, not much lower than the height I'd died from in countless HALD simulations.

"Drop. Drop. Dr—"

We plunged into the sky surrounded by a fireball, chunks of destroyed dropship and the colossal roar of rushing atmosphere. I glanced up in time to see Tellane and her copilot arch upward, then down. Her copilot and his parachute suddenly burst into flames.

"Anti-air laser batteries," Radley said. "Scatter. Release fairings. Reflector shields u—"

Whatever else Radley had to say stopped when a FLAK artillery battery filled his airspace with shrapnel and smoke like something out of an old movie. Another exploded just below me. Before the smoke cleared enough for me to see if Radley had survived, my unschooled motions sent me into the same wild spin I'd caused in the simulator. Everything inside my cockpit dimmed. I closed my eyes, more to see with my pinplants than to hide from Death.

My pinplants did the math, and I moved in response. To my utter shock, the CASPer righted. I took care to stay upright as I juked every which way trying to stay alive.

Bottom line, I made it. Others didn't. Darkness crowded my shell-shocked world, but I managed to land my CASPer. The blackness swallowed me but spit me back out.

The dim light from my Tri-V painted the interior of my CASPer with a forest of gigantic trees that looked like columns in a mausoleum. A thinned section of the overwhelming canopy showed where I'd broken through the upper branches. Old leaves carpeted the ground which was mostly bereft of grass and brush.

I'm alive. That's good. What now?

Attempts to use the radio returned only static. According to my topographic map, I was quite some distance from Hannibal's Hammers' garrison. The CASPer's fully-charged capacitors barely had enough juice to go the distance. If something happened to the CAS-Per or its power, the hike would take days. Unlike the simulated jungle from my HALD, the space between the massive trees gave me enough room to bound using jump juice. Using the jets might help stretch the capacitor power, but I resisted. I'd used a lot of fuel trying to keep from repeating my simulator failures and didn't want to exhaust what remained frivolously. And my simulator-honed jumping ability wasn't all that trustworthy.

I marched toward the garrison, my feet already hurting. Strange noises filled the forest, and I hoped they signaled a lack of predators.

A sudden burst of radio traffic made me jump. In a CASPer, that translated into hopping several feet, tripping over a large root, and staggering into a tree as wide as a house. Another amber light appeared on my status panel.

"—ello?" <*squelch*> "—nyone read...is—"

Tellane? I lurched away from the tree in case it was blocking her transmission. I received a few more bursts that were too garbled to understand, but they helped the system mark her approximate position on the map.

Her little, red dot blinked behind me, to my right, closer than the garrison waypoint. I chewed my lip, glancing at the damage I'd done to my CASPer just trying to move around. Even though the garrison was farther away, getting her help seemed far better than charging off to rescue her myself.

Another garbled message tugged me away from safety.

I'd interviewed Tellane. She'd seemed like a bright, capable pilot, and, while not some pageant contestant, she was the kind of attractive woman who passed me up for beefy mercs like Radley or Brooks.

I turned my CASPer toward her signal and took a single step before turning back toward the garrison. My sudden change of direction caused me to stumble just as a laser shot burned a chunk out of the tree that should've been behind me.

I stumbled sideways, trying to open my laser shield as another shot barely missed one leg. My eyes followed the path of the second shot to a blue-striped, grey felinoid reloading a medium chemical laser rifle behind cover.

I fired my light MAC in a loud staccato, the rounds impacting the tree, as my pinlink connection reacted to my instinctual defense and adjusted the reticles. My attacker dodged behind a massive trunk. My shot had been reflexive. I hadn't thought, I'd just reacted. The sudden reality of being attacked by aliens on a strange planet crashed down on me a moment before a second alien creased one of my legs with its laser.

I managed to bring up my reflector shield before it loaded the next chemical round. The trees were great cover, but I was too big to dash left to right, presenting the shield then firing while they reloaded. I could leave the shielded arm visible, reflect a hit, then risk my arm by folding the mirror to shoot my high-velocity machine gun.

Another chunk of tree exploded into flames.

Crap, nothing for it. I jumped from behind cover, using a little jump juice to amplify the CASPer's superhuman jump capabilities. I fired the MAC at the first alien, shifted the reticle to the second and cut loose with the machine gun before I hit the ground.

Unable to shoot aliens and land at the same time, I bungled the landing and stumbled sideways into yet another tree. Trying to keep from falling, I missed the second alien.

I glanced at my first attacker and caught it just as it emerged to take another shot.

I fired.

A fountain of blood and violent death throes from the cat signaled my first kill.

An accelerator round punched through the armor just below my right arm like it was tin foil. I ducked back behind a tree and took a moment to get my rampaging breath under control. Neither of my first two attackers had fired MACs. Who knew how many aliens were trying to kill me, and I'd already expended a lot of rounds to take out one.

I looked down at my belt and smiled. "If you can't beat them man to man, blow them up."

I threw a grenade with a little help from the computer's flight arc assist, and it went too far. The exploding K2 was far less spectacular than I anticipated, but the explosion did throw my second attacker, screaming and wind-milling its arms, through the air before it landed unmoving on the ground.

That just leaves whoever had the MAC, unless I got them with the grenade too.

I held out a hand from behind cover. I waved it a little. No one shot it. I risked a look around the other side of the tree, my MAC ready and waiting. No one shot me.

I stared at the cats lying dead on the ground. My search hadn't turned up any cat merc races like these, and the Pushtal were known pirates. *Who else would try to interdict a system and attack a merc company in transit?*

I didn't feel killer's remorse even though I wasn't in a simulation. I'd killed to defend myself and taking out two trained mercs by myself left me feeling smug.

Tellane's voice crackled over my radio again. "—ching hostiles, pinn—own...please assist."

Maybe Dad was wrong. Maybe the gene didn't skip me. I turned my CASPer toward Tellane's waypoint and ran across the unknown planet.

I caught sight of her parachute before I saw her. The silver fabric draped down to seemingly severed ropes dangling above a handful of Pushtal. At first, I thought I was too late, but then I realized they were searching the area. I caught sight of Tellane and realized she had climbed upward into the canopy.

A sudden clunk against my armor caused me to turn until another CASPer slid into view on my Tri-V. It pointed to where the head belonged and gestured several times.

"Hello?"

The Pushtals whirled at the sound of my voice.

"Idiot." The other CASPer slapped the top of my cockpit, shoved me behind a tree and bounded backward to his own cover. A sudden barrage ripped up my tree, stealing my attention, and caused me to lose sight of the CASPer. I ducked out to fire and lost my MAC to enemy rounds.

I jerked back into cover, armed only with my CASPer's reflective shield, a mostly depleted, high-velocity machine gun, and an arm blade.

An unfamiliar merc's tinny voice drew my attention toward a damaged CASPer staggering cover to cover from fifty yards away. "Get in the fight."

Before I could follow his advice, a single-shot rocket slammed into the CASPer's lower torso. Heat, noise, and raining metal filled the forest.

I tensed to run. There were too many of them. I wasn't trained to fight like this. I wasn't a merc. I wasn't anything, just like my father said.

I heard a shout through my translator, "There's the Human, in the canopy!"

My eyes fell upon the CASPer's limbs smoking on the ground nearby. I was in a CASPer like I'd wanted since childhood. Tellane was a sitting duck in the canopy, wearing nothing more than a lightly armored flight suit. Someone had to help her.

I ducked out of cover and snatched the dead trooper's right arm. A laser blast set my cover on fire. I didn't have the time, tools, or training to shift his MAC over to my suit even though the manuals said they were modular, so there seemed little point in risking death for the other arm.

Should've grabbed one of the dead Pushtal's rifles.

It took time to detach his reflective shield. Holding it in my left hand and mine in the right, I charged around the tree trunk screaming at the top of my lungs. A round punctured my suit's armor just beneath the shield and my left arm. Another bit a chunk out of one leg. Lasers reflected off both shields.

I wanted to cry.

I wanted to run.

Run after she's safe.

I bowled over a Pushtal, rammed the borrowed shield into another, emptied my machine gun into a third, and extended the retractable blade to gut the alien at my feet.

Wide eyes stared at me as I reared back to strike. A MAC round knocked my arm backward. The blade and most of the mechanical hand were gone. I snatched up a cat's fallen laser rifle. Heavy fire drove me back before I could stomp him or assess the rifle's charge.

Tellane screamed overhead. I whirled and shot from the hip. Lasers impacted a tree near a Pushtal's ear. It screamed and slapped at its burning pelt.

"It's crazy. Run!"

Tellane jumped.

I didn't think. I reached out, catching the pilot in a clumsy, damaged basket of arms. We landed gracelessly, and she tumbled out of my arms and hit the ground hard.

At least you didn't crush her.

Not taking time to check on her condition, I raised the rifle and swept the area for hostiles. Rifle parts exploded, followed immediately by my CASPer's left hand.

The pain followed, and I blacked out.

* * *

Kalae led a lightly armored felinoid into the garrison CO's office, checked the hall, and shut the door. Quall stood, greeting his guest with an overly elaborate bow that replaced their handshake. "Director Varmao, I welcome you to my..." Quall glanced at the Spartan office. "...tree?"

She returned the bow, smiling indulgently. "You greet me in the old way. You are pleased with our performance, Commander? Like your forebears?"

"Absolutely. Your troupe performed magnificently."

Kalae laughed. "Gerard thought you were Pushtal."

Varmao's long tail flicked up. "Pushtal? Only a nose-blind kit would make such a mistake. Grednwah performances are renown throughout the Union."

Quall held up his hands. "You don't have to convince me. He couldn't tell when he was or wasn't in VR."

Varmao displayed sparkling teeth. "Our performance was enhanced by Lady Kalae."

"I understand things went off script. Were any of your troupe seriously hurt?" Quall asked.

"Osburin's pelt was burnt, and Tothrian hasn't stopped complaining about being cut by exploding metal after nearly being stabbed—"

"Sorry about that," Kalae said. "We gave him dummy rounds and misaligned his MAC reticle, but we never expected he'd go hand-to-hand."

Varmao's tail tip bobbed back and forth in her version of a shrug. "Theater is life and life is pain. Besides, Tothrian is a whiny prima donna."

"We've paid your contract with the 50% hazardous audience bonus. Our shuttle will return you to the *Codicia* when you're ready."

"We will not have to spend time in your crates this trip?" Varmao asked.

"No."

Varmao circled Quall with her tail up before striding away without a backward glance. Quall dropped back into his chair as First Sergeant Radley entered.

Kalae sat opposite Quall. "As much as I hate to admit it, Gerard didn't do too badly for a greenhorn."

"We *should* recruit B-Line," Radley said.

They frowned at him.

Radley shrugged. "Hammers gave him a call sign."

"Can't," Quall said. "He fought with us—"

Everyone laughed.

"After everything we put him through, Gera-, I mean B-Line, thinks he's a Hammer. Having him champion us from inside the IRS would protect us and alleviate our need to hire the Grendals again."

"And it would keep us from having to sacrifice any more CAS-Pers," Kalae said. "Poor Giles."

Radley snorted. "That CASPer was mostly duct tape."

"Let Giles shoot B-Line," Kalae said. "He'd feel better."

"Speaking of which, you were supposed to graze him," Quall said. "Not shoot off body parts."

Kalae leaned back in her chair, head cradled in both hands. "He wanted to give us that finger anyway."

# # # # #

Midnight Diplomacy
by Tim C. Taylor

1

"You know, Captain Blue, on a propitious day like today, one is reminded of the remarkable nature of this hidden world through which we are traveling. We must not permit the weeks that we have spent in meticulous diplomatic endeavors to blind us to our good fortune in simply being here. Don't you agree, Captain?"

Blue hungered to tell Brown Owl exactly where he could shove his propitious day. Ferrying the incompetent Buma diplomat to yet another failed meeting with this ice moon's denizens was the biggest test of her life. Instead, she glanced across the bridge of Submarine Number 6 at Venix, the Zuparti installed by the owner of the Midnight Sun Free Company to keep an eye on her.

He shook his furry head and silently signed. Putting the back of one hand into the open palm of the other.

Money.

They were being paid a lot of credits to escort the Buma delegation to these first contact negotiations.

The ambassador blinked his huge black eyes in his feathered head, but although they were so large he looked like an overdrawn anime character, Brown Owl failed to see the exchange going on around him.

Blue's sister had insisted everyone on her crew learn the Midnighter sign language. Venix wasn't strictly a merc, but he'd obviously been learning because he now drilled upward with the index finger of his right hand.

First.

This was the Midnighters' first official contract. Escort two Buma delegates to negotiate Galactic Union entry for a newly discovered race. Then let them screw the rubes out of everything they could, before bringing the diplomats home with 'no-one-of-consequence' dying in the process.

"Captain?" queried the Buma. "Do you not agree?"

Venix was right, of course. The whole company was relying on her to make this first contract the cakewalk success it deserved to be. All except Venix, whom she suspected of wanting her to screw up.

"Captain?" Brown Owl rose from his seat to his full four-foot height and swiveled his head around to fix her with those damned anime eyes.

"I do *not* agree, Ambassador..." Blue bit her lip. She needed to say Brown Owl so very much, but she forced the diplomat's proper name through her lips. "...*Reshila.*" She used her newly-implanted pinplants to take control of the bridge's main Tri-V screen. "If the submarine had windows, this is what you'd see outside right now."

"Ahh, I understand," said the patronizing alien without bothering to look at the fathomless darkness on the screen. "You Humans developed on a planet abundant with illumination. You are uncomfortable in the attenuated light."

"Attenuated light? It's brighter in the gulf between the galactic spiral arms. The ice above our heads is four miles thick. I think it's rather telling that the Tyzhounes you've been trying to cut a deal with never bothered to evolve eyes. No, I do not like this world. It's a freaking ice tomb."

"Come now, Captain Blue. It is a natural splendor. The arrangement of moons around this gas giant is just enough to warm the sub-ice oceans through gravitational tidal heating, but not so strongly that the seas boil."

"Jupiter's Europa," Blue mumbled.

"And the polar ice geysers through which the Tyzhounes launched the space probe that led to our delegation here are a unique wonder of the galaxy."

"Saturn's Enceladus."

"I beg your pardon."

"Nothing. They are but savage Human words that express my admiration for your sophisticated insight, Ambassador Reshila. All my people feel such a debt of gratitude to the Buma race above all others. For it was the diplomatic mission to Earth by the exalted Ambassador Shinalra and his auspicious aide, Chisayl, that dragged my poor, benighted race out of ignorance. If not for the Buma, we would have remained ignorant apes scratching our naked buttocks at each other."

"Well said, Captain. Your humility does your species credit."

Blue bowed deeply.

Choking noises emanated from the pilot's station. Lieutenant Norton was not only a skilled helmsman but a giggler too, though he kept his guffaws contained for now.

"Forgive me," she begged Brown Owl. "I must not keep you from your vital preparations."

Blue shut her eyes and reached out to the sub's controls using her new pinplants. The trick to them, she was finding, was to think about what she wanted and ignore how the pinplants were making it happen. She relaxed until she could form a 3D mental image of the vessel's nav map. A dotted line showed Submarine Number 6's journey, starting beneath the Midnighter forward base at the vents through the ice at the south pole. From there it ran a dozen miles below the surface of the ice moon. Then a hundred to the north, on its way to the negotiation chamber set inside the peaks of an underwater mountain range.

The route was not a direct one. There was a detour. This was the seventeenth time she had escorted Brown Owl to meet the Tyzhounes, and every time there had been a different detour, a little kink a short distance from their destination.

Her feathered VIP had no idea about any of this, but it maddened her that she knew little more than the stuffed owl. Today, though, she would find out.

At the waypoint ordered by Venix—only a mile from their destination—she opened the outer doors of the main hold, and whatever the sub had been carrying fell into the ocean. Two minutes later, she opened the doors of the secondary hold.

She marched over to Venix and leaned in close to his sensitive ears. "What are you not telling me?" she whispered.

"Whatever you're not supposed to know."

"I could torture the truth out of you. I'm so desperate to know that it would be worth it. What is in those crates I've been dropping off?"

"Torture is not always effective, Captain."

"Don't be so sure. I've had practice."

"I don't doubt it, but I cannot reveal what I do not myself know. If your sister were still with us, she would have told you that."

Blue felt her face chill and knew her skin was switching to its translucent state. She stepped back from the Zuparti as if slapped. "We don't know Sun is dead," she warned.

"She was exposed to a bio-weapon. In any case, alive or dead, it makes no practical difference. She's not here on this contract."

Pinpricks flashed across Blue's cheeks. To Venix, it would look as if demonic lightning were discharging across her face, a side effect of recreational nanites that had long ago gone rogue. Most people learned to be nervous around her in this state, but not Venix. He snapped her a defiant look, then softened his tubular body and looked away. "Perhaps I spoke insensitively. I apologize. I respect your sister a great deal, and I hope we return to find her recovered."

"Accepted. And maybe…" She waited until the firebolts left her cheeks. "Maybe it was unprofessional for me to threaten you with torture in front of the crew."

He lifted the whiskers on one side of his face and lowered them on the other—a Zuparti display of amusement. "Only because you threatened the wrong target." He looked pointedly at their VIP client with the brown and cream feathers.

Blue sighed. She could torture Reshila as much as she liked inside her mind for the crime of being an incompetent buffoon, but in real life, he represented a paying client, and he could fail as much as he liked.

She returned to her station and tried to act how she imagined a professional chauffeur should behave.

Her mind kept drifting high above to where the company's cruiser, *Midnight Sun,* orbited the moon. A great deal of money was being wagered on how long it would take the eminent Ambassador Reshila to realize the Tyzhounes didn't want to sign up to his Union accession deal. Even if they had wanted that outcome, the various factions would rather die than actually agree on anything.

No, nothing and nobody could unite the Tyzhounes.

Maybe if she explained to them what an exhilarating thing it was to travel the stars.

Lucrative too.

Blue laughed at the idea that she of all people could be a diplomat. She just had to wait patiently until the Buma realized they were wasting their time here.

Just so long as they didn't get themselves killed.

Then the Midnight Sun Free Company would still be paid for their first ever contract. In full. And she would make her sister proud.

2

The alien steadied itself on its back feet and lifted its long skeletal tail as a counterbalance. It stood erect, an act that clearly required great exertion in this meeting chamber that was filled with air, not seawater.

Without the buoyancy of their natural environment, every movement of the Tyzhounes was a strain, and they needed bubbling rebreather collars to breathe. The Buma had explained the aquatic aliens had insisted on meeting in such an environment to demonstrate they were not the weak party in these negotiations.

Blue didn't doubt it. It was what she would have done in their place. The way Ambassador Reshila trembled as the leader of the hermit faction placed her hands on the Buma's shoulders and looked down on the diplomat, the Tyzhounes also knew how to intimidate.

The exposed vertebrae of the long spine, which swept out into the paddle-tipped tail on the Tyzhounes, reminded Blue of fossilized sea reptiles from the age of dinosaurs in the museum she used to visit as a kid. Unlike the plesiosaur fossils, the Tyzhounes were the smooth black of coastal pyrite pebbles washed ashore by the waves. Even the armored fan that swept back from the head to protect its exposed back resembled a stretched mussel shell. And with the rounded dome of its eyeless head, the Tyzhoune resembled the Mark 8 CASPers that Blue had brought to the party as a ceremonial escort.

A *heavily-armed* ceremonial escort. The Human drivers inside the personal mecha lifted their coil gun arms and pointed them at the Tyzhoune getting too close and personal to the Buma.

Blue gestured for them to stand down. It had taken Reshila weeks to get this faction to send a representative to the meeting. Gunning her down during the introductions would do nothing to speed up the negotiations.

As the moment stretched on, Blue began to wonder what the hell the Tyzhoune was playing at. Probably something with religious significance, she told herself; pretty much everything was around these parts.

Although large, the meeting chamber was a crude cavern hewn from the mountain's heart, unadorned except for paintings on the walls of the Sacred Chimney. And at the chamber's center was a five-foot-high representation of the same chimney in gold and more precious minerals and metals. The chimney they portrayed was a real thing. One of thousands of deep ocean hydrothermal vents, but their religion insisted this was the one from which life had first spilled forth into their hidden world.

The hermit faction—whose representative was giving Brown Owl the shivers—wanted to preserve the chimney exactly as it had always been. They hated the warming of the seas and the pollutants from the burgeoning underwater civilization. Aliens such as Humans and Buma were off-the-scale badness.

Every bit as committed to their religious convictions, the faction Blue had named the godly adventurers despised the apostate hermits because, let's face it, if you needed to give God a hand by fencing off His most sacred creation, then you didn't really put much faith in Him. Despite their fetish for this thermal vent, it was the godly adventurers who were most enthusiastic about joining the Union. Just so long as the filthy aliens kept their hands off their chimney. That faction's symbol was the moon itself, which suggested they thought of their place in the wider galaxy.

Blue referred to the other main faction as the United Nations. Mostly secular, though sometimes not. United around power blocs—which continually disagreed with each other—the United Nations were the representatives of politicians, industrialists, warlords, and celebrities. They didn't call themselves that name of course, but they reminded her of the Human representatives who had answered when the Buma first called on the Earth and asked if humanity was coming out to play.

Ambassador Brown Owl gave a sharp squeak of pain, and the Tyzhoune lowered herself to the ground. "You must regard me as primitive," she said through her translator pendant, "but it is important to us to touch those with whom we deal and feel their vibrations."

Primitive? Blue wasn't convinced. True, the Tyzhounes had nothing to compare to the Mark 8 CASPers, or the ancient stargate through which *Midnight Sun* had journeyed here, but they had metal smelting, had developed rebreather collars, and had enough of an industrial base to launch a space probe. Developing all that while living underwater was impressive.

"I perfectly understand," Brown Owl replied, although Blue doubted that very much. "Uncontacted species are often overawed by more advanced races such as mine." He ruffled his feathers. "Now, with that...*display* over, will your faction sign the deal? I require evidence that at least 70 percent of your species agrees to its terms, and as representatives of the three dominant factions on the moon, I will accept as evidence the agreement of all three of you. Regrettably, if you cannot agree, I shall be forced to leave you unprotected by the Galactic Union, and at the mercy of any who cares to pass through the gate."

The hermit faction leader lifted her tail and coiled her limbs as if to strike. "Don't threaten me!"

"Steady on," the Buma pleaded. "I am an authorized representative of the Trade Guild, not a marauder. I issued no threats, and you have nothing to fear from the Union."

"Don't we? The jump gate in our system was built thousands of years ago, and we have known its existence for centuries. Haven't we, Shiyu-Alk-Tox?"

"It is why we launched the probe," confirmed the alien Blue assumed was the godly adventurer representative, given the moon symbol embossed on the coral torc he wore around his neck. "And you have confirmed our suspicions. Our star system was selected as a perfect location to conduct experiments in artificial generation of F11. The technique worked, but always required more F11 as input fuel than was ever produced as output. The operation was abandoned, and our system with it. You're only here because automated systems remained that detected our probe, and with the gate infrastructure already in place, the cost outlay for your negotiation is minimal. All you needed were your Merc Guild thugs."

"How do you know that?" squeaked Brown Owl.

"Perhaps our people are not so divided as you believe," said the hermit leader.

What was that supposed to mean? Blue didn't know, but she sensed the godly adventurer tense as if wary. Or guilty.

"If we join the Union," said the hermit, "the Sacred Chimney will be defiled. It is bad enough that the technocratic fools brought unwelcome attention with their space probe, but that is nothing to the interest we will awaken by entering your Union. I say no. Not now. Not tomorrow. Not ever. Whatever you attempt to bribe us with, it will never justify the risk to the sacred plume."

"You and your ridiculous sea chimney," snapped Blue. "It's just a freaking hydrothermal vent. It's a fissure releasing mineral-laden superheated water—your moon's core farting its effluent into your fathomless ocean. I've seen it a million times before on a thousand worlds."

She marched toward the sacred gold statue at the center of the negotiation chamber and pulled back one arm to knock it down.

The reaction from every Tyzhoune there was immediate. They lowered their heads and raised their hands, distorting their fingers, fusing them into wicked points like lance heads.

Blue lowered her arms slowly. "Fine. Don't let me stop you obsessing over your sacred vent."

"Captain Blue," thundered the Buma with unexpected force, "perhaps your vessel requires your immediate attention?"

"Oh, for crying out loud. All right, then. I'll just go stretch my legs, eh?"

She turned to her CASPers. "Don't let anybody die," she ordered. "Especially people we like. Or our clients."

Feeling the hatred of the Tyzhounes scorching her back, Blue left the chamber. She was in no danger, but if the locals attacked, the CASPers would gun them down, and performance penalties on the contract would begin to bite into her bonus.

It had been a difficult balancing act. With every step she took toward the sub, her tension lessened, and her grin widened.

A concerned MinSha met her as she boarded, all blue chiton and worried compound eyes. "Problem, Captain?"

"Not at all, Ensign Flkk'Sss. Everything is going according to plan. I'm just popping out for a swim. Don't worry, I'll be back before it's time to go home."

Five minutes later, as she waited in the submarine airlock, basking in the memory of the bamboozled MinSha and with the water rising over the helmet of her pressure suit, the first doubt hit home.

What would big sis say about this escapade?

Ever since the nanite incident when she'd been a kid, she had relied on Sun to steer her away from her wilder schemes. In this case, she imagined her sister rewarding her with one of those rare smiles and telling her she should have gotten imaginative sooner.

The exterior airlock door slid open.

"Thanks, sis," said Blue as she swam away into the darkness of the subterranean sea.

3

"**M**ajor Sun!" The Jeha's multitude of legs thrashed in an uncoordinated scramble, to simultaneously rise to a respectfully-erect posture and to flee the unexpected arrival of the terrifying Human merc.

He fell off his workstation couch.

Luckily, this gravity ring of the massive Port Hektatus station orbiting Tau-Rietzke was simulating only 0.8g, and the four-foot segmented arthropod was a lot tougher than he looked.

"It's a pleasure to see you, ma'am," he lied.

"Stow that shite, Jenkins. If you'd jumped out of your carapace any more, I'd need a shoehorn to stuff you back inside."

"Well I didn't...I mean, how? Should you be here at all? Is it safe? And anyway, how?"

Sun was smiling as she took in the office space they had rented for a song. Other than the Midnight Sun crest and motto mounted on the far wall, it looked like a frontier world cantina after the police had arrested everyone for brawling. Jenkins had regained his couch in front of a bank of slates, Tri-V screens and processor blocks. Everything else was broken and heaped in one corner, and had been that way since the previous occupants left suddenly a decade ago. In biohazard bags.

"I know you've been checking on my progress every day," she told the Jeha data analyst. "Only trace amounts remained of the bioweapon the assassins used in this compartment all those years ago, and it was never intended for Human victims. I'll be fine. And thank you, Jenkins. I mean it."

"Yes, but what I really wanted to know was—"

"How come the company's finest data analyst was fooled by a false data trail that said I was still planetside? Simple, because I wished to test our latest recruit. Her name's Kl'ch'hk, and here she is."

A smaller version of Jenkins scurried inside the Midnight Sun office from where she had been waiting out in the passageway.

Jenkins practically back flipped in consternation. "But she's...She's..."

Sun sighed, recalling that Jenkins had an intense amorous streak that had gotten him into trouble before. "She's what?" Sun demanded.

"She's a *child*."

Oh. Sun hadn't expected that.

"I am not!" Kl'ch'hk protested. "I am an independent legal entity who makes her own decisions."

"Of course you're a child. You're only three feet long!"

Sun snapped her fingers. "Enough! Kl'ch'hk has proven her worth to me. And you, Jenkins, are now her superior and mentor. Act like one."

She pulled a couple of padded stools out of the heap, squatting on one of the slashed seats and offering the other to Kl'ch'hk. "Seeing as I'm here in this dumpster mess—Operation Room Detritus, I'm naming it, but don't let me see it in this state again, Jenkins—let's have an update."

Jenkins proceeded to tell her how the money they'd thrown into equipment and bribes was paying off. The digital antennae he extended from this office were feeling their way into many vital intelligence sources, which would give them the edge over other merc outfits. The news was good, and Jenkins was excited, but her attention kept drifting to an ice moon many light years away. They had received one message pod so far from Tyzhou. Blue's report had managed to sound both tense and bored, but at the time, her sister hadn't known whether Sun was going to live or die. Well, Doctor DiMassi had given the all-clear an hour ago. It was time to let Blue know.

Sun noticed Jenkins had stopped the clicking and leg rubbing that passed for Jeha speech.

"She'll be all right," he assured her. "I'm sure of it."

She rapped him affectionately on his head plate. "That's very kind. But my sister is a thrill addict. You do know what that means, right?"

"Yes. She's insane."

Sun winced and tried to explain what really ailed her sister. "Her need for excitement clouds her judgement. Occasionally she can't distinguish between a course of action that's the right thing to do, and one that is the most...alluring."

"That's what I meant, ma'am. She's insane. But with you sick, Mister Venix is there to look after her, so she'll be okay."

Hmmm. Sun wasn't convinced that would work well. The Zuparti thought the company's silent owner had made a big mistake in appointing Blue as its captain and made no secret of his opinion. "Besides," Jenkins continued, *"Midnight Sun* is ferrying a Buma diplomatic mission, not entering combat."

Sun laughed dangerously. "What could possibly go wrong? Is that what you're telling me, Jenkins?"

"Yes, ma'am."

She shook her head. "It's a dangerous galaxy. A wild one too. *Everything* could go wrong."

Instantly, she regretted her words. She asked Jenkins to explain his operation to Kl'ch'hk. She turned off her translator pendant, stewing in her fear for her sister as the two Jeha scratched and hissed in the background.

Five minutes later, Jenkins gave a jerk and turned Sun's pendant back on. "Major Sun?"

"Yes?"

He curled his antennae, reluctant to speak.

"Go on. What is it?"

"You were right, ma'am. I think something's gone wrong."

4

Swimming blind through the endless dark of the subterranean sea, guided only by her pinplants pinging geolocation requests to *Midnight Sun* up in orbit, Blue had begun to check the air reserve on her rebreather with increasing frequency when she found the floating life pod precisely where she'd dropped it out of the sub's secondary hold and squeezed inside its pressurized interior.

Stripping out of her sub-aqua equipment, she contemplated the waiting CASPer that made every movement inside the pod awkward and put extreme stress on the pod's power cell as it attempted to keep the pressurized bubble at a consistent depth.

Several minutes later, Blue reentered the underwater perpetual darkness wearing the latest personal combat assault system. This Mark 8 was underwater adapted, with shaped charge harpoons mounted on one arm and a coil gun on the other with special underwater rounds. Instead of shoulder-mounted weapons pods, the personal mecha mounted an underwater turbine motor and faring to reduce drag. She used this to bullet through the water toward the location where she'd dropped the much larger crate.

Nothing would give her greater pleasure than to try out the exploding harpoons in her anger. As much as she longed to blow shit up, Blue reminded herself that doing so would probably be counterproductive during a delicate diplomatic mission. Instead, she activated the sensor pod she'd had the techs strip from a scout model.

The Tri-V bank wrapped around the inside of the cockpit burst into life. On her way to the pod, her surroundings had been so uniformly black that she might as well have been swimming through a sea of crude oil. Now the ocean took on form and differentiation. She perceived currents flowing, patterns of bubbles and dirt. Ghostly translucent worms the size of torpedoes crowded around her, just out of reach, the fronds ringing their open maws angled in her direction. There were hundreds of them. Had these monstrous creatures followed her all the way?

Shining through these worm bodies, which had never developed any need for skin pigmentation in this Stygian gloom, was a source of light her HUD informed her was artificial.

Blue felt a kick of excitement in her gut and changed direction, flying straight at the light and making the worm creatures coil away to avoid contact.

She slowed as she approached the light source: beams emanating from a floating submersible that illuminated a scene of activity. The craft itself was armored, and the rail running over its upper surface looked like a weapon. The mini sub was far smaller than Submarine Number 6, which was the underwater equivalent of a heavy shuttle. It was small enough to fit inside the crates she'd been secretly depositing and retrieving while the Buma had been dickering with the locals. She had no doubt this was the secret Venix hinted he didn't know.

Who were they?

Teams of Tyzhounes were coming to the end of an operation to ferry equipment crates from the mini sub to far more primitive craft. These were the Tyzhoune equivalent of underwater trucks, and the moon symbol embossed on the cab doors was that of the godly adventurer faction.

They had always been the most positive about contact with the Union. Was this why? Someone in the Union was arming them.

So what? If one bunch of deep sea killers wanted to bring in advanced weaponry to win the millennia-long argument over a stupid deep sea chimney, it was not her problem. So long as she still got paid.

But no matter how many times she told herself this, the idea of becoming an arms smuggler would not sit easily.

She tried to identify the species that crewed the mini sub, but the only individuals she saw were on a floating platform crowded by Tyzhounes and...equipment. She realized what she was seeing. The secret aliens had uncrated several missile launchers, secured them to the platform, and were demonstrating their operation to the Tyzhounes. Other than the portable launchers, this was the same Svalinn SLAM system mounted in Number 6. A properly deployed submarine-launched air missile system could clear the skies above these waters of air assets. And despite the small size of the moon, it did have a dense atmosphere—mostly nitrogen with a little methane and trace amounts of hydrogen. But so far, Blue had seen no evidence that the godly adventurer's rivals had developed air assets.

What they *had* seen were holes being drilled through the ice crust at widely dispersed locations. Holes large enough to fire missiles through.

The mystery of these secret arms supplies was as intoxicating as it was dangerous. So much so that Blue almost missed the critical threat alert on her HUD.

Someone was coming at her from behind!

She activated the turbines on her back, shooting up, then swiveling at the hips to employ the impellers in the CASPer's lower legs to arc her around in a loop and bring the intruder into view. Blue was upside down, but had a clear target for her harpoons.

It was a strange alien creature with six long limbs and a bulbous head. The targeting reticle locked onto the alien's center of mass. At the same time, the sensor pod highlighted the way the alien was clasping pairs of its hands together...in the Midnighter sign for *friend*.

Blue realized who she was on the cusp of blowing apart. It was Flkk'Sss. And the MinSha was right to maintain radio silence.

Meeting ended, signed the MinSha. *Bird-being is stupid. Follow me!*

Blue raised her CASPer thumbs and followed her ensign back to Number 6, signaling her life pod to sink to the seabed as she passed.

It was time to act as the chauffeur again while she figured out what the hell was going on.

5

"I've detected a xenocide contract," Jenkins explained. "Well, actually I've detected that a mercenary company has been awarded a xenocide contract, and this has been logged by the Mercenary Guild."

"I thought xenocide contracts were illegal," Sun replied.

"They are," said the youngster, Kl'ch'hk, "which is why the contract terms will have been worded in a flexible manner that permits plausible deniability of their true intent."

"The youngling is correct," Jenkins accepted—grudgingly, Sun reckoned—"but in this case the target is not a member of the Union. Strictly speaking, there are de facto laws preventing the extermination of extra-Union races, but no practical way to enforce them. Essentially, no one is incentivized to care. Theoretically the strongest protection is Guild Law, but seeing as the contract is being awarded by a powerful Veetanho faction, it's not surprising the Mercenary Guild has not challenged this."

"Why is this xenocide contract of significance to us?" Kl'ch'hk asked.

"I imagine," Sun answered, "Jenkins has forgotten to tell us that the target is a moon called Tyzhou."

"I was just getting to that."

"The situation is hopeless," said Sun. "If Tyzhou were a member of the Union, then not even Veetanho-contracted mercs would dare nuke the planet from orbit. They would have to launch their strike from below the ten-mile attack altitude limit. It might give the Tyzhounes a chance, but the last report from Blue said our Buma ambassador couldn't negotiate a drink at a bar."

Jenkins eased a sly curve into his segmented body. "But the Tyzhounes *could* be probationary members of the Union by now."

Sun shook her head. She felt sorry for the Tyzhounes, but the dangers were more personal. Their own contract was to escort the Buma and secure a safe negotiation environment. If the moon was nuked, they would fail to deliver on the company's first contract, and the mercs doing the deed might want to clear away any witnesses.

"Who took the contract?" she asked.

"Experienced Goka outfit."

Damn. Goka were killers who were highly skilled and loved their trade. "Theoretically, we could have the protection of the Union by the time the mercs turn up," she said. "But realistically, there's very little chance."

"What if we weren't being realistic?"

Sun recognized the audacious tilt to Jenkins' antennae. It was weird but the Jeha reminded her of her sister. The other Human mercs were fond of Jenkins but thought of him as an inoffensive coward. In Human terms, he was. But in his alien way, he was as much a thrill addict as Blue.

"We just need to make one tiny assumption," he explained, "that the Tyzhounes are signed up probationary members of the Union. Then the Peacemakers will have to get involved."

Was Jenkins proposing a daring move or signing a death warrant for the entire company? Sun wasted a few moments trying to decide before concluding that the answer would only be revealed once they'd tried.

"Okay," she said. "Let's do it. Let's lie to the Peacemakers."

6

"I'm sorry for your loss." Blue felt a sudden urge to stroke the feathers of the Buma. Deputy Ambassador Lykalah's plumage was a striking pattern of dark and light grays with iridescent blue and green strips. If her poisoned boss lying under a sheet on the medi-bed had looked like an overstuffed brown owl, Lykalah was more like a giant pigeon with a MinSha grandparent. "I assure you that the treachery will be met with painful repercussions if you so order it, and that safety will be massively uprated for your future meetings with the Tyzhounes. No Tyzhoune will approach within ten feet of you without getting a face full of 15mm autocannon rounds. No one else will die on my watch."

"You are right that there won't be any danger," Lykalah replied, "because I'm never going back down on that moon." She roared—a most un-avian sound that made every merc in sickbay tense. "You failed to protect my superior, Captain, and I do not trust you to protect me. Only an idiot would go back down and negotiate with those dangerous savages."

"But...the contract. It will be withdrawn...a failure."

"Your contract is no concern of mine, mercenary."

"The captain refers to your contract to negotiate this deal on behalf of the Trading Guild," suggested Venix.

It wasn't true, but the Buma had been grinding what sounded like gravel in her neck. Venix's talk of the cost of failure stopped it. Was Lykalah reconsidering?

"We are all in shock," said Blue quickly. "And grief. Let us not make hasty decisions."

The Buma tilted back on its heels and looked up at Blue, who was only a few inches taller than the four-foot alien. "Nothing you can say or do will persuade me to go back into that moon."

"You don't need to," said Blue. "You're licensed to approve a deal to bring the Tyzhounes into the Union, but you don't have to be the one who knocks their bony heads together."

Lykalah's black anime eyes stretched to absurd dimensions. "Are you suggesting that *you* will negotiate a trade deal, Human?"

"Certainly not. I meant Mister Venix."

The Buma twisted her head around to stare at the Zuparti for several seconds before flouncing out of sickbay, ruffling her feathers.

"She didn't actually say no," Blue observed once she'd left.

"But I *am* saying no." Venix teased the whiskers on his snout between finger and thumb, as he often did when in deep thought.

Blue left him to think for as long as her patience would permit, which amounted to several seconds. "Why the hell not?"

"I'm a Zuparti. You younger races call us the most paranoid species in the galaxy. I prefer to think of us as the most adept at risk management. Before we picked up the Buma, I considered hundreds of risks that threatened the success of this contract. I have mitigation and contingencies worked out for all of them, some of which I discussed with the owner. She was insistent that should the current situation arise, *you* must negotiate this deal. You must rescue both our contract and the Buma's. She was very insistent upon that."

Blue couldn't believe what she was hearing. A diplomat? Her? "Mister Venix, it is true that our professional relationship has so far lasted only a few months. Nonetheless, from what you have learned of me during that time, do you regard me as suitable for leading a diplomatic mission?"

"Captain Blue, I can think of no one less suitable than you."

"I will fail."

"Almost certainly. Nonetheless, I represent the company's owner, and if she were here she would order you to complete the mission objective. And that is what you must do."

"But why? Why would she insist on this?"

Venix tugged at his whiskers again. "She detects in you an annoying habit of succeeding despite—or possibly *because*—of your many inadequacies."

"And you, Venix? Does your snout detect this same annoying trait?"

He snorted. "Why else would I be here?"

7

Blue was out of ideas.

She paced her captain's room, her mind rejecting every scheme she devised for rescuing the situation. Situated just off the CIC, which was near the engines housed within *Midnight Sun's* inner section, the pseudo gravity from the cruiser's spin was low, meaning Blue's pacing consisted of a single bound off the deck alternating with tumble turns off the bulkheads.

Normally, it helped her to think, but a solution to this mess eluded her.

As she floated through the air toward the spinward bulkhead, it suddenly came alive, an embedded screen showing the worried face of Lieutenant Norton. "A Peacemaker ship just emerged through the gate," he announced. "It's hailing us. Sending initial lag estimates. Standby...and we have news! A message pod came through with the Peacemaker. One of ours! Omega priority. It has Major Sun's signature." Norton paused a moment to control his excitement. "Putting it through to your personal data node."

The Tyzhou system's emergence area was currently seventeen light minutes away, but the Peacemaker craft had transitioned in with a velocity that would bring it to Tyzhou within seven hours.

As Blue took in the hard data, the news from Sun and Jenkins made her simultaneously cold with fear and hot with excitement. So, the Veetanho wanted the Tyzhounes snuffed out before they could join the Union? That had to be connected with the undersea arms smuggling she wasn't supposed to know about. The Goka the Veetanho had contracted were due to emerge from the gate in around three hours. Which was why, warned her sister, they'd summoned a Peacemaker under false pretenses. Sun hoped they would have a signed treaty in time.

Way to up the stakes, sis!

"Ma'am?" prompted Norton. "What do we say to the Peacemaker?"

"Lieutenant Norton, you are an officer of this company. Use your initiative to stall."

"Stall? A Peacemaker?"

"Yes, Norton. What species is it?"

"XenSha."

"The killer bunnies? Norton, they're three feet tall and think close quarters combat is something you do sitting down with a video game controller."

"I don't know, ma'am. It's still a Peacemaker. It will be an elite specimen of its race."

"Nonetheless, an elite specimen easily distracted by lettuce and salad vegetables."

"Are you serious, ma'am?"

"About the lettuce, no. But I'm deadly serious about everything else. Keep that Peacemaker off my back for a few hours." She grinned. "I've got an idea."

8

Giving credit where it was due, the Sacred Chimney was more than just another vent on the seabed where intense heat burst forth from the moon's core.

As Flkk'Sss and Blue dove below the black cloud of sulfides that belched from the chimney top and spread for miles, the foothills leaped into view. Abrupt splashes of color after the featureless wastes of the seabed, they were writhing masses of plump red worms that clung to the coral-like base structure. Spindly-legged spiders chased each other across the worm fields.

And then the chimney itself towered into view. It looked like a gnarled termite mound; wreathed in gleaming minerals and a tight band of exotic sea life, it stretched upward for over a hundred meters.

Of course, none of that would normally be visible in the permanent night of this hidden sea—which was a shame because it really *was* one of the prettiest sights she'd ever seen—but the mini sub she'd stolen from the hold of her own submarine had powerful illuminating beams and image enhancement built into the holographic display.

"You figured out how to fire that thing yet, Flkk'Sss?" she asked of her co-conspirator.

"I believe so, Captain. I cannot tell for sure until I activate the system."

"Well, give me a moment. I want to take one more tourist fly past."

By now, Blue had mastered the basic controls of the mysterious underwater vessel, although she still hadn't figured out how to sit in the pilot's station, which was designed for a dramatically different physiology. She took a lazy loop around the glorious tower of deep sea life. She had heard of many wonders in the galaxy, and she felt privileged to see one for herself.

Unfortunately, it had to go.

She came about and turned toward the chimney again, but this time it wasn't sightseeing. This was an attack run.

"Target set on the structure's base, Captain."

Blue leaned over and pressed the control Flkk'Sss had indicated to her earlier. As captain, it was her responsibility to fire.

The mini sub throbbed with sudden power from the rail that ran over the top of the craft. Just slow enough to follow its progress with her naked eye, a tunnel stretched out from the weapon, the water churning white within its diameter. When the tunnel met the chimney, the ancient structure exploded outward in green-tinged flames.

Blue feathered the maneuvering controls to cut the beam along the bottom of the chimney.

One pass. That was all it took. After countless millions of years, the Sacred Chimney that the locals venerated as the wellspring of all life on this moon toppled to the sea floor.

"Let's get out of here," Blue said. "I think the locals might get a little vexed when they learn what I've done."

9

"**R**adar lock!"

"Launching countermeasures."

"Altitude—22,000 feet."

Blue sat still in her couch and let the shuttle's crew deal with getting the hell off the moon before the Tyzhoune faction she herself had helped to arm figured out how to blow them out of the sky with their SLAMs.

For once, leaving her crew to do the job was easy. For a start, they were thrusting so hard that if she moved an inch, she felt sure all her ribs would pop. Even without the considerable weight of the submarine she'd left beneath the polar vents, the pages of the heavy shuttle's playbook for evasive maneuvers were entirely blank.

A lamp built into her station announced an urgent incoming communication. A moment later, Lieutenant Norton's worried face appeared in the station's ruggedized slate. "Peacemaker Kellen-Hyri is demanding to speak with you."

"All hands," announced a computerized voice over the roar of acceleration that swept the shuttle's flight deck, "brace for maximum survival thrust."

Blue clamped her jaw together and opened her lips, which were instantly ripped back by the intense Gs. "A little...busy...right now," she told Norton.

A grunt of pain escaped her chest as the thrust ratcheted up to a pummeling new level. She abandoned her attempt to close her lips over her teeth, and let them flap loose like a dog strapped to a high-speed hover board.

"He's halfway through a forty-second countdown," Norton explained from the calmness of *Midnight Sun's* CIC. "If you don't answer him, he'll arrest us all and execute you."

"Unghh," she told him, and Norton's Human face was replaced by that of XenSha with gray fur, twitching nose, and a vague resemblance to a terrestrial rabbit that ended with the array of tentacles that crested its head. Tentacles which gave it senses Blue barely comprehended.

"At last, the elusive Captain Blue. Please explain why you feel the need to flee that moon in such haste?"

"Radar locks lost," announced the pilot. "Easing off the gas."

"Diplomacy," Blue replied through clenched teeth, as the Gs relaxed from insane to merely intense. "A bump in the path of peaceful negotiation."

"Exiting estimated effective range of enemy missile defense."

"Enemy?" queried the XenSha. "I'm no expert, but I would say your diplomacy is in trouble. As is your continued existence, Captain. I was told of an impending illegal attack on a Union world from what I had believed was an impeccable source. A mercenary force did indeed emerge shortly after I did, but I do not believe what I am told about the race who inhabit this moon. Are they Union members or not?"

"They are, Peacemaker. Signed up and secure in the bosom of the Galactic Union."

"And your evidence?"

"Aboard our cruiser, the *Midnight Sun*. I'm old school. Had the agreement signed in ink. Dock, and I'll show you in person."

The XenSha narrowed his eyes and bared his teeth. "You had better be telling the truth." The frond of head tentacles straightened, pointing at Blue like plump darts. "But I don't think you are. I was going to levy an impressive fine for wasting Peacemaker time, but your lies go too far, Captain Blue. It is important from time to time to make examples of those who seek to abuse the Peacemakers. You shall be my example, Blue. As will your crew. Do not leave orbit. I shall dock in three hours. Kellen-Hyri out."

The Peacemaker's image vanished, replaced by Lieutenant Norton.

"Tell Flight-Sergeant Jackson to prep a dropship," Blue told him. "And get that useless Buma on board. Oh, and bring plasti-paper and ink."

"The Buma won't go."

Blue felt the pigment drain from her face as her anger welled up. She was tiring of this Lieutenant whose first instinct was forever to tell her what she could not do.

"Make her go," she growled. "We're paid to deliver results, not be nice to our client representatives. And when you've packed her securely into the dropship, I want you to organize communications from orbit to all the main Tyzhoune factions."

"That last won't be a problem. They're demanding to have a word with you. Although, Captain…"

"Get on with it, Norton."

"They don't sound very happy."

10

"Y ou can't take your revenge on me or defend against those Goka unless you first sign the treaty," Blue explained to the Tyzhounes, praying she would never have to meet them again in person. "And until you are a Union member, anyone who wants to can sit in orbit and irradiate your world with impunity. Anyone, such as the Goka fleet which is going to do exactly that in just a few hours."

"No. We will never agree. We will never join your Union."

"But you could—" Blue was about to suggest they hire a Depik assassin, but some dangers even she would never encourage. "You could hire your own mercenaries," she said as a safer alternative.

"What we wish is for you to return to our world and stand trial for your sacrilege."

"Who? Who wishes this? Which faction?"

"All of us. Congratulations, Captain. After centuries of bitter division, you have finally united us—in our hatred of you."

Blue closed her eyes and flushed with pleasure. Her plan was working so far. She felt a tap on her shoulder followed by Norton's whispered voice. "The xenocide mercs are hailing. Patching through now."

"This is Flotilla Commander Gzalt," announced the Goka, a member of an insectoid race of near-indestructible killers. Gzalt's long antennae swept back aggressively.

"Who is this?" demanded the Tyzhoune on the other channel, but Norton had patched the simultaneous conversations so the Goka were unaware the Tyzhounes were listening in.

"I am Captain Blue, commander of the *Midnight Sun*. State your intentions in this star system."

"Our intentions are not your concern. I order you to power down weapons, or we shall fire upon you."

"I have reason to believe you intend to commit xenocide against the people of this moon."

"Interfere and we shall destroy you too."

"As a good Union citizen, I cannot stand aside and permit you to commit an illegal act. The Tyzhounes who dwell here are probationary members of the Galactic Union."

"You lie. There is no record of any treaty negotiation. We may attack this moon with impunity."

"Did you hear that?" Blue asked the Tyzhounes after Gzalt severed the comm link.

"We did, but this does not make us allies."

"True, but before you come after me to take your revenge for the act I carried out to unite your people, you first have to survive the attack from these Goka mercenaries. Turns out, it's your lucky day. Because I have a solution. I'm sending a dropship down to the southern ice crust vents with a treaty for you to sign." Blue made a quick mental calculation. The Peacemaker would dock in ninety minutes, and the Goka ship reach orbit two hours later. "If you want to prevent the Goka raining death from orbit, I need that treaty signed within the hour."

11

"Cut the crap," barked the Peacemaker when Blue met him by *Midnight Sun*'s airlock. "Where is your evidence?"

Blue activated a slate built into the bulkhead. It showed the Buma on an icy wilderness surrounded by Tyzhounes. Flight-Sergeant Jackson was there too, her grin clearly visible through her bubble helmet.

"That Buma does not look happy," said the Peacemaker. "Is it under duress?"

"No, Peacemaker. It is under contract. A contract to deliver a trade deal. Hold it up, if you please, Deputy Ambassador Lykalah."

On the moon below, the Buma held up a stack of plastic paper sheets to the hovering camera view.

"I can't see," said Peacemaker. "They keep icing up. Deputy Ambassador, please confirm that this moon is now a member of the Union."

"It is so," the Buma replied.

"I confirm that we are the legitimate representatives of over 70 percent of our world's population," said the hermit faction Tyzhoune.

The XenSha's head tentacles writhed. Everyone present knew he would check the truth of what he was being told, but Blue hoped he would now have no choice but to place the moon under his protection.

"One more thing," the Peacemaker demanded of the Buma. "If you are the deputy ambassador, where is the senior member of your delegation?"

"You're with her now. It is Ambassador Blue."

The Peacemaker literally jumped off the deck in surprise before recovering his composure. "I see. It appears, *Ambassador* Blue, that your execution is temporarily postponed. I shall return to my ship and observe developments."

12

"Izlian-built *Pyhkayl*-class heavy cruisers," commented Flkk'Sss as the three Goka warships descended below *Midnight Sun*'s orbit. "They have the ability to conduct an orbital bombardment and are full of dropships. They would make formidable opponents if we took them on."

Blue drummed her fingers on the arms of her command station. The MinSha tactical command officer had never before volunteered that a potential opponent could prove dangerous. Knowing she couldn't take them on in a fair fight didn't make it any easier to watch them pass and do nothing.

"Peacemaker Kellen-Hyri to Goka mercenary commander." The XenSha's openly broadcast image appeared on the CIC screen. "I have studied your contract and judge it to be illegal. I will not permit xenocide against a Union world."

A Goka head was added to the screen as the reply was broadcast. "I am Gzalt, and I command here. Thank you for bringing your judgement to our attention and preventing a crime. We have struck all illegal clauses from the contract and are invoking secondary success criteria. We shall degrade the target's industrial and technological capability, and we shall do so below the ten-mile bombardment limit using lawful weaponry."

"I have seen *degraded* worlds that have lain barren for millennia. What you propose is reprehensible but not illegal. If there are to be repercussions it is for the Mercenary Guild to deliver them. I shall notify them of your action."

"Oh, the Merc Guild won't be a problem. Not for us. Thank you for your service, Peacemaker. Keep a safe distance and watch. I'm sure you're listening in, Midnighters. That goes for you, too. We have powerful backers. Do not make us your enemy. Gzalt out."

The Goka warships were orbiting stern first. Each fired its main engine and extended a huge parabolic dish to act as an upper-atmosphere brake. The dishes began to glow red as the ships dropped out of orbit.

"We can't sit back and do nothing," cried Lieutenant Norton.

"Are you recommending we engage in combat with these warships?" Blue snapped back. "We are outnumbered, and we are not contracted to defend this moon. Would you have me risk the lives of everyone aboard *Midnight Sun,* and our owner's capital investment, on a matter of principle? The strong take from the weak and keep them weak so they can take again tomorrow. It happens the galaxy over, every single day. Are you unable to stomach that truth, Lieutenant?"

"No, ma'am. But this is different. Those Veetanho bastards put out a xenocide contract. How can you sit back and watch these Goka carry it out?"

Blue sensed Venix's attention, but then she looked around CIC and saw all eyes, snouts, and antennae were hanging on her response.

A rapt audience was such a thrill!

"The galaxy can be a harsh place," she said, addressing everyone there. "There may come a time when I call upon you to take a stand on a matter of principle, but not here and not today." She pointed at the main screen. "Because today, we don't need to. Stand down your moral qualms, Norton, and watch what happens next."

13

S afely below the ten-mile limit, the Goka ships began playing energy beams along the ice crust above the Tyzhoune capital, cutting a hole in preparation for pouring through a rain of deadly munitions.

But the Tyzhounes had been drilling their own holes through the ice for a long time.

The Svalinn SLAM system was designed to scale up to a planetary defense shield for entire water worlds. Blue hadn't inadvertently delivered enough to do that, but when thirty missiles rose from the ice, she knew the Goka were beaten. The cruisers threw out countermeasures and tried to gain altitude, but the Svalinn missiles were not so easily distracted.

They slammed into the bellies of the invading craft, blowing out chunks of debris. The ships glowed blue as the methane in the atmosphere burned.

Badly damaged, all three fled for the safety of orbit, but one didn't make it. By the looks of it, the fire ripping through its belly reached a magazine because it blew apart in a spectacular explosion.

No more missiles rose from the ice in pursuit, though, and the Goka were still dangerous. Once they'd limped through the upper atmosphere, dropships launched and formed up, ready to land and wreak revenge on the moon dwellers.

"Putting a Tyzhoune communication on screen," Norton announced.

"You sold us a lie," said a representative of the godly adventurer faction. "You all did. We do not have enough missiles left to take on this new attack, and the Peacemaker refuses to prevent it. Union membership is not enough to protect us."

"That's not how this works," Blue explained. "Union membership allows you to employ mercenary companies. It is your good fortune that there is one here available on my ship, the Midnight Sun Free Company. Would you like to employ us to clear away your Goka problem before it gets to the ground?"

"What payment do you demand?"

"To give me and my company a full pardon, sworn on sacred oaths by all of you. You will explain to your people that although I cut through your sacred chimney, it was divine will that guided my hands in order to unite your people in your time of greatest need, and that the chimney is not dead but shall be renewed in good time. Payment in advance. Oh, and that gold chimney in the negotiation chamber. I want that too."

The Tyzhounes fumed and cursed her, but they agreed as she knew they would. But by then, Captain Blue had already withdrawn behind her darkened control glasses and entwined her mind around that of the *Midnight Sun*. For the ship was alive, and together they were learning a dance of destruction such as the galaxy had not experienced in eons.

She felt the machinery of war energize her being, but there was a pang of regret too. Ensign Flkk'Sss had been wrong in her assessment. There was no challenge here; the Goka didn't stand a chance.

14

Blue caressed the craggy rim of the golden artifact strapped securely into the vacant Second Officer's station. There were still too many vacancies aboard this ship—she glanced at Lieutenant Norton—and maybe some surplus to requirements. Still, the Golden Chimney of Tyzhoune! What a trophy! If she chopped the base off and plugged a flat section into its top, it would make an awesome night stand in her apartment.

"Captain, please reconsider."

She looked up at the Buma whose arrogance had returned since the trade deal had been signed, and the Goka wiped out by the fury of *Midnight Sun*. "Deputy Ambassador Lykalah, can you confirm you have everything you need to take this deal back to the Trade Guild?"

"Yes, but that's not the point. We're leaving orbit and we've not even begun to monetize the first contact situation. If you understood the statistics for how lucrative initial transactions with a fledgling Union race can be, then you would understand the need to remain here for a few weeks at least. I can offer you a ten percent commission on all transactions from this moment until our departure."

Using her pinplants, Blue instructed the helm to accelerate their departure from orbit. Lykalah stumbled, and grabbed onto Blue's chair.

"You wish to reinforce in my mind that you Buma are the premier race licensed by the Trade Guild as first contact negotiators. You are the closest thing the Galactic Union possesses to a diplomatic corps."

"It is a truth often spoken."

"Good. Before we discuss your request to remain in orbit, I desire to call upon your professional judgement as a diplomat. After the success of this first case of Midnight diplomacy, I'm going to apply to the Trade Guild to license the Midnight Sun Free Company as a hybrid mercenary–diplomatic organization. What do you say to that?"

Lykalah's feathers fluffed up to twice their normal thickness. Her huge black eyes blinked at the irreverent Human before her. Then she fled CIC.

Blue ignored her. There were more pressing matters. "TacCom, report!"

"The Tyzhoune missile's guidance systems failed at an altitude of 125 miles. That is 52 miles higher than their previous attempt. I estimate we shall be gone before they adapt their SLAM to fire in true sea-to-space mode."

"Agreed, Ensign. They're just sending a message. Received and understood—we're clearing off and not coming back."

"Midnight diplomacy?" queried Venix a few minutes later, when they had safely left orbit. "You *were* just toying with the Buma, weren't you?"

She regarded the Zuparti. At first, she'd taken an instant dislike to the way he poked his whiskers into her business, but now she saw that his natural caution might prove an invaluable balance to her...*issues*. He might even be the one to sniff out the deadly secrets she was fronting for the company's owner. For that to work, Venix needed a proper place in the chain of command. A senior one.

"Licensed diplomats?" she replied. "Who knows? I don't believe in limitations, but one thing is for sure. With the Midnight Sun Free Company, anything is possible."

His whiskers stopped twitching, and he did something she didn't even know was possible for his race.

Venix smiled.

# # # # #

Desperta Ferro by
Eric S. Brown &
N.X. Sharps

Lieutenant Gregan Mazzey sat in a chair designed for inhuman proportions and hunched over a glass of amber liquid. The synthesizer may have whipped up something chemically resembling fermented grain mash, but whiskey it was not. He drank the final finger of alcohol and contemplated what he had left on his person to pawn for another bottle, or at least another glass. His hand strayed to the hip holster, absent a laser pistol. His slate had purchased the last round and his pistol the round before that. He considered pleading with the bartender to open a line of credit again but figured his fellow patrons might be more generous. After all, a glass of faux-whiskey was a small price to pay to hear about his glory days with the infamous Graveyard Whistlers, was it not?

He decided to end his self-imposed seclusion, dismounted the awkward chair, and turned to scan the Voluntary Exchange for a drinking buddy. He found the Merc Pit virtually empty, save for the Lumar bartender who stood at the counter, disassembling and cleaning a familiar-looking sidearm with its two pairs of hands, and a bored-looking Sirra'Kan prostitute. Light strained through the shuttered portals of the Exchange, but with Tobobo's confusing day/night cycle, it was difficult to guess the time. Mazzey called up his pinplant's chronometer, but the program failed to boot up, flashing an error code. He cursed the capricious nature of the outdated computer integrated into his head and wondered what value it might have.

Even in his inebriated state, he quickly came to the conclusion that whatever paltry sum he pocketed wouldn't be worth risking back-alley brain surgery. He patted himself down, desperate for one last drink before he had to stagger back to the Mongrels' billet located in an even sketchier neighborhood than he currently found himself. He couldn't tell what he dreaded more, First Sergeant Bahtia's pity or the rest of the platoon's contempt.

"I like your boots. What size?" asked the bartender.

"What?" asked Mazzey.

"Your boots, I like them. What size do you wear?" asked the bartender.

"Size twelve," responded Mazzey, bewildered.

"Close enough. I'll trade you another pour for 'em," said the bartender.

At last, Mazzey understood. He shucked off the combat boots without hesitation and padded across the grimy floor to deposit them on the counter. The Lumar set aside the Colt-Casio 10kJ laser pistol lens he had been polishing to examine the boots. Presumably pleased with the quality and condition of the footwear, he stashed them behind the bar and poured three fingers of faux-whiskey into a clean glass. Mazzey opened his mouth to protest that the boots were worth significantly more than three measly fingers of the synthesized spirit, but the expression on the bartender's face and the empty holster on his hip persuaded him otherwise. He took the glass and skulked back to his corner of the Exchange, socks adhering to the floor with every step. He sat back down and nursed the drink, determined to make it last.

To Mazzey's credit, he did make it last until a band of boisterous young bucks strolled in like they owned the place, hooting and hollering like kids fresh off of taking their VOWS. With his calm irreparably damaged, Mazzey knocked back the last of his beverage and turned to leave. He saw the shaved heads, tacky gold chains, pristine white and teal track suits, and growling bear badges of the Bruiser Boys sewn on the shoulders. Upon noticing who they were, he turned right back around and developed a sudden and intense interest in the bottom of his glass. The Bruisers conversed with the bartender in thick accents and ordered a round of imported Russian vodka.

"Za Zdarovje!" they cheered.

Empty shot glasses thudded against the countertop, and the Bruisers enthusiastically ordered, "Another!" Mazzey scoffed at the absurd tab being rung up for an inferior liquor. The front door of the establishment swung open, interrupting his musings, and heavy footfalls sounded on the tile. A hush descended over the revelry.

"You best not be drinking," said a gruff voice.

A moment of silence stretched on uncomfortably long.

"You best not be drinking without me, anyway."

The Bruisers erupted with cheers. Mazzey recognized the voice, but he glanced over his shoulder anyway. Major Aleksei Brusilov, executive officer of the Bruiser Boys mercenary outfit, strode into the Voluntary Exchange and saddled up to the centrally-located bank of terminals. He stood stock-still and ramrod straight in his pressed white dress uniform as he watched streams of data scroll across the Tri-V screens. A slight adolescent with an acne-scarred face brought the Major a glass of clear liquid. He took the offered drink, sipped it without diverting his attention from the screens, and nodded once to dismiss the boy. Mazzey put his head down and shrank in his seat. He debated the merits of trying to sneak past Brusilov and his goons or hiding in the corner and hoping they minded their own business.

Fifteen minutes passed. The Bruisers continued to indulge themselves, one even having escorted the Sirra'Kan prostitute to a side room for a quick romp, while Mazzey cursed his second-in-command for not protesting harder against his insistence to go have a drink. It was all her fault for refusing to stock their billet with alcohol in the first place. The least she could have done was unlock the spend limit on his Universal Account Access Card, so he wasn't left pawning his meager belongings for few drinks, the selfish shrew. Occupied with a subject to blame his misery on, Mazzey passed the time thinking of ways to avenge himself upon Sergeant Bahtia until Major Brusilov declared an end to the festivities.

"Time to go lads, we've got a new contract," said Brusilov to a chorus of protests.

"You'll have plenty of time to rest when you're dead or after I've ejected you from my outfit. We've got a substantial payday lined up to retrieve some classified information from a band of pirates."

"What good do all these credits do if you're always cutting leave short before we can spend them?" asked a broad-shouldered lad with a lazy eye.

"Consider your daily wages docked for insubordination, Private Grankin. Problem solved. Now settle your tabs and shuttle up to the

Rostislav. Anyone unaccounted for by 1900 earns themselves a dishonorable discharge from my employ. And will one of you please make sure that oaf Lutrova visits Doc Gurevich for an inspection before we lift off? I don't even want to imagine what types of venereal diseases you can contract from a Sirra'Kan hooker."

The last line earned some chuckles. Brusilov began to leave and Mazzey sighed, relieved to have avoided the Major's notice. He sighed too soon because once Brusilov reached the Exchange's front doors, he stopped, pivoted on his heel, and stared directly at Mazzey in the corner.

"Could that possibly be the infamous Captain Mazzey I see?" asked Brusilov.

Mazzey fought the urge to sink further into the alien chair. He took a deep breath, puffed out his chest, and clothed himself in the shreds of his long-forsaken dignity as Brusilov approached.

"None other," said Mazzey, not bothering to correct Brusilov regarding his rank.

"This man is the hero of Cho's Folly," said Brusilov, addressing his men.

Liking the turn things had taken, Mazzey shrugged, affecting an attitude of nonchalance.

"Last we crossed paths was what, during the Rykwon Raid? How are the Graveyard Whistlers? I'm frankly surprised an outfit of your caliber is slumming it out here on the margins," said Brusilov.

"I'm actually commanding the Iron Mongrels now," corrected Mazzey.

"The Mongrels." Brusilov chortled the platoon's more commonly used abbreviation. The Bruiser Boys joined in, but, when Mazzey's expression failed to change, the laughter died out.

"The Mongrels?"

"The Iron Mongrels," Mazzey confirmed.

The Major mulled that over for a second, absorbing the man's disheveled state—the glassy eyes, the reek of booze, the empty holster, and shoeless feet—before clapping him on the shoulder.

"We all fall on hard times," said Brusilov.

He placed a credit chit on the table in front of Mazzey and spoke softly but still loud enough for the troopers to hear.

"Buy yourself a decent pair of shoes, courtesy of the Bruiser Boys."

Mazzey glared at the chit until Brusilov and his goons left. After the doors closed behind the final mercenary, he picked it up and rubbed it between his fingers. He licked his lips, well aware that he could now afford several bottles of imitation swill or even a few sips of genuine, Irish whiskey imported all the way across the stars from the cradle of mankind. He hadn't tasted the good stuff in years, yet something in the depths of his mind prevented him from acting on the desire—be it Brusilov's unwanted pity, the derision with which the Bruisers regarded his admittedly-inferior platoon, or the reality of sitting alone and shoeless in a bar. He slipped the chit into his front pocket instead, stood up, and stumbled over to the bank of Tri-V terminals.

* * *

Seven minutes later, Mazzey left the Merc Pit and began the lengthy trek to the Mongrels' billet. He picked his way around the shards of glass and bits of scrap metal littering the neglected streets, keenly aware of the absence of his combat boots. Layers of graffiti smothered the walls in a riot of shapes and colors, though whether it was of Human or alien composition was anyone's guess. Motorists of a variety of races, operating an assortment of ground cars, barreled down narrow lanes with little regard for other drivers and zero consideration for pedestrians. Freight containers screeched by without any sense of urgency on overhead rails and, farther out, flyers could be seen ferrying passengers between the more affluent wards and the starport.

A quarter mile out from the Voluntary Exchange, Mazzey passed an alley bisecting a row of shuttered storefronts and picked up a tail. He admonished himself for the lapse in situational awareness. He wasn't well versed enough in alien body language to predict whether the three Pushtal wanted to strangle him or snuggle but experience living in human-majority cities suggested they were up to no good. He increased his pace and, if that made him xenophobic, then so be it. He heard the padding of feet increase behind him and longed for his Colt-Casio or at least his combat boots. Thugs were generally cowards, whatever their race, and cowards tended to prefer unarmed prey. And if they were the rarer, bolder breed of thugs? Well, Mazzey had never missed an opportunity for target practice, unless of course he had hocked his gun to drown his regrets.

He felt, more than heard, the stalkers draw near, and his muscles bunched up for the imminent confrontation. He had fought and won fist fights before, even in various states of impairment, but against three potentially packing Pushtal? He didn't love his odds. Even so, better to seize the initiative than wait for the thugs to make the first move. He spun around and adopted a half-remembered fighting stance. The trio of felinoids halted in midstride. Mazzey lunged at the nearest of the three, and it flinched back from him. He bared his teeth and growled. Perhaps the behavior translated into comical-

282 | KENNEDY & WANDREY

crazy rather than dangerous-crazy or maybe they just realized he was unarmed because they began to tighten the noose.

None of them saw the ground car hurtling toward them, nor did they hear the subdued hum of electric engine. One moment Mazzey stood braced by a few mean looking aliens, and the next moment, one of the thugs lay crumpled and yowling under the front tire of an automated taxi while its companions fled the scene. Mazzey stood there stunned as the car's horn blared, and an electronic voice hurled randomly generated obscenities at the still-twitching roadkill. The wipers activated and began to smudge the Pushtal's vital fluids back and forth across the windshield, revealing a very flustered woman with an athletic build and cappuccino skin sitting in the back seat. Too busy yelling at the taxi's navigation system, Sergeant Bahtia failed to notice Mazzey standing by her window until she opened the door to exit.

"Lieutenant? Lieutenant!" she exclaimed.

"Scoot over," ordered Mazzey.

"Did you not just see what happened? We need to get out of this death trap." she said, opening the door of the ground car and sliding across to the adjacent seat.

"That Pushtal and its friends were about to jump me when you came along. Besides, we're safer in here than we are dodging these 'death traps' out on the streets," said Mazzey, shutting the door behind him.

"Where have you been? I must have sent a dozen queries to your pinplant. I was starting to worry," said Bahtia.

"I never got them," Mazzey lied, "you know how finicky my hardware can be."

"Please input destination," said the taxi.

"Take us back to the tenement stacks," said Bahtia.

"Belay that. Deliver us to Topopo Starport, Berth 26C."

The ground car shifted into reverse, executed a tight turn in the narrow avenue, and sped off back in the direction it had come, leaving a horribly mangled Pushtal in its wake.

"Sergeant, send out a general recall and have everyone meet us in orbit on Topopo Station. I want *Pugnacious* to be stargate bound no later than 1600. Anyone unaccounted for by that time earns themselves a dishonorable discharge," Mazzey gave his best Brusilov impression.

"Sir, yes, sir," replied Bahtia. Her quirked eyebrow indicated curiosity, but professionalism stayed her tongue.

"What's our current disposition?" Mazzey asked.

"As it stands, we are woefully short on firepower. Between the units you've instructed me to sell to cover expenses and those lost to natural attrition, we may have one understrength squads' worth of CASPers. The only relatively modern models in the entire platoon belong to Sergeant Whoolery and myself—the rest are antiques in different levels of disrepair. That leaves another three squads of light infantry with standard ballistic armor and small arms. We're not equipped to assault a hardened military target if that's what you're asking," she said bluntly.

"We don't need to be," said Mazzey.

"What have you gotten us into?" asked Bahtia.

"I've accepted a contract to reclaim a data cache stolen from an Information Guild courier ship by Riagian corsairs."

"Have you ever even fought Riagians?" she asked.

"Once when I was a Whistler. They're an ex-mercenary race that's grown fond of piracy since their ousting from the Guild. We

284 | KENNEDY & WANDREY

called 'em 'squatches on account of the fact they resemble the big, hairy, upright-walking ape from North American folklore. They're nasty buggers too. I've seen mature Riagians crack open CASPers with their bare hands," said Mazzey.

Bahtia shuddered.

"Why would anyone trust the infamous Iron Mongrels with the retrieval of sensitive information anyway?" she asked.

"Simply put, a lack of options. I'm sure we wouldn't ordinarily be our employer's first choice, but their rivals have already signed a contract with a competing firm and time is of the essence," said Mazzey.

"What competing firm?" asked Bahtia.

Mazzey grinned.

"What firm?" she asked again.

His grin widened.

"Mazz?"

"Brusilov's Bruiser Boys."

* * *

Theoretically, Mazzey's imposed deadline of 1600 hours should have put *Pugnacious* in space well ahead of the *Rostislav*. In reality, however, Sergeant Bahtia was left wasting precious time rounding up the fractious Mongrels while the more disciplined Bruisers reported back to their ship the second they received the order. Laggards were still trickling aboard *Pugnacious* when a transit conveying a final load of track-suited goons arrived at the station to embark upon the *Rostislav*. Already irritated by Bahtia's refusal to allow him to repurpose medical nanites from the infirmary to kill his hangover, Mazzey declared anyone still missing to be AWOL and ordered *Pugnacious* to dust off.

His mood only worsened when Second Sergeant Whoolery, nicknamed "Mammoth," rescinded that order on behalf of Daimyo Ichiro Matsui, the platoon's benefactor and license holder. Many of the Iron Mongrels, including two of the four men yet unaccounted for, were indebted to the Daimyo and served in the capacity of bonded labor. Mazzey fumed at Matsui for contradicting his orders and pointed out just how many credits the Daimyo stood to lose if the Bruiser Boys fulfilled the contract first. Whoolery capitulated, and *Pugnacious* vacated Berth 26C without the four men but still hours behind schedule.

The peculiar restrictions hyperspace transit imposed upon smaller vessels forced the Mongrels' corvette to link up with *Profit Motive*, a bulk hauler headed in the general direction of their mission. They bribed the captain, a Bugitar merchant, to make a slight deviation from her standard route. *Rostislav* possessed the capacity to generate enough fusion power to stay in hyperspace on its own and, unfettered by such limitations, departed the system in short order while the bulk hauler lazily navigated the vagaries of Tobobo's space traffic control. Mazzey raged at the density of congestion for such a lightly-populated planet. Bahtia refrained from mentioning that lightly populated though it might be, Topopo was situated along one of the region's major corridors of commerce; and with hostilities constricting a few of the other passageways, it only made sense Topopo would experience a surge in traffic. Finally, after half a day of maneuvering, *Profit Motive* arrived at the stargate as it activated. The pilot entered the sequence to trigger the hyperspace shunts and a formless, featureless nothing enveloped the freighter, corvette, and crew.

Nerves fried, Mazzey retired to his quarters to sleep off his hangover while Bahtia and Whoolery pored over the details of the contract and began planning for the mission ahead.

* * *

Precisely 170 hours after they transitioned through the Topopo stargate, the bulk hauler emerged seventeen light years away in the Nesplud system with *Pugnacious* latched on. An alert chimed in Mazzey's quarters, summoning him to the Combat Information Center on the double. The Lieutenant unzipped his sleeping bag, climbed out of his niche, and donned the cleanest t-shirt floating within reach. He laced up a pair of boots he had purloined from a private under the guise of punishment for an imagined infraction and slicked back his graying hair. Satisfied he looked passable, Mazzey left his claustrophobic cabin and glided down the hall, using conveniently placed grips to propel himself onward. Few other Mongrels occupied the cramped halls of the habitation cluster at that hour, but he did have to jockey around a few on his way through the corvette. Along the way, he bumped into the bearded space Viking, otherwise known as Sergeant Whoolery.

"You look like spit," said Whoolery.

"I think you mean, 'You look like spit, sir,'" corrected Mazzey.

"You look like spit, sir," said Whoolery.

They reached the portal to the CIC, and Mazzey pinlinked with the door lock. He commenced the authentication process, but his pinplant's operating system crashed, and *Pugnacious'* security suite rejected him. He booted up the software and made another attempt, but it crashed once again, and security rejected him, this time with a warning in the form of a shock delivered directly to his parietal lobe.

He winced and rubbed his head. A third failed attempt and the firewall would incapacitate him—it was an effective system for preventing unwanted access to the brains of the ship.

"Let me," offered Whoolery.

Mazzey unplugged from the lock and flattened himself against the wall. The corridors of *Pugnacious* were narrow enough already, but the entry to the operations rooms was designed specifically to form a bottleneck in the event it needed to be defended against boarders. The Lieutenant and Sergeant shared a regrettably intimate moment scooting past each other, and Mazzey got two nostrils full of the other man's body odor. No amount of no-rinse body wash could compensate for a week without bathing, especially for a man who sweated like the Mammoth. Once in place, Whoolery pinlinked to the lock, and the blast door opened a second later. The large man grabbed a handle and hauled himself inside, segueing from the microgravity of the hab cluster to the artificial gravity of the spinning CIC module.

"I should've pawned you when I had the chance," Mazzey mumbled under his breath to his pinplant and followed suit.

Mazzey paused and closed his eyes after crossing the threshold, battling back of a wave of nausea as his body acclimated to experiencing weight again. Alcohol withdrawal didn't make the adjustment any smoother.

"Are you okay, Lieutenant?" came the friendly voice of Sergeant Bahtia.

"Prime, thanks," said Mazzey.

He opened his eyes, and the blue and orange-tinged ambiance of the Combat Information Center invited him in. Nothing so inessential as a window compromised the structural integrity of the module, but a series of high-definition Tri-V screens depicted views from external cameras, overlaid with pertinent data and markers in a rainbow of colors denoting specific details. A crew of six attended recessed workstations, arrayed in a ring around a central dais. Compact and immaculately groomed, Captain Fukuda, commander of the *Pugnacious*, sat upon the dais and observed his flight team like a hawk as they managed navigations, communications, detection and tracking, weapons control, and dozens of other tasks beside. Sergeant Bahtia flanked the dais along with a mangy mutt named Patches who served as the platoon's unofficial mascot.

Ever the faithful second, Bahtia snapped a sharp salute as Mazzey approached. Whoolery, joining her mere moments ahead of Mazzey, didn't bother. Tail wagging, Patches limped over and nudged his head into the Lieutenant's crotch. Mazzey waved aside Bahtia's salute and gave the dog the head scratch he so desperately desired. Patches thanked him with sloppy kisses and a burst of flatulence.

"SITREP?" he asked.

"We have entered hostile space," reported Fukuda.

"Can you elaborate, Captain?" asked Mazzey.

Fukuda entered a series of commands into the dais, and scores of green markers blinked into existence across the Tri-V screen.

"Each one of those indicates a clutch of void mines. Someone has seeded a minefield across a large swathe of the emergence point," said Fukuda.

"The Riagians?" Mazzey asked.

"It corresponds with corsair modus operandi. Cripple ships as they leave hyperspace and then commence with the pillaging," said Bahtia.

"So why weren't we attacked as soon as we emerged? Surely *Profit Motive* is a ripe enough target?" asked Mazzey.

"You may notice that, despite the proliferation of mines, there are substantial gaps in the coverage. I would say we owe *Rostislav* our gratitude for clearing a path and keeping the marauders too occupied to replenish the trap," said Fukuda.

"Any sign of Brusilov nearby?" Whoolery asked.

"Scans have detected the wreckage of what we suspect to be two vessels in the vicinity—neither match the characteristics of a human-built destroyer like the *Rostislav*. It is more likely that the debris belongs to past victims of the marauders or the marauders themselves. We have, however, detected energy signatures emanating from a space station orbiting the planet Luclites," said Fukuda.

"Wouldn't you expect to see energy signatures around a space station?" asked Mazzey.

"Generally, yes, but records indicate that no permanent Union settlements exist on Luclites, and the space station is officially categorized as derelict," answered Fukuda.

"Sir, I've got the captain of *Profit Motive* on comms. The mines have her spooked. She's requesting *Pugnacious* decouple so she can return to her standard route," announced a lifeform resembling a lemur with the aid of its translation pendant.

The Maki communication officer was one of only a few nonhuman members of the crew. How the alien had become indebted to Daimyo Matsui was a mystery to Mazzey. Then again, so too was the proper pronunciation of the Maki's name. Both issues could have been resolved with a functioning pinplant.

"*Pugnacious* will disengage and proceed on, but if the captain wants to be paid for her troubles, she needs to stick around. She's our ride out of here after all," said Mazzey.

"Per our agreement, *Profit Motive* is not to vacate the system until we have accomplished the mission or perished in the process. Any divergence from these conditions, and she will be held liable for any and all incurred damages," recited Bahtia.

"Well stated, Sergeant," said Mazzey, marveling at the reality that in the Union even bribes were governed by contracts.

The Maki relayed all this to the captain of the freighter and, after a succinct exchange, informed Captain Fukuda that they were clear to detach. *Pugnacious* disconnected from the bulk hauler and performed a series of attitude adjustments as the crew plotted the safest possible course through the minefield. Once aligned with a gap opened by *Rostislav's* passage, the Captain gave the order to engage the drive thrusters. The corvette boosted away, clearing the hazards with minimal difficulty. Once *Pugnacious* gathered sufficient momentum, the thrusters switched off and it coasted onward, effectively invisible in the empty expanse. Mazzey, Bahtia, and Whoolery observed the hushed professionalism of the flight crew in silence. Whatever quality, or lack thereof, the rest of the Iron Mongrels exhibited, Captain Fukuda's team was topnotch. As the maxim went—second-rate spacers don't live long.

As they drew nearer the orbital complex, the Tri-V screens provided an increasingly clear picture of the situation. A cursory scan located yet more ship debris drifting through the void. Analysis of larger segments confirmed that the wreckage belonged to vessels of Riagian manufacture and, while long range image captures revealed damage to *Rostislav's* hull, it appeared to be superficial. Evidently, while *Profit Motive* had spent a good twelve hours jockeying for position in the Topopo stargate queue, Brusilov had been busy slaying pirates. Even nearer, and the displays began depicting scenes of boarding craft departing *Rostislav* under fire from the apparently-not-so-derelict space station. The brave souls piloting the boarding craft relied on a number of defensive measures to close the distance, latch onto the space station, and disgorge their deadly payloads. Not all the pilots rose to the challenge. Mazzey watched as a boarding craft evaded one missile only to be intercepted by its twin. The ship and its complement of mercenaries vanished in a brief, spherical burst of light. With the last of its insertion teams launched, *Rostislav* retreated to a distance judged safe from enemy attack.

"I don't understand. Why are the Bruisers risking the losses when *Rostislav* is sufficiently equipped to pound the facility into radioactive particles?" asked Whoolery.

"Brusilov must believe the objective is stored somewhere aboard the space station," said Bahtia.

"Why not at least eliminate the emplacements?" asked Whoolery.

"Even if Brusilov knew the objective's approximate whereabouts, I doubt he would chance it. There is no such thing as a 'surgical strike' when the slightest error in calculations could result in a massive chain reaction," explained Fukuda.

"In that case, we need to launch a boarding party of our own if we're going to have a snowball's chance at recovering the objective before the Bruisers. I'll go prep the platoon for action," said Whoolery.

"Wait," said Mazzey, halting Whoolery midstride.

Bahtia tore her gaze from the Tri-V panels and looked at Mazzey with those copper-jacketed eyes. She had spent so long with him that she could almost perceive the turning of gears inside his pickled brain as he peered at the external feeds. Magnified, the superstructure of the artificial satellite drifted in orbit over the alien planet. The scene was almost serene, if not for the projectiles streaking into the void at high velocity.

"Sir, what's on your mind?" Bahtia asked.

"Hypothetically, let's suppose you were engaged in a capital crime, something severe enough to incur the wrath of the Peacemakers, say piracy, and let's even suppose you stole classified information from an Information Guild courier. Would you keep the evidence of your crime, your only leverage in the event of capture, on you? Or would you stash it somewhere safe, somewhere you could return to reclaim it if you had to make a hasty getaway?" asked Mazzey.

"But the corsairs aren't attempting to flee," challenged Bahtia.

"What do they have left to flee in? I suspect that, by the time they realized the threat *Rostislav* posed, it was already too late," said Mazzey.

"So where do you think they've stashed the objective?" asked Bahtia.

"Captain, can you perform a full sweep of Luclites? I want radar, lidar, maser—I don't care; give me everything," asked Mazzey. Fukuda nodded and commanded it done.

"You really think it's planetside?" asked Whoolery.

"The maritime pirates of Earth buried their plunder in remote places for safekeeping. Why not alien space corsairs?" asked Mazzey.

"Are you drunk? What are you basing this on?" asked Whoolery, incredulous.

"Robert Louis Stevenson mostly," said Mazzey.

They disputed the merits of classic literature informing military strategy while *Pugnacious* scoured the surface of Luclites. Sergeant Whoolery looked about to boil over when the sensor officer spoke up.

"Sir, I think I've found what you're looking for. There's an outpost a few miles from the original failed settlement. It's well concealed, I passed right over it several times, but I'm detecting signs of recent activity," she reported.

"There we have it. While Brusilov wastes valuable resources cracking the corsair base open, we're going to fly down to Luclites and steal the data cache right out from under his nose. Simple smash and grab," said Mazzey.

"Sir, don't you think that we should take the time to craft a better plan of attack than 'simple smash and grab'?" asked Bahtia.

"There's no time. The space station has the Bruisers tied up for the moment, but it won't last. Besides, what makes you believe our little band of misfits can handle anything more sophisticated?" said Mazzey.

"This is asinine. We aren't even certain the objective is down there," interrupted Whoolery.

"Once I've paid off the Daimyo and you're in charge of the Mongrels, you can make your own asinine decisions, *Sergeant* Whoolery, but while I'm your superior, you will follow my orders. Now go prep the platoon for planetfall," commanded Mazzey.

Whoolery left the Combat Information Center to ready the men for battle, but not before first giving a sarcastically crisp salute.

"You're also dismissed," Mazzey said to Bahtia.

"Sir, can we speak for a moment in private?" she asked.

Mazzey nodded and stepped aside from the command dais with his first sergeant in tow. The modest room lacked any real semblance of privacy, but it would have to suffice.

"You don't look well," she said.

"So, I've been told, though in blunter terms. I assure you, I'm prime," said Mazzey.

"You're sweating, your eyes are bloodshot, your hands haven't stopped trembling since you entered the room," Bahtia said, "You should direct the operation from here and let me take point on the ground. Mammoth doesn't like me, but he does respect me, and you know I can keep the Mongrels in line."

"As much as I appreciate the concern, I told you—I'm prime. Besides, we don't have enough CASPers as it stands," said Mazzey.

"Thanks to you," said Bahtia.

"Be that as it may, we still can't afford to bench any players. I don't have the patience to argue it any further, so will you please go make sure Mammoth isn't organizing a mutiny against me?"

"Sir, yes sir," said Bahtia.

Now who am I going to send after her to make sure she isn't organizing a mutiny, Mazzey asked himself as Bahtia stalked away, clearly annoyed.

* * *

As *Pugnacious* flitted into range, a pair of forms separated from the corvette and cast their silhouettes across the planet. Having sold off all of the military-grade combat dropships for an interest payment, Mazzey and his platoon of Mongrels descended through Luclites's atmosphere in the storage holds of repurposed cargo shuttles. The aircraft were bulky, ponderous, and uncomfortable. They carried little in the way of defensive or offensive measures, save what had been spot-welded on, but at least they were marginally functional and capable of transporting weapons platforms like the CASPers.

The shuttles fell like bricks dropped from the thermosphere. Their pilots risked waiting to activate their thrusters and decelerate until the last possible moment. It was a gamble, given the intended purpose of the shuttles, but one that paid off when no surface-to-air missiles smashed them out of the sky. They swooped in low over the jungle canopy and unloaded racks of rockets on the outpost's air defense batteries before they could react. The unguided munitions reduced the automated turrets to burning bits of scattered wreckage but left the shuttles defenseless. The pilots zoomed a quarter of a mile past a string of prefabricated buildings to touch down on a pair of camouflaged-but-still-accessible launch pads, drawing small arms fire from a handful of the quicker-witted Riagians patrolling the area. Cargo doors clattered open before the landing gear even finished settling, and Mazzey led the platoon's six CASPers out onto the tarmac, where they opened up on every target within range. Shoulder-mounted chain guns shredded any corsair caught out in the open. Lasers lanced out at technicals and gun emplacements, slagging steel and incinerating fur and flesh.

Despite the ferocity of the opening salvo, the Riagians recovered quickly, taking cover and returning fire with oversized rifles an unaugmented Human would have struggled to lift, let alone shoot. A stream of magnetically-propelled rounds hammered Mazzey's Mk 5 suit, gouging furrows in the layered plating and fraying his nerves, but failing to penetrate the pilot compartment. He pivoted to address the assailant and hosed the offending 'squatch with his laser carbine, then led the other CASPers across the landing pad and down the ramp, drawing the fire away from the shuttles.

Behind them, those Mongrels without powered armor disembarked and sought cover under the leadership of Corporals Weese, Okeke, and Villalobos. Most reached the meager shelter provided by concrete barriers, freight crates, and trucks, but a few caught stray rounds from the Riagians. In his peripheral vision, Mazzey saw one man hurled bodily across the platform, his ballistic vest doing little to deflect the tremendous power of a coilgun. Once under relative cover, the light infantry added to the CASPer fusillade. Their smaller rounds and less-potent lasers proved ineffectual against the molded lorica and thick hide of the Riagians, compelling the squads to focus their fire. The rudimentary tactics suited the indentured servants of Mazzey's platoon just fine, and they successfully suppressed the corsairs while the CASPers mopped up the token defense force.

As the platoon began to report to Mazzey over the shared comms, he found himself transfixed by the sight of a dying Riagian. Blood gushed from a profusion of exit wounds, slicking the alien's lorica and matting its pelt, only to soak into the thirsty tarmac. Singed hair and crisped skin indicated burns from the lower-intensity handheld laser weapons. The mangled fingers of its lone remaining arm grasped for a rifle well out of reach, yet still the corsair bared its teeth and glared at Mazzey through eyes such a vibrant hue of yellow they practically glowed. In the distance, shattered air defense batteries smoldered and smoked.

"Lieutenant?" asked Bahtia over the comms.

"Mazz?" she asked several seconds later over a private channel.

"Yes?" he replied, snapping out of the trance.

"All squads have reported in; the area is secure. Judging by the sound of it, the Riagians are mobilizing a response. They could arrive at any minute. Your orders?" asked Bahtia.

"We've seized the initiative. I see no reason to hand it back. Proceed to the outpost with haste but order a squad to scout ahead. I don't want to walk straight into an ambush and lose our big guns. Better to risk the expendables, economically speaking," he said.

"Uh, yes sir, will do, sir."

Mazzey returned to staring at the corsair snarling, twitching, and most noticeably bleeding out at the feet of his Mk 5 suit.

"Are you okay Lieutenant?" Bahtia asked.

"I need a drink, and, unless you're prepared to offer me one, would you kindly stop asking?" snapped Mazzey before delivering the *coup de grace* to the wounded Riagian in the form of a point-blank blast from his carbine.

Bahtia killed the private channel without another word and directed Corporal Weese and his boys to take point. Weapons at the ready, the nine-man vanguard stepped into the undergrowth skirting the landing zone. Their traipsing generated nearly as much commotion as the one-ton CASPers, sending indigenous critters fleeing from their path. Once again, Mazzey found himself longing for the hardened operators he led during his stretch with the Graveyard Whistlers. Even if stealth wasn't especially important on this mission, he still hated to see displays of such sloppiness. But what else could be expected of reprobates like the Mongrels?

Sergeant Whoolery, encased in his Mk 8 armor, guided the other five CASPers down the paved road to the outpost at a brisk trot. With a reaction force already mustering, they elected for the speed afforded by the level surface as opposed to the moderate conceal-

298 | KENNEDY & WANDREY

ment of the bordering thicket. Of all the suits in the *Pugnacious's* inventory, Whoolery's, a gift from the Daimyo, was by far the most modern, and only Bahtia's Mk 6 featured anything close to comparable specs. The other four armored Mongrels piloted antiquated suits, maintained through a combination of scrap parts and sheer stubbornness. Much like he longed for the superior troopers of the Whistlers, Mazzey yearned to pilot the cutting-edge armor of his glory days. Still, he confessed to himself, even a third-rate Mk 5 suit beat slogging through the jungle in ballistic plate and combat boots like the scouts up ahead, or the two squads of light infantry flanking the procession of CASPers. He was busy chiding himself for not focusing on the contract at hand when the metallic zip of coilguns collided with the throaty roar of Human rifles and machineguns.

"Contact!" shouted Corporal Weese over the comms.

A deluge of incoming fire scythed through the jungle, ripping apart plants and mercenaries alike. Spongey alien trees shredded under the sustained barrage, as did any Mongrels hiding behind them. Errant bullets whined off Mazzey's armor, ricocheting off into the brush, but less than fifteen feet in front of him, Private Giordano's suit erupted in a ball of oily flames when struck by a magnetically-propelled grenade. Bahtia invoked command privilege to mute Giordano's anguished cries from carrying over the comms as the CASPers scattered. Mazzey trampled a Human body underfoot, cracking the ballistic shell like an egg in his rush to get off the road. He spoke a silent apology and hoped the Mongrel had already been dead.

Mazzey brushed the thought aside as his eyes roamed the displays, scouring his surroundings for enemies. He squeezed off short, controlled bursts from his chain gun as the Mk 5's targeting software highlighted likely targets darting through the dense foliage, though whether the bullets felled any Riagians was another matter entirely. He spared a moment to assess the platoon and realized they were dumping massive quantities of ammunition down range with little to no cohesion. Spray and pray.

"Armor needs to move up and attack the corsairs before we lose what's left of the infantry," said Bahtia over the command channel.

"No need to advance, the 'squatches are coming right to us," replied Whoolery.

The incoming barrage slackened, and a chorus of bestial roars echoed through the jungle, sending a primal chill down Mazzey's spine. A second later, his Mk 5's translation program converted the howl to English: battle cry, Riagian.

"Helpful," mumbled Mazzey. "What's that sir?" asked Bahtia over the muffled stutter of her own chain gun.

"Armor will hold the line. Bahtia, have the infantry disengage and regroup to support by fire. Whoolery, lead the assault," ordered Mazzey, instinctively ducking as a magnetically-propelled grenade detonated within the trunk of a sponge-tree nearby, showering him in sappy chunks of pseudo-bark.

"Yes sir," they answered in unison.

Bahtia relayed the Lieutenant's orders to Squads Okeke, Villalobos, and the chewed-up remnants of Weese. They began an orderly withdraw, maintaining contact with the enemy while retreating back toward the CASPers, until three dozen space apes came barreling out of the forest and sent them into a full-blown rout. Coilguns slung across their backs, the Riagians pounced on the laggards, rending flesh and pulverizing bone with their immense paws. Mazzey watched as Private Murphy, a new addition to the platoon, was scooped up by one extraordinarily muscular 'squatch and dashed against the ground until he hung as limp and featureless as a noodle. The fleeing Mongrels, fast enough to outpace the Riagians—or at least faster than their less fortunate comrades—surged past the armored suits like a river flowing around boulders. Mazzey wondered if they would just keep running until they reached the shuttles instead of regrouping to support the five CASPers. He didn't have long to wonder because, less than a minute later, the corsairs were within spitting distance.

Guided by the targeting system, the chain gun on his shoulder lit up, decapitating one Riagian before traversing to liquidate another. The sizzling barrels discharged twenty-four more rounds before clicking empty. The surprise almost cost Mazzey his life when his target, wounded and enraged, capitalized on the opportunity to close with the Lieutenant. The corsair slapped his laser carbine aside and proceeded to batter the cockpit. Unable to bring his carbine to bear, Mazzey grappled one-handed with the 'squatch, fending off blows to the best of his ability. The alien's radiant eyes and spittle-flecked teeth filled his monitors as it ceased hammering on the suit, only to begin prying open the clamshell seams of the cockpit. The groan of buckling armor prompted a burst of desperation from Mazzey, and he punched the Riagian and felt bone fracture under the impact. He punched again and again in the same vicinity, feeling the fractures widen and finally snap. The alien pulled back a little but enough for him to leverage the carbine between them and open fire. At that range, the laser beams speared through its torso, incinerating its innards. The aroma of flash fried meat assailed Mazzey through a freshly torn rent in his Mk 5. He shoved his victim away and loaded a full magazine into the carbine.

Around him, four other CASPers contended with three times as many Riagians. Bahtia, armor dented and scored, and Private Beck traded shots with several of them while Whoolery defended Private Lawler's disabled suit from a pack of baying 'squatches. The Mammoth tore through the corsairs like the Viking berserker he was, utilizing his state-of-the-art Mk 8 to its fullest extent—deploying shields to deflect ranged attacks, boosting from one foe to the next with the jumpjets, and then butchering them with retractable arm blades. Mazzey felt another pang of envy for Whoolery, who reminded him so much of himself in his youth. He ground his teeth together and lent the fury of his carbine to the fray, dispatching a couple more Riagians with precision shots. It wasn't enough. There were only five CASPers, four if you discounted the alive-but-useless Private Lawler. They weren't prepared to face so many enemy combatants.

"Where's our support, First Sergeant?" asked Mazzey over the command channel.

"On the way, sir," Bahtia replied.

"Before or after we're 'squatch chow?" questioned Mazzey.

Bahtia started to respond when a cry escaped her lips midspeech. Mazzey spared a glance in her direction and saw one particularly bold Riagian had managed to pierce her armor with some type of spear. He raised his carbine to shoot the alien, but Bahtia beat him to the trigger, unleashing a torrent of rounds from her chain gun that shredded it into splinters of lorica and bloody scraps of fur. She wrenched the spear out with her free hand.

"Are you okay?" he asked.

"Prime," Bahtia said, giving her best impersonation of his voice, "surprised me is all. Nearly breached the cockpit."

Back in the direction of the shuttles, a cacophony of coilguns erupted. Mazzey swung around as fast as the bulk of the Mk 5 would allow, fully expecting to be slain in a double envelopment by the corsairs. Instead, to his astonishment, he spotted Mongrel infantry advancing. More astonishing yet, they had abandoned their ineffectual rifles and lasers and were hauling coilguns pilfered from fallen Riagians. The weapons were so massive and packed such a kick they required multiple men to aim and shoot, but they were laying down a punishing fire. A long dormant sense of pride suffused Mazzey at the sight of his Mongrels, and he pounded a fist against his suit.

"Desperta Ferro!" shouted Mazzey, using a battle cry the platoon had appropriated from a class of 13th century soldiers called the Almogavars but never had much cause to utilize.

He hoisted his carbine, unsheathed his retractable wrist blade, and charged into the mass of corsairs. Puzzled by the sudden reversal, the Riagians hesitated to act. It spelled their demise. The reinvigorated Mongrels rolled right over them and, for a few beautifully frenetic moments, Mazzey remembered what it meant to be a warrior. He blazed away with his laser carbine and, when the magazine lost its charge, he clubbed 'squatches to death with it. When the gun flew to pieces under repeated strikes, he resorted to blade work. Alongside him, Mammoth bowled through the corsairs like his namesake. The Riagians attempted to break away and make a run for it, but Bahtia and Beck cycled through the last of the rounds in their ammo hoppers to prevent their flight. Not more than fifteen minutes after the return of the infantry, the final Riagian fell, slain by a wild-eyed Corporal Weese who had implausibly survived to rally the troops.

Mazzey watched Whoolery kneel down alongside a mortally wounded Private Fleischer, one of the youngest members of the Mongrels. The Second Sergeant held the boy's hand in one gauntlet and spoke the traditional words absolving the indentured servant of his debt to Daimyo Matsui in death. Fleischer took several more gulps of air and ceased breathing before Whoolery finished. The Second Sergeant closed Fleischer's eyelids with a tenderness that shouldn't have been possible with a CASPer. Mazzey diverted his gaze and called up the squad bio-signs on his monitor. He saw that a little more than half the platoon was dead or injured.

"Bahtia, take Beck and a squad to evacuate the wounded. Once you've got the critical cases onboard a shuttle, lift off. Don't wait for us. I want them set up in the infirmary and attended to ASAP," directed Mazzey.

"Yes, sir," she replied.

"Come on, let's go dig for buried treasure," Mazzey said to Whoolery, clapping him on the pauldron and gesturing to the prefab buildings a short jog away.

The two CASPers and an understrength squad of infantry seized the outpost without firing another shot. They did encounter two more Riagians, but these threw down their coilguns and surrendered without a fight. The aliens were stripped of their lorica, frisked for hidden weapons, bound, and placed under Whoolery's keen eye while the other Mongrels completed their sweep of the outpost. They struck out on their search of the two nearest prefabs, one of which was a mess-cum-slaughterhouse. The reek of butchered meat stewing in the jungle humidity emanated from the building and slipped into Mazzey's nostrils. He felt the urge to open his cockpit and vomit, but he resisted, knowing that to do so would only expose him to the full bouquet of charnel house scents. The mercenaries accompanying him had no such protection against the stench and ejected the contents of their stomachs where they stood.

The second prefab they explored appeared to be the 'squatch equivalent of a billet, but its smell was only a minor improvement over the first. Animal hides and skulls lined the walls and large sleeping mats cluttered the floor. Bone totems decorated racks of coilguns and lorica. Mazzey knew very little Riagian history but, given the primitive nature of their living conditions, he wondered just how developed the race had been when the Union made first contact. Private Halvorsen interrupted the line of thought when he pointed out the trinkets strewn about the room. The baubles stood out as foreign objects, likely minor prizes claimed in raiding parties, in the midst of all the crude junk on display, and Mazzey felt optimism radiating from the generally cynical roots of his brain. He ordered the Mongrels to move on to the next building in the row.

Unlike the first two buildings, one glance at the reinforced blast doors of the third prefab told Mazzey it would require a concerted effort to break into, but this obstacle gave him an even greater degree of hope. The Mongrels adjusted their laser rifles and used them as improvised cutting torches, along with the delicate application of high explosives and the brawn of the Lieutenant's Mk 5 suit, but still they failed to gain entry. With enough time, they might have been able to force their way in, but Mazzey didn't want to be caught planetside when Brusilov finished up on the space station. He called for Whoolery to bring up the prisoners. He started by asking them politely to open the doors, allowing the CASPer to translate his words into the Riagian dialect. The bigger of the two 'squatches croaked and growled, and the program converted the alien dialect into a rather complex insult. Without better comprehending the corsair's culture, the remark lost much of its sting, but Mazzey understood the sentiment well enough. He shot it through the chest with a coilgun he had taken as a replacement for his shattered carbine and turned to address its buddy. The other Riagian submitted without further threat, yielding the door's passcode. Just like that, they gained access to the building.

The doors groaned open, stuttering just a bit on tracks warped by the prior attempts to get in, and Mazzey beheld a vault teeming with valuables. Crates stacked upon crates of plunder filled the warehouse—everything from bulk nanite containers and weapons systems to sophisticated medical equipment and automated agricultural tools. Somewhere amidst all that loot, awaited the objective. The platoon may have suffered grievous losses to the savage space apes, but the haul from this contract would be enough to clear his various debts, pay to have a replacement liver grown, and retire to a life of leisure. A smile split his face from ear to ear, and he whistled.

"There's your payday gents," he said over the comms to the hooting and hollering of the assembled Mongrels.

"It's not buried," joked Whoolery.

"A minor technicality," replied Mazzey.

"But it is treasure, I'll give you that," said Whoolery.

Mazzey laughed to himself. He rarely, if ever, felt this good sober.

"Alright, time is wasting! We can celebrate later. Go commandeer some trucks from the landing zone, and let's get all this packed onto the shuttle," he barked.

Four men sprinted down the road, the promise of riches temporarily edging out their weariness, while the other two men stayed with

306 | KENNEDY & WANDREY

Mazzey and Whoolery and began to conduct an audit of the vault's contents. No sign of the objective was forthcoming, but the Lieutenant decided something of its worth wouldn't be stored near the front of the building anyway. Twenty minutes later, the four runners returned to the outpost steering two trucks. They explained that only three of the industrial loading vehicles had survived the initial skirmish unscathed, and the capacitors on the third had died on the drive back. The Mongrels started stowing crates aboard the trucks, but the process was slow. A majority of the crates required the effort of multiple men or a single CASPer to lift, and some even necessitated that both suits carry them together. They had just begun securing freight on the second truck, having sent the first trundling back down the road toward the shuttle, when Bahtia established a private channel with Mazzey and Whoolery from aboard *Pugnacious*.

"Please tell me you have the objective," she said.

"Not yet, but you'll never believe the hoard we've found here. I'm sure the cache is stashed away in here somewhere," said Mazzey.

"No, Mazz, it isn't. We've intercepted communications between the boarding party and *Rostislav*—Brusilov says they are in possession of the objective. He's dispatching a squad to transfer it to *Rostislav* while they mop up the rest of the Riagians and free the hostages," Bahtia said.

"Huh, our client excluded mentioning any hostages," Mazzey mused.

"I told you. I told you this was asinine from the beginning, and you didn't listen. Why wouldn't the Riagians keep something that valuable with them at all times?" spat Whoolery.

"Even a blind Xiq'tal dismembers its prey once in a while," Mazzey quipped with a shrug.

"By the authority invested in me by Daimyo Ichiro Matsui, I am hereby relieving you, Gregan Mazzey, of command."

"Stow it Whoolery, you can relieve me of command after our contract is fulfilled. The objective is still in play, and I still intend to claim it," said Mazzey before switching over to the squad channel.

"Drop whatever you're carrying and leg it back to the shuttle, double time."

"But sir, there's still a fortune in there," said Private Halvorsen.

"Leave it Mongrel, the real prize is getting away, and the clock is ticking," said Mazzey.

The young mercenary looked to Whoolery as if begging him to countermand the order. A long moment stretched out, and Mazzey wondered how the Mammoth would react.

"You heard the Lieutenant, you cur, don't make me repeat him. Move it!" bellowed Whoolery.

With sighs of resignation, the troopers dropped their loads and hastened for the shuttle.

"I hope you know what you're doing," said Whoolery.

"I understand you're not big on classic pirate literature, but how do you feel about heist movies?" asked Mazzey.

* * *

A shudder vibrated through the hull of *Pugnacious* as its docking clamps engaged with *Profit Motive* and Mazzey massaged no-rinse body wash into his skin. He did so gingerly so as not to elicit unnecessary pain from the collection of bruises he had obtained on Luclites. He would have preferred to skip the waterless bath in favor of crawling into his niche and sleeping until they transitioned into the next system, but the smell of his own

308 | KENNEDY & WANDREY

body odor had persuaded him otherwise. An alert chimed in the stall and a voice spoke.

"We are receiving transmission from a Major Brusilov of the Bruiser Boys mercenary company. Shall I patch him through to you, Lieutenant?" asked the voice of the Maki communication officer.

"That won't be necessary, thank you. I'm wrapping up here now. I'll head directly to the CIC," said Mazzey.

"Understood," answered the voice.

Eager for what he was expecting, he shrugged into a clean shirt and pants, the fabric adhering to patches of cleansing gel that had yet to dissolve, and left the stall behind. He floated through the corridors and felt the absence of so many Mongrels tugging at his conscience. That certainly wouldn't do—a drink was in order, first thing upon arriving at their destination. He resolved to give the fallen mercenaries a proper send off, Irish Wake style. He arrived at the CIC, and his pinplant miraculously cooperated to grant him access on the first try. He stepped inside, and Patches welcomed him with a salvo of sloppy tongue-kisses.

"Up on the screens, please," requested Mazzey, and a second later, the perfectly groomed face of Brusilov populated the Tri-V.

"Greetings, Aleksei," said Mazzey.

"Listen to me you villainous little whelp. I am your superior. I am your better. You will address me by rank with the respect I deserve," snarled Brusilov.

"Yes, Major, my apologies," said Mazzey with feigned contrition.

"Don't you dare mock me, you wretch! What, in the good name of the Union, do you think you're doing?"

"We are currently preparing to transition into hyperspace, so we can fulfill our contract and collect our reward," said Mazzey.

"Your scoundrels hijacked my boarding craft," said Brusilov.

"Now that's not fair. You got the craft back intact, didn't you?" asked Mazzey.

"Intact? Intact? You disabled the thrusters, breached the troop bay, and spaced a squad of my Bruisers," said Brusilov.

"We spaced CASPers. Nobody died per my explicit instructions," said Mazzey.

"You stole the data cache my men fought and bled to secure. You're no better than the blasted Riagians!" shouted Brusilov.

"You've wounded my pride, sir. And to think, we left you a consolation prize in the strongbox," responded Mazzey.

"A credit chit? What am I going to do with this paltry sum?" asked Brusilov.

"Buy yourself a decent pair of shoes, courtesy of the Iron Mongrels."

# # # # #

The Deadly Dutchman
by Kevin McLaughlin

The clamor of alarms woke him with a start. Corporal Ted Wilson snapped his head up hard enough to crack his helmet against something. Stars flickered across his vision, mixed with red lights from his HUD. Damn, he had a hell of a hangover. Where was he? Groggy, he looked at the read-outs on his display. He was in his CASPer, a Combat Assault System, Personal. OK, that part made sense. He didn't remember suiting up, or what happened after. That part made somewhat less sense. Ted's thoughts were fuzzy, so he shook his head, trying to clear away the cobwebs.

His cameras were down, part of the comprehensive damage that had shut down about half the systems in his suit. Damn, what happened? The backup cameras were still functional. He activated them and got his first look outside his suit.

All Ted could see was stars. Stars everywhere, against a field of black. He turned on one camera after another, but it was the same in every direction. He was adrift in space. Alone. In a suit that was so badly messed up, he wasn't sure how it was still maintaining life support.

Shit. Some days, it didn't pay to wake up.

Memories began drifting back. He'd armored up as the troop transport, *Orca*, exited hyperspace. It was standard protocol for his merc unit, the Yaalaay Hlgalgan—The Black Ravens. They weren't expecting trouble, but it never hurt to be careful. They were just basic precautions.

It had paid off in spades this time. They were ambushed at the emergence point. A warship waited for them, a battlecruiser. The *Orca's* captain tried to get away, but it didn't happen. He jettisoned the dropships carrying his troops in an attempt to save them.

But that hadn't been enough, either. The enemy launched boarding pods. Ted didn't know what happened to the other dropships, but one of the pods smashed into the side of his, blowing right through the port-side hull. Then the nose of the pod opened, disgorging its contents.

They were Tortantulas, giant spider-like aliens. He wasn't sure how many, but it seemed like more than enough at the time. Ted fought alongside the others in his squad, trying to defend the dropship. Then someone fired a MAC—magnetic accelerator cannon. He heard the boom as it creased the air close to his head, even in the thin atmosphere remaining after the hull breach. A second later there was an explosion, a fireball that came from the aft of the ship and washed over Ted's CASPer.

He didn't recall anything else until he woke up, adrift in space.

How had he gotten there? It didn't speak well for the fate of the rest of his squad. There was no way they'd have left him out there if they could have recovered him. Had the Tortantulas jettisoned him, leaving him for dead? That didn't sound like the spider-like aliens. They were more likely to eat their fallen opponents than to eject them into the void.

"First step, see if there's anyone out there who can help me," Ted said. He'd need to be careful about that. If the enemy were still about, they'd pick up any signal he broadcast. But he wasn't just floating in space. If he'd been blown off the dropship, he would be moving at velocity. Every second was carrying him further from rescue and opening the search window that much wider.

"Damned if I do, damned if I don't. OK, what still works on this thing?" Ted asked. He found talking to himself preferable to silence. If he sat in the CASPer staring into the cold void for too long, he'd start gibbering. Talking to himself was preferable, even if it was weird.

The answer was, not much. His jumpjets were damaged. The laser rifle he'd been carrying was sheared off. His MAC still worked, which was something. He had half a drum of ammunition for the thing left, too. Primary sensors were out. The explosion must have torn him up pretty badly. Secondaries were working OK, and he started using passive scans to examine the space around him.

The worst was the life support situation. His oxygen was decreasing at an alarming rate. Ted checked the time. He'd been unconscious for about fifteen minutes, which was good, because if he'd been out much longer, he might not have woken up at all. The alarms that roused him came from the suit, telling him his O2 level was nearing critical. That shouldn't have happened!

"I ought to have plenty of air left. So why..."

There had to be a leak somewhere that the CASPer's automated systems hadn't been able to seal completely. The suit was keeping positive pressure around him, but there was a slow leak someplace. His air was venting into space, and there wasn't a lot he could do about it. He needed a refill tank, or better still, to get the hell out of the broken-ass suit.

"One step at a time," he said. Who won the battle? Ted didn't think there was much chance his people were victorious, but you never knew. It was always possible, especially since the Ravens were damned tough fighters.

A quick pulse of active scans would tell him a lot more than the passive images he was receiving. But he hesitated before activating them. Even a brief pulse might show up if anyone out there was looking. If the bad guys had won, he'd be lighting a signal flare that said 'come get me.'

He didn't have a lot of choice, though. He couldn't make any decisions blind. Crossing his fingers for luck, Ted flipped the switch, sending a scan pulse into the system around him. Just as quickly, he shut it down. He hoped the little burst of energy was too small to be noticed. Of course, his luck had been crap so far that day...

The scan gave him a decent feel for the space around him. There was a debris field floating alongside and nearby. It was traveling at roughly the same rate he was—a slow drift away from where the *Orca* had jumped into this system. He suspected the debris was probably from his dropship, ejected at the same time he was by the explosion.

His on-board computer was able to triangulate the point of origin from the debris vectors. Now Ted knew where he came from. That was a good start.

Unfortunately the scan hadn't picked up the signatures of any Raven ships. It had spotted three enemy warships, though. Ted realized a lot more debris was drifting around than there should have been. He ground his teeth together, frustrated by his impotence.

"Tore up my friends and my ship, they did. We'll see about that," Ted said.

The battlecruiser was still on station, waiting. Why? If their mission was to pick off the *Orca*, they'd certainly accomplished it. One battlecruiser didn't seem like enough to adequately interdict the system though. There could be more out there somewhere, but Ted didn't think so. There'd been no word about more ships as his dropship took off.

No, they were waiting for a specific target. Somehow, they knew Second Company was coming. It hadn't been in the initial plans. They were only going to send a single company for this mission, but Second Company had finished a contract early and become available. After a quick refit, they'd join First Company on garrison duty.

Somehow, the beings on those ships knew that. Ted felt sure of it. They were waiting for Second Company to come along. If they exited hyperspace into the same ambush, they'd be torn up the same as the *Orca*. That would be it for the Ravens and would just about finish the Haida peoples' venture into space. They only had two companies. Losing both of them at once would be a blow they'd never recover from.

Damned if he was going to let that happen.

* * *

There was no sign of any First Company elements still active in the system. From all the debris around the exit point, it looked like the *Orca* had bought it. If any of the dropships had made it away, they were keeping quiet, which was smart. It would keep them alive a little longer. But it was damned inconvenient from his point of view. A dropship might be able to mess with those warships enough to save Second Company when they came plowing into the system in a few hours.

Ted looked at the scattered bits of debris drifting alongside him again. There wasn't much of it. Where was the rest of his ship? If the thing had blown entirely, there'd be a lot more debris. Plus, he would probably have been torn to shreds in the blast. No, it was more likely the blast blew a hole in the side of his ship, blowing him away at the same time. Was there anything left of his dropship? He might be able to get O_2 refills, ammunition, weapons, and other supplies if he could get there.

"Crappy time for my jumpjets to be on the fritz," he said. The boot-mounted thrusters made steering in space a simple thing.

If he didn't find a way to arrest his velocity soon, he'd be doing a full Dutchman. The last of his air would give out first. Then the suit's power would run out. He'd be one more frozen corpse drifting forever through space. The thought made him shiver. There were good ways to die and bad ones, but the idea of floating off alone, forever, chilled him to his bones.

"Not me. Not happening," he said. There had to be a way to survive and save the rest of the Ravens.

What did he have that might help him get back to where the dropship ought to be? He didn't have enough air left in his tanks to use them as controlled thrusters. He wasn't sure how he would have managed it, but it wasn't a viable solution anyway.

The MAC might work, though. The thing had a hellacious recoil. Even in a CASPer, you had to brace pretty well to fire it. The thing could knock you on your ass. It fired a magnetically impelled round at incredibly high velocity. The tricky part would be steering. Ted wasn't at all sure he could stay in a relatively straight line. And he only had limited ammunition. Would it be enough?

"The longer I wait, the farther away I'm going," he said.

There didn't appear to be any better options. Ted tried to angle the weapon so that it was facing opposite his direction of travel. Trouble was, he had some spin, probably from the air leak. There was no way to stabilize the spin, and the air was still leaking. He'd just start spinning again. That meant he had a narrow window each rotation to fire the MAC if he wanted to stay in anything close to a straight line.

"If it was easy, they'd have an officer do it instead of an NCO," Ted grumbled. He'd borrowed the phrase from First Sergeant Jones, who'd used it often. He smiled at the memory, but the smile crumpled when he realized Jones was probably dead along with the rest of First Company.

Ted held his breath as the first opportunity to fire his MAC came around. He tapped the trigger when the computer told him it was time. The heavy weapon jolted in place and spat a chunk of metal into space. He couldn't tell if his plan was working. He checked the passive scans, but the readings were too fuzzy for him to determine whether he'd slowed down much.

He fired again when the spin brought him back around, and then a third time. After the third shot, he felt a patter as bits of metal bounced off his back. That had to be more pieces of the dropship! He was slowing down relative to them, so they were zipping past. The MAC was doing the trick!

He took each shot carefully, waiting for just the right second. If he missed the target by more than a little bit, he'd end up drifting off into deep space in a different direction. But little by little Ted managed to overcome his velocity and accelerate in the direction he'd come from.

He kept his eyes peeled for any signs of the dropship. If he could see it, it would make using the MAC as a thruster that much easier. But the ships were designed to be hard to spot in space. Finding it wasn't going to be easy.

The ammo count kept dropping as he pushed on. If there were any Tortantulas left on the ship, he was in a lot of trouble. Ted decided to save the last six rounds just in case he ran into something that needed shooting.

A beep told him he was nearing the origin of the debris. Ted looked around with the cameras, hoping to catch a glimpse of the active ship. But he saw nothing except blackness. Was the dropship completely destroyed, after all? It was certainly possible the spiders had finished it off after it was damaged. He hoped that wasn't the case, but scuttling a captured ship wasn't uncommon if the ship was too damaged to be of real value.

If they'd blown up the dropship, he was sunk. Ted couldn't think of anywhere he could get enough air to survive. He guessed he could always radio for help from the attackers, but somehow he didn't think that would help.

"Where are you?" Ted asked.

According to the computer he was drifting right through the center of where the dropship ought to be. It wasn't there. Ted didn't see anything even vaguely resembling the hull of a ship. There wasn't much debris, either. What had been blown off the dropship was drifting around further out.

The ship couldn't have been completely destroyed in the first blast, and for a terrible moment Ted was afraid the enemy had gone to the trouble of scuttling the wreck. Hell if he knew why they'd do that. It was a waste of ordnance. But who knew how these aliens thought?

If it was gone, he was toast. The CASPer said his O_2 level was nearing critical. Another hour, tops, and he'd be out of air.

"Of course!" Ted exclaimed. He slapped a hand against the side of his helmet, realizing where he'd gone wrong.

Action and reaction. The same force which propelled him far from the ship would also have impacted it. If it was still relatively intact, it ought to be somewhere in the space opposite the direction he'd first drifted. He might find it somewhere up ahead.

But he probably wouldn't see it on passive sensors. The ship was dark, the engines gone or at least damaged enough to shut down. Plus, the blast might not have carried the ship in a directly opposite course to his. It could be almost anywhere out there, nearly invisible, drifting. The only way he was going to find it was to use the active sensors again.

Ted's hand was sweaty as he flipped them on. Just a quick pulse. That wouldn't hurt, right? Just a short burst. He was a lot closer to the warships this time, though. If they'd spotted the first sensor pulse, they could be watching this area for another.

He'd know soon enough.

"There you are!"

He spotted a big block of metal, drifting slowly away from him. It wasn't too far away. The sensor ping gave him a reading that matched the identification of his dropship. That was home base, all right. He flipped the active sensors off. With luck, nobody had seen them.

Problem was, he was off course again. The ship was drifting at an acute angle away from him. He had the computer plot its projected course. He couldn't afford another sensor ping. Two had been risky enough! But the CASPer's on-board computer should give him a decent idea of where the ship would be.

The computer now had a much better read on precisely how much acceleration the MAC gave him. It spat out directions for the next firing sequence much faster. Trouble was, he was only going to have three rounds left when he arrived at the ship. He wasn't expecting to meet trouble, but being without any means of defending himself while surrounded by enemies wasn't appealing.

He fired the gun, altering his course so he would float closer to the dropship. He couldn't help using the ammo. He hoped there were some spare weapons or extra MAC ammunition on the ship. After a few more shots, he was well on his way.

The minutes ticked away. According to the computer, he would arrive near the dropship in one hour and fifteen minutes. His air would run out in an hour and twenty. That didn't leave him a lot of wiggle room. Ted fired the MAC again. It was the last shot he had to make. The remaining three rounds were his backup in case he needed to make course adjustments at the end of the run.

He had over an hour left to go before he arrived at the dropship and nothing to do but sit in his metal coffin and think. For the first time since signing up, Ted wondered if he'd picked the wrong career. Not that there were a lot of better prospects back home. His family was dirt poor, living in ramshackle housing just outside Vancouver. The only jobs worth having were in the center of town, around the starport. Everything else was either busy work or subsistence-level survival shit.

His people had gravitated toward the latter. The government was handing out subsidy food to anyone who wanted it. You didn't really have to work anymore. The taxes pouring in from the merc units were enough to keep everyone on Earth fed and housed, more or less. You weren't going to starve, but the food might be crap. Everyone had shelter if they wanted it, but it might be a crappy old tenement shared with half a million cockroaches.

The Haida had been living off the land since before the Europeans arrived, though. Sure, some stuff had been forgotten, but when things suddenly got 'easy,' his parents' generation got suspicious. They moved further and further off the grid, relying on the old ways of surviving. It worked for them.

But surviving wasn't enough. That's how the Black Ravens were born. The only real way to make a living on Earth was through the planet's primary export to the rest of the galaxy—mercenary forces. If you weren't in a merc unit, you could make money providing services to them, but the easiest way to make bank was to join up.

Or start a unit. It had taken a decade of pooling resources for the Ravens to be able to afford their first squad of CASPers. They'd taken jobs supplementing larger units at first, and that had brought in enough credits for them to build up their force. By the time Ted signed up, the Ravens were almost two companies strong. In the two years since he enlisted, they'd grown even more.

Half of that was undone now. If First Company was gone, which seemed likely, they'd lost half their people. But what if Second Company was killed as well? There wasn't a backup force. This was all his people had. They might be able to put together enough credits to bankroll a squad again, starting from scratch. But he wasn't sure they'd have the stomach for it after losing so many of their young all at once. His people had just barely begun rising to a place of dignity. Now all that was at risk.

It was up to him to save the day. The idea shook Ted to his core. He wasn't a hero...He was just trying to get by, and learning to fight in a CASPer had been the best way forward for him, his family, and his people. Ted scored high on the aptitude tests he took. That was pretty much the end of the decision chain. His family hadn't needed to apply pressure to get him to sign up. He'd done that himself. They needed the income badly. Going into space gave his family a huge financial leg up.

But this was too much for him to shoulder alone! He was good at taking orders, good at making the CASPer do what he wanted it to, and excellent at shooting. This sort of making shit up as he went along, though? It didn't play to his strengths.

Nobody asked him what he wanted. He'd just have to figure it out, somehow.

The computer chirped. The dropship was close. He might be able to catch a glimpse of it on the cameras. Ted trained the devices toward where the ship should be and upped the magnification as much as he could. Nothing was there but empty space.

Shit, shit, shit! Where had it gone? It must be out there, somewhere. He set the computer to move the cameras around, looking for even the smallest sign of the ruined ship's hull. It wouldn't be easy to spot.

Another warning bell caught Ted's attention. He checked the longer range passive scanners and saw the plume of a small ship's drive. It was leaving one of the warships and heading his way! They must have seen something that bugged them. Maybe they picked up his last active scan pulse. Or perhaps they spotted his MAC fire. He didn't know, and it didn't matter. They were sending a small ship to intercept him.

It wasn't going to reach him before he made it to the dropship according to the computer's calculations. Assuming, of course, he could find his ship! He returned to the search. If he missed the ship and shot past it, he wouldn't have to worry about the enemy vessel coming after him. He'd be dead of oxygen deprivation long before they found him.

A tiny mote of light that hadn't been there before caught his eye. Ted turned the camera toward that spot and watched. There it was again! Just the smallest gleam of light reflecting off some surface. It was probably the hull breach, since the dropship was painted to be anti-reflective. He fed the data into the CASPer's computer.

He was off-course, but not by much. The computer calculated a course correction. He would have to use two more of his precious MAC rounds. Ted fired the first shot at just the right time. There was no room for error. He had to do it perfectly, or he'd miss the target.

Ted waited, holding his breath, as seconds ticked off on his HUD until he reached the window for the second course correction. His shot was perfect. The computer said he was only eight hundredths of a second off, which was about as close as he figured he could expect under the circumstances.

The hull of the dropship became increasingly visible as he drifted closer. In fact, it was quickly looming larger. It looked like he was going to make it! He activated the magnetic boots on the CASPer. There was no sense risking bouncing off. He set the boots to their highest power level, so he'd get a nearly unbreakable grip on the hull.

"Damn, how fast am I going?" Ted asked. The ship was getting bigger alarmingly faster. He felt like he was falling straight at it.

The computer obligingly gave him the answer: too damned fast. He was going to smack into the dropship at a speed that...well, it was going to hurt. He might shatter bones, even though he was protected by the reinforced armor. It was designed to take some serious damage and soak up impacts from big falls, but this was pushing its design parameters even if the suit was undamaged, which it wasn't.

Ted looked at his Mac. He had one round left. If he fired it in the direction of the ship right before he landed, it might slow him enough. But then he'd be completely defenseless, and the other ship was still on its way, probably loaded with Tortantulas who'd missed lunch.

"What the heck. One MAC round won't stop a squad of aliens in body armor anyway," Ted said.

Once he decided, he waited until he was close enough to the vessel that he could fire a braking shot without hitting it. The dropship was dead in the water. Shooting yet another hole it in probably wouldn't make things any worse than they already were. But you never knew. All he needed was to rupture the oxygen tank or hit something else vital.

Ted took the shot. It skimmed past the vessel's hull, just missing the outer armor. The computer told him it had slowed his fall about ten percent, but it didn't feel like it. The ship was looming huge in his cameras now. Ted winced as he rocketed toward the hull like a meteor.

The impact reverberated through his CASPer. He was slammed against the bottom of his suit with bruising force. For a minute it was hard to catch his breath, but it didn't feel like he'd broken anything. Better yet, the boots held. He was securely locked to the outside of the dropship.

"With about three minutes of air left," he muttered, turning down the magnetic grips on his boots so he could walk across the surface.

Time to find some oxygen. He knew it ought to be in the CASPer loading bay. Whether it was still there—and still intact—was another matter.

* * *

At least getting inside wasn't going to be a problem. The alien boarding vessel was gone, leaving a big hole in the hull. And just aft of that penetration was an even larger breach. You could have flown a small ship right through the second one. Something had breached the engine section. Ted didn't know enough about the ship's engines to know what it might have been, but whatever it was blew through several decks, tearing the hull apart on each before venting into space.

If his squad had been any closer to the blast, he'd never have survived. As it was, he wasn't sure how he lived through an explosion this big.

Ted decided to enter through the Tortantula's hole. That was where he was when he lost consciousness. Maybe he could learn something more there. He swung himself in, then stuck his boots to the floor again. The lights on his suit illuminated the CASPer bay. Its walls were scorched, burned black by the blast. Here and there, he could see the ripped deck and wall plates where rounds from allies and enemies tore up the ship. There were pieces of CASPer armor floating about as well. One bumped into his suit, and he looked down and saw a frozen bit of Human protruding from it. Ted looked away quickly, horror and disgust warring with rising anger.

These aliens had wiped out his company. Worse, they were trying to erase his entire people. Ted wasn't about to let that happen.

His CASPer beeped a loud alarm. Shit, it was the oxygen tank warning! He was out of time. There was nothing left in the tank to maintain positive pressure in his suit, which meant he wasn't just going to start breathing CO_2, he was going to be breathing vacuum in a few minutes. Ted hurried over to the oxygen storage tank. It looked OK. He plugged his suit in, waiting for the hiss that indicated air was flowing.

Nothing happened.

What had he missed? Oh, shit! The tank was electronic. It ran off the ship's power. No power, no oxygen. He could bypass it. The tank was designed to run off a CASPer's internal power in an emergency. Ted unreeled the power conduit from his suit. His head hurt. Each breath was a gasp. His lungs strained for the smallest bit of air as the atmosphere in his CASPer thinned.

Attach the cord, turn the knob to latch it in place, activate the sequence to switch the power source...Ted worked his way through each step of the procedure. He'd drilled on it dozens of times, but it wasn't something he expected to use! There, that should do the trick. Just one more switch. He crossed his fingers and flipped it.

Air rushed into his suit. The CASPer immediately refreshed his atmosphere as O_2 flowed into its tanks. Ted inhaled deep lungfuls. Being able to breathe had never felt so good! The needle in the gauge rose as the reserves refilled. It didn't stop the leak, but it would buy him a lot of time.

The hull beneath his feet shook, a vibration running through the deck plates. Something hit the ship hard enough to send tremors through the whole structure. Ted uncoupled from the tank. His reserve was only about a quarter full, but it would have to do for now. The impact was probably the alien ship. It had arrived to check out the dead dropship.

Ted glanced around wildly, looking for something to defend himself. Nothing was at hand. There might be some working weapons in the storage lockers, though. He turned off his boots and pushed off hard from the wall, floating across to the other side of the bay.

Two of the lockers closest to the engines had been damaged. There might be something salvageable in them, but it would take too long to pry them open. The third was still intact and he activated the magnets in his boots to hold him next to it. With shaking hands he keyed in the code to open it. The lid popped up, revealing a row of heavy lasers.

They should do the trick! They weren't as good as his MAC, but they should punch through the light armor Tortantulas wore. He grabbed one from the box and scooped up a handful of magazines. The laser didn't fire rounds, but each magazine held a stack of little chemical cartridges. The laser used one for every shot, then ejected the spent casing. He'd need to be cautious about ammo, but there was enough that he felt confident for the first time in a while.

His confidence vanished as soon as he turned around. A ten-foot tall spider was crawling through the hole he'd used to access the interior. It froze for a moment when it saw him. Maybe it was surprised to find a live Human in there. But it recovered quickly and rushed toward him, its auto-cannon blazing.

The rounds pinged off the hull plates to Ted's right. He raised the laser rifle and snapped off a shot. It glanced off the Tortantula's body armor. The spider was still closing, now within ten feet, and coming fast. Ted forced himself to hold position and fired again.

This time the laser struck a lightly armored spot and punched straight through. Gouts of fluid gushed out of the spider, freezing into a stream of dirty ice. The beast's rush turned into a tumble. Ted sidestepped it as it crashed into the wall near him and rebounded off.

Two more Tortantulas came through the gap, one at a time. He lined up the first in his sights. This time he aimed carefully for an unarmored spot. The beam sliced through the spider's body, and it floated free from the deck.

The third Tortantula didn't come right at him, using the dead one for cover instead. It held the corpse in front of it and advanced, picking up speed. Ted snapped off one shot after another, but the body was an efficient shield. Nothing he sent his attacker's way was getting through.

Ted tried to dive sideways. The Tortantula shoved hard against the body of its dead companion, sending the huge bulk crashing into Ted's CASPer. The momentum broke the connection between his mag boots and the floor, sending him flying backward into the bulkhead. He shoved hard against the dead body, trying to get clear before the other alien could get to him. He wasn't quick enough. The Tortantula pressed hard from the other side of the corpse, using its mass to keep Ted pinned in place.

The whole battle was like an eerily silent bar-room brawl. They were at close combat range now, and the Tortantula had a hell of an advantage over him despite his armor. He needed to find a way to nullify that edge, or he was going to end up spider food.

Ted slammed his boots down—not against the floor, but against the wall behind him. Cranking the mag power all the way up again, he grabbed hold of the alien corpse with both hands and twisted his body with as much force as he could. His opponent pushed as hard as he could, but suddenly it had nothing to push against. The corpse sailed past Ted and slammed against the wall beneath his feet. The live spider followed, landing right underneath him. The Tortantula looked up. Ted could see its snarling face through the plate glass mask of its body armor.

He pushed off from the wall, dropping onto the Tortantula's back. It writhed and shook, fighting to dislodge him. Ted hung on for dear life. If he dropped off, the thing would pick him apart. He was on its back, the only place he was a little protected from its wild and furious attacks.

Ted still had the heavy laser. He armed the weapon and chambered a round. He laid the muzzle near a lightly armored part of the spider's back.

"Sorry, dude. I need your ship," Ted said. Then he fired.

* * *

An hour later Ted was ready for the next leg of his mission. There was only one way he could think of that might allow him to make a dent in the enemy ship. One CASPer wasn't enough to take down a battlecruiser. He didn't care how many times it had been done in vids; it wasn't realistic, and he knew it.

But one CASPer, a busted up dropship, and an operational cutter? With all those moving parts to work with, he might have a chance.

The aliens were squawking bloody murder at him over the radio as he sat in the Tortantulas' cockpit. His computer translated some of it. They wanted him to report in, wanted to know what the hell he was doing, and so on. They'd sent a second cutter. Ted was pretty sure there were more than three spiders on board this time. They knew something was up. But he wasn't going to hang around waiting for them.

Ted managed to attach two lines from the Tortantulas' cutter to the wrecked dropship. The first was a tow line. He slid into the cockpit seat. It was a poor fit for his body, having been designed for a giant spider, not a Human.

"At least it's big enough for me to keep my suit on," he said. Having the armor around him made him feel better. There was atmosphere in the cutter, so he could probably take it off if he wanted, but the extra layer of defense around him was a comfort.

Small comforts were a good thing. He had too few of them as it was. He shut off the radio, tired of listening to their yammering. The second cutter was still a ways out. He had time to act, if he could figure out how to fly the thing.

Ted had taken a familiarization course on dropship flight. That helped some, but not as much as he hoped. The instrumentation was wildly different, and the control surfaces were like nothing he'd ever seen before. He searched the CASPer's computer database for some sort of instruction manual. It was doubtful he would find one, but it was worth a shot.

"Holy shit," Ted said, watching the instructions scroll past his HUD. Damned if the armor didn't have the manual he needed after all. Maybe his luck was finally turning around.

The engines warmed up and engaged quickly. The tow line went taut, and Ted heard the whine of the engines increase as they strained to move the heavy dropship. His plan was working, but he wasn't going to make great time. That meant a direct assault path wasn't in the cards. He needed to get past the other cutter. The battlecruiser was the real threat.

If he tried a straight run, he'd have to exchange fire with the other cutter, which he might or might not live through. It was better not to take the chance.

He darted toward the nearest planet. His pursuer obligingly followed, close on his heels. Ted had the computer plot a slingshot course around the planet. It would bring him around the other side with a lot more velocity behind him. That might not be enough, but it was the best he could do.

The other cutter followed him into the long loop. The extra mass of the dropship actually worked to his advantage. More mass equaled more momentum, which increased the force of the slingshot. Force was converted into acceleration in this case. The computer projected the other ship would overtake him just after he reached the battlecruiser. Perfect.

One enemy ship at a time, just the way he liked it.

"Oh hell. Who am I kidding, eh? This is nuts," Ted said. He let the Gs he was pulling push him back against his seat. There was little left to do but wait and hope he could get close enough to the enemy to strike a mortal blow before he died.

* * *

A short while later alarm bells blared, alerting Ted that the battlecruiser had opened fire. He wasn't surprised. It had turned toward him. The enemy obviously planned to catch him in a pincer between the battlecruiser and the cutter pursuing him. Ted wondered what the spiders thought when they saw him continue on the same course, heading directly toward them. They were playing a giant game of interplanetary chicken.

Of course, the battlecruiser had strong shields. Even if he rammed them at full speed, it wouldn't be enough to bust through the shields and take out the ship. He might scratch their paint a bit, but he needed to do more than that.

He'd been watching the scans actively pinging away. No sense trying to hide where he was anymore! The cutter's fusion torch blazed behind the ship like a tiny sun. Half the solar system could see him now.

Maybe some of his brother and sister warriors were still alive out there. Ted hoped so. If they were, they could see him. It was nice to think someone might be able to bear witness to everything he was trying to do. But whether they were there or not didn't matter in the end. He was doing what he had to do.

The battlecruiser launched a full spread of missiles. Ted was impressed. They clearly thought he was a serious threat! There were a dozen ship-killing rockets. The ordnance was a fortune to spend on such a little target. They'd also blow him to kingdom come long before he got anywhere close enough to do any damage. He was sure that was the point of using so damned much overkill.

"Got a surprise or two up my sleeve for you, though," he said. He slipped a slate out of his pocket and keyed a command sequence.

The second cable he'd attached to the ship was a power lead. The engines on the dropship were toast, but the cutter had a powerful drive. It wasn't strong enough to get everything on the dropship running, but Ted managed to divert enough power to make a few key systems functional.

First, the anti-missile defenses came online. He launched decoys into space on either side of the ship. They would spoof a ship's radar signature, trying to throw off the missiles' guidance systems as they drew near. He opened fire with the anti-missile guns, spewing flak into the missiles' paths.

"Now for the best part," Ted said. He pressed a second key, and fired an alpha strike of missiles. One after another, like a stream of rockets from a Roman candle, the missiles streaked away into the void.

He had enough power for about a minute before the conduit burned out. After that the dropship went dead again. But that was enough. He had scared them! The battlecruiser was turning, trying to maneuver clear of the missiles he'd sent their way.

But they were too close and moving too fast. It wasn't going to be nearly enough, but he was in the same situation.

His defenses worked. Flak blocked seven of the incoming missiles, and five more went after decoys. He'd stopped the entire volley, which was damned lucky, but it didn't matter in the slightest. The battlecruiser responded to his alpha strike with something similar. Two more volleys were coming his way, and he had no power left to defend himself. The cutter had a couple of anti-missile lasers, but they weren't going to be nearly enough to keep him alive. There were too many of them, and even if he survived those, he would soon be within laser range.

Ted had always known this was a one-way trip. He opened the radio channel, broadcasting on every frequency, just in case anyone was listening.

"Yaalaay xiidang, shitheads," he said. The Raven is flying. Damned right it was. Right into the teeth of the enemy that hoped to take it down. That was it for this step. Ted jumped from the cutter and worked his way hand over hand back to the dropship.

Missiles blew the cutter to bits moments later.

His missiles slammed home about the same time. The Tortantula defenses blocked some of the strike, but they were overcome by the sheer number of missiles Ted sent. The shields of the battlecruiser were considerable, and they blocked almost all of the incoming blasts before they went down. EMP waves from the nuclear tips on a few of the missiles knocked out much of the delicate electronics on board the battlecruiser for a precious few seconds.

That was long enough for them to miss seeing the plume of flame jetting from the dropship as laser fire breached an oxygen tank, igniting the gas as it seeped out the hole cut into the ship's side.

It was also long enough for them to completely underestimate the threat the dropship posed. It was a hulk, they thought, unable to accelerate or steer. They had plenty of time to get out of the way.

Until they didn't.

The dropship slammed into the side of the battlecruiser. With the shields still down, the ship took the full brunt of the impact. The velocity carried it deep into the enemy ship, shattering one bulkhead after another. Finally, the dropship struck a critical system within the Tortantula ship. One system blew in a secondary explosion, then another, and a third. Finally, the alien ship lost fusion containment and was incinerated by the blast.

* * *

"But what happened to Ted, Grampa?" The child's inquisitive eyes were bright with unshed tears. The story was an emotional roller-coaster. She'd been on the edge of her seat the entire time.

The old man leaned back in his seat. He didn't like to reminisce about the old days, but sometimes it was worthwhile. Kids needed their heroes. Even if he knew there were never any real heroes on the battlefield. They were just men and women, fighting to stay alive and keep each other alive.

"He jumped into space right before the dropship hit," the old man said.

"Did he live?"

"He did, indeed. Second Company came through and picked him up a few hours later," the elder told her. "He came home and never went into space again. He stayed on Earth and raised a family, instead."

"That's silly. He was a hero," she replied with a snort. "I'm gonna be just like Ted, Grampa. I'm going to be a hero and blow up bad guys just like him!"

He smiled indulgently at her. "Go on now. Story-time is over. Go play with your friends."

"OK. Thanks, Grampa! See you soon!"

Then she was off. Theodore Wilson watched her go, shaking his head. He'd encouraged her to become a warrior, as he had been. Would that lead to her death? If she died in the void, would that be laid at his feet? As old as he was, he didn't have all the answers he wished for.

"No, child. I don't want you to be like me," he whispered. "Warriors don't hope their children will grow up to be like them. Warriors wish for a time when their children will never have to fight at all."

Sadly, Ted didn't think that would happen anytime soon.

# # # # #

The Felix
by RJ Ladon

Carl touched the pinplants behind his ear. "Gurgul, incoming." The bright purple, bear-like alien was easy to spot among all the other species congregating in the shopping area.

"Piss him off," Teela responded through the pinplant link.

"Excuse me?"

"You heard me," she hissed.

"As you wish," Carl mumbled, rolling his eyes, wondering why he agreed to work for family. He turned off his communications. "Why? That's all I want to know. No one in their right mind makes an Oogar mad." Carl sighed, then returned to the back of Teela's Salvage Emporium, trying to make it look like he was busy.

"Acquisitions," snarled the gravelly voice.

Carl looked up from his slate, where his neglected inventory paperwork glowed. "Good morning to you, too, Gurgul." He flashed a smile at the fearsome Oogar. "What can I do for you today? Would you like a crate of gears?" Carl nodded to a wooden box sitting on a pallet. "Or a couple of Mk 1s?" Carl waved toward two boxy, humanoid shapes. They stood guard at the door like ancient suits of armor. Someone had added a rusty, steel bar, meant to represent a sword, to one of the CASPers. The other had a bit of orange plumage in its helm. "Or perhaps I can interest you in this drive shaft, fresh from a Mk 7 'overhaul.'" Carl used his hands to scratch quote marks in the air. "You'll have to ignore the microcracks and the pitting and don't run it any higher than 2,000 RPMs. Otherwise, it's perfectly fine."

The Oogar leaned down, putting its purple muzzle closer to Carl's smiling face. Gurgul snorted, billowing the Human's hair. "Acquisitions," the Oogar grunted again, louder.

"What? No pleasantries? Fine, fine." Carl adjusted his body armor, picked up his laser rifle, and led Gurgul to Teela's office, then hesitated. "You know, she's been busy. Perhaps you ought to come back later."

Gurgul pulled his lips back into a feral growl. "Go suck an Athal, Human."

Carl blinked twice as a disturbing image flashed through his mind. He shuddered. "I'll pass, thank you." He rapped on the door, shouting through it. "Gurgul is here to see you."

"Tell him to come back later."

The Oogar roared, knocked Carl forcefully aside, and broke into the narrow room. "You'll see me now," he bellowed at Teela.

Teela shoved star charts and documents into the desk's metal drawers. "Gurgul, so good to see you again." She stood, walked around her desk and sat on its front edge, blocking the bear-like Oogar from getting any closer.

"Your brother is an ass," Gurgul snarled at Teela, his fur bristling. Rotten meat and musky body odor hung like a robe around the Oogar. The smallness of the room seemed to condense the stench further.

"I know. He's bored playing salesman." She leaned to her left and looked around the Oogar's bulk. Carl rose from the floor, patting dust from his clothes and armor. He stuck his tongue out at the back side of the bear. She returned her gaze to Gurgul. "Why are you here? What do you want?"

"I want to know why you keep avoiding me." Gurgul poked a long, curving claw at Teela. "I want you to hire my crew for your mission in the Cimaron region."

Teela's eyes widened, then narrowed. "What mission would that be?"

"We heard you're going for the *Medusa*. Her salvage value is legendary." Gurgul leaned over Teela and tapped the top of the desk with his claws. "I'll wager your maps and charts are right here." The Oogar stepped back, his eyes glittering and his mouth salivating. "My crew and I will gladly accept 20% of the haul to keep you and your *Felix* safe."

"I would love to find the *Medusa*. It's the most sought after military salvage out there. There's enough unused Mk 6 CASPers on it to buy a fleet, not to mention the munitions and the value of the ship, itself. But I don't know where it is. Whatever you heard is false." Teela sauntered over to the wall and leaned on it, trying to show that the desk and its contents were unimportant. She fingered the revolver at the small of her back.

A deep growl emanated from Gurgul's chest. "Lies!" he barked at Teela.

"Suppose I do know where it is." Teela pulled the gun and cocked it.

"I knew it. You have a map." He approached the desk. "It's in here, isn't it?"

"I don't know where the *Medusa* is." Teela sighed, rolling her eyes and tossing her arms in the air. "I was theorizing. I don't have a map. But if I did…why would I need your crew of Oogar mercs? Are they going to classify the find?" Teela tapped him on the chest with her revolver, as he huffed at her insolence. "Are they going to help move the munitions or hardware? Are they going to fill out forms? Do you know how hard it is to find help with paperwork?"

"My crew are killers, not accountants." Spittle flung from his muzzle. "You'll need protection from pirates!" Gurgul slammed his forearms on the metal desk, bending the surface where his flesh kissed the steel.

Teela jumped back, away from Gurgul's windmilling arms. "Why would I need you?" she shouted over the racket. "You don't know where the *Medusa* is. That keeps it safe." Teela attempted to make herself smaller as Gurgul continued attacking the desk.

"You know nothing, Human," Gurgul spat out. His purple-hued claws dug into the desktop, removing chips and thin spirals of steel.

"Besides, I have protection. You've met my brother, Carl. He is ex-military."

"You mean, ex-junkie." An ugly smirk twisted his muzzle.

The gentle hum from Carl's laser rifle was barely discernable over Gurgul's heavy breathing. "Get out," Carl said.

Gurgul snarled at the two Humans and the weapons pointed at him. "This isn't over." He stomped from the office, making sure to knock over shelving and crates while leaving the storefront.

"Okay, he's pissed off. Mission accomplished." Carl studied his sister. "Why did you do that?"

"He's so mad, he won't be able to think straight for hours. That means we can leave the system without him following us." Teela waved Carl out of the office. "We can discuss this later. We've got to go. Lock the store down and gather supplies for 30 days, and I'll get everyone on the *Felix*." Teela picked her way around the freshly-strewn merchandise.

Carl watched his sister depart, wondering why she had to keep everything so secret.

* * *

The *Felix* waited in formation with dozens of other ships for the hyperspace gate to activate. A battleship cast a long shadow over the smaller cargo ships and freighters. Teela tapped on a viewport. "I wish I could be certain Gurgul and his mercs weren't out there."

Light and color swirled, indicating an open stargate.

"If there is a problem, perhaps we ought to wait," Kartikki said over steepled fingers. The Pendal's secondary hands manipulated the controls, keeping the *Felix* in line, moving slowly with the other ships toward the stargate. "Approximate time to transition, ten minutes."

"It would give me time to run diagnostics," Trk'tk complained. As the ship's engineer and maintenance technician, the Jeha was never satisfied with the state of the *Felix*.

"Wait? I can't chance that," Teela said, floating above the seats of the cockpit. Her long blonde hair moved like seaweed in a gentle ocean.

"Please explain," Carl said. "What exactly can't you chance, dear sister?" He steadied his position by holding onto Elagabal's chair. The Sumatozou was secured in her chair, taking notes with her bifurcated trunk and studying star charts. The green markings under her eyes were light, barely there, indicating her youth.

"I think we can all agree that Gurgul is an idiot," Teela said.

Kartikki nodded silently.

Carl, Trk'tk, and Elagabal responded boisterously with shouts, clicks, and the clomping of plate-sized feet.

"That idiot figured out we are planning to salvage the *Medusa*. That means someone else knows too, maybe more than one someone. He had the nerve to suggest we align with him and form a partnership."

Trk'tk's mandibles clicked. "Why not accept his proposal?" The Jeha's shiny carapace undulated as his many arms and legs rippled along his body.

"When a ship is lost for more than ten years, it's considered abandoned by its previous owner, which opens up the salvage rights to the public. Anyone with a salvor's license can claim ownership by bringing the ship into any space station. Claiming the *Medusa* will be easier than our normal salvage jobs. We don't have to go into hot zones or deal with natives.

"Partnering with Gurgul is a bad idea." Teela sighed, wrangling her hair into a bun and securing it with a short, metal rod. "He can't be trusted. He would rather kill us than share the spoils. We've all heard the rumors—he takes what he can and only shares when the odds are even."

"So, what you're saying is, we should have killed him at the store," Carl said with a sardonic grin.

"If only it were that simple. He thinks we have charts and maps showing the location of the *Medusa*. Until she's recovered, we are a target to Gurgul and any of his allies. At least we know what his ugly face looks like."

"We could go to another section of the galaxy and lay low," Kartikki suggested. "Approximate time to transition, five minutes."

"That is an option, but not one I would readily take. I don't want to keep looking over my shoulder for Gurgul's nasty, purple grin. If anyone wants to disembark after emergence, I'll understand." Teela looked out the viewport and watched as the ships ahead of them moved into the stargate, then disappeared with a flash of light. "Our jump is approaching, get seated."

Teela left the cockpit and entered her quarters, where she waited for the jump and the moment of unmaking that came with it. She never understood Carl's attraction to space travel and military life.

* * *

"One-hundred-seventy hours of jump time. One-hundred-seventy hours to search your soul. Nothing is more boring than waiting for the end of transition," Carl said to himself. "At least I have something to do." He pulled his favorite weapon off the wall, a Smith and Wesson 500, and rubbed oil on its surface, carefully looking for any signs of biological contamination or corrosion. Suddenly he stiffened, spun in zero G, pointed the handgun at nothing in particular, and said, "Pew-pew…pew-pew." He blew on the imaginary smoking barrel and placed it back on the wall.

Carl pushed away from the wall to admire his assortment of weapons, armor, and toys. The daunting task of cleaning and maintaining them would have upset him at any other time. "We have seven days to be together, alone and uninterrupted, my beauties."

A maniacal light gleamed in Carl's eye. "I wonder if Teela would object to zero-G weapons training." He grabbed a different weapon off the wall, stuffed a magazine in his pocket, then left the room. He pushed off the walls, floor, and ceiling, looking for his prey.

Trk'tk clung to a surface with a couple of hands while tightening a bolt with another. "You two better not break anything," he said to Carl, eyeing the weapon in the Human's hand. "Took me months to fix her last time you did this."

Carl placed his finger to his lips and shot the engineer a Cheshire cat grin.

Kartikki watched Carl's antics, waving at him with an inner hand while munching on a ration with an outer one.

The hum of *Felix's* engines did little to hide the noise of Carl's approach. Every push off made a sound. He found them, thick as thieves, talking quietly to each other, one blonde-headed Human and one grey-brown-headed elephant. Carl couldn't help but think of the terrestrial African or Asian elephants when he saw Elagabal. The thought was fleeting, but it was always there. He shook his head to clear away the distraction.

Carl set up the shot, aimed, and pulled the trigger. The bullet left the barrel like gossamer. It flew true, hitting Teela in the back of the head. Carl was pushed backward slightly due to Newtonian law.

Teela turned and saw the now spent foam bullet suspended between her and Carl. "Damn it, Carl, can't you see we're busy?" She flicked the bullet aside.

Flummoxed by not arousing the ire of his sister, Carl continued shooting, emptying the magazine and taunting her, "I killed you. I killed you."

Teela dodged the slow, clumsy foam bullets by rolling her body and pushing or pulling on surfaces as needed. "I don't have time for this nonsense, Carl," she shouted at him.

"You've got 170 hours," Carl retorted.

Teela tensed, glided to the hatchway, gave Carl her best, 'Try it and die stare,' and then pulled the door closed.

Teela turned back to Elagabal. "Do you think we have another choice?"

The Sumatozou twisted her trunk. "I don't know." She wrote some equations on an erasable board and, using a slide rule, solved them. "I've got more trajectories to calculate before I'll know if it is possible." Elagabal continued to write, erase, and hum while she worked, appearing content. After an hour of figuring, she placed a mark on a star chart and drew a line using a straight edge. "I have to do that same calculation five more times, then recalculate it with a different equation to confirm the math. Once I have the math confirmed, I'd like to double check with the guild. To be safe, I want to know what is in the emergence area. If they refuse my request, you may have to offer the guild something…" Elagabal let the sentence hang.

Teela didn't respond, lost in thought.

"I could use a ration or two if you don't mind," the Sumatozou said.

"Yeah, sure." Teela left Elagabal to her work.

* * *

The *Felix* emerged in the Formalhaut System with 20 or 30 other ships. All of them moved slowly, in formation. Kartikki piloted the ship to Aeternum Starport which orbited the star just outside the Goldilocks zone. They waited a few hours for a docking bay to become available so they could secure fuel for the rest of their trip.

Even though the crew complained about Gurgul for the bulk of the transition hours, no one disembarked.

The *Felix* moved away from the area of commerce and traffic to an area free of planets and exoplanets. Before anyone could disagree, Teela directed Kartikki to charge the shunt and transition to the co-ordinates Elagabal put into the computer. The *Felix* jumped.

* * *

"What were you thinking?" Carl leaned toward his sister. "The *Felix* can only handle one jump. Now we don't have a backup."

Trk'tk nodded. "He is correct."

"Relax," Teela said. "This is the only way to avoid a shadow. The *Medusa*'s specs show she has her own shunt. She has been missing for some time, all her solar batteries will be charged. We can put the *Felix* in the hold and transition back the moment we find her."

Carl slapped his forehead. "You don't get it; you were never a merc." He looked at his sister incredulously. "If Gurgul shows up, we have no escape."

"He won't. He can't."

"Purely out of spite—he will," Carl said. "I've worked with that Oogar before, we all have. He's mean and underhanded. Hell, he's downright evil."

"If he knows where the *Medusa* is, he wouldn't have come to me for the charts," Teela said.

"Where did you get those charts? Maybe there are copies out there."

"We didn't get them anywhere. They have taken years of study and translation to develop. Honest to goodness detective work."

"You didn't pull the information out of the air. Where did it come from?"

"It came from different sources. Sound maps, radar, beacon transmissions, telemetry models, and some educated guessing."

"Guessing? We are mid-jump to a salvage we aren't sure is there, with a crazed Oogar on our ass?"

"No, he has no idea where we're going."

"Well…" Elagabal started. "I sent my calculations to a friend who confirmed the trajectory. Once confirmed, I sent them to the guild to be certain that we're not jumping into a sun or planet. If Gurgul intercepted that transmission he would have our coordinates." Elagabal stopped and swallowed, staring at the disbelieving faces. "But…but…but he would have to know I was transmitting to look for my message. Do you have any idea how much data is sent every second? There is no way he'd find it, translate it, and understand my math."

"If there is no way, why did you mention it as a chance?" Carl raised an eyebrow.

".0001% is still a chance." Elagabal twisted her trunk. "I thought you should know."

Carl moved to the weapons room where he counted the explosives, bullets, and magazines, hoping they would be enough. "All we have are hand-to-hand equipment and small arms. We don't even have a CASPer. What the hell was she thinking? We are not prepared to take on an angry Oogar, let alone all the Oogar mercs he employs."

* * *

The *Felix* emerged in a small solar system consisting of a red dwarf and a lonely gas giant nearly half its size. The giant traveled around the star in a long, elliptical orbit.

"I can't find her," Kartikki said. All four of her hands worked knobs and toggles, delicately adjusting equipment. She watched various screens, looking for dips and spikes on the displays.

"Her solar equipment ought to still be active. Keep trying," Teela encouraged.

"Wait, I've got something." Kartikki pointed at a spike on one of her displays. "She's orbiting the giant, but she appears dead, no electrical or audio. No transmissions of any kind."

"No wonder she remained missing for so long."

Kartikki's hands paused, hovering over the controls. "I don't like it."

"What don't you like?"

"She has no power, yet she is in orbit as if someone purposely put her there."

"Couldn't she have drifted into orbit after she went astray from the military caravan?"

"I don't believe so; at least not on her own. Some ships have safety equipment to prevent outright collisions with asteroids or comets. But to put a ship in orbit, intentionally, without direction or coordinates? No, I don't know of any ship that has that capability."

"The crew could have put her there before the power failed," Teela suggested.

"Agreed." Kartikki fidgeted. "But…" Her hands danced over the control console. "This situation is more than a logistics problem. This system has two objects that compete for gravitational dominance." Kartikki pulled up a display showing the projected orbit of the giant around the dwarf. "See how the dwarf wobbles as it approaches perigee? The competition would pull or push a powerless ship down to either surface or, perhaps, tear it apart."

Teela pointed at the image of the gas giant. "How quickly does the giant orbit around the dwarf? Your representation appears fast."

"About 19 Terran months."

"And how many of those months are in perigee?"

"Approximately one-third."

"A little over six months. Wait a minute, are you telling me the *Medusa* had no stable orbit?"

Kartikki nodded. "Its current orbit will fail within a few months." The display showed the giant moving into the tighter orbit of perigee and the *Medusa* representation falling toward the red dwarf. "They all fail within 13 Terran months." The Pendal swept her outer arms. "That's why there are no other planets or moons in this system; it's too volatile."

"Shit!" Teela realized the implications of Kartikki's postulations. "The *Medusa* has been lost for decades. Not months."

The Pendal nodded.

"Any other ships in the vicinity?"

"Scans are clear."

"Who put it into orbit? And why? Have we wasted our time?" Teela said aloud, not expecting an answer. "I want to dock and take a look."

* * *

"Ｎo power, no air." Carl donned his helmet, staring at his sister as he clipped every weapon he could to his suit. "It's a good thing there's also no Gs. I wouldn't be able to walk with all these weapons."

Teela returned his stare through her helmet. "I know what you're thinking, but it isn't a trap."

"It's a trap, Teela. Maybe not Gurgul-designed, but it's still a trap." Carl continued to add weapons and finally a large bag. "You know, we're going to die."

"You say that every mission."

"This isn't a mission. This is suicide." Carl turned away from Teela, then added the remaining weapons to Elagabal's suit. "Want some C-12?"

"If you're offering, yes. I can add it to the doors and hallways in the docking bay to cover our escape," Elagabal said. "Best to be prepared."

"Don't I get any weapons?" Teela asked.

"You're not a merc. You've never had training. You should stay here. Elagabal and I can run reconnaissance."

"No. This is my salvage. I'm going. Give me a weapon." Teela thrusted her open hand toward him.

Carl reached into the bag and shoved a foam bullet pistol into her glove.

* * *

Kartikki maneuvered the *Felix* toward one of a handful of docking bays on the side of the *Medusa*. The dull thunk of metal on metal rang throughout the *Felix*.

Elagabal manually secured the locking mechanisms. She waved the Humans into the airlock, closed the door, and prepared for decompression. "Looks like there is no pressure on the ship; she's a true derelict," the Sumatozou said.

After equalization to the *Medusa*, Elagabal opened the inner and outer hatches and floated through the openings. The lights on her helmet illuminated a vast, open area. "Docking bay is empty. Three ports are associated with the bay. Investigating now," she reported over the comm. She maneuvered to the nearest door. Elagabal used the manual override to open it, looked around, returned, and finally placed a C-12 charge near the door's manual controls. She addressed each of the doors in the same way.

Carl and Teela waited patiently for Elagabal to secure the area and set a perimeter. The Sumatozou took pride in her defensive tactics.

Elagabal nodded to the Humans. "Everything is clear. I'll hold this location until you return."

Teela grabbed Carl's suit and forced him to face her. "Look, I know you have no respect for me as a leader, but we need to address this situation and get back to the *Felix* as quickly as possible."

Carl rolled his eyes, which he knew would irritate her. "Time?"

"No more than 20 minutes. Keep comms open and report."

Carl saluted Teela sarcastically, nodded to Elagabal, then left through the nearest bulkhead door to explore. "First room vacant." He pulled his way to the next room. "Vacant," he reported. Then he stopped and looked closer. The door was not just open; it was missing. He scanned the inside of the room, carefully, tapping on the walls. The panels that covered the walls were loose. Carl moved one aside and saw something very strange; nothing. Carl grabbed another loose panel and threw it aside, letting it float. There was nothing behind it either. "Teela, you need to come and look at this."

"On my way," Teela answered.

By the time she appeared in the room, Carl had removed all the panels, floor, ceiling, and walls. "What do you see?" he shoved the panels into the passageway.

"Nothing, other than the struts of the ship, the bones." Teela turned to look at Carl. "Am I missing something?"

"No, you're correct. There's nothing here. That's the problem. These bulkheads should have cables, wires, tubes, plumbing, and ventilation running through them. But it's all gone. Someone has already salvaged this ship. All that's left is a façade."

"Are you fucking kidding me?" Teela looked at the walls. The light on her helmet reflected off the cut and ground steel. "They even took their time cutting each tube and pulling each wire. That's insane." Teela's eyes became vacant, lost in thought. "We salvaged a small transport. It took us a couple of months, and all it had was a cockpit and crew area, nothing this extravagant."

"That was the four of you? You, Elagabal, Kartikki, and Trk'tk?"

"Trk'tk is pretty quick with tools. He's equal to at least three or four Humans." Teela touched one of the struts with her gloved hand. "Salvaging to this degree, on a ship this size, would take the four of us years. Ten to twenty, I'd think."

"I wonder how many Oogar it would take?" Carl asked.

"I don't like what you're suggesting," Teela retorted. "I'm going to command to see if there is any way to move this ship out of orbit. Would you check engineering? There ought to be an alternate piloting station there."

"Sounds like a plan," Carl said.

Teela went down the corridor, and Carl followed. At the end of the passageway was a secured door.

Carl opened the hatch, revealing a ladder. "Command should be up a few decks and engineering down a few." Carl looked around. "I hate zero Gs; it's always hard to know up from down."

"Come on," Teela said, pointing to a sign that read 'Topside.' She proceeded to follow the sign. Carl went the opposite way.

Carl stopped when he noticed a red stripe in the corridor. Most large ships had one color-coded level, which usually held engineering, medical, and the mess. If you were on a military ship, and lucky, you could find bars, tattoo parlors, and other forms of entertainment.

The comm crackled. "I found central command. Everything is gone, except for the pilot's chair. I'm going back to the *Felix*. Report what you find in engineering."

"Roger." Carl continued following the red-striped corridor, until he found a closed door. He opened it, exposing the contents of the room.

"I found something," Carl said, his voice cracking.

"What do you have?"

"Bodies."

"Repeat. I'm not sure I heard you."

"I've got a room filled with bodies." Carl punched the wall. "Not just military or merc either. There are children in here, civilians, each one with a hole in their head, execution style. Some are…fresher than others. I think I know what the *Medusa* is. She's bait, and we took it."

"What?"

"It explains the façade of the ship. Some sucker, sorry Teela, finds a map or hears about something that leads them to a prize more fabulous than all their dreams put together. They go for it, only to find out the prize is not the golden egg they thought it was. They are killed, then their ship is taken and sold. The bait is set again, waiting for another sucker to pounce. From the look of these bodies, this bait has been set quite a few times. I think I know the evil, underhanded mind that would come up with that kind of plan."

"I hope you're wrong, but if you're right, we need to go. Get back to the *Felix*."

"But I haven't checked engineering yet," Carl said.

"I've got a blip," Kartikki said over the com. "It came from behind the sun. I didn't see it until now." The *Felix* rumbled, and the comm audio stuttered. "Taking fire."

* * *

The *Medusa* was struck numerous times, but with no power to deflect the energy, the laser-like projectiles burned holes through her hull. The derelict ship creaked and whined.

The ceiling and walls seemed to fall and crash upon Teela, like millions of gallons of water. Unbound by gravity, she bounced around, hitting the walls and ceiling with startling force.

Teela shook her head, trying to keep her senses. The display on her arm was shattered, it blinked unintelligibly.

"Carl, are you ok?"

There was a long radio silence before he responded, "Yea." His voice didn't contain the sarcasm Teela expected.

"Get your ass to the *Felix*."

Teela pulled herself along the corridors, heading back as quickly as possible. "Bastards knew we were here, if they hid behind the sun," she complained. "Kartikki, do you recognize the ship? Does it have any transponder codes?"

"No, IFF is only displaying origin Uuwato System. Could be merc or pirate," Kartikki said. "Two more blips, same point of contact."

"Three ships? Shit." Teela continued moving toward the *Felix*. "Trk'tk, damage report."

"We've got some damage, mostly superficial."

"Carl? Report. Are you on the *Felix* yet?"

* * *

The bodies floated aimlessly, some moving into the corridor, others bumping into Carl. He stirred, regaining consciousness, looking at the faces of terror, frozen in time. They were of species of all types, all ages; no one was neglected. Some had been there for a long time and looked more like mummies than their species.

Carl remembered Teela yelling for him to get back to the *Felix*. He moved, grabbed his helmeted head, and groaned in pain.

"Carl?" Teela's voice came over the com, sounding very much like their mother's.

"I'm here," Carl said, his voice croaking. "What's going on? Weren't we taking fire?"

"We had to disengage from the *Medusa*."

"What? You left me?" Carl noticed a crack in his helmet, running down the left side.

"We didn't have a choice."

"We thought you died," Elagabal interrupted.

"We thought you were captured," Teela corrected.

"Captured? By whom?"

356 | KENNEDY & WANDREY

"Gurgul and his crew. He said he had you, and we couldn't raise you over the comm, so we believed him. He wants us to turn over the *Felix* in return for your release."

"Don't be stupid. If you give him the *Felix,* he will kill all of us." Carl paused, looking at the faces of the dead bodies before him. Some of them looked alike, like family members. They were bargaining chips. "No, it's best you leave me. Save yourselves."

"Mom would kill me if anything happened to you. Besides, we already used our shunt. We don't have a jump. We can't outmaneuver all three of his fleet. We'd be run down sooner or later."

"Make arrangements to meet him an hour from now and expect a fastball." Carl hoped his sister would understand his code. He turned his comm to a different, unused frequency. Without the buzz and static of the comm, the silence was eerie. His breathing and heartbeat and minor noises from his suit were the only sounds he heard.

Carl left the bodies, moved down the corridor, and entered engineering. The core was still in place, unpowered. With the computers removed, the fusion core was worthless as an engine, but he didn't need an engine. Carl adhered C-12 charges all around the tranquil core, setting the timer for 60 minutes. He realized the Oogar had probably determined where his communication with the *Felix* came from. They would eventually search the engineering level and discover his little surprise. Carl took the time to rewire the C-12 charges to make sure they would detonate if anyone tried to disarm the cluster.

He left engineering and heard his comm's static peak, then disappear. "Comm interference," Carl mumbled. "That means someone is close." He pulled his Smith and Wesson 500. He continued talking quietly to himself. "Oogar tend to get angry when you shoot them. I wonder how many have felt the sting of a .50 caliber bullet." He giggled, then snorted.

Carl double-checked both directions of the corridor. He reached up, turned off his helm light, and moved toward the room with the bodies. He used the walls to help guide his way.

The lights of a distant spacesuit glowed against the walls of the hallway. Carl readied the 500, pointing it in the general direction of the spacesuit. The helm's edge appeared first around the corner, followed by the ugly, grizzly mug and the helm light, blinding Carl for a moment.

Carl aimed and fired before the Oogar could report his position.

He was tossed back like a ragdoll, ricocheting off the floors, walls, and ceiling. Carl felt his head and back slam into a solid surface. The .50 cal broke free. His momentum slowed. Carl threw out his arms to grab something. He located a doorway and stopped.

Carl coughed to catch his breath. A shriek-like whistle startled him. He turned on his light. The hairline crack in his helmet was longer and wider. He reached in his bag, pulled off a chunk of C-12 and used it like caulk to patch the hole. He lost 20% of his vision. It wasn't a permanent or perfect solution, but it would work.

Carl moved back along the corridor and found his gun tumbling barrel over handle. Further down the hallway was the Oogar, clearly dead. Globules of purple blood floated freely until they connected on a surface or coalesced into larger balls.

The Oogar's helmet had been torn off by the impact of the bullet, leaving ribbons of flesh and bone floating in zero G. The .50 caliber was too strong for the situation. Carl reattached it to his suit.

He rounded up the Oogar's laser pistol and rifle, putting them in his bag. Carl added five grenades to his collection. He looked at the readout on the bear's arm and noticed the frequency of the comm.

Carl moved into the room where the bodies were stored. He changed his frequency to the Oogar channel and turned off his microphone. Snarls, grunts, growls and guttural tones filled his ears. It took a moment for his computer to decipher and translate. "It's just one Human. You call yourselves Oogar. I need proof that we have him. Go to the engineering level. Take as many as you need."

Carl turned off his light and lowered the volume on his comm. He joined the rest of the floating bodies and waited.

Chatter came over the comm, but the volume was too low for him to hear clearly. Lights passed the room where he hid. Suddenly there was a burst of Oogar-speak. "Hagthar killed, weapons gone." Vociferous roars filled his helm.

Carl turned off the comm, then slowly maneuvered through the bodies. Hidden by the blind of corpses, he watched as the Oogar angrily attacked walls and each other. Their muzzles bellowed silently behind their domed helms.

The bears dispersed in pairs, weapons drawn. Two pairs moved toward Carl. He slithered back to hide deeper within the room, nudging a body, causing it to turn.

One of the Oogar pointed. They spoke to each other, then moved closer.

Thinking he was spotted, Carl drew two laser pistols and waited.

The Oogar shot the body of a Pendal that reminded him of Kartikki. They laughed as it tumbled in lazy circles. Carl could see the enjoyment on their faces. He hated them for killing innocent people, especially children.

Before he could think it through, he pulled both triggers, aiming at a bear-like face, and shouting retribution. The shattered glass and splattered blood were satisfying.

A hot burst of red burned past Carl, striking a dead Sumatozou wearing armor.

He moved, pushing a body aside, and shot, striking an Oogar.

The gasses escaping the spacesuit propelled purple blood. The wounded Oogar pushed off the wall and charged through the room, shoving bodies aside, creating more chaos and leaving his weapons behind.

Carl aimed, released his breath, and fired, hitting helmet and face.

The last two Oogar assaulted the room, tossing corpses into the corridor, trying to find Carl.

He fired at them recklessly, connecting a few times, burning holes in their suits.

The Oogar brought the attack to Carl, forgetting their ranged weapons, and swiped at him with their clawed gloves.

Carl continued to fire until his weapons were spent. He didn't know if they'd died from bullets or exposure. The thought of dying by asphyxiation caused Carl to look at the readout on his arm. He had 45 minutes of air and 30 minutes until his fusion bomb detonated.

"Time to move." He left the spent laser pistols behind.

One of his reckless shots had torn a ventilation or crawlspace port off the wall. Carl had a crazy idea. "What better way to avoid detection?" He clambered inside. It was a tight fit—tight enough that he was certain no Oogar could follow. Carl imagined the only thing an Oogar would see, if it chose to look in the hole, would be his hind-quarters. "A full moon." He giggled, then shimmied faster, afraid of a bullet.

With his arms stretched out in front of him, he felt an edge. He turned on his light. He saw a room with tubes on one side and pin-holes on the other, reminding him of a hub or transfer room. He pulled himself in and noticed more openings that might be crawlspaces. Some were smaller than the one he came through, while others were much larger, big enough for an Oogar.

A flash of red light entered the room from one of the other openings. It was followed by another from a different opening, and another. The volleys of laser fire intensified.

The openings in the floor and ceiling remained clear, as did the Oogar-sized openings. "Of course, they know where I am, it took years to salvage this ship. I should have expected this kind of trap." Carl opened his bag and pulled out a C-12 charge. He set the timer for one minute and climbed into a crawl space in the floor.

A hatchway stopped his progress. Carl turned the handle and pulled the door inward, which forced him to back up. He pulled his body through the door, then closed and secured it. With his hand still on the handle, he felt the vibration from the C-12 explosion. Carl was surprised by the subtleness of the bomb. Then he realized the charges were exposed to the vacuum of space. Without atmosphere, the explosions would be much smaller, but the shrapnel would have a much larger radius.

Shrapnel did wonders to space suits. Carl smiled. He turned his comm back on and was rewarded with the sounds of pain, no trans-lation needed. Disgusted by his morbid curiosity, Carl turned off the comm.

He tapped the hatchway as if to say thank you, then continued through five more hatchways. The last emptied into a room containing defensive turrets. There were no rounds for the weapons. Not that it mattered, any round big enough to fit in the barrel would have been impossible to lift or maneuver.

He climbed into the barrel of the large weapon and emerged on the outside of the *Medusa*. From his vantage point, he located Gurgul's docked fleet. As Carl descended from the lip of the barrel, his bag moved strangely, sometimes pulling him, other times twisting and banging into his back. "Gravitational eddies?" Carl wondered.

Once off the massive weapons, Carl used hand holds to maneuver across the *Medusa*'s surface. He slowed when he came closer to the fleet.

One of the ships left the *Medusa*. The other two remained. Each of them was connected to the larger ship by a mechanism near the nose of the smaller craft. Carl climbed to the maintenance panel and pried it free, exposing the hard, mechanical connection. Carl placed a C-12 charge, smashing it into the gears and cables, and set the timer for five minutes.

He clambered from one smaller ship to the other, staying in the shadows, trying to avoid viewports. He opened the second maintenance panel and placed the second C-12 charge, setting the timer for two minutes. He moved as quickly as possible away from the ships. Once clear of the blast radius, Carl turned on his comm and microphone and set the frequency to that of the *Felix*.

He pulled the 500, imagined a line between the *Medusa* and the center of the star, held the gun tightly with both hands and fired.

The Newtonian forces pushed him backward, away from the star and the *Medusa*. His hands, arms, and shoulders ached. He began to spin slightly. Carl studied the *Medusa*, looking for the docking bay, and saw two flashes of light as the C-12 detonated.

"Carl to the *Felix*, over."

Static answered.

Again, Carl tried his best to aim at an imaginary line between the *Medusa* and the star.

He fired. His shoulders screamed. Carl folded his arms across his chest, hoping to ease the pain.

"Carl to the *Felix*, over. Fastball incoming. Come on, Teela, where the hell are you?"

Static.

"Carl is that you?" Kartikki's voice came over the comm. "We are trying to stay out of Gurgul's firing range."

"I thought he wanted the *Felix* to sell, not destroy," Carl responded.

"He—" Kartikki's voice crackled and vanished.

Gurgul's voice growled through the comm. "You killed 11 of my men, Carl. I always knew you were an ass. Your sister is going to pay for your insolence."

Carl looked at the readout on his arm. "Are you sure I only killed 11? My count seems so much higher." As if on cue a flash of bright light emitted from the *Medusa*.

Gurgul roared.

Static.

"What did you do?" Teela's voice filled his ears. "He broke off; he's no longer chasing us."

"I went beyond pissing him off." Carl watched as a speck of space grew larger. "I think he is going to kill me."

Huge bolts of plasma struck above Carl, then below, and then to his side.

Gurgul's ship passed Carl and slowly turned about near the *Medusa*. The derelict ship appeared to have been propelled toward the gas giant, and the Oogar's ship struggled to break free from its gravity well. Gurgul pulled the ship around and aimed it at Carl. The ship was close enough to fire but didn't. Gurgul planned to run him down, like a bug in a headlamp.

Carl aimed his 500 at the viewports of Gurgul's ship and fired. He flipped in response to the Newtonian forces. Carl tucked into a ball, trying to become smaller.

The ship passed and turned back.

Carl's arms and shoulders couldn't handle the stresses of the gun. He looked at the readout on his arm; only a couple minutes of air left.

He was going to die. He closed his eyes. His body tumbled erratically.

* * *

Kartikki's delicate hands manipulated the dials and toggles. Her head tilted a little. "I think Gurgul's ship may have been damaged. Look, he seems to be pulling to starboard."

"That asshole is trying to kill my brother. Is there anything we can do?" Teela questioned.

"Yes. While Carl distracts him, we can fire a couple of precise rounds," Elagabal said. "It's like Gurgul doesn't see us."

"A furious Oogar is a blind Oogar," Kartikki quoted her favorite writer. "We are in position, Elagabal, fire when ready."

The Sumatozou pressed a button with a short, fat finger.

Two plasma blasts hit Gurgul's main engine, causing it to fail, and the ship began its inexorable descent toward the gas giant as the gravitational forces pulled it in.

Can we get him now?" Teela fidgeted, clearly wanting to save her little brother.

# # # # #

The Heart of a Lion
by Terry Mixon

Commander Rick Betancourt followed his escort up the tube between decks. Even if protocol hadn't demanded it, he'd have been grateful for the guide. The battleship *Lion* was easily the largest ship he'd ever been on, not counting freighters or liners.

Those didn't really count though, as the areas where passengers had access were carefully restricted. No one wanted the untrained or unknown wandering their corridors. And, since he *did* have an escort, he supposed it was true here, too.

They stopped at a hatch guarded by two marines in unpowered combat armor, without helmets. His escort announced Rick's name, and the lean woman with hard eyes on the left brought up a slate and scrutinized it—and him—closely before activating her comm unit with her chin.

"Commander Betancourt from the *Hermes* is here to see you, Admiral."

Moments later, the hatch slid aside, and the woman gestured for Rick to go in. His escort turned back the way they'd come, but the woman followed him in. No doubt she'd do something painful to him if he even looked cross-eyed at her boss.

366 | KENNEDY & WANDREY

The compartment was large but only spartanly appointed. A wooden desk dominated the room, taking up a full quarter of the space. The bulkheads lacked the racks of trophies and awards that some mercenaries kept on hand to impress visitors. Here the walls were bare, only showing off the neutral gray favored on the *Lion*.

Admiral Hawthorne, a beefy man with salt and pepper hair cut in a flattop, rose and shook Rick's hand across the desk before gesturing to a chair and resuming his seat.

"Welcome aboard, Commander." The admiral's voice was deep and gravelly, as powerful as the sea.

"I apologize for the chaos during your approach. We just wrapped up the final pre-raid briefing, and everyone is on their way back to their ships."

Rick eased himself down into the chair. "It was no problem, Admiral. I'm sorry if my delay caused any hitch in your schedule."

The larger man waved his apology away. "Not at all. I need to make certain your portion of the operation goes smoothly, too. We only get one chance at this, and I won't see it wasted.

"You have my complete and total attention for the next twenty minutes, so I can make certain you have the best chance possible for mission success. Honestly, I think you have the most difficult job during the raid.

"I know I'm paying you top credit for this, but I cannot overemphasize how important your mission is to me. Any resources you need will be made available to you, if they'll make any material difference. The sky is the limit."

Rick nodded. "I'll let you know if I think of anything."

Hawthorne cleared his throat. "For the sake of clarity, I'll go over the raid plans with you. Once the fighting starts, I want you to know what any possible set of commands or maneuvers means so you can adjust your operation.

"Major Hawke will accompany you. She has the battle plan memorized and is completely aware of how I think. She's been with me for fifteen years and knows me better than anyone."

That last came with hint of pain, but the older man didn't stop to explain.

"First, the history. I had to limit the background information in our contract to keep word of this operation from getting out. My apologies if that offends, but while you and your people come with impressive recommendations, you're not Lions."

"I'm not offended, Admiral," Rick said genially. "The contract explained this, and I came in with my eyes open."

The large man considered him closely for a moment, then nodded. "Excellent. One never knows how that kind of thing will go over. You're just as professional as your reputation implies. Let's go over the battle plan.

"This strike force is leaving for the Aventari's system in a bit more than two hours. Have you heard of them?"

Rick shook his head. "I can't say that I have."

"Big bastards, like a cross between a massive badger with a bad attitude and a starfish with knives on its arms. They're xenophobic, and they'll shoot first and never bother asking questions. Oh, they also eat their own kind and any aliens they capture alive in combat. They consider them delicacies.

"They're technically not a mercenary race. Even though they can fight, they don't ever venture into the Union. They got lucky when they found a source of F11 in their system, and they managed to hang onto it after the discovery. They've used the money it brought in to upgrade their weapons and ships extensively."

Rick felt his eyebrows rising. "That seems unusual. The scent of F11 usually brings someone more powerful to take it away."

Hawthorne nodded. "They made an initial exploration deal with a well-connected corporation, allowing the company to take a significant cut of the earnings in exchange for a large defensive force. One significant enough to deter incursions."

"If they're so xenophobic, how does the F11 extraction work?" Rick asked, his lips pursed as he considered the possibilities.

"They grudgingly allowed the corporation to set up the facility and somehow found a few of their people who could restrain themselves from eating the techs. From my understanding, there were never very many techs anyway. As much as possible was automated.

"Ten years ago, the Aventari finished upgrading some of their ships to modern standards and dismissed the protective mercenaries. That was enough of an opening for someone to contract mercenaries for a raid.

"My older brother, Andy, commanded the Lions back then. He died on the raid when everything went to hell. The Aventari were everywhere, in far greater numbers than our intelligence estimates had led us to believe."

The older man shook his head grimly. "Let my experience be a lesson for you, Commander. Never count on spies. If they don't know the answers, they'll make things up. It was a bloodbath."

The other man stared at the desktop, his jaw working. His eyes were unfocused, and Rick knew he was reliving the events from a decade ago. Horror and pain were etched into his expression.

Rather than say anything, Rick let the silence grow until Hawthorne recovered and stepped back from the abyss.

His eyes came up to meet Rick's. "My apologies, Commander. My brother's ship, the battleship *Lioness*, held them back to allow as many of us to escape as possible. When I last saw her, she was engaged with four times her tonnage and already dead, though her crew was too defiant to admit it.

"I lost my brother and my heart that day. The Aventari took them from me."

That last was accompanied by real tears, a sight one didn't often see from a grown man, much less a tough-as-nails mercenary commander.

"That sounds like something out of a saga, Admiral," Rick said softly. "I'm sorry for your loss."

Major Hawke edged forward and handed the admiral a handkerchief, seemingly unconcerned the man would lash out at her for her temerity. Rick had no idea where she'd found it in all her armor.

Hawthorne nodded his thanks as he wiped his eyes. "Thank you, Ava."

He turned his attention back to Rick. "I assume you're familiar with the story of Thermopylae. Of how King Leonidas and the three hundred Spartans fought to the death against King Xerxes of the Persian Empire and his overwhelming forces.

"Legend would have us believe it was three hundred Greeks against a million Persians, but it was more like seven thousand Greeks defending against several hundred thousand Persians. The *Lioness* wasn't outnumbered quite that badly, but her defeat was just as inevitable. She fought to the death to allow us time to escape, much like King Leonidas did."

"Are you familiar with the term 'Molon Labe,' Commander?" Major Hawke asked.

"Come and take them," Rick responded immediately. "It's a very popular phrase in the circles I frequent, though it's not usually the kind of defiance I favor."

She nodded. "When Xerxes sent an emissary to King Leonidas to demand the Spartans' weapons, that was his response. Directly translated, it means 'having come, take.' That was the final transmission from the *Lioness* as she charged the Aventari, giving us those crucial last few minutes. I'm sure they weren't actually given the option to surrender, but that wouldn't have changed anything."

"We transited out before the *Lioness* died," Hawthorne said. "Still, we know what happened from the stargate crew. The *Lioness* wasn't destroyed. She was crippled and boarded. The monsters took anyone alive they could, though they told the mercenary guild there were no survivors. They ate them."

For the first few seconds, it was as if someone had doused Rick in ice water. Then his vison went red. He didn't trust himself to speak, so he kept his mouth shut.

Hawthorne nodded approvingly. "I see I chose the right man for this job. You're as angry as we are. Perfect.

"Let's fast forward ten years. The Aventari have been strengthening their military forces aggressively since that battle. Six months ago, they broke the contract with the corporation mining the F11 and expelled them from the system for contract violations.

"The evidence they presented to the Union held up, angering the people involved. I guess even monsters can occasionally have the facts on their side. But that isn't stopping the corporation from trying to take the F11 for themselves.

"The corporation hired the Lions to head the raid. We have skin in the game. We've recovered in the last decade, and we're ready to fight those bastards again. We've assembled enough firepower to eliminate everything they have in space."

Rick cocked his head slightly. "Can you afford that kind of confidence, Admiral? Forgive me, but I'd wager your brother thought the same, and it didn't work out the way he planned. What if they're significantly more powerful than you expect?"

Rather than getting angry, Hawthorne smiled. "No, I'm not sure. Even though I've gathered as powerful a force as I can, I'm still taking a gamble. That explains why you're here.

"The corporation that hired us gave us as much data as they could on the system, including the fact that the *Lioness*'s wreck is still there. The Aventari put it into orbit around the dead world between their home and the innermost gas giant. It's a planet much like Mars where they've begun building a shipyard.

"Their intent, I'm sure, is to salvage the ship once the yard goes operational. I want to recover the dead crew that almost certainly still populates her before that happens. Every single person, Commander. And I want to recover our battle standard from the *Lioness*'s flag bridge. It's the company's heart."

Understanding filled Rick. "My mission is to get in there while the fighting is still going on and recover the dead and the Lion's Heart, in case you don't win."

"Precisely. We'll detach a couple of destroyers to see you to your target and protect you as best we can," Hawthorne said with a nod. "With any luck, the Aventari won't notice your ship because of all the ruckus the main force is generating. If we win, you're going to have all the time in the world to complete your operation. If not, you're going to want to finish as quickly as possible and hurry to the stargate."

"Understood," Rick said. "In addition to the good major, I'd like to request complete plans for the *Lioness*, a crew roster to compare with the bodies we find, and as many people as you can spare that know her layout. With battle damage, I'd prefer damage control people, but I know how badly you'll be needing people with that type of training. Any personnel will help since we may have to cut a lot of the bodies free in a hurry."

"We're already ahead of you," Hawthorne said. "My chief engineer has been training teams to assist you for the last six months. The *Lion* is identical to the *Lioness,* and we've been operating with a double complement of damage control specialists, preparing for this moment.

"In addition, Major Hawke will bring marines trained to assist with damage control efforts. When the time comes to search every section, you'll have people intimately familiar with everything."

Rick blinked in surprise. "I'm grateful for all the help, but that sounds like as many people as I brought. You could've carried off this mission in-house. Why bring in an outsider?"

"Because you and your ship are the absolute best at search and rescue. My people are good. Yours are better. This mission has no room for ego, and I cannot stress how important your success is. I won't allow you to fail because I didn't give you the support you needed.

"You might not be fighting, but as far as I'm concerned, your success is one of the primary raid objectives. If you fail, we will both have failed the Lions and those who sacrificed themselves for us. I will not see that happen, Commander."

"I won't let you down, Admiral."

Hawthorne stood and extended his hand across the desk. "I know you won't, but just to sweeten the pot I'm adding a hefty success bonus if you make a clean sweep. Recover at least eighty percent of the crew, and I'll double your take home pay.

"If you can only get the battle standard and bodies from the *Lioness*'s flag bridge, I'll still pay you the base amount we agreed on. That's your core mission, Commander."

Rick took the man's hand. "I'll bring your people home, Admiral. You have my word on it."

* * *

The *Hermes* wasn't a huge ship, but she was designed for search and rescue and didn't have space devoted to offensive systems. Speed was her strongest defense, as was the fact she was damned hard to detect when hidden.

They'd been in transit for almost 170 hours. Hyperspace trips always had the same duration, no matter the distance. Because of the vagaries of hyperspace physics, travel was much more fuel efficient for larger ships, so the *Hermes* was attached to one of the larger combatants in the second wave.

As soon as they arrived, she'd cut loose and separate from the combatants. The destroyers would cover them once they matched the *Hermes*'s vector.

Another oddity of hyperspace travel was that while ships kept the velocity they had when entering hyperspace, the exit vector was random. It was possible the *Hermes* would be going in the wrong direction when they arrived, so Rick was preparing for the possibility of a few minutes without the destroyers.

Luckily, their ride would cover them for the first thirty seconds. The battlecruiser *Apollo* could protect them unless they were under heavy fire. In that case, the *Hermes* might be screwed.

"Five minutes until breakout, Commander," Adrian Vanderbilt, his helmsman, said over the suit comms. "I have multiple courses laid in so we can make a clean break as soon as we disengage from the *Apollo*."

"Excellent," Rick said. The screen still showed the blank whiteness of hyperspace. That never changed, even if ships were right next to each other. No one understood why, and that probably wouldn't change during Rick's lifetime.

And, if he wanted his life to last more than the next ten minutes, he needed to focus on his job.

"Ping all department heads for their final status," he said calmly. "The moment we emerge, we're going to be under fire. The heavies are going in first, but we're right behind them. Make sure everyone has their suits sealed."

"Copy that," Lacey Sturtevant, his scanner officer said. "I imagine we're about to emerge into a target rich environment, but I'll do my best to get us away from the fighting as quickly as possible."

She was an exceptional scanner operator and had the best people the industry could offer supporting her in a backup control room deep inside the ship. If anyone could discern a path clear of the fighting within five seconds, it would be Lacey.

On most mercenary ships, the officers had ranks, but he'd never felt the need. Search and rescue didn't require the same hardening for the chain of command. Even his "rank" of commander was only for outsiders. Inside his tightknit crew, everyone knew their jobs and how to do them.

The countdown timer seemed to drag, with the last thirty seconds lasting an eternity. When the counter finally hit zero, the screen abruptly cleared and showed them what was waiting.

An enemy fleet was already locked in combat with the first wave. Missiles, laser beams, and particle beams shot in every direction, and several ships were already critically damaged or had exploded. Not just the enemy's, either.

"Detaching now. Engines to max," Adrian said, his tone grim. "The *Apollo* is taking fire. I'm using her hull to shield us from the closest enemy formation. That won't last long. I need a vector."

"We're heading away from the inner system," Lacey said. "There are four small ships ahead of us. I'm sending the best course I can find to you, Adrian."

"Got it. If we can keep them off us, we should be clear of the Lagrange point and the fighting around it in a couple of minutes. If the raid keeps the enemy ships pinned down, our destroyers can cover us."

Rick leaned forward. "Where are the destroyers?"

"They came out facing the opposite direction," Lacey said with more than a hint of disgust in her voice. "It looks like they're coming around, but we'll be uncovered for at least sixty seconds."

While the ships in front of the *Hermes* were engaging higher priority targets, they weren't simply ignoring the search and rescue vessel. One ship fired a spread of missiles that raced toward the *Hermes* with unsettling speed.

Thankfully, the *Apollo* still had an eye on the *Hermes*. The battlecruiser used its antimissile defenses on the incoming salvo, decimating it. Where there had been a dozen missiles a second earlier, there were now two.

One of them was going to miss cleanly, but the other had locked onto the *Hermes*. Luckily for them, their lack of offensive weaponry did not mean a lack of *defensive* capability.

"Engaging the remaining missile with antimissile defenses," Lacey said. "Multiple hits, missile destroyed."

"One of our destroyers has come around and is drawing off the ships ahead of us," Adrian said. "The other one hasn't disengaged from the main fight yet."

"And she's not going to," Lacey said grimly. "She just took a particle beam meant for the *Apollo*. She's gone. We're down to one escort."

The remaining destroyer exchanged missile fire with four smaller vessels as she charged into their ranks. Two of the enemy vessels promptly exploded and one was severely damaged, but the destroyer took numerous hits on the way in. She continued trading missile fire with the remaining vessels and destroyed them within twenty seconds.

"Incoming communication from the destroyer," Lacey said. "It's going to be bad news. I can already see that their engineering compartment took extensive damage."

"On screen," Rick said, his heart sinking.

The image of the battle was immediately replaced by a bridge somewhat larger than the one on the *Hermes*. Smoke poured from one of the consoles in the background, and the officer in the center seat had a gash on his suit's arm. Another officer was patching it.

"*Hermes*, this is Commander Dunn of the *Rapier*," the man said. "I'm afraid we're not going to be able to escort you any further. Our engines are severely damaged, so you're going to have to carry on without us. I'm sorry, but we're going to turn around and rejoin the main melee."

Rick turned his attention to Lacey. "What's our current situation? Is anyone paying us any attention?"

She turned slightly in her seat so she could see him through her faceplate. "All enemy forces appear to be fully engaged in the raid. I'm no expert, but I believe the Lions have enough strength to crush the units at the Lagrange point. The Aventari don't dare take their attention away from them to come after us."

Rick focused his attention back on the screen. "Commander Dunn, we have time to evacuate your injured and noncritical personnel and are standing by to do so."

The commander pulled off his helmet and scowled at Rick.

"Dammit, Commander, you have a mission to perform. You *have* to get the Lion's Heart."

"I can walk and chew gum at the same time, Commander," Rick said. "You know the odds are stacked against you. Don't let your people die when the chance to save them is right in front of you."

Dunn stared at him for a few long seconds, then pressed a key on his armrest. "All hands, this is the captain. I want all noncritical and secondary personnel to move to the escape pods. Leave enough pods for the critical personnel, but I want you off this ship within sixty seconds. Medical, send any personnel needed to take care of the injured. The *Hermes* is standing by to pick you up. Captain out."

Dunn had never taken his eyes off Rick. "I appreciate this, Commander. If we somehow manage to survive this fight, rest assured we'll be buying all the drinks you and your crew can handle. *Rapier* out."

Moments later, dozens of escape pods jettisoned from the damaged destroyer. They shot across the distance to the *Hermes* and queued up for retrieval.

Without waiting for orders, his crew sprang into action and began using the remote arms to bring the pods to the docking stations designed for them. Teams would pull people free as quickly as they could, then jettison the empty pods.

Picking up escape pods was one of the primary tasks of a search and rescue vessel. They had all the equipment they needed to retrieve the pods without exiting the ship. As that wasn't true for most combat vessels, this was one of the areas where the *Hermes* shone brightly.

The *Rapier* finished ejecting its pods while the recovery process was still underway. The damaged destroyer turned and moved back toward the fighting.

Rick really hoped they made it, but he knew the odds were against them. If any of the enemy combatants targeted the crippled destroyer, they'd probably kill it and everyone on board.

That was out of his hands. He had his own mission to think about.

A few minutes later, Lacey reported that all the pods were emptied and discarded. The medical teams down below were seeing to the injured. It was time to make their way to the *Lioness* and start a whole different kind of recovery.

* * *

Even taking the most circuitous route toward the Mars-like planet the *Lioness* orbited, the *Hermes* still managed to arrive before the main task force, as the relative distance was shorter, and they weren't fighting for every meter.

The Aventari resistance was stronger than the Lions had hoped it would be. That meant the recovery operation was still on shaky ground, particularly without the pair of protective destroyers.

The *Hermes* came in from the outer system, above the plane of the ecliptic, to reduce the chances of being spotted. As they got closer, they kept the bulk of the planet between them and the partially-constructed shipyard.

If they could get into orbit without drawing the attention of the aliens, they might be able to sneak in and accomplish their mission.

Thankfully, the battle deeper in the system would've drawn any mobile units stationed around the dead world to protect their home.

That didn't mean Rick and his people could just waltz in and do what they wanted. Anyone with half a brain would arm their shipyard. It would be one of the very first systems brought to readiness there.

After all, a shipyard capable of producing capital warships was worth a lot of money. One certainly wouldn't want some uppity mercenary sneaking in and blowing it up.

He'd relocated to the main conference room for the final briefing. That gave them enough room for all the major players. Barely.

His conference table was about the same size as Admiral Hawthorne's desk and could seat six people, if they didn't mind bumping elbows.

He sat at the head of the table. On his right were Kimberly Livingston, his chief engineer, and Andrew Nesbitt, his senior rescue specialist. On his left were Major Hawke and Lieutenant Commander Donovan Rutan, the *Lion*'s number two damage control officer.

At the foot of the table sat Lieutenant Antwan Malave, one of the *Rapier*'s junior tactical officers. His left arm was in a sling and part of his dark, curly hair was covered by white bandages, but he seemed to have his wits about him. From what Rick had heard, the console on the destroyer's bridge had exploded in his face.

A mockup of the strategic situation around the dead world was on the screen mounted to the bulkhead. It showed their current location in orbit and the locations of the shipyard and the *Lioness*.

"Ladies and gentlemen," he began. "It looks like we've caught a little bit of luck, and there are no mobile units in orbit around this world. Unfortunately, the wreck is somewhat closer to the shipyard than we anticipated. I'm not certain we can get the *Hermes* into position without their noticing us."

"Then we'll have to do this the hard way," Hawke said. "We always knew this might be our only option, so you've got plenty of shuttles strapped to your hull. Far more than the ship was designed to carry.

"We'll load everyone into them, come around the planet, and use the wreck to block the shipyard's view of our approach. If they don't see us coming, we should have plenty of time to scour the *Lioness* and get our people off. If we're lucky, we'll be gone before the admiral trounces them on their home world."

Or gets trounced by them, the pessimist inside Rick insisted glumly.

"We won't be able to fit all the bodies in the shuttles for a single trip," Andrew said. "There'll be too many of them, even if we stack them like cordwood."

"I understand your wanting to show the dead as much dignity as possible, and I respect you for that," Commander Rutan said slowly.

"But we have to let the realities of the situation dictate our actions. The dead won't mind any passing indignities, if we get them home. Stack them in the bays or strap them to the hull. Do whatever you have to do to get them out of there."

Rick turned his attention to Kimberly. "What kind of conditions are we expecting on board the *Lioness*? Will the emergency power systems still be operational?"

His chief engineer shook her head. "Not after a decade. We've brought a couple of power packs to plug into the emergency system. That'll get us light for six or seven hours. If we're not done by then, we'll be working in the dark."

Commander Rutan shrugged. "That should be more than enough time to get everyone except those trapped in the most damaged areas. Perhaps even them. We won't know until we see inside."

Rick looked at Major Hawke. "I understand most of your people are going to be dedicated to search and rescue operations, but some of you will be in CASPers. How long will you be able to hold off boarding parties sent from the shipyard, if they spot us?"

She smiled coldly. "For as long as it takes. If they blow up the ship, that's one thing, but if they just send troops our way, I think we can hold. After all, what size combat force would they leave in the shipyard while we're invading their system?"

"Good point," he admitted with a nod. "Lieutenant Malave, you're the most senior officer from the *Rapier*. Are any of your people able to help us speed recovery efforts?"

The man looked pained when Rick mentioned that he was the senior officer. The statement was true in multiple ways. The *Rapier* hadn't survived the fight at the Lagrange point. She'd been lost with all hands. Commander Dunn would never have the opportunity for that drink.

"We're about half-and-half, Commander. The most seriously injured would be a hindrance, but we have several noncritical and secondary personnel who can help.

"If we recover those not needing extraction, it frees up trained personnel to go after the more difficult cases. We're at your disposal. Admiral Hawthorne has placed us in your command for the duration of this raid."

Rick did a few calculations in his head. If they stuffed the shuttles, they could get everyone over to the wreck in one run. Returning with the bodies would be more challenging.

"Can we put the dead in the ship's escape pods and program them to rendezvous with the *Hermes*? The shipyard is in a geostationary orbit, so they can't chase after us. If all the escape pods launch at the same time, they should be able to get behind the planet before the aliens start shooting."

Kimberly nodded and raised an eyebrow at the damage control specialist. "The power in the escape pods should still be good. It won't be hard to enter the destination and set them to jettison on a general signal. That will leave the shuttles free for us to use."

"I agree," Rutan said. "That sounds like an excellent plan, Commander Betancourt. When should we execute it?"

"There's no time like the present," Rick said, rising to his feet. "Let's make this happen, then get the hell out of here."

* * *

When their probe showed no signs of unusual activity in the shipyard, Rick ordered his personnel to board the shuttles and queue up for the run around the planet. All the equipment had been preloaded and getting everyone on board took twenty minutes.

The battleship's wreck wouldn't completely cover their approach, but it would add some clutter to the yard's scanners. It also didn't hurt that most of their attention would be focused on the battle for their home world.

Hoping the aliens *were* suitably distracted, Rick ordered the small line of shuttles to slowly approach the wreck. They seemed to inch around the planet, then both the wreck and the shipyard came into view.

The shipyard was significantly larger than the battleship, but it was also farther away. The outer edges of the shipyard would be visible until they got closer to the *Lioness*. If the plan was going to go sideways, it would happen now.

Time seemed to drag until the wrecked battleship took up half the sky. By then, they were close enough to the *Lioness* to be certain the shipyard couldn't see them.

Rick let out a breath, thanked whatever gods had been watching over them, and activated the shuttle's short-range comm. Even if some of the signal leaked around the wreck, it would only carry a couple hundred meters.

"Alpha shuttles, this is the *Hermes* Actual. Execute phase two."

Four of the shuttles moved ahead of the pack to preselected docking ports. They were filled with marines wearing CASPers. They'd do the initial sweep to be certain there were no guards.

Ten minutes later, they saw the running lights on the docked shuttles begin to pulse. That was the signal to move in.

"All remaining shuttles, this is the *Hermes* Actual. Go for docking."

He'd picked a docking port that was close to the flag bridge. He needed to get in and assess the situation as rapidly as possible. If things went to hell in a hurry, he'd still be able to recover the battle standard and the dead before making a run for it.

Minutes later, his shuttle jarred to a halt as the pilot locked them down.

"Let's go," Rick said, releasing his crash harness.

While she wasn't wearing a CASPer, Major Hawke was armed and armored. She and a couple of her marines would provide overwatch for Rick's team. Lieutenant Malave, his arm still in a sling, was with them.

Once Major Hawke opened the outer door, they rapidly made their way into the dead battleship. Only it wasn't quite as dead as they thought it would be. The emergency lights were on.

"What the hell?" Rick muttered before activating his suit com. The low-powered signal would bounce from suit to suit inside the hull until it reached its intended recipient.

"Kimberly, are you seeing what I'm seeing? We seem to have emergency power."

"I see it. The batteries should've died years ago. We're just entering engineering now. Holy shit. We have power here. I think the Aventari repaired at least one of the power plants."

Rick frowned. "Why would they do that? It's just wasted resources on a wreck like this."

"Maybe they think she's salvageable. We also have pressure back here. The atmosphere isn't Earth standard, so it must be Aventari. There are no bodies. They must've moved them elsewhere."

"Copy that. Make certain your damage control people start checking the areas they're assigned to. I want to know if the Aventari have repaired any other sections of the ship, and we need to figure out where they've moved the bodies."

By then, Rick's party had reached the flag bridge. It was sealed, but Major Hawke entered a code on the keypad. Moments later, the massive hatch slid aside.

Just like the rest of the ship, the flag bridge was in vacuum. From the looks of things, it had lost pressure during the fight that destroyed the ship, and the Aventari had never bothered looking inside.

The dead were still in their seats. The center console seemed intact, but an explosion on the starboard side had scattered fragments of metal throughout the compartment. A long spar had impaled the admiral commanding the ship.

Several dead bodies sat around the remaining consoles. All of them must have been killed in the explosion as it appeared that no one had tried to assist anyone else.

The most haunting image was of a woman seated at the tactical console. A fragment of debris had shattered her helmet and left her head fully exposed to the vacuum. Her blonde hair floated around her head like a golden halo in their lights.

Her expression was one of determination, so Rick suspected the impact had killed her instantly.

Rick pushed himself into the room, stopped at the admiral's console, and stared into the dead man's eyes. "Admiral Hawthorne. We've come for you, sir. It's time to go home."

Thankfully, the escape pod set aside for the flag bridge personnel was on the opposite side of the compartment from the explosion. One of the men assigned to his team signaled Rick with a thumbs up after looking inside. It was still operational.

"Okay, everyone, let's get busy. I want these bodies secured in the pod before we get started on the rest of the ship."

While they were working, Rick turned his attention to the battle standard on the rear bulkhead. It was a big one, two meters across, showing a lion standing on a spur of rock, snarling defiantly at some unseen foe, on a light blue field.

Like the crew, it had caught some shrapnel. Numerous tears covered its surface, but it seemed salvageable. Hell, the Lions might leave it like that, battle damage and all. He seemed to remember that's what others had done throughout history.

He motioned for two of his men to secure it in the escape pod with the bodies.

"Commander, I've got something strange here," Lieutenant Malave said from the tactical console.

Rick turned around, stopping his rotation by placing a hand on the back of the command chair. Someone had already removed the woman's body, and the injured lieutenant was now seated in her place. He had the console online.

"Shouldn't that be dead?" Rick asked as he propelled himself over to join Malave.

"As long as there is emergency power, primary systems on the flag bridge should be operational. In fact, we can probably raise the lighting in here to something approaching normal. But that's not what I mean. Look at this."

One of the screens showed a compartment elsewhere in the ship, most likely the primary bridge or a backup control center. Normally, on a ship this large, the flag bridge was reserved for fleet operations, not for control of the ship. Though, if circumstances called for it, the people seated at the flag bridge consoles could certainly run things.

But, the control room on the monitor seemed completely alien.

"What am I seeing?" he asked.

"That's the *Lioness*'s bridge. Unless I've lost my mind, it looks like the Aventari tore out the original controls and replaced them with something more suitable. And see the shadows? There's no sharp demarcation with the light. It looks pressurized."

Malave turned toward Rick. His expression was very worried. "I can only think of one reason they'd do that. This isn't a derelict. They think they can salvage it."

Rick clutched the back of Malave's chair and stared at the image for several seconds. "Can you find out what other systems are functional?"

"On it."

Major Hawke pushed off the bulkhead and stopped at the scanner controls. The system came online when she touched the console.

"Be really, really careful," Rick said as he went to join her. "If they detect any unusual readings on this ship, we're going to have visitors."

"Copy that. I only have passive scanners online. And, they *are* online. Even the active scanners are available. Either they were not significantly damaged during the fighting or someone has made basic repairs to the system."

That was unsettling and more than a bit scary to Rick. What could those bastards be up to?

388 | KENNEDY & WANDREY

"What do the passive scanners tell you about the shipyard?" he asked.

She worked the console for half a minute, then swore. "I'm not an expert on Aventari shipyards, but I think this one is fully operational. Worse, it seems to be opening up."

He leaned over her shoulder and stared at the readings. The structure did appear to be unfolding like a flower facing the sun. It hadn't been like that when they came around the planet twenty minutes earlier.

"Can you tell what they're doing?"

She shook her head slightly. "Not with passive scanners. But, I suspect they have something inside they want to get out. They've likely been working on a ship of some kind, and they intend to get it into the fight."

"Work on identifying that ship. We may have to send a signal to Admiral Hawthorne. He's already in a tough fight, but if this is something big, he needs to know about it."

His suit com chimed with an incoming call from his chief engineer. He answered immediately.

"Talk to me, Kimberly."

"Someone's been busy down here. All four power plants have been repaired. It looks like they've slapped in some jury-rigged parts, but it's Union technology. Only one of them is operating on more than standby. Rick, they've also repaired the drives. This ship can move."

"Why would the Aventari render this battleship operational?" he asked slowly. "It would have taken more work to fix it than to scrap it and build something new."

"I think I can answer that," Lieutenant Malave said. "If the ship was in marginal condition, they could've repaired it and used it for defense while they got the shipyard online. Now that the yard is operational, they don't have to man it anymore and will probably scrap it at some point."

"That's what I see when I run a system check," Kimberly said. "The primary weapon systems are functional and in standby mode. Even the spinal mount."

Just like the *Lion*, the ship had a very powerful particle weapon running through her core. It was the kind of weapon that could take out a capital ship with one shot, if the shooter got lucky.

"We have another problem," Hawke said. "I think there are four ships inside the shipyard. All are at least as big as this ship. Two of them seem to be under construction, but the other two show indications of being under power. I think we're looking at a pair of mostly-completed battleships wanting to join the fight."

Rick hit the com channel for all hands. "Everyone, we need to expedite. Load all the bodies into the escape pods. Don't be overly gentle. Just get them in. Rick out."

Rick sat at the command console in the center of the flag bridge. It took him a moment to bring up the scanner readings of the shipyard. The data was limited, but the *Lioness* was far closer than any warship should be allowed to get to such a vulnerable target.

He could just make out the ships inside the yard. The two with power were being towed by small tugs to clear the yard. Once they were away from the structure, they'd be able to bring their engines online.

"Kimberly, how long will it take to bring all the power plants up to full output?"

"Fifteen minutes. I can have the one already spun up at maximum output in ten. What are you planning?"

"Let's just say we might need to move in a hurry. Are you sure the drives are going to work?" he asked.

"As sure as I can be without testing them."

"Then pray the Aventari do good work."

He killed the channel and focused on Lieutenant Malave. "You said the spinal mount is functional. How long to charge it?"

The tactical officer turned in his seat, his face paler than it had been before. "Once the first power plant is at full output, I can begin the process, but it will take every erg of power we can get. These things are power hogs. I should be ready to fire in less than five minutes once I start charging. The cycle time will improve as other power plants reach full output."

"You're not seriously considering firing on those ships, are you?" Hawke asked. "The battleships will be free to fight before we can run, and we don't have a combat crew on board. They will tear us apart."

"We probably won't get off more than a single shot with the main gun," Rick admitted. "Then we'll have to abandon ship, get back to the *Hermes*, and run like hell. But if we don't do what we can now, those ships could be the difference between victory and defeat. If the Lions lose, we lose everything. Remember, the Aventari eat live prisoners."

He considered Malave. "Have you ever fired a spinal mount?"

Malave shook his head. "Only in simulations. Also, the missile launchers are going to start failing quickly once we start shooting. They're a little finicky under the best of circumstances. Without crews to man them, they'll start jamming before we can empty the magazines."

"How many salvos do you think we'll be able to get off?"

Malave shrugged. "It's not going to be that clean. Some missile batteries will empty their available supply. Others will lock up after firing a single missile. Think of it this way. During the first launch, just about every missile battery will work as expected. We'll probably lose five or ten percent on the next salvo. After that, the rate of failure increases. That's why crews man them."

"Do the best you can," Rick told the tactical officer. "As soon as we start firing, eject the escape pods. We'll only keep a minimal crew in engineering. When the Aventari start returning fire, we'll abandon ship."

It took Rick several minutes to figure out how to bring up the spinal mount monitor on his display. Thankfully, the particle accelerator seemed to be functional and the batteries were charging quickly.

He watched the charge bar slowly climb. It would be ready to fire about the same time as the remaining power plants reached full output. They might be able to get off a second shot, if the universe smiled on them.

When it was time to fire, he ordered everyone to the shuttles except for Kimberly's people, the crew on the flag bridge, and the marines.

Minutes later, Hawke swore. "I think they just spotted us. I'm detecting a strong comm signal directed at us. It looks like they're trying to access our security feeds."

"Can you stop them? What can they do if they get in?"

"I'm working on it. If they get in, all they'll be able to do is monitor the security cameras. Ships like this aren't designed for remote

392 | KENNEDY & WANDREY

operation, and nothing I've seen indicates they've changed that. They won't be able to shut down the power plants, the weapons, or anything else.

"I'm also detecting half a dozen shuttles headed our way. We're going to have boarders about the time we fire the main gun. I'll move my marines into position to repel them."

Rick turned his attention to Lieutenant Malave. "Can we stop those shuttles?"

"The systems that normally deal with those situations are offline. I'm trying to get the antimissile defenses to lock onto them, but they weren't designed for that. So, I'd say no."

"Do the best you can. How long until we can fire the main gun?"

"Ninety seconds. What do you want me to target?"

Rick considered his console. Passive scanners weren't receiving enough data to help him choose the best target. He needed a little more time and better resolution.

"Are they still trying to access the security feeds?" he asked Hawke.

"They're trying, but so far, I've managed to shunt their access to dead parts of the ship. That probably won't work much longer."

"Give them the feed to this compartment," he ordered. "Focus the camera on me. As soon I give you the sign, I want you to kill their access again, if you can."

She looked at him in confusion but nodded. "Will do. Feed on you in three...Two...One..."

Rick stared at the video pickup and stuck his chin out defiantly. He proceeded to sing the chorus to *Never Gonna Give You Up* by Rick Astley. When he was done, he made a slashing gesture across this throat.

"What the hell was that?" Malave demanded. "That was gibberish!"

Major Hawke stared at him, her expression thunderstruck. "No. Way. You did *not* just fucking Rick Roll the Aventari."

"I told you 'Molon Labe' wasn't my style. Take the scanners to maximum while they're confused."

Kimberly pinged him through his suit comm. "Power plants at maximum output. All systems available at your command."

He brought up the helm controls on the master console and began accelerating the warship toward the shipyard. It moved significantly quicker than he expected. They wouldn't have time to get off a second shot from the spinal mount.

The feed from the active scanners began filling in the data he was missing. The two battleships being towed out of the shipyard were ninety percent complete. Significant sections of their hull plating were not installed, but it looked as if their engines and weapons were functional.

The first battleship cleared the side of the shipyard and immediately fired missiles. Moments later, a barrage of missiles rose from the shipyard itself.

"Antimissile defenses at full," Rick ordered. "Fire all missiles at the first battleship. Eject all occupied pods except for those for engineering and the flag bridge. All shuttles detach and head for the *Hermes* at maximum acceleration. This is it."

Missiles accelerated at several hundred gravities, making them dangerous weapons in space combat, because ships had little time to dodge. At this ludicrously short range, the missiles didn't have time to reach full acceleration before impact.

Two battleships exchanging missiles at point-blank range was like a knife fight in a closet. The ships couldn't stop most of the damage coming their way.

But Lieutenant Malave managed to somehow stave off more than half the incoming missiles.

The missiles that got through were enough to significantly damage the *Lioness*, but not enough to cripple her. The console in front of Rick lit up with damage indicators. Thankfully, the main gun wasn't damaged. It was heavily protected, but one never knew what would happen in a fight.

"We have boarders docking at six locations," Major Hawke said. "Marine teams are moving to repel them."

"Main gun is ready to fire," Lieutenant Malave said. "I need a target."

"Your target is the second battleship," Rick said as he leaned forward. "Burn it down. Keep missiles focused on the first one."

The lights dimmed as Malave fired the main gun. It felt as if the ship was putting every single bit of itself into the one strike.

Rick watched on the screen as the bright blue gout of energy tore through a few of the shipyard's girders and struck the enemy battleship. A section of the ship glowed brightly for a moment, then the beam ate into the hull like a blowtorch cutting through butter.

A moment later, the battleship exploded, causing significant damage to the unfinished ships and the shipyard. The explosion coupled with the missiles they were still pumping into the first ship caused it to explode a few seconds later, further wrecking the shipyard.

Missiles from the shipyard continued to slam into the *Lioness*, causing the overhead lights to fluctuate and go out. The emergency lights came on a second later.

"Bridge, engineering," Kimberly said. "One of the power plants is offline and another one is entering a runaway state. I think that hit wrecked the jury-rigged safety controls. We're less than a minute from what I'll generously call an 'unfortunate incident.'"

It was time to leave. "Get into the pods. Good luck."

He killed the channel before she could reply and looked at Hawke. "Can your people disengage, Major?"

"They're disengaged now, Commander," she said with a grin. "None of the boarders was wearing anything heavier than basic combat armor. My people thrashed them and are racing back to the shuttles. We need to get out of here if we're going to go with them."

Rick brought up the autopilot and locked the ship onto a collision course with the shipyard. Then he raised the acceleration to maximum. The console indicated impact in thirty seconds. It was time to go.

"Everyone to the escape pod," he said as he undid his harness.

They all raced to the escape pod and strapped themselves in. Twenty seconds later, they closed the hatch, and Major Hawke slammed her fist against the emergency launch button.

The G-forces as the escape pod jettisoned from the doomed battleship pinned Rick against his restraints. The small screen at the front of the pod showed the *Lioness* as they ejected. He had a ringside seat as the doomed warship slammed into the section of the shipyard housing the main fusion plants.

He didn't know if the impact detonated one of the alien plants or if the out-of-control plant on the *Lioness* blew at just the right time, but the explosion was epic. It seemed to fill the sky before guttering into darkness. There was nothing left.

Returning to the *Hermes* was somewhat anti-climactic.

* * *

Twenty-four hours later, the fighting was over. It had been a tough fight, but the Lions had beaten the Aventari. They'd destroyed every vessel in space and all the orbital assets around the planet that had fired on them. If Rick understood the situation correctly, that had been all of them.

With the system secure, the *Hermes* made the trip to the Aventari home world. They'd been very lucky, and everyone had made it back from the *Lioness*. Some were injured, but everyone was breathing. It was a real win, considering the odds.

In preparation for his meeting with Admiral Hawthorne, Rick arranged for one of the storage rooms aboard the *Hermes* to be converted into a viewing room. It felt like a wake, but it seemed like the only tasteful way to prove he'd accomplished his mission.

The Lions' battle standard hung on the rear bulkhead. In front of it, arranged in a line, the bodies from the battleship's flag bridge laid in state, covered to their necks in bright white cloths.

Major Hawke had changed into a black and gold dress uniform. She looked sharp.

"The admiral's shuttle is on final approach," she said as she stepped toward Rick. "Before he gets here, I want to take a moment to congratulate you and your people.

"I know the admiral will eventually tell you this himself, but his attention will be elsewhere for a while. He'll be grateful, just as we all are. You've done the Lions a great service."

Rick shot her a slight smile. "I just did what anyone would do. Nothing more, nothing less."

She laughed a little. "I somehow suspect getting into a knock-down-drag-out fight with a pair of battleships wasn't in your original plan. Neither was commanding a major unit in battle.

"Congratulations on that, as well. The admiral said you've earned your people a combat share and that you should damn well list it in your resume. Not many people can claim the privilege and honor of commanding a battleship in action."

"You were there," he said dryly. "That's not quite how it happened."

"That's *exactly* how it happened," she said firmly. "You recovered far more of our dead comrades than we hoped for. Ninety percent! Then you led us into battle against a stronger enemy. Don't sell yourself short, Commander.

"But that part of the story isn't what people will be talking about when they gather in bars and tell your story. No. We'll be telling everyone how you Rick Rolled the bastards. That was amazing and, as far as I know, unparalleled in the history of Human warfare in space. A true first and one worthy of free drinks for eternity."

Before he could respond to that outrageous statement, an announcement came over the speaker. "The shuttle from the *Lion* has docked, Commander. Admiral Hawthorne is en route to the viewing room."

Rick adopted a somber expression and turned toward the hatch. This was going to be a powerful moment. The man had lost his brother and now he had him back.

The hatch slid aside and Admiral Hawthorne stepped into the compartment, his face stiff as he scanned the room. His dark eyes took in the battle standard and the line of bodies with his brother at the center.

Without a word to anyone, Hawthorne walked toward his brother but stopped short when he saw the woman whose helmet had been shattered in combat.

He knelt beside her, searching for and finding her hand. And then he began to weep.

"His wife, Emily," Hawke said softly. "Lionel never got to say goodbye. He never got to bury her. She was his heart—the Lion's Heart—and you've given her back to him. For that, the Lions owe you a debt that can never be repaid."

It finally dawned on Rick that he hadn't understood the scope of his mission. His throat tightened, and he fought back tears.

"I'm glad," he finally responded, his voice raspy. "Should we step outside and give him time alone to grieve?"

"No one should be alone at a time like this. Wait with me."

The two of them stood as silent sentinels, watching the broken man who knelt beside his dead wife and sobbed.

# # # # #

What Really Matters
by Chris Winder

Tizona, Low Orbit, Planet Jeatov

Colonel Ty Jackson unsealed the black plastic pouch with some trepidation. Apparently, his food vendor had decided that not labeling the packages added a delightful element of surprise when an unsuspecting hungry Human opened them. He disagreed with the delightful part.

As the seal gave way, he held his breath. Even though he was holding his breath, the smell of the contents hit him like a spanner falling through a maintenance compartment, right in the nose.

"Holy Hell," he sputtered. "I wasn't ready for that!"

"Which one did you get?" Master Sergeant Timothy Brocado asked around the plastic spoon hanging from his mouth.

Ty coughed, holding the half-open food package away from himself as if it were a grenade. In his mind, he didn't consider that too far from the truth. "Can't you smell it?" he inquired.

"I know I sure can," Captain Rosa Conway said from her spot at tactical. She was pinching her nose and staring through squinted eyes over her hand. "You got the barf bag, didn't you?"

"I think so," he said with a note of sadness. "Barf bag" was a dysphemism for what someone had the audacity to call lasagna. To him, it smelled like a rat, long forgotten in a trap, locked in a sealed, old house on a cattle ranch in the middle of summer. "Anybody want to trade?" He surveyed the room, although he didn't really think anyone would do it. The rest of the crew broke eye contact and pretended to be busy with their own activities.

Ty leaned forward in his command chair to get a better look at what everybody else was eating. All the black bags were identical, and none of them had any writing on the outside.

"Sergeant Newton," he said to the gaunt, bald, young man sitting at the weapons station. The man launched himself from his seat to stand at attention. "First of all, quit doing that. This is a ship's Command Information Center, the CIC. I need your ass in that chair. Secondly, what did you get?"

Newton sat down, glanced from his already-open black pouch to his Colonel's and back again. "I'm pretty sure I got the little piggies," he said hesitantly.

"Little piggies" was their name for what some confused person liked to call "spaghetti." Ty wasn't sure where they got these recipes. He didn't even know if it was Humans who performed the cooking or processing of the slop. For all he knew, the cook could've been another mercenary company trying to sabotage his own by making them too sick or hungry to fight.

"Little piggies, you say?" Ty asked, stroking his chin thoughtfully. "Why, that's my favorite one. Thank you for volunteering to trade yours for mine."

Newton frowned, glanced at his meal, then at his commander's. Then he stood, brought his meal to the command chair and swapped food pouches.

"Just hold your nose, Newton," Tim said as he chewed. "Then it'll taste just like strawberries!"

Newton didn't look convinced, but tried it anyway. His gag proved the Master Sergeant's theory false. Conway gagged in sympathy. Ty greedily chewed and ignored his subordinate's suffering.

The Crimson Corps was small compared to most mercenary companies. The one thing they did well—the one thing they did better than most other companies—was outthink their opponents. It was for this reason they'd been offered a subcontract by the Yorktown Dragoons, just in case things did not go according to plan. If it came down to it, the Corps was supposed to pull their asses out of the fire.

Newton took a deep breath, eyes watering, and squeezed the rest of the gelatinous, thick concoction into his mouth. He gagged again, chewed as fast as he could, and swallowed hard.

"Well," Ty said with a wry smile, "if we get boarded, I'll just have Newton breathe on the enemy. If they don't flee, they'll surrender for sure." The bridge erupted into laughter.

"Sir," Lieutenant Francisco Herrera asked, "permission to turn up the filtration system?" He had one hand covering his mouth and was staring at the now-empty black bag as if he was afraid it would attack him at any moment.

Ty smiled, showing his teeth, which he knew would be covered by a thick layer of the food-like substance he'd forced into his gut.

Francisco, who liked to be called "Cisco," tried to hide his dismay, but failed miserably.

"Denied," he said. "We need to keep our power signature to a minimum. If the Jivool have a spacecraft in the area, we don't want to attract its attention. So, denied. I will do one thing, though."

Cisco's brows shot up.

"Captain Conway," Ty said to his tactical officer, "please make a note for when we get back home. Let's fire this supplier and find someone who can make a meal that doesn't stink like dirty Oogar butt."

"Yes, sir," Conway said enthusiastically as she jotted the note into her slate—a small, flat computer she kept with her all the time.

A tone sounded from her terminal, and she turned to address it. "Sir, Fifth Battalion has arrived. They've started launching dropships."

"Very well," Ty said from his position in the command chair near the rear of the bridge.

"Tim," he said, addressing the Master Sergeant standing to his right, "join our troops. Make sure they're ready. The Yorktown Dragoons are tough, but they hired us for reason. Make sure the men understand how serious this is."

"Yes, sir," Tim said through the huge, gray mustache that covered both his lips. Then he performed a perfect about-face and marched from the bridge.

"Incoming transmission, sir," Cisco reported. "Narrow-band communications laser. They're a lot farther away than we thought they'd be. There also seems to be a lot of debris or dust between us and them. I've informed their comm officer. They adjusted the transmission. We're receiving less data, but it's clean."

"So, we aren't going to see the whole picture?"

"Yes, sir. It's a little slow, and we're a little blind, but it allows us to remain stealthy. Anything you want to say to their comm officer?"

"Yes, please ask them how we are supposed to know if things aren't going well. Also, ask if they plan on relaying everything to us from the ground. Remind them our transmissions are poor, and we

can't be sure we'll be able to get there in time if we don't get telemetry. Also inform them that this is beginning to sound a lot like breach
of contract. As we have arrived and performed our responsibilities, if
they refuse to provide information—their part of the contract—then
we're done here. I can turn the comms off, sit on my ass, and collect
my payment, regardless of how the day goes."

There was a delay of 30 seconds between sending the message,
the crew of *Shield Maiden* processing it, and their reply. "Sir," Cisco
said, "the *Shield Maiden* has provided access to the general communications channel they're using. We'll be able to listen to everything
they're transmitting between their vessels and the ground. We'll also
receive some basic telemetry. Shall I send it to the main Tri-V?"

"That'll work," Ty said. A bit of stress left him like a weight being lifted from his shoulders. There was no such thing as too much
information, not when lives were at stake. He began to wonder how
serious the Yorktown Dragoons were about his contract.

The Yorktown Dragoons were paying the Crimson Corps well to
have the *Tizona* available if needed. However, if they wanted the
Corps to succeed, if they wanted Dragoon troops saved if the worst
should happen, Ty needed everything.

Speakers concealed within the walls of the CIC of the *Tizona*
burst into a cacophony of transmissions. Requests, status updates,
and data bursts crackled through the room like shotgun blasts.

Cisco used his terminal to channel the signals into their types and
adjusted the volume. "Sorry about that, everyone. I'm filtering out
the stuff we don't need right now and homing in on the transmissions from the dropships. They did a good job setting signal priori-
ties. It'll make the most urgent ones take priority." A few seconds
later, the transmissions played through the speakers again, but in-

stead of being a loud, jumbled mess, they were played one at a time. Whichever craft was making the transmission was highlighted on the Tri-V.

"Touch down in two minutes," one of the landing craft pilots sent.

"Incoming!" another transmitted. "Looks like short-range rockets." The dropships widened their formation to avoid dozens of dumb rockets which soared past their vessels.

"Returning fire," another pilot said. His ship's icon indicated it had begun to use its rail guns, strafing an enemy emplacement. The rest of the dropships in the immediate area also opened up.

"Resistance neutralized," one of the pilots said. "Ten seconds."

"Well," Ty said, more to himself than anyone else. "That was easier than I thought it would be."

"Sir," Conway said, "I have a tactical overlay available. It's going to be delayed as I try to figure out where everybody is, but it's the best we're going to get with the amount of data we're receiving. Would you like me to add it to the display?"

"Make it so," Ty said as he leaned forward in his command chair. Conway would use her pinplant to create a map of the battlefield based on the data she was receiving and the communications they could all hear.

The original tactical display on the Tri-V dimmed considerably and was overlaid by Conway's new information. Eighteen dropships had been launched from the two cruisers the Fifth Battalion had brought. The cruisers themselves were far too large and heavy to enter the atmosphere.

Sixteen of the craft landed and began to disgorge their troops. The other two began circuitous patrols of the perimeter as it grew.

Most likely providing close air support, he mused. *It's what I would've done.*

He watched as dozens of icons appeared outside of the landed dropships. The icons multiplied several times as the troops separated, forming rough, protective formations around their landing zones. When all the troops had disgorged from the sixteen dropships, the transports launched into the air.

"Conway," Ty ordered, "show me how far away their first objective is."

A new icon appeared on the display. "How far is that from their troops?" he asked.

"Two, maybe three miles," Conway breathed, her voice distant like it always got when she concentrated on something else. "It's hard to be sure. We didn't get a lot of details with the mission briefing. We know what we're supposed to do, but not what they're going to be doing. The first target is a fortress of some kind to their northwest, magnetically speaking."

"Well, it should only take them a couple minutes to get there if they hurry," Cisco said. "They've got Mk 7s, right?"

"Looks like it," Conway said.

"It would only take five minutes for us to make that distance in our old Mk 6s," Ty added. "Although that's only if we didn't run into trouble. But the Jivool have to know they're coming. I mean, the contract was advertised. It wasn't a secret."

Everyone in the CIC murmured in agreement.

The target's icon shifted closer to the icons for the troops on the ground as Conway adjusted the image with new data. "Sir," she said in her dreamy voice, "the Dragoons have engaged the enemy."

"Switching to the transmissions from the ground commanders," Cisco said.

The channel was almost silent. The Dragoons performed their duties with practiced, efficient lethality. Ty watched the Tri-V as threat icons appeared, then disappeared. "Damn," he whispered. "It's a slaughter."

"Sure is," Sergeant Newton said as he craned his neck and watched the battle. "Are the Jivool even fighting back?"

"Oh, the Jivool are fighting back," Cisco said. "But damn, the Fifth is hitting them hard!"

As the battle continued, its pace slowed but only a little. The troops continued to advance. Threat icons appeared and disappeared. The enemy, it seemed, had gotten themselves in way over their big, furry heads.

Ty watched the hologram with a mixture of shock, horror, and amusement. The Jivool, part of a syndicate known as *Moklek's Hand*, had captured a red diamond mine and its nearby ancient fortress from another syndicate. At least, that was the story.

The Yorktown Dragoons had been hired to take it back. If they were successful, there would be a bonus. Ty's Crimson Corps, however, would not get a bonus unless there was someone for them to rescue. They had to enter the battle at the request of the Dragoons. Otherwise, their job consisted of maintaining stealth and staying out of the way.

Ty watched the battle progress, leaned back in his chair, picked up a water pouch at his side, took a sip, and glanced around the room. Sweat glistened on Captain Conway's forehead. Ty checked the chronometer at the bottom of the Tri-V display and realized she'd been tapped in, updating the tactical display of the battle, such as it were, for over three hours. According to what he could see, it would be over in another ten minutes.

"Captain Conway," Ty said, "why don't you go ahead and take a break? I think we know how this battle's going to end."

"I can keep going, sir," she said. Her voice sounded strained, tired.

"That's an order, Conway. Disconnect. Take a break. I can get you a barf bag if you want," he said. "I'm sure we have some more in supply."

Conway disconnected from her data terminal and chuckled, turning tired, watery eyes his direction. "No thanks, sir. You know, we can always keep those nasty things and feed them to troublemakers instead of bread and water. It might be more effective."

"It might," Ty said, "but who really gets punished then, us or them?"

The crew snickered.

Cheering from the CIC's speakers alerted the crew that the battle was over.

"What?" Ty asked himself as he leaned forward and checked the chronometer again. "It's only been two hours, and the first objective is secure?" Thoughts of upgrades to the ship, a vacation, maybe a nice night, or a dozen nice nights on the town seemed far away. Ty frowned and began mentally scratching things he'd wanted to purchase off his list.

The slate near Ty's right hand beeped twice indicating an incoming transmission from onboard. He answered it, and Master Sergeant Timothy Brocado's gray, bushy mustache and eyebrows filled the display.

"It's over?" Tim asked.

"Sure looks like it, Tim. What the hell happened?"

Tim looked to his right, to his own slate, and shook his head thoughtfully. "It doesn't look like the Dragoons have too many troops for the mission. It was only one battalion against twice as many Jivool. So, either they're more badass than we thought, communications security was better than we thought, or the Jivool seriously underestimated them."

The two men were silent for several seconds, each lost in his own thoughts about how much money the Dragoons had made in such little time.

"Well, I guess we're stuck with the flat fee. Are they going for the secondary objective?" Tim asked, pale, blue eyes watching his commander's face.

"I sent Conway on a break, so my info is limited, but I'd continue on, wouldn't you?"

"Yes, sir, I would," Tim confirmed.

Both men listened to the next transmission. The Dragoons were leaving one platoon behind to hold the fortress while the rest redeployed to the east.

"Sounds like they read our minds," said Tim. "This might be where the real battle begins. Confined spaces, chance of cave-in. Gotta be careful what weapons you use in a mine. CASPers are tough, but not thousands of tons of rock and dirt tough."

"Agreed," Ty said. "They still have all the dropships and what looks like all their troops. Damn, they stomped their target hard."

Tim chuckled, which always gave Ty goosebumps because it sounded like someone shaking a bag of gravel. "Yep. Mind if I feed my troops?"

"Go ahead," Ty said. "I don't think we're gonna see any action today."

Ty thought about having a snack, but instead he decided to make a list and prioritize what he'd upgrade and repair once they'd been paid. This time, he'd have to shorten the list to just the essentials. No frills. No upgrades. No party. No fun.

Ty knew it was time to be responsible. It was time to make sure the ship kept flying, the crew was fed, and there was money socked-away to purchase more F11 for when this was all over.

Tim's troops would perform most of the maintenance on the *Tizona* with Tim himself acting as maintenance chief. That, along with the man's responsibility as security chief, would have earned him an additional portion of the bonus, money which was clearly not coming in anymore. The crew would have to listen to the grumbling and complaining for days to come.

Ty knew Tim performed both duties well. They were still flying, and nothing was on fire, at least for the moment. It's all he could expect from the old Cayuse-class fast frigate. He'd bought her, along with three other vessels, after receiving his inheritance. His father had served with the Yorktown Dragoons' First Battalion, had been promoted several times, and died during an operation. The circumstances were unclear, but money was involved. Money was always involved in the big tragedies. It was his father's dream that his son would someday start his own mercenary company. To help with that dream, he'd squirreled away as many credits as he could.

That money, along with the death benefit from the Dragoons, provided Ty with enough capital to get started. He himself had served with two other companies but was dissatisfied with how they ran their businesses.

Once he'd bought his first three ships, he hired Timothy, Newton, and Cisco, along with some temporary engineers, to bring his idea to fruition. From those three ships, he'd envisioned and developed the *Tizona*. He called it a "sleeper"—a vessel that looked like it was made to haul foodstuffs and furniture, chugging lazily through the galaxy on another boring delivery, but was so much more.

Fitted with an additional three power plants, the *Tizona* could generate enough power for a battlecruiser and then some. He also transferred all the point-defense laser systems from the other ships and integrated them into her systems.

The point-defense lasers only produced two-megawatt beams apiece, but there were eighty-three of them. Individually, they could intercept most incoming rockets and missiles. Together, they, along with their quick-charging capacitors, could produce a potential 120 MW pulse of energy every half-second, depending on how many happened to be pointed in the right direction. The effects were devastating.

The reactors and three concealed fusion drives used up a lot of internal space. So much so, that the ship's normal freight capacity was cut by more than fifty percent. As a general transport vessel, she was inefficient and useless. In a hostile environment, she was formidable.

His team compensated by automating the ship's functions as much as possible. The construction had almost tapped him dry. The most expensive part had been purchasing enough F11 for five fusion reactors, but there was no such thing as spaceflight without F11.

"Looks like they're going to take their time with the mines," Cisco reported. "They've slowed their assault. They're setting patrols and...yup, entering the mines."

The CIC was silent for several minutes as they listened to the incoming feed. Then Cisco had a grim idea. "What if it's a trap, sir? That battle went pretty easy. What if the Jivool are waiting for most of the Dragoon elements to enter before detonating some bombs and burying most of them alive?"

"Oh, good point," Conway confirmed. "What do you think, sir?"

"I agree," Ty said as he stroked his chin. "But, the Dragoons are more experienced than us, and it's their ass on the line. I'm sure they've thought of it." He thought for a moment and added, "Captain Conway, is there anything within sensors that looks dangerous, hostile, or otherwise demands our attention?"

"Nothing within sensor range, sir. Two Yorktown Dragoon cruisers station-keeping above the battle zone. Lots of Dragoon troops on the ground. And us, sitting here all nice and pretty, dark as a hole in space. Looks like this is going to be an easy one, sir."

"Just what I wanted to hear," Ty said as he stood and stretched. "Captain Conway, I'm setting a watch. I'll take the first three hours, but there's no reason for all of us to be up here staring at a battle when we know exactly how it's going to go. I'll keep one eye on the sensors, and the other on the one reactor we have running. Go get a snack, some sleep, or whatever. Be back to relieve me in three hours. Cisco will relieve you after that."

"Yes, sir," both Conway and Cisco said in unison. The rest of the bridge crew yawned, stretched and exited.

Ty tapped a few commands into his slate, brought the power plant status up, and added the data to the main Tri-V display. The fusion plant was only running at five percent of its maximum power, just enough to keep the tiny sun at its core fed. Satisfied, Ty stood, removed his slate, and began pacing back and forth across the small

CIC, planning how he wanted to spend the money the Corps would earn.

* * *

Tim sat at the head of the long table, listening to his troops trade insults, sea-stories, and jokes they'd told each other a dozen times before. Their battle armor hung from hooks along the walls behind them, ready for deployment, but unpowered. It would only take a few minutes for them to lock each piece in place and power them on. Nobody thought they'd need the armor, but he insisted they keep it close.

He spun his coffee cup, now empty, in small, partial rotations on the table. He thought about his age and wondered again if he should retire. Seventy was old, even by his own standards. He'd seen a lot, been through a lot, and lost a lot of friends. He was thankful his troops would not be in harm's way on this mission, but he was also counting on the bonus to finally pack it all up and leave mercenary life behind him.

"What do you think about that, Master Sergeant?" one of his troops asked.

Tim hadn't been listening, so he had no idea what the man was talking about. But it didn't matter. He had a response prepared, one he'd canned and could slop out whenever he wanted. "It's garbage," he said. "All garbage."

"B…but, Master Sergeant," the man stammered, "I was going to…"

"Shaddap!" Tim snapped. "What you were going to do is shut your coffee-hole and go clean your armor!" The man got up from

the table without another word and began doing as he was instructed.

Tim dragged his gaze across the rest of the men at the table.
"Well? You telling me your armor is clean, ready to fight, perfect,
and ready for me to inspect?"

"Yes, Master Sergeant!" his men roared in unison.

"Bullshit," he said, slamming his fist on the table. The echo from
his strike on the metal furniture echoed in the now-silent room for
several seconds. "I say it's not clean enough, so clean it again!"

He understood that most of his rage stemmed from the fact that
he'd have to complete at least one more mission, probably two or
three, before he could retire, but that didn't stop him. The troops
would learn, one way or another, that there was no such thing as
over-prepared.

* * *

Ty was still pacing when his slate flashed an alert across
the top, indicating there was a new player in the field.
At first, he didn't understand what he was seeing. His
mind had been on supplies, foodstuffs, and the lack of funds to
make the upgrades he'd wanted.

He turned his attention to the main Tri-V and felt his stomach
hit the floor. He hadn't realized the three hours had passed until
Conway entered a moment later and gasped.

"Um, who is that?" she asked as she rushed to her station.

"I don't know," Ty said. "Get me some info."

A few seconds later, she responded. "This isn't good, sir. They
aren't Dragoon craft. I'm not sure who they are. I'm seeing six de-

stroyers, four battlecruisers, and two battleships. Oh, hell, and at least thirty interceptors!"

Tim activated the quiet alert system which would bring everyone to battle stations without giving away their position to the new fleet.

A second later, a low, rhythmic thrum pulsed through every room and passageway, a war-drum tattoo that sent the crew to their battle stations. As sound wasn't transmitted in the dark void of space, the chance that his alert would be detected was extremely low.

Thirty seconds later, the CIC was fully crewed again, though Sergeant Newton at the weapons station slumped in his chair.

"Wake up, Newton!" Cisco snapped. "We might need you to kill something."

"I'm good, sir," Newton said as he twisted both his fists into his eyes. "Just woke up is all. Standin' by."

"Keep it cold," Ty ordered. "Don't power anything on until I say so. It doesn't look like they spotted us."

"It does now, sir," Conway reported.

Ty's eyes shot to the Tri-V, and a shiver ran up his spine. Three small vessels had launched from the nearest battleship and were headed in their direction. "Boarding craft," he whispered.

"Confirmed, sir," Conway agreed. "Those look like *Brrkarr*-class vessels. We have three points they could board from, and it looks like they're going to use all of them."

"Any chance they're someone else?" Ty asked.

Conway studied the data for a few moments, then said, "No, sir. They're on course to intercept us. Estimated time of arrival is 10 minutes. We could have the fusion plans online, maybe run before that happens, sir."

Ty considered his options for a moment and studied the Tri-V. It looked like the syndicate had a different kind of trap in mind. It looked like they wanted to take out the entire Fifth Battalion, and it looked as if they had the means to do it.

"What's going on?" Tim demanded as he barged into the CIC, fists clenched.

"Looks like we're about to be boarded," Ty said. "Do you think you can arrange a welcoming committee for our guests?"

A wicked grin spread Tim's mustache wide. "I'd love to, sir," he said. "I'll make sure the party favors are ready too." Then he nodded to Newton, who chuckled and mashed an icon at his terminal with his thumb. "It'll be a party they won't soon forget," Tim said before turning and leaving the CIC.

"Incoming!" Conway reported. "Two low-yield missiles. They're heading toward our stern. Probably targeting our fusion torches. Looks like they want to disable us."

"We should already look like we're disabled," Cisco scoffed.

"Yeah," she said. "We should, but it looks like they're not gonna take any chances. Hell, they haven't even tried to contact us yet."

"Now they have," Cisco said as something flashed on his screen. "Sir, do you want me to put this up on the Tri-V?"

"Please do," Ty said.

A second later, a hairy, toothy visage appeared. It growled, snarled, and snapped its jaws. The computer translated the language instantly.

"Unknown vessel, you are in a battle zone. Therefore, you will be detained until we can determine your origin, purpose, and threat potential. If you attempt to flee or activate shields, you will be destroyed."

"They warn us after they've launched missiles?" Newton asked. "Also, sir, I don't have any power to shoot those things down. Can we spin up another power plant?"

Ty thought about it a moment before answering. "Negative. Let them in. We have enough surprises for them, and hopefully the rest of their fleet will turn their attention away from us so we can figure out what to do next, like possibly earning our bonus."

"The missiles are still coming, sir," Conway reported. "Five minutes until impact."

"Damage estimation?" Ty asked.

"Those will take out our two visible fusion torches for sure. Beyond that, I don't know. I just can't be sure. Especially since we don't have any shields up at the moment. Engineering should be empty."

"Very well. Let's get them nice and close before we teach them a lesson."

* * *

"You've got two whole minutes to get your damn armor on, get sealed, and be ready to fight!" Tim ordered. "Do you need me to hold your hand and show you how it's done?"

"No, Master Sergeant," the men shouted back.

"Then get your asses moving, now!"

Tim charged to the closest man who appeared to be having trouble getting his seal secure.

"What are you waiting for, Matthews? You waiting for me to say please, for me to ask nicely, for me to bribe you with credits so you don't get dead? Did you forget *all* your training?"

"No, Master Sergeant," the man stuttered, "it's just . . ."

"It's just what?"

Tim's blood boiled as he waited for the man to continue his explanation or pathetic excuse, whatever was. He glanced down and saw the problem.

"I'd ask you when's the last time you cleaned your armor's seals, but I don't have time to listen to your stupid excuses."

Tim snatched a forgotten butter knife from the nearby galley table and dug a colorful piece of gunk out of the seal. He took a moment to sniff it and eyed the man suspiciously. "We'll talk about the candy you're hiding later—if you survive," Tim hissed.

"What about you?" Tim roared as he vaulted across the table to the opposite wall, scattering dishes across the floor. The man he approached looked terrified.

"Master Sergeant," the man said, "I think...I think my suit is dead in the water."

"Dead in the water? I don't see any water, Private. What are you talking about?"

"I don't have any power, sir. My battery is busted."

Tim stomped the floor in a small circle and when he rounded on the private again, he reached in with both hands and ripped the man's helmet off his head.

"Next time," Tim roared, "it will be your head! Get out of my sight. Grab a rifle if you can manage, and get your ass to the CIC. You're going to be their security detail while I play with our new guests. Move—now!"

The man scrambled, stopped for a moment at the weapons locker to grab a rifle and extra ammunition, and fled the room.

* * *

"**B**esquith here? Who invited them?" Ty was beside himself, pacing back and forth in the CIC, frustration almost making him glow with rage.

Then the missiles detonated, causing the *Tizona* to shudder.

"Damage report!" he snapped.

"Minimal damage, sir," Cisco reported. "The drives they were aiming for are offline. One minute until their ships intercept, sir."

"Well, it's no use pretending like we're a hole in space anymore, but I'm still curious how they found us."

Sergeant Newton cracked his knuckles. "They've locked onto the hull, sir. Standing by with the party favors."

"Sir," Conway said, "the Dragoon cruisers have engaged the enemy. Looks like they're going to try to hold the beasts off until they can get their troops back on board. I don't see how they're going to do it."

Ty studied the Tri-V for a moment. "They're not," he confirmed. "Have we received an extraction request yet?"

"Negative," Cisco replied. "You want me to ask?"

"Yes. Inform them we're being boarded. Soon as we can knock these ticks off our ass, we'll go get them." There was a long pause before anyone said anything else.

"Problem, sir," Cisco said. "It looks like the explosions also got our transmitter. We can still receive, but we can't send anything."

Ty opened his mouth to speak and then closed it again. There wasn't a clause that allowed him to take the initiative and enter the atmosphere without a request from the Dragoons. The Crimson Corps would be paid for the service they already completed. They'd shown up and were waiting in orbit, but he couldn't guarantee they would earn the bonus. He glanced at his crew in the CIC and thought they might be thinking the same thing. Each of them was glancing from their consoles to the Tri-V, weighing duty and survival.

"I'm the commander," Ty said. "I make the final decision, but I want your input. There's no guarantee we'll get a bonus if we go to the surface. But, do we want to leave the Dragoon troops behind? Is that the reputation we want to set for the Crimson Corps? Don't answer now, but as soon as we've taken care of the intruders, we'll need to quickly decide what our next move is."

"Here they come," Newton reported as he hovered his finger above a set of icons at his terminal. The Tri-V in the center of the room changed to display a view of what was happening near the bow. The enemy ships had mated with the three hatches. The invaders were cutting through the hatches with lasers. A few seconds later, the access portals fell from their frames. There was no sound from the Tri-V, and to Ty's mind, it almost seemed as if he were watching a movie instead of real life.

"Boom!" Newton said as he mashed two fingers down on two separate icons. A thick, armored panel, roughly half the size of the opening the intruders had cut through the hatch, shot out of the wall on powerful, extending electric solenoids. The first lightly-armored Besquith to step through was crushed under the force of the armored plate. Though they couldn't see what happened to the other invaders behind the first, there was a cloud of blood and what appeared to be intestines wrapped around the now-stationary panel.

Ty looked to the outer-view of where the vessel was docked, half-expecting to see several Besquith bodies punch out of the other side of the craft. He was disappointed it hadn't happened and almost laughed.

The other two vessels must have been warned because their troops backed up into their ships, and from the relative safety, fired their laser rifles through the breach to disable the mechanism on the other side of the passageway.

Ty glanced at Newton and noted the man was frowning.

"Status of the enemy fleet?" Ty asked.

"They're still advancing on the cruisers," Conway said. "There's a lot of missiles in the black, and it's not looking good for the Dragoons. We need to hurry up and sweep out these invaders if we're going to do anything."

"Did you hear that, Tim?" Ty said to the air.

"Yeah, I heard," Tim grumbled. "Just waiting for Newton's confounded gadgets to soften them up before we finish 'em off."

The weapons officer watched his display and his hands hovered over several more sets of icons, deciding which ones to use based on the movement of the enemy. Obviously, one or more of them had reached another trap because he stabbed an icon triumphantly and then moaned in disappointment when the trap failed.

The Tri-V displayed the trap—a pair of jaws that snapped from the deck on a hinge and met in the middle—meant to literally chop a man-sized invader in half. Besquith were big, though, and it was more likely to cut them right about their groin, which would've been fine if the trap worked. Instead, only one side of the trap had launched. The other side appeared to be stuck, and one Besquith lay curled on the ground, both hands on his groin, while his comrades destroyed the trap.

Tim's gravelly snicker filled the air of the CIC. "Looks like you blew that one, Newton," he teased.

The weapons officer didn't respond. He pouted and watched the invaders advance.

"Where are they headed, Sergeant Newton?" Ty asked.

"Looks like the first two squads are en route to the bridge, sir. The last one looks like it's patrolling for the Master Sergeant's team. Not sure. They might be confused or worried. I hope they get movin' again. I got way more surprises for 'em!"

"Contact!" Tim reported.

Ty took his seat in his command chair and reattached his slate. *I need to calm down*, he told himself. *I need to maintain control, confidence, and stay aware of what's going on.* He watched as five of the icons designating Tim and four others engaged the Besquith stragglers.

"We got three of them, but there are still about a dozen left," Tim transmitted. "We're backing up to the next surprise, Newton. You'd better be ready."

"I got this," Newton said. "Just keep 'em coming after you."

"Not gonna be a problem," Tim grunted.

The weapons officer jabbed three more icons.

"Don't move so fast, Master Sergeant," Newton instructed. "I want to get them all at the same time if I can."

"Don't tell me how to do my job!" Tim yelled, but his icons indicated he was slowing down.

"Almost," Newton whispered. "Just a little more. Just a little more. Got you!" He jammed his finger down on an icon and cheered in victory.

Ty watched as the advancing Besquith looked around in confusion. Both doors, which had previously been open to the room they found themselves in, slammed shut. Less than a second later, their expressions turned from confusion to utter disbelief as the outer wall of the 30-foot long room popped off into space and they were sucked into the void. Five seconds later, the gap began to close as the hatch of what use to be a hanger groaned into position and sealed the room.

Newton grinned at his commander, pure joy on his face.

"You are one twisted son of a bitch," Ty said, but he was also grinning.

"The situation down below has gone to shit, sir," Conway reported.

Ty wondered how worse the situation could get. "Report," he ordered.

"Besquith dropships have landed, sir. We didn't see them around the other side of the planet. The ground forces are engaging them, but they are outnumbered."

"Best guess?"

"Two-to-one, sir." The temperature in the room seemed to drop a few degrees, and everyone was silent, except for Newton, who jabbed another icon with a hiss.

"They're getting slaughtered down there, sir," Cisco said, his voice trembling. "We should go down there. Drag the damned boarding craft with us. Just seal up the holes. Hell, just blast them now. If we hurry…"

"Silence!" Ty snapped. "Do you think I built this company on my generosity?" He pointed at the Tri-V, which clearly displayed the retreating line of Dragoons and their advancing Besquith enemies. "Do you think they would do the same for us? No! That would be foolish. This is business—that's all! Mercs sign up to throw themselves at whoever their enemy is today. If they want our help, they'll ask for it, and then they'll pay for it. End of discussion!"

The bridge remained silent for nearly a minute, beside the speakers' crackle of hurried, panicked orders being barked among the Dragoons.

"They're attempting to reform their line, sir," Conway said. "It doesn't look like they have a chance, though. They're all going to die. You know what Besquith do to their dead enemies."

Ty ignored the comment. Sympathy didn't win battles, and it didn't repair starships.

"Sir, we just received an official call for help from the surface," Cisco reported.

"Well, that's more like it," Ty said, straightening his slate-gray uniform, the least expensive color he could find. "Okay, let's take care of these doggies and go rescue whoever we can. Cisco, bring up three of our power plants."

"New report from the Dragoons, sir," Cisco reported. "The Besquith aren't just attacking them. They're attacking the Jivool as well. It's a slaughter."

"The Jivool didn't hire the Besquith company?" Ty stared in bewilderment at his communications officer.

"Doesn't look like it, sir. We have a third party involved."

"Another call for help, sir. A...Lieutenant Novak. Apparently, he thinks the name means something."

Ty watched the Dragoon line crumble. The enemy was among them, and soon, through them. Icons representing the Human warriors vanished. He swallowed and felt his breath catch in his throat. He had to cough before he could speak again.

"It doesn't," Ty said. "I don't want to hear of any more calls for help. I already know."

"Tim," Ty transmitted, "we need to get those dogs taken care of right the fuck now. We need to move. They're getting slaughtered down there. Do what you have to do, just don't blow us up."

"Yes, sir," Tim replied, sounding grim and determined.

"Sir," Newton reported, "one of the squads has reached the bridge. Looks like they're going to cut through."

Conway changed the Tri-V display to show a view of what the enemy was doing. They were creating a hole in the armored hatch, but it seemed too small even to reach one of their large arms into.

"What are they doing?" Ty wondered.

His question was answered when one of them struck the spot they'd been working on, a small circle only a little larger than one of their large fists, and tossed a grenade through the hole. As soon as it exploded, they continued to cut around the door and entered, looking confused.

"Yep," Newton said, "that's where they expected us to be. They never expected a frigate to have a CIC." Then he laughed.

A series of beeps caught Newton's attention. "Finally," he said. "Hey y'all, watch this! This one's my favorite."

The crew turned their attention back to the Tri-V, some of them having to get up from their seats to see it. A squad of Besquith were advancing through a long corridor between a storage room and a secondary engineering bay, which contained the life-support system and one of the power plants, currently offline.

"Here it comes," Newton squeaked. A second later, he gently tapped an icon at his terminal.

The two Besquith in front, slinking forward shoulder-to-shoulder, were impaled when the floor in front of them suddenly snapped itself vertically and extended foot-long spikes.

The two Besquith at the rear backed up a few steps, right into another trap, and were similarly skewered.

Those in between seemed uncertain of which way they should go, but all had their attention turned to the ground expecting another trap. The trap didn't come from the ground, though. Instead, long spikes folded out from the ceiling, and when it fell, it impaled them from above. Thousands of little pieces of confetti followed the falling ceiling and filled the air, swirling about before settling on every surface.

"Happy birthday!" Newton cried as he stood holding both hands above his head, cackling madly.

Three *Tizona* troops emerged from their hidden ambush locations in engineering to survey the scene.

"Really?" Tim transmitted. "Confetti?"

Newton sat back down, and his smile faded a little. "Yes, Master Sergeant," he said.

"I hope you know I'm not cleaning up this mess," Tim said.

"Yes, Master Sergeant," Newton replied. Ty was impressed that the man could sound sad while still grinning from ear to ear.

"How many are left?" Ty asked. The communications among the Dragoons was beginning to become sparse. He forced himself not to think about how many his hesitation had...*No*, he told himself. *The Besquith killed them, not me.*

"Just two," Conway replied. "The rest have been taken out by other squads and traps."

Newton pressed another icon on his terminal.

"I stand corrected," Conway said. "The boarders have been neutralized."

"Good," Ty said. "Now, get those ticks off the *Tizona's* ass. Get us down to the surface now!" The crew breathed a sigh of relief. Help was on the way, and they were the help.

"Yes, sir," Newton said before jabbing three icons. The CIC shuddered as shaped-charge explosives—hidden around the hatches through which the invaders had entered—blew, sending thousands of pieces of shrapnel through the vessels.

"Spin up the rest of our power plants," Ty ordered. "Deploy our other three fusion drives. Let's go earn our bonus."

The *Tizona* vibrated a little and something in a nearby wall rattled loose and began to bounce and tumble to a lower deck. Ty hoped it wasn't something important.

The remaining fusion torches came online and sent him back into his seat. Some of the crew leaned a little to one side, because their stations weren't pointed directly at the bow of the *Tizona*.

Normally, such a maneuver would have been difficult for a pilot who was unable to lift his or her arms. However, Conway was also the pilot, among her other duties, and all she had to do was concentrate. Her thoughts and pinplants did the rest.

Ty watched through watering eyes as the Tri-V display in the center of the room showed their progress. The 300-foot-long, squashed sphere-shaped craft bucked once as the bow collided with the outer atmosphere of Jeatov. Something tore loose with a screech, then bounced and smashed along the skin of the ship, barely heard but felt from the center of the five-deck craft as it careened toward the surface. Ty found himself again hoping whatever fell off wasn't that important.

Conway cut the power to the thrusters and let gravity and momentum draw them closer. The bridge crew took a deep breath and straightened themselves in their chairs.

"We have interceptors incoming, sir," Conway reported. "Twenty minutes until they reach us. There are six of them."

"We need to hurry, then!" Ty barked. "Let's not tangle with any more than we must. Get us down there! Newton, destroy anything with fur. The Yorktown Dragoons don't employ non-humans. Therefore, if it's not human, it dies."

"Yes, sir." Newton was hunched over his terminal, nose almost touching the screen, his usual pose when he was getting ready for a fight. "Should I warm...*it*...up?"

The crew glanced at their commander, almost in unison. The *it* Newton had referred to was not an option Ty wanted to consider. However, Newton was right, and he knew he should keep his options open. Ty opened his mouth to answer in the affirmative, but the stares of his subordinates closed it again. He was afraid his voice might crack, or he might sound happy about it. Instead, he simply nodded. Newton did likewise and tapped an icon.

Ty had acquired his weapons officer from a planetary government, for which he had completed a contract. It was only simple cargo movement, one of those don't-ask, don't-tell jobs. Six large boxes, and what was inside was none of his business. While having dinner with the local governor, the man expressed his deep appreciation, bemoaning all the trouble he was having and how much crime in his district was costing him. It was an obvious attempt to get out of paying the full price for the contract.

When Ty expressed his own need for the money so he could hire a weapons officer, his client's eyes lit up. He happened to have a

428 | KENNEDY & WANDREY

prisoner who had been captured from a vessel committing piracy in his region. The prisoner claimed to be a weapons officer. After dinner, Ty met Newton and bought the man from the governor, who happily transferred ownership to Ty for half of the contract payout.

Technically, according to the planetary laws and the receipt the governor provided, Ty owned the man. He would not, however, enforce the ownership. There was no way to officially give the man his freedom, so as far as Newton knew, he was a free man. Ty liked it that way.

"I have a landing zone, sir," Conway reported. "Looks like the troops on the ground have cleared some trees for us. It'll be a tight fit, might get some scratches on the hull, but we can make it."

"Good, take us in. Newton, keep us safe."

"Tim, do you copy?" Ty transmitted.

The old man double-clicked his comm, indicating he did.

"Stand by! We're heading into a hot zone. We're going to pick up some troops. This may be all we get. How copy?"

Another double-click. Ty knew that Tim would have his men stationed at the loading dock, rifles and grenades at the ready to help whoever was still alive make it to their hold.

Ty opened his mouth to deliver another order but gasped when his body was whipped painfully to the right.

"We've been hit!" Conway reported. "Energy weapon from the surface. Looks like a tank."

"Got 'em!" Newton yelled from his station. Blood flowed freely from his nose which he'd smashed into his console during maneuvers. He wiped his sleeve across his blood-flecked terminal screen and turned several lasers toward the enemy.

The lasers consisted of an emitter and a vibrating mirror which moved 120 degrees back and forth several times per second. In this way, the lasers did not have to be aimed. The weapons officer could pick a target, fire, and whichever lasers happened to be pointing in that direction would blast the target. It wasn't perfect—there were small dead-zones here and there—but usually it meant that the time it took to aim the lasers was nil.

The first tank, camouflaged and hiding amongst dense trees, exploded in a shower of sparks, setting fire to everything around it. Newton began to pepper the area near the tanks in an ever-widening cone, destroying three more he couldn't even see.

"Damage report," Ty ordered.

"Decks four and five have been breached, and the power plant near engineering is offline. I don't think it's been damaged, but it's not responding. Power plants one through four are still operational. Shouldn't affect our ability to pick up survivors."

I've given the Besquith time to set up, to support their front line, Ty realized. *I've made things worse.*

Newton wiped fresh blood from his terminal screen and gasped.

"Incoming!" Conway reported. "Rockets from the surface!"

She banked hard so the lasers along the *Tizona*'s keel could provide better point-defense. Newton pressed and held an icon to allow a point-defense algorithm to run. It was the closest thing they had to an artificial intelligence, the closest thing anyone had so far as they knew. An entire power plant output was routed to the laser emitters and, instead of charging and discharging, thirty-two of them simply switched on and thirty-two arcing beams of energy cut through the air, incinerating missiles, trees, and Besquith.

Two seconds later, Newton pulled his thumb away and craned his neck to look at Captain Conway. "Did I hit any of the friendlies?" he asked. "Please tell me I didn't."

"You didn't," she said. "But the Dragoons have been overrun. We probably bought them some time, but I don't know how much. We need to pull up, get out of here, and try again."

"Do it," Ty ordered. A sick feeling settled into his gut as they pulled away from the surface. He tried to take in the Tri-V display, the data pouring into his slate, and the transmissions still coming through the speakers. It was all going to shit. The Fifth Battalion was essentially gone. They were too late.

"Options?" Ty asked his crew.

"Interceptors are five minutes out," Conway reported. "Whatever we do, we need to do it in four minutes."

"We can head to Sector Seventeen," Cisco offered. "We can probably get a couple dozen there."

"The rainmaker is warmed-up," Newton offered, his voice quiet and sober.

The bridge grew very silent. The instruments, the crew, and even the transmissions from the surface seemed to grow quiet and still. Rockets struck the belly of the *Tizona*, but Ty barely noticed.

He'd forced this decision, he knew. He'd never be able to evacuate the Dragoons now. The soldiers were running, fleeing, but they wouldn't make it unless someone slowed the enemy down and gave them a chance. Ty wondered if it would be enough. *Maybe*, he thought, though he didn't believe it.

"Okay," Ty said, turning unfocused eyes to his weapons officer. "Let's do as much as we can before we evacuate. Make it rain."

Newton scanned the data at his terminal and selected the target, three miles wide and nine miles long. He marked it and sent the location to Conway, who turned the *Tizona* hard to the left to line up for their run.

The weapons officer glanced once at his commander, who nodded grimly. Then he tapped a few icons which opened small sliding panels on the outside of the hull. A new icon, this one of a skull and crossbones, appeared in the center of his screen. Beneath it was a green circle—the icon that would disarm the rainmaker should he change his mind.

Ty watched the Tri-V as they closed on their target. The *Tizona* began taking hits from ground-launched rockets, but the crew ignored them. They could take a lot of damage before they went down.

"Ten seconds to target," Conway reported. The ship rattled a few more times, impacted by rockets.

Ty watched as Newton's finger slowly closed on the skull and crossbones icon until it finally touched. When it did, small, black orbs poured from the hatches opened earlier. The spheres soared through the air. Some barely rolled out of their tubes, landing directly under the hull. Others were launched with a bang and stopped rolling a half-mile away.

The orbs landed. Nothing happened. The enemy stared at the devices and waited. Nothing happened. Some approached, others backed away. Some were curious and picked them up.

However, as soon as the *Tizona* began to climb, reaching for the safety of space at full power, Newton tapped his terminal's screen with a shaking, sweaty hand.

Every fourth device was filled with a chemical compound known as Compound-A. The rest were filled with Compound-B. Alone, each was an irritant, but only mildly so. When they met, however, they erupted in a powerful exothermic reaction.

The Compound-B was released first. The spheres exploded, slightly injuring anyone too close to them, but that wasn't the point. The chemical gas they released quickly expanded and hung like an evil fog.

A few seconds later, the canisters containing Compound-A popped open, and the world within the fog erupted into Hell.

Ty knew he would later blame the tear streaks on both sides of his face on the intense gravitational forces that ripped liquid from his eyes. He could barely breathe, but there was no choice. They had to escape the interceptors; they had to get to hyperspace.

The chemicals burned and formed heavier elements, which first rose, then fell as fiery drops of reactive rain. They reacted again, formed clouds above the screaming, burning Besquith, and repeated the process.

The expanding cloud of hellfire would continue until the chemical reaction ran itself out, which, in the oxygen-rich environment of Jeatov, might take three or four days. The ancient fortress, the forest, and possibly more would be ruined for all eternity. If the fires continued unabated on the fuel-rich, forest planet, it could change the weather permanently. Enough ash in the air would block the sun and lead to a winter which could last generations. The planet would become a lifeless hunk of rock.

The Dragoon icons on the Tri-V hesitated for a moment, apparently awed by the spectacle, then continued their retreat. The Besquith at the front of their line, the targets of the rainmaker, were consumed by the rainmaker's rage.

It felt like it took longer than normal to reach the black, and he was beginning to see sparks in front of his eyes as his lungs burned for air that he didn't have the strength to draw in anymore. Thankfully, once they broke the atmosphere, Conway reduced the thrust to two gravities, which was still difficult to breathe in but not as difficult as the five which had been crushing his lungs for the past several minutes.

"Interceptors incoming," Conway wheezed.

"I've got them," Newton said, stretching his arms as far on his data terminal as he could without leaning forward. "I need you to start spinning us so we don't have any laser dead spots. The dogs have launched missiles. I need everything we've got."

Conway followed his instructions, suspending power to the thrusters. She used the maneuvering thrusters to start spinning them about six revolutions per minute.

She then displayed the location of the missiles to the Tri-V for the benefit of her captain, who quietly watched them work. Fourteen icons appeared for fourteen missiles. They weren't the small ones used against the *Tizona* earlier. These were standard-sized missiles, any three of which could turn the *Tizona* into an expanding cloud of gas.

But the missiles never had a chance. Newton vaporized them while they were still fifteen miles away. He waited until the Besquith lasers began striking their shields, and then, with a push of an icon, he vaporized the pursuers as well.

"That's all I got," Newton said.

"Let's get out of here," Ty said.

Conway rotated the ship back on course and activated the fusion drives, shoving the air from their chests again.

* * *

Ty sat on the floor and nursed the bottle of whiskey he'd smuggled onboard. It had been meant for celebration, but now Ty drank it with purpose and determination.

The room was dark, except for the dim light cast by his slate as he scrolled through images of the dead. The Yorktown Dragoons had provided him with their roster in advance so he could provide them with a list of whom he'd rescued. Ty knew the memory of that conversation would haunt him for the rest of his life.

He scrolled through the faces. Most of them grim—their owners doing their best to look tough, bulletproof and unafraid. He stopped when one in particular made his breath catch in his throat. He stared at it, squinting, and turned his head first one way, then the other.

The man looked familiar. Ty tried to place him with eyes that refused to focus, steered by a mind that swayed, staggered, and declined cooperation. However, the picture held him fast. The name underneath was difficult to read, but he saw it: Robert Anderson.

"It's the eyes," he whispered. Eyes like his father had—deep, brown eyes that seemed to peer right into his soul. Eyes that could extract the truth with a glance. Eyes that were knowing and wise. Eyes that said more than his father had ever expressed in words. Kind when Ty had needed them to be. Frightening when his father was angry. A Dragoon. His father had been one of them, once, and he had failed them.

"I'm sorry, Dad," he slurred. He lay on the floor and wept.

# # # # #

Headspace and Timing
by Robert E. Hampson

"No shit, there I was. Murthering great battle on, and my heads-up goes red, and I see the warning 'Critical systems failure. Communication lost, Pinplant T00A7. Emergency eject.'"

The four men were clustered around a small table at the bar. Tall glasses, half-filled with beer, sat in front of three of them, and a shorter glass containing a dark amber liquid sat in front of the fourth. The pitcher of beer was half-full and the storyteller, Ginzberg, grabbed it and refilled his glass.

"I hated those damned models. Give me a Mk 7 with full combat overrides." The new speaker, Jackson, refilled his own glass, emptying the pitcher in the process.

The third person at the table only grunted and muttered under his breath.

"Wait," said the fourth person. It was the newbie, Kaizo, or Kaishwan, or something like that. (The others just called him Kaiju since he was new and hadn't earned a nickname name yet.) "Did he just say 'chicken pluckers'?"

"Yeah, Angus swore off swearing after that last battle," Jackson supplied.

"Um, why did he swear off swearing?" Kaiju asked. "And why did he do it if he can just mutter and make it sound like he was swearing?"

The object of his curiosity muttered again. "Not our story to tell, kid," Jackson translated.

"Yeah, in this crowd, if a merc doesn't volunteer his story, you don't ask," Ginzberg interjected. "Besides, you have to earn the right to hear it." He picked up the pitcher and looked pointedly at the kid. "Speaking of which, junior buys the drinks."

"Hell no." Kaiju responded. "I know my rights. I know how to earn his story, too." He reached into a pocket and pulled out a shiny coin, rapped it on the edge of the table, then laid it flat on the surface. It was hexagonal and bore the image of a man on horseback.

"Nice one, junior, so shiny. Which means it's new, like you." Jackson pulled out a well-worn coin with a German eagle on the face, as did Ginzberg. Angus grunted, dug deep into his pocket and pulled out a silver coin with lettering on it. The silver was blackened with age, but the lettering was crisp and clear: 'C-H-A-O-S.'

"What does that mean?" Chagrinned, Kaiju put his coin back in his pocket.

"It means Angus is an old soldier." The bartender raised his voice, so he could be heard across the room. It wasn't hard, the room had been quiet, except for some slight rustling sounds, ever since the kid rapped the table. "He was given that coin by the man they used to call 'Mad Dog.' It also means you need to learn a bit more about the challenge coin tradition, kid." He spread his arms and indicated the rest of the patrons in the room. In front of every single patron was a coin, shiny or tarnished. The entire tavern had responded to the call.

"I don't see his." Kaiju pointed to a grizzled veteran sitting at the bar.

"I did," the bartender replied, and several patrons nodded. "You don't just wave a DFT around."

"DFT? What's that?" Kaiju's eyes went wide. "You mean he's got a Depi—"

"Just stop right there, kid. You don't just say the name in public, either." Jackson had put his hand on the kid's arm. Ginzberg had a hand up as if to cover the kid's mouth, and a rather wicked-looking knife had appeared in Angus' hands. "Just...leave it. Besides, you made the call, and everyone in the room produced their coin. That means you buy the drinks...for everyone."

"Oh. Oh, shit," the kid said, but he pulled out his Yack, checked the balance, then nodded to the bartender.

Once the pitcher had been refilled, and Angus had a fresh glass of whisky, Ginzberg resumed his story. "See, told ya, kid. I'll tell my stories for free, just buy my beer. Now, where was I?"

"He was on Fors, getting ejected from his CASPer," Jackson whispered to the kid.

"I thought it was Orcut?" Kaiju whispered back.

"Doesn't matter, it changes each time, just listen."

"So, there I was, no shit. Big honkin' battle on Kr'ss-9, and my heads-up goes red, and I see the warning 'Critical systems failure. Communication lost, Pinplant T00A7. Emergency eject.'"

"Hated those suits," added Jackson. Angus mumbled about rams and ruck marches.

"Ejected right onto the battlefield, buck naked."

Kaiju held up a hand and interrupted. "Whoa, what did you do?"

Jackson grinned and gestured at Ginzberg with his beer, sloshing a bit on the table in the process. "Dude, you had your haptic suit on."

Kaiju snickered. Angus snorted and went back to his whisky.

Ginzberg glared at the other three. "So I was next to buck naked, in the middle of the battlefield."

"Wool shirts. It launched you 2 miles toward the rear lines." It was the first time Angus had spoken clearly. Perhaps the whisky was loosening him up.

Kaiju's expression was all screwed up as he tried to parse the meaning. He was mouthing the word 'wool' when Jackson leaned over and whispered "Wool shirts. Bull shit. I guess it makes sense if you're Angus."

Ginzberg focused his glare on the Scot. "Rear lines, my ass. I hit the ground right in the front of a charging Oogar who was screaming at me. The whole time I kept hearing 'Critical systems failure. Communication lost, Pinplant T00A7.' So, I couldn't even open a link to call for help!"

Angus snorted and went back to staring into his glass.

Kaiju was still working through what he'd heard. "Wait, pinplant A7? That's like..." It was obvious he was trying to calculate a number.

Jackson spared him the effort. "One hundred sixty-seven, kid. It's Hex."

"Wow, Ginzberg! You were one of the first to get a pinplant? What was it like?"

"It's worse than that." Jackson drained his glass with a gulp and refilled it from the pitcher. He looked at Ginzberg, and, knowing the story that was coming, topped his off, as well, and motioned toward

Kaiju. "Oh yes, it was worse than that, kid, they started the numbering at Ay-Zero. Slick here was number eight."

"That is so cool!" Kaiju's beer was mostly untouched, so he waved off the refill.

"Wait a minute. I'm telling you about how I faced down a charging Tortantula on Sevalax wearing only my CASPer long johns and a belt knife..." Ginzberg tried to regain the floor.

"But, pinplants!" Kaiju interrupted. "Man, you've got to have 'plants if you want to drive the Mk 8s. After I finish my first contract term, I've got an option for 'plants. What's it like?"

"Pure hell if you ask me." Jackson said.

"Um, wow! You have 'plants, too? Geez, who are you guys?"

Angus looked up from his whisky and muttered. "Feather dusters. No one of any consequence."

"Who am I?" blustered Ginzberg. "The one telling this story, that's who! As I was saying, no shit, there I was, on Tic'k!t'ock, squaring off alone against the Zuul when my godforsaken pinplant lost contact..."

"I thought it was Orcut, and the Oogar were charging you..."

Jackson leaned over and, with a slightly tipsy slur, said, "Ignore him, kid, that story changes every time. Next thing you know, he'll be saying it was a school of Selroth, and all he was wearing was a Speedo and a breath mask."

Ginzberg spat out his beer and started to raise a fist toward Jackson. Angus held out a hand, palm down, between them, and the pair sat back down.

Once the beer was again refilled, Kaiju picked up right where he'd left off. "So, what was it like? Getting pinplants?" He turned to Jackson. "Which number were you?"

Jackson sighed. "Number T00B2. Eleven grunts after Slick, and we all had to sit and listen to him screaming about tentacles..."

* * *

It was not a good area for Humans to roam in groups of less than company size. Frankly, no station that catered to mercs was a 'nice' place to visit, but this district was giving Ginzberg the creeps. He'd survived Jakarta, Detroit, and Pr!lax IV, but he'd never felt the sheer sense of unease he had the moment he set foot in the To'Os.

It wasn't that this place seemed particularly dangerous; it was more a sense of uncaring. High on Flake? No one cared. Overcharged at the Bar? Not their concern. Mugged by a G'nish? Too bad, Human, you shouldn't have come alone.

But he wasn't alone. He had a whole squad of Riedel's Rächer with him (including Jackson, his friend since cadre), but it didn't seem to matter. People entering the To'Os had been known to disappear, and there was a rumor that at least one merc company had never been heard from again after daring to go to To'Os.

"The KAS isn't working; I can't pull up a map of this area," one of his squad mates said. The Kartenausschnitt, or KAS, was equal parts GPS, inertial navigation, blue-force tracker, and infogrid terminal. If the KAS couldn't map an area, it didn't exist, or someone wanted to make sure that it couldn't be found.

"That's because the Tossers don't want anyone wandering in here, map or not," Jackson told the soldier. "It doesn't matter. The place we want is down this street, left into the alley, then halfway down on the right."

"You've been here before." Oberstabsgefreiter Beitel didn't phrase it as a question.

"We both have," answered Ginzberg. "Didn't like it then, don't like it now, but when Oberst Riedel inquired about equipping us with pinplants, he was referred to this place."

"If you've already got your 'plants, why are you here?" That was Schmidt, the gefreiter—private—who'd been fiddling with the KAS. He still acted like a raw recruit, even though he'd come on for the latter half of the Pr!lax campaign. He still hadn't learned to keep his mouth shut and listen to his sergeants—Feldwebel in the official German rank structure used by the Rächer. Beitel smacked him in the back of the head, her armored gauntlet ringing against his helmet.

"Scheisskopf. We were here for pre-op. They don't see too many Humans in To'Os, so Squiddy needed morphometric data. He's done a few since then, and they've all worked fine, so the colonel sent us to make sure you get 'planted safely."

What was left unsaid was that they were all expendable. Riedel's Rächer—Revengers in English—needed NCOs and officers with the implanted biomachine links to be able to compete with the off-world merc companies. Before Oberst Gernot Riedel dared risk his officers, he sent Ginzberg's squad. It wasn't that they were worthless guinea pigs, after all; Ginzberg and Jackson were NCOs with training and experience in both Earth and Galactic campaigns. Beitel was likely to head up the training cadre once she got a bit more rank and seasoning, and the privates would become Headquarters specialists running computers, communications, and logistics. It was more that these troops weren't in the direct command structure now, so the Company could afford the personnel shortage and recuperation time needed to recover from surgery and training.

There was one last unspoken reason—to see if the implants were successful. That had been the reason for Ginzberg's and Jackson's preliminary visit, but this was the real thing. Riedel had arranged for a discrete Human clinic on W-K Station to study the soldiers after they were released, just in case of complications. The fact that they were interested in duplicating the implants in the future was just a bonus.

The party turned down the alley and immediately lost the scant light from the glowstrips overhead. The indirect light left shadows everywhere, and many of those shadows moved. Jackson had led since he had better position sense than most (and was usually assigned as a guide to the Leutnants who were forever getting lost on field exercises). He stopped and turned, holding up a clenched fist to instruct the rest of the party to freeze, but it was too late to dodge the object that had been tossed at his head.

With their point man down, Ginzberg tapped Beitel on the shoulder and motioned for her to guard the rear. He then moved up to the front and scanned the surrounding area before checking Jackson. The latter was moving, albeit slowly, so Ginzberg continued looking for the attacker. He'd bent at the knees and kept his back straight, so he could spring into action if necessary. Very slowly, he reached up to the side of his helmet and touched the switch that deployed his night vision goggles. The greenish lighting in his NVGs wasn't much better than the indirect lighting of the alley. There were heat sources all around. Most were cooler than the bodies of his Human companions, but that didn't mean much in a Galactic Society with thousands of races ranging from cold- to hot-blooded and insectoid to giant slime molds.

The sergeant held up his hand and the squad froze. He was at a right angle to the rest of the party, staring at a particularly dark pocket of shadow. He was perfectly still for long moments, then burst out from his squatting position and dove into the shadow, coming up with a small creature. Ginzberg's quarry was struggling, biting, and howling, but he held it firmly with both hands clasped around its neck. One hand of the creature held a piece of brick like the one on the ground near Jackson.

Now that the other Sergeant was up, he reached for his belt and pulled out a powerful flashlight. He shined it on the creature in Ginzberg's grip, revealing an immature dog- or wolf-like creature with a mouth full of sharp teeth. It kept trying to bite its captor, but Ginzberg held it at arm's length, and its teeth were unable to reach him. Likewise, the pup kept trying to swing the brick at him, but its arms were too short to be effective.

"Besquith," Jackson said. "Juvenile, which is good for us. What are you going to do with it?"

"Grab the med kit." Ginzberg grunted, dodging the brick the pup had finally decide to throw at the man who held it by the throat. "'Bes-kit's' can be knocked out with some of our stronger pain killers. Get a fentanyl stick...um..." He bounced the pup up and down a few times to estimate its weight. "Twenty kilos, give or take. Five milligrams should do it."

"Where? He won't stay still!"

While the other sergeant readied the injection, Ginzberg carefully shifted his grip. "Back of the neck, right below my hand. And if you value your life, do NOT stick me with that thing!"

It took a few moments to get the autosyringe in position and then for the pup to stop moving after the injection. The rest of the squad stayed alert, but nothing else came out of the darkness. Jackson flashed his light back into the shadowy area where the pup had been hiding, revealing a sleeping nest, empty food packs and a pile of bricks. He pushed at the nest with his foot and uncovered a pile of material that glittered in the light.

"Gutter rat," Ginzberg pronounced as he laid the pup back on its nest. "Come on, we're going to be late."

"You're just leaving him here?" asked one of the privates.

"It's where he lives," supplied Beitel, then slapped the private on the back of the head. "Feldwebel said move it."

The sign on the door was lettered in alien script. They'd had no other encounters during the short trip down the alley. Ginzberg called a halt, directed the squad to check the perimeter, then nodded to Jackson to open the door. Beitel did a clearance entry, hugging the doorframe with her sidearm held at low-ready, with Jackson right on her tail.

A synthesized voice boomed through the doorway from inside. "Damned mercs, always doing a combat entry! I run a clean establishment!"

Jackson answered, "It's nice to see you too, Squiddy. We got ambushed in the alley."

"One wolf cub hardly counts as an ambush, Human!"

Ginzberg had motioned to the rest of the squad, following them through the door into the clinic. "You were watching? Why didn't you do anything?"

"What was I to do, Human? I am a humble surgeon, not a big, strong mercenary like you!" The voice came from a series of small speakers around the room and from the conveyance of what appeared to be a four-foot octopus. It sat on what looked like a tall bar stool with motorized wheels. The "seat" of the chair was roughly cup-shaped and held the body of the creature plus a small amount of water. There were several articulated "arms" sticking out from the chair, holding various medical devices and scanners, and a control console with multiple screens directly in front of the cephalopod's single eye. Its tentacles were draped over the various instruments and arms. They were in constant motion, reminding Ginzberg of snakes. They moved with purpose, however, constantly adjusting and controlling the chair's attachments.

"You're a menace, that's what you are, Squiddy. Anyone who knows you would be afraid of you if they knew you were entering the fight." Ginzberg's voice was light, and it was clearly meant to be a jest, but the members of the squad could tell there was a grain of truthfulness in the statements, as well. "I suppose I should introduce your victims. You remember Jackson, right?"

"We Wrogul never forget, Human. It is good to see you again, Sergeant Jackson."

"Corporal Beitel, Private First Class Giorgios, and Privates Markos and Lomidze. Markos is the one with the dents in his helmet from getting smacked in the back of his head for asking dumb questions. PFC Giorgios is the one with his back against the door, shaking. Giorgios, I know you tested low in xenophobia, what's your malfunction?"

"S-sn-snakes. I h-hate sn-snakes, s-s-sir!"

"Oh, hell. I'll overlook that slur on my parentage for now. How the hell did you end up in an expeditionary force with a fear of snakes?" Ginzberg was frustrated. Given the various species a merc was likely to encounter, fear of other species was usually weeded out.

Rage, anger, aggression...those were acceptable, but fear usually drummed a recruit out of cadre.

"N-never c-came up, s-sa-Sergeant!"

Ginzberg noticed Jackson going for the medkit and nodded slightly. They didn't need this right now.

"If it makes you feel better," the Wrogul's voice boomed throughout the room, "they are tentacles, Private First Class Giorgios. I understand my kind are very popular in your Japanese film industry."

Beitel gulped and turned red.

"As physicians!" The Wrogul's voice came from all speakers, as before, but then switched to the speaker closest to the junior NCO. "Why? What did you have in mind, corporal?"

If anything, Beitel turned even redder. Markos laughed, and Jackson started coughing while trying to hold in his laughter.

"Excuse me a moment, Squiddy," Ginzberg interrupted. "Obergefreiter Giorgios! Beachtung!"

The soldier snapped to attention, eyes forward, allowing Jackson to slip out of his field of view and apply the auto-injector. The PFC held at attention for a moment, then relaxed. He didn't quite collapse, but his eyes fluttered closed, and his chin settled into his chest. After about 30 seconds, his eyes opened, and he straightened out. "Thanks," he mumbled.

"Hmph. Val-Z?" Ginzberg asked Jackson. The latter nodded, acknowledging he'd only delivered an anti-anxiety drug and not a sedative. "Good. I wouldn't want to have to adjust his meds. Right, Squiddy?" He turned back to the surgeon.

"Indeed, Sergeant Ginzberg. You Humans are so septic, it's a wonder you don't get terribly sick every time you get punctured. Oh...wait...you do!"

Jackson laughed, but Ginzberg just scowled. "Okay, let's get this over with. Who's first?"

"Me," said Beitel. "Just one thing though, how does this work? And how do you implant it?"

They knew the basics, pinplants were in use as essential brain-to-computer interfaces (BCIs) throughout many of the Galactic races. There were some who frowned on it and others for whom the implant was...problematic. However, as long as a species had a dedicated cognitive ganglion—a brain in Human terms—they could be fitted with a pinplant. Earth had experimented with BCIs since the late twentieth century, the earliest being used to restore hearing by placing an electrode in the inner ear and electrically stimulating the cells that connected to the hearing centers of the brain.

In the twenty-first century, BCIs consisting of thumbnail-sized chips with hundreds of fine metallic spikes were placed in the brain areas controlling muscle movement as well as the touch-sensitive brain regions for those same muscles. Rudimentary artificial limbs could be controlled by mental signals alone, and one team actually used a similar technique to boost memory capability, but they'd never become widespread due to the surgery required to place the interfaces into the brain.

Galactic nanotechnology and Wrogul surgical techniques changed all of that. Nanites were injected into the appropriate brain areas and self-assembled into a mesh connecting the movement, sensory, language, hearing, and vision areas of the brain to an interface 'Pin' placed just behind the recipient's ear. Computers, comm units, exoskeletal suits, even CASPers could be connected via a hard-wired cable. Some species, such as the Wrogul, built wireless communications directly into the nano-mesh, but Humans had to settle for attaching a thumb-sized transceiver to the Pin.

Squiddy had explained it during the Sergeants' prior visit—Human brains were complex chemical and electrical machines, but very low powered. The Wrogul had not yet figured out how to power some of the more advanced pinplant functions without using an external power source, although he assured them he had a colleague who was building a 'model' Human brain to try to figure it out. Thus, these pinplants would not be capable of some extreme functions such as cognitive enhancement. Furthermore, certain functions such as memory caching and increased processing speed would only be available when hardwired to an external device capable of providing additional power to the pinplant. Given that the main anticipated uses for mercs were computer interfacing and control of their war machines, the power requirements were not thought to be a problem.

In response to Beitel's question, Squiddy manipulated one of the articulated arms on his chair. One part of the arm was a vial filled with a silvery liquid that sloshed very slowly as it moved. "I will inject these nano-assemblers into certain parts of your brain. The assemblers will build the neural mesh required to connect to the pinplant pedestal." Another arm held up a flat disk with a one-centimeter pin sticking out at right angles. "Then I'll need to figure out where to put the power supply." Several tentacles surrounded a 5-centimeter-diameter sphere and appeared to lift it with difficulty.

Beitel paled and swallowed audibly. Markos stepped back and Lomidze gasped.

"I kid, I kid." Squiddy said, tossing the ball easily from tentacle to tentacle. He squeezed it, and it squeaked. "I just keep that to tease Humans." He squeezed it several times with different tentacles, sounding like a dog playing with a toy. "It's also good for strength exercises."

Beitel gulped again and continued in a much more subdued voice. "But, how do you get the nanites into my brain?"

"With these, of course!" Squiddy held up two tentacles. They were slightly different from the others, much smoother and tapered to extremely fine points. They were no less functional, though, since he was able to curl them all the way up, then extend them all the way straight. They were at least two feet long.

There was a thud, and the squad turned in time to see Giorgios hit the floor. He'd been tracking better the last couple of minutes, but now he was out cold. He'd apparently fainted.

"I think he goes first," said Jackson.

* * *

Ginzberg woke to the sound of sobbing. He thought it was Giorgios, but it was hard to be sure. After a few moments of listening he could make out, "The tentacles, the tentacles..." Yes, that was Giorgios.

"That's it?" Ginzberg asked.

"Yes, the primary matrix is inserted. It will take several days for the mesh to fully develop." Squiddy's voice came from a speaker somewhere to the left of the couch Ginzberg reclined on.

"What about the others?"

"While we speak, I am finishing up with Corporal Beitel and starting on Sergeant Jackson." The voice now came from two different speakers off to the right. Ginzberg turned his head and could see instruments moving above the two closest couches. Three more couches were occupied, including the moaning Giorgios. "I do not understand why you Humans will not allow me to develop a full-cognitive integration system. Multi-tasking is okay, but full hyper-threading is better."

Having developed the pinplant technology to its current state of the art, Wrogul had taken it to an extreme by fully integrating computer technology into their brains. Mercs were being pinned to better function on the battlefield but didn't quite trust the idea of merging with a computer and letting it make battlefield decisions.

"I know the power supply is a problem," Squiddy continued, "but I can make a device that can be carried externally. After all, Human males carry important reproductive databases externally! What's one more 'appendage'?" The voice returned to the speaker on his left. "There, I have finished with your Privates." Ginzberg instinctively lowered his hands to the vicinity of the aforementioned 'reproductive database' and flinched.

Scratchy laughter filled the room from all the speakers: "Ha! You Humans, so gullible! No, I meant that I have finished with Markos and Lomidze. Beitel should start waking up, now, and Jackson should in another twenty of your minutes."

Ginzberg lay back and closed his eyes. He only knew one Wrogul, so he had no idea if the rest of the alien race shared Squiddy's crude humor. He had to admit, it was somewhat appropriate for a seedy clinic catering to mercs. The humor would not be out of place in any combat surgical hospital. It was just...bizarre...hearing it from an intelligent octopus that had just had its tentacles up vari-ous...orifices.

Giorgios might be right. Best not to think that way.

"How do we...know if the...pinplants...are working?" Beitel asked slowly as the effects of the surgical field wore off.

"They are currently blocked, until I release them," Squiddy said over the speakers. He was currently located at the head of Jackson's couch and appeared to be fully...immersed...in that procedure while still carrying on the conversation. "The mesh will not be fully mature for several days, but you should be able to access basic functions in a few hours. Since your Kommandant Riedel would not allow me to include integrated power supplies..."

Ginzberg could have sworn he heard the words 'wink, wink, nudge, nudge' come from the speaker beside his head.

Squiddy's voice continued: "...I have applied an auxiliary power module to your pin." All the soldiers who were awake raised their hands to a point behind their right ear, where they encountered a device covering the pin that extended up over their ear like a hearing aid. "It's supplying power for the nanoassemblers building your mesh and will function as your wireless interface once I unlock the function links. For now, you should rest, and I will show you how to access your plants when you wake up."

There was a strange resonance as Ginzberg heard the word 'rest.' The voice had come from all the speakers and seemed to reverberate throughout the room. He suddenly felt very sleepy. Was this another function of the pin—?

* * *

When Ginzberg awoke the second time, all the medical instrumentation was gone, and Squiddy was nowhere to be seen. What was present was a voice in his head droning on about something...let's see...“...command syntax for the model H-stroke-alpha mark-three pinplant. Commands may be thought or spoken. Guild authority recommends that users practice command syntax in the spoken form before attempting non-verbal commands. Please note that all verbal pin commands must be preceded by the activation code-phrase 'pin command.' Commands are as follows: 1 of 492, 'Able'. The Able verb command activates the option subset for subsequent verb activation commands. Options from the Able command can be used to modify...” He shifted his attention to the rest of the room, and the voice seemed to fade into the background.

The rest of his squad were sitting up on their couches. Some looked confused, like Beitel, others looked distracted, like Jackson. Giorgios had a wild look in his eyes; the 'voices in his head' might prove to be a problem.

“Squiddy?” Ginzberg asked, but there was no immediate response.

“Are we done?” asked Lomidze in his near incomprehensible Georgian (the country, not the state) accent.

“Yes, my friends, you are done.” Squiddy's voice came from all the speakers, like the booming sounds they'd encountered when they first entered the clinic. “I was just reviewing the results of your PET scans. The sleep command was a very specific test of the feedback interface. The appropriate brain areas responded exactly the way they were meant to. You may go on your way.”

“Good,” said Ginzberg, standing up. “We need to get back to base.”

"Wait," said Jackson. "Let's not forget we left an angry, tranquilized Besquith pup out there. Perhaps we need to recover a bit more, so we're not distracted..."

"Um, did you say pet scan? As in dogs and cats?" asked Markos. Beitel reached over and slapped him on the back of the head.

"No, Private Markos, PET scan as in Positron Emission Tomography. It's an imaging technique used to see what part of your brain is metabolically active following a stimulus. I stimulated your pinplants and watched to see which brain areas were active. It's a standard procedure even Humans use. On their dogs and cats, even!" Squiddy's speakers produced his near laugh again.

"Wait...positron emission..." Beitel grimaced. "YOU INJECTED ANTIMATTER INTO MY BRAIN?" She began looking for something to punch and was about to settle for punching Markos, when Jackson held out a hand and restrained her.

"Technically, no. I injected a radioisotope of fluorine into your brain. When the isotope breaks down and emits positrons, the scanner records where that occurred. If it makes you feel better, your brain produced the antimatter!"

"THAT'S NOT ANY BETTER!" shouted Beitel. Jackson moved to intercept her as she moved away and contemplated restraining her with both hands.

"...and the fluorine-18 produces gamma rays as well!"

"Not helping!" shouted Jackson as Beitel screamed in rage.

"Perhaps it is time for you to go." A door opened in the blank wall, and they could see the alley outside the clinic. "Perhaps I turned up the aggressive/alert functions a bit much when I tried to give you a competitive edge over that poor little puppy dog. The furniture sank into the floor and the back wall started moving to force them outside. As the door closed behind them, they heard: "Good-bye! Have a nice day! Remember to refer all of your friends to Squiddy's!"

The trip back to the docks and their transport was uneventful...if one considered subduing a pack of five adult Besquith backing up the gutter-rat pup they'd encountered earlier, a brawl with a dozen Human mercs that came spilling out of a bar wrestling an inebriated Oogar as the squad passed, and the platoon of Lumar security goons the bartender called in to escort the whole lot to the brig or their ships uneventful.

Perhaps Squiddy had set the pinplants to stimulate the aggression centers a bit too much.

* * *

It was late, and the bar was emptying out. Jackson was staring into his beer. Kaiju was at the bar arguing with the bartender about his not-inconsiderable tab. Angus had fallen asleep several times and had been helped back to his quarters by a couple of patrons wearing uniforms similar to the inebriated Scot's. Only the old soldier with the DFT remained at the bar. Rumor had it he lived in a back room. Having a DFT meant a powerful race of near mystical assassins owed him a favor. It also made him a target. Ginzberg hadn't seen the man enter or leave. He was just...there.

They sat without talking for a while.

The problem with 'plant-assisted memory was that when you called it up, you got everything, right down to the smell of the battlefield. The 'plants had gotten better over the years, and he'd made many return visits to Squiddy for upgrades. They'd finally fixed the power requirements, and Ginzberg's last upgrade had given him the full memory-caching capability.

It wasn't without a price, he thought as he continued to ruminate in silence.

He remembered clearly how it had felt when the pinplants came fully online a week or so after the surgery. All his senses were alive with the ability to amplify and enhance at will. The first time he'd plugged into a battlefield information system, he'd felt like a god. The ability to see everything in one glance, to know without doubt where his squad mates were located, seemed like the ultimate advantage.

That memory triggered another—associative memory cascades were a bitch for a pinned soldier who'd gotten too deep into his wine. The first time he'd gotten into a 'plant-capable CASPer. He didn't just wear the war machine, he was the war machine, and all the excitement and power and elation came flooding back, lifting his spirits, even if temporarily. But then there was the time they came back from a deployment and found Colonel Riedel dead by his own hand. He'd pinned into the administrative 'net, started sorting through the comm traffic of the last few days, and discovered the company was bankrupt. He was going to have to explain to the troops that the Rächer were disbanded and couldn't pay them what they were owed.

The good and the bad, the beautiful and the ugly. You only got out of the 'plants what you put into them. Ginzberg turned his attention back to Kaiju. It was hard to believe that he and Jackson had been that new, that...shiny...once. He looked over at Jackson. "Do you think he bought it?"

"I doubt it. You and I know it, and he's been in long enough to know full well they don't serial number the 'plants. At least, not in standard."

"I thought your line about '...listening to him screaming about tentacles...' was inspired. I especially liked how you acted it out. You looked just like that PFC, what was his name?"

"Giorgios. Bought it on Orkutt."

"Oh, yeah. Somehow, I should have remembered that."

Jackson looked at him in disbelief. "Markos is a businessman, can you believe it? Import/export out of Piquaw. Lomidze went officer. Was trying for that Swiss outfit."

"Beitel."

"Yeah. Damn shame. She would have made a good sergeant."

"Right. One person. ONE PERSON in our company had an allergic reaction to nanites and it was Beitel." Ginzberg raised his almost empty glass. "To absent companions."

Jackson nodded, then drained the last of his beer. He stopped, and a wry grin appeared on his face. "Do you think they still employ that Jeha scanner mech tech at Peepo's?"

Ginzberg smiled in return. "Yeah. They do. I had to get a scan last month." His grin grew larger. "Why? Are you thinking what I'm thinking?"

Jackson's grin matched Ginzberg's. "Oh yeah. I mean, can you imagine the kid's face when he's being prepped for his pre-pinplant scans and in walks a six-foot centipede in coveralls, carrying a toolbox?"

# # # # #

Return to Sender
by Benjamin Tyler Smith

"What do you mean the shipment's not coming?" Captain Philips snapped. "Nuchols,
my men are depending on the munitions
you promised to deliver!"

The mud-caked receiver in Philips' hand crackled to life. Zuparti
chittering overlaid with the digitized voice of a translator program
filled the cramped underground chamber. "*Apologies, Captain. Your
goods were in my possession, but I received an emergency request from a client on
another of Krieben 7's moons. Their need was greater.*"

Their wallet was greater, you mean. Philips ground his teeth. The men
and women who made up his command staff did their best to avoid
eye contact with their enraged commander. Philips rested an elbow
on his stiff, aching knee and put the receiver right to his lips. "We
reserved that shipment weeks ago, Nuchols. I paid good money for
it!"

"*And you will get your shipment,*" Nuchols promised. "*It is simply delayed.*"

Delays resulted in dead mercs, and he had enough of those already. He sighed. "How long?"

"*I assure you we will do everything we can to expedite—*"

Philips pounded the cracked stone wall. "*How long?*" he roared.

Another pause. *"Five weeks. Two for a skip drone to reach the home office, another to gather the order—"*

Philips tossed the receiver to Corporal Rienard, who fumbled to catch it. "Shut it off before I break our only working comm system!"

He rested his chin on clasped fingers and stared at the chamber wall. A distant explosion shook the earth around him. Another crack formed in the wall. How much more punishment could these underground ruins take? How much more punishment could his men take?

It was supposed to have been a cake walk for the Philips' Phalanx mercenary company—land on one of Krieben 7's many moons, secure the ancient ruins the Science Guild wanted to investigate, protect the dig team once they arrived, get paid, then head back to Karma to get laid. Three months of light garrison duty, in a temperate forest where the greatest predator was the size of a house cat, but with scales and more legs. Easy contract, right?

Wrong. First the Caroon diggers hadn't arrived as scheduled. And when the oversized anteaters finally did show up—weeks late—they had Lumar mercs hot on their heels. A shit-ton of Lumar mercs. He and his "Philippians" had been dug in pretty well, but they were burning through their ammo faster than a hungry GenSha could polish off a hay bale.

It didn't help that the four-armed freaks could soak up a lot of punishment before going down. The tall humanoids weren't bright, but they were tough. If Philips had known he was going to be up against them, he'd have brought ten times the amount of munitions. As it stood, the Philippians would run dry in a few days. And if it came to a melee, four hands beat two.

"Hey," one of the men whispered, "wasn't there an arms dealer back on Karma who claimed she could make rapid deliveries? 'We're just in time or you don't pay a dime' or some crap?"

Philips cocked his head.

"Oh, yeah." Sergeant Hector tore open a ration pack with his teeth. "There was this smoking hot woman on the Tri-V, advertising for a weapons delivery outfit."

"The only outfit I remember was the camo bunny girl costume she was wearing!" another called.

The men laughed. The few female mercs rolled their eyes and groaned. Philips hid a smile behind a callused hand. It was juvenile, but at least his soldiers could joke around. They were still in the fight.

"What was her name again?" Hector asked. "Tammy? Cammy?" He snapped his fingers. "Wait, it was Candy! Of the—"

* * *

"Justin Warren Munitions Conveyance Company, Jackie speaking. How can I help you, Captain Philips?"

Jacquelyn Candace Warren, founder and CEO of the fastest growing arms delivery company in the sector, pulled the bunny ears from her head and set them on a table laden with makeup and bandoliers of magazines and power cells. She ran a hand through her long, raven-dark hair, her fingers brushing against the wireless transceiver connected to the pinplants behind her ear.

After a moment's delay, a gruff voice filled her head. *"I'll cut to the chase, Miss Jackie. Your company prides itself on rapid munitions delivery, and that's what I need: munitions, delivered rapidly."*

She smiled. "We aren't called the Justin Timers for nothing, Captain. What do you need, and what are the conditions on the ground? You're on Krieben 7-h, correct?"

Jackie arched her back and removed the puffy tail connected to her bikini bottom, then settled back into her leather chair. A glance around the small studio confirmed that the Tri-V film crew greatly appreciated the sight as they set about cleaning up. The director mouthed "Great shoot today, Candy!" and gave her a thumbs-up as he walked from the room, his steps more like little hops in the deck's low gravity.

Riku gathered up the bandoliers while one of the stagehands packed away her makeup and costume props. Riku was the youngest of her bodyguards, a slender Japanese-American in his mid-twenties. He handled the munitions used in the ad shoots, as the marketing staff didn't work with live ammo. Months earlier, the director had even suggested they use mockups of all the military hardware her company could provide for safety reasons, but that had seemed...wrong.

Not to mention terribly tacky. The average merc could tell in an instant what was real and what was fake, with weapons and...other things.

"You look great as always, JC," Riku murmured as he slung the bandoliers over his dark suit jacket. She couldn't see his eyes beneath his bodyguard shades, but she knew his gaze lingered in certain all-natural areas.

Whatever improved morale and boosted sales, she decided. Back when her company had been small, she'd opted to be its mascot rather than pay someone else. Now she was stuck with the role. She didn't wear camo bikinis for fun.

Well, maybe a little fun.

Jackie patted Riku on the arm and pointed at her slate. When he handed it over, she saw it already displayed information about Philips' Phalanx, its current contract, and the number of Philippians deployed. The mercenary company specialized in site security, from planets to space ships. Very similar to what Warren's Wardens had done back in its prime.

Captain Philips read off an extensive list of supplies, ranging from arms and ammo to rations and water filters. Jackie compared it to what she had aboard the transport ship *Wardens' Justice*. They had just finished equipping two companies of mercs on Krieben 6, but there were more than enough supplies and equipment in the hold for Philips and his crew. Her smile broadened into a grin. They could definitely handle this job and make a tidy profit while they were at it.

"And to sum up the situation on the ground, it's FUBAR. Rhymes with Lumar, and I've got those to spare. How much will this cost?"

Jackie ran through the math in her head: inventory cost, fuel, transit time, and potential for combat. "Ten thousand on delivery, plus five percent of your current contract's proceeds. When you collect, of course."

"Five percent? That's robbery!"

"That's reality, Captain Philips. We don't only ship weapons to customers in safe starports. Our teams risk their lives to resupply our clients, directly on the battlefield if need be. We will stop at nothing, but that dedication comes at a price."

"Not even the junior officers get that much of a mission cut. Hell, after costs, neither do I!"

"We're offering you these terms because we know the reputation of you and your Philippians." She tapped the slate and skimmed the reviews left by the mercenary company's many satisfied clients. "We believe you can succeed, and we're willing to help you do that. But, if these terms are unfavorable, we will demand all the money up front."

After a much longer pause than could be accounted for by distance delay, Philips said, *"How soon can you be here?"*

"Give us thirty-six hours."

"That's...a lot better than our previous dealer's estimate."

She sent Marcus a summons through her pinlink. "You're fortunate we're in-system. Otherwise it would have taken us at least two weeks to reach you."

"Still better! The next time I see that fat weasel..." There was another pause. *"You have a deal. See you in thirty-six hours at the following coordinates—"*

The door slid open as the transmission ended. A middle-aged man in P.T. gear entered the room, his lined face slick with sweat from whatever grueling training he was putting the rookies through. "Hello, Marcus," she said to the leader of her bodyguards.

"A new job?" he asked, eyes firmly on Jackie's face rather than her mostly exposed body.

Such a good and proper man, she thought with a flash of annoyance. When was he going to stop seeing her as a little girl and start...She brought up the invoice on her slate and tossed the device to Marcus. "Get this to the foreman and tell the captain we leave for Krieben 7-h as soon as refueling is complete."

* * *

Jackie and Marcus floated side-by-side in the cargo bay's zero gravity. She had changed into a dark shirt and trousers that clung to her curvy frame. He wore the haptic suit he would need to pilot his CASPer.

"I really wish you'd reconsider coming," Marcus said as they angled their way to the ramp of the dropship, *Bunker Hill.*

"And I wish you'd quit wishing for that." She traced the round patch on her shoulder. It bore a silhouette of her Gun Bunny Candy persona, with JWMCC printed beneath and the phrase "Ready to hop when you need a drop!" wrapping the border. That particular patch was quite popular at their GalNet souvenir shop.

"We can handle this on our own. You do enough already."

"Papa always led from the front. That's what I'm going to do."

Marcus grunted. "You're a Warren, all right. Stubborn as mules, the lot of you."

They pushed against the *Bunker Hill's* ceiling and drifted toward several blue cargo containers, each filled with enough small arms, CASPer ammunition, and foodstuffs to supply the Philippians for a month. She stopped at each container long enough to connect her pinlink to its security panel. No one was getting into a container unless she manually unlocked it.

"What's in the green one?" Marcus asked, pointing at it.

"A few Camille H5 automated sentry guns, miniguns loaded, capacitors charged, and target of choice already set for Lumar combatants." She locked it and shrugged. "I figure we can upsell Captain Philips when we get there."

"Stubborn, and opportunistic. Yep, definitely a Warren."

"Quiet, you."

The forward portion of the cargo bay had been set aside for the *Bunker Hill's* passengers and their equipment. Three CASPer Mk 7's lined one wall, their sturdy frames secured behind steel cages. Jump seats lined the other wall, where she and her men would be restrained for the atmo-drop. She rubbed her butt. Those seats sucked.

Riku was already strapped into one of the jump seats next to a squat man with a bushy red beard. Both wore haptic suits, and both waved when they saw Jackie. "Big Al, your favorite water nymph is here!" Riku said.

"Och, so it would seem." Big Al flexed his bulging biceps. "And who shall we smite today, me blue-eyed lass?"

Jackie giggled. Back when she was a child, she had made the mistake of comparing him to a dwarf from one of her favorite stories. "You'll never let that slide, will you?"

"Him?" Riku asked. "Never. He's a nerd for life."

"Guilty as charged!"

"Don't encourage them, *garota*," a feminine voice muttered from above. Sayra, a petite Brazilian woman in her forties, sat cross-legged on the ceiling. She looked down from examining her sniper rifle, a small smile on her brown face. "You'll only make them worse."

"Come on, Mom," Riku objected. "We're not that bad."

"I am not your mother!"

The cockpit door slid open, and a big black man stuck his head out. "Welcome aboard!" pilot Terrence Tremain said, eyes hidden by the aviator glasses he always wore. He grinned. "We ready for some fireworks?"

Jackie returned the grin. "Double-T, I can only hope the show is exciting, especially after all this hurry up and wait."

"With you, it's always exciting! Isn't that right, Ed?"

Double-T sidled over, so a sandy-haired man could peek out. "Excitement's what we live for, JC. Give me a target, and this ship's guns will sing!"

The others voiced their agreement, even taciturn Sayra. Jackie beamed with pride. These were her best men. No, *Papa's* best men. Each of them had served in Warren's Wardens, all the way to the bitter end. They had been the only survivors.

Her hands reflexively clenched, and she fought to relax them. "All right, Justin Timers! The Philippians have promised us a secure LZ, but you know from experience how quickly that can go sideways. We're going in hot. Be prepared for anything!"

* * *

"Phalanx Actual, Phalanx Actual, this is *Bunker Hill*," Double-T said. "Requesting confirmation of LZ coordinates, over."

Static played over the cockpit's speakers. Double-T looked over his shoulder. "That's all I've been getting, JC. I've checked and rechecked the coordinates. We're in the right spot, but no one's down there."

"I know I said to be prepared for anything, but I didn't expect nothing." Jackie chewed the inside of her lip. "Make another pass over the site. We'll give them one more chance, then pull back into orbit."

"Roger. Stay frosty on those guns, Ed!"

Double-T banked the *Bunker Hill* to the right. The Tri-V monitors suspended above the forward viewport showed the ground below, everything shaded in the bright green of the camera's enhanced night vision. Dense forest covered much of this area of Krieben 7-h, but the area designated by Captain Philips was a grassy field filled with giant, fallen columns and the occasional stone tower.

They circled around in a lazy arc, with Double-T repeating his hail, over and over. Only static answered. Were they too late? Jackie's heart sank at the prospect. Thirty-six hours was fast by in-system transit standards, but it was several lifetimes on the battlefield.

Before she could tell Double-T to return to low orbit, the radio crackled. "Bunker Hill, *this is Lieutenant Eckland. Coordinates are confirmed. You are clear for drop. Over.*"

A sense of excited relief flooded through Jackie. She keyed the receiver. "Lieutenant Eckland, this is Jackie Warren. Where is Captain Philips? Over."

"*Indisposed at the moment, ma'am.*" Eckland's voice sounded strained, as if he were fighting back tears. Had something happened to the captain? "*You really are a sight for sore eyes.*"

"Where are you, Lieutenant?" Jackie studied the Tri-V. "We're not seeing anything on our monitors, and we don't want to land in the wrong location."

"*You're going to...land? Not drop the supplies?*"

Jackie frowned. "The agreement was for us to land and assist with site security while the transfer took place. Captain Philips didn't tell you that?"

"*No, er, yes! Yes, he did! We will...*" There was a long pause, as if he were speaking with someone off-mic. "*We will set down flares. Stand by.*"

"*Something's not right,*" Marcus said, his voice broadcasting from inside his CASPer. "*I don't trust this guy.*"

Jackie's frown deepened. Was Captain Philips dead? If so, that could explain why Lieutenant Eckland didn't know all the particulars of the agreement.

Two bright balls of light fell from one of the towers near the center of the pillar field. The camera zoomed in, and a pair of Humans came into focus. They waved at the circling *Bunker Hill*.

"Stay or go?" Double-T asked. "It's your call, but for the record: I don't like it, either."

Jackie hesitated. They could be walking straight into a trap set by the Lumar. But, if the Philippians were still down there, bugging out would be a breach of contract. Her company's reputation would suffer, and so would the bottom line. And if she left, she'd be no better than—

"Take us down," she said, her voice tight.

Moments later, Double-T gently set the *Bunker Hill* down near the chemical flares, on a patch of grass devoid of any rubble. The dropship's thrusters kicked up clouds of dust before he powered down to a steady idle. "We're ready to fly the moment you give the word," he promised.

Marcus's metal feet clanged down the ramp. He cut a wide berth around the tower, looking left and right. "*Clear.*"

Sayra ventured out next. She moved slowly, scanning the area through her rifle scope. Jackie followed close behind, a compact FN-P90 tight across her armored chest. Even though the select-fire bullpup was more than a century old, it was hard to beat for personal defense. It was reliable, concealable, and damn sexy; her kind of gun.

The upper limb of Krieben 7 peeked over the treetops, the gas giant's yellow atmosphere as bright as a supermoon back on Earth. Jackie crouched behind an enormous column as big around as a centuries-old oak tree. The others were of varying sizes, but all had toppled, sliced through at the base like a scythe through wheat. What kind of weapon would be needed for that? Was that what the Science Guild had come for?

And if not, how much could she sell it for?

"*Little Miss, we've got company,*" Marcus said.

A man Jackie assumed was Lieutenant Eckland jogged from the tower's open entrance, flanked by a pair of his men. All three looked bedraggled, their uniforms ripped and stained with mud and blood. Eckland's head was covered in a dirty, blood-soaked bandage. The corporal to the left had his arm in a sling and sported two black eyes. The private on the right was hunched over as if he were in a lot of pain, his bulky frame draped in a big coat, face hidden behind a closed helmet. Several more men hung back in the shadow of the tower, their features lost in the gloom.

"Thank God you're here!" Eckland said, breath misting in the cool air. "We didn't think we'd make it. The Lumar have been relentless."

"I can see that." Jackie glanced from Eckland to Corporal Slinger to Private Hunchback. "Do any of you need medical attention?"

"We've already had a lot of hands on us, especially him." Eckland jerked a thumb at the ailing private. "We'll get checked after we're done here. Can we offload the supplies? We'll see they get to Captain Philips."

"We'll handle the offloading. Once your captain signs the contract, they're all yours."

"He'll be here soon," Eckland promised. "We radioed him as soon as we saw your dropship."

Then why had it taken so long for anyone to respond to their hails? The skin around Jackie's pinplants was starting to itch. *Danger,*

Jackie Warren. She tapped her transceiver. "Start offloading." Then they could get the *Bunker Hill* back in the air for overwatch.

Big Al and Riku stomped down the ramp and took up positions on either side. Big Al slowly scanned the area while Riku flexed his mechanical hands and waited. *"Activating conveyor,"* Double-T said. *"Time to put my baby on a diet!"*

A loud whirring drowned out Double-T's laughter, then the first container slid down the ramp onto the grass. Riku shoved it out of the way as the next one flew down. Within a minute, all six crates were present and accounted for.

Private Hunchback muttered something, then groaned piteously. Eckland glanced at him, frowning. He turned back to Jackie. "So, uh, what's in that container?" he asked, pointing to the green one.

"Rations," she lied, her skin itching even more. "We like to keep them separate from the munitions." She glanced from Eckland to Private Hunchback. "Are you sure he's all right?"

"Oh, he's fine," Eckland said. "A little stomachache. He and his brothers got into a ration-eating contest the other night, and he won *and* lost, if you know what I mean. Which is interesting, considering he's the smallest of his siblings. The others are the tallest in the unit! Why—"

As he rambled, his gaze flicked from Jackie to Private Hunchback. Slowly he reached up and scratched behind his right ear, on the same side as Jackie's pinplants.

Jackie rubbed her forehead, her hand covering her eyes and the telltale glassiness that accompanied a pinlink dive. She accessed her wireless transceiver and reached out for any active transmissions. She found one, encrypted and broadcasting in Private Hunchback's helmet. She assumed it was Philippian radio chatter, but there had been something in Eckland's eyes...

She activated the decryption program. Within a few seconds, the chittering squeaks of the Zuparti language filled her head. A few seconds more, and her translator kicked in: "*...getting tedious. If they won't leave, deal with it. It's only a few CASPers and a couple of Human females. Kill them!*"

Her hand dropped toward her P90 as Private Hunchback rose to his full seven-foot height. He threw back his coat, revealing four arms. Two of his ham-sized fists aimed laser pistols at her. She wouldn't make it in time!

Eckland crashed into her, sending both of them to the ground. Corporal Slinger threw himself at the Lumar in Human's clothing, and the two grappled for a few seconds. The whining crack of a laser pistol rang out, followed by a gurgling scream. Another crack, and the scream cut off.

The Lumar turned back to Jackie, who used her nanite-enhanced strength to lift Eckland enough to get her P90 out from between them. Before the Lumar could fire, she pointed the short-barreled bullpup at the creature's groin and squeezed. She held it steady and rode the recoil up the Lumar's body, stitching a line of 5.7mm bullet holes from crotch to face. Lumar might be tough, but this one had been unarmored to aid in the deception. A gasp escaped the broken faceplate, and he collapsed into the dirt.

Unseen laser beams scorched lines of grass and bullets shattered against pillars in sprays of alabaster chips. "*Lumar!*" Marcus growled over the comms.

"*They're pouring out of the tower! They—oh, those bastards!*" Big Al roared.

Jackie rolled onto her stomach and raised her head. Eight armored Lumar charged out of the tower, each holding a laser rifle in one pair of hands and a Human in the other. A dead Human, judging by the way the uniformed Philippians flopped around.

"Damn them," Eckland said, his voice low and flat. "They ambushed us, took us prisoner, and said they'd kill us if we warned you." He laughed bitterly. "They keep their word, these aliens."

Jackie fired a burst at one of the Lumar, but he saw her and raised his dead hostage as a shield. The hypervelocity rounds blew through the slain Philippian, but barely scratched the Lumar's armor. He pointed his laser rifle.

Riku stepped between her and the tower, shield raised on his left arm. Laser pulses bounced off the reflective surface. "JC, stay behind me!" he shouted through his CASPer's external speakers as his shoulder-mounted chain gun shredded three of the Lumar. The others dropped their Human shields and dove.

Jackie ducked to switch magazines. She glanced at Eckland. "How many men were with you?"

"Nine, including Rienard." He pointed to the dead corporal, then picked up one of the laser pistols dropped by the alien formerly known as Private Hunchback. "I'm all that's left."

More Lumar charged from the tower, but the inside still teemed with them. And Eckland's whole squad was dead, so...She keyed her pinplants. "Take that building down!"

"*Don't mind if I do!*" Big Al spread his legs and fired his shoulder-mounted missile launcher. The missile flew straight through the doorless opening. The entire first floor disappeared in a fireball. Pieces of Lumar sailed out of narrow windows, their bloody remains bouncing against columns and rolling through the grass.

472 | KENNEDY & WANDREY

"Excellent work!" Marcus called.

"How do you like that?" Big Al laughed. *"How do you—"*

Something exploded against his back. He struck the ground face-first, his thousand-pound Mk 7 crushing a small column into powder. "Al!" Jackie cried.

"I'm all right!" Big Al pushed himself to his feet and reached for his laser carbine. *"Enemy to the rear!"*

Dozens of Lumar surged out of the woods on the edge of the field, firing wildly with all kinds of energy and ballistic weapons. Jackie kept behind Riku's protective armor, firing burst after burst at the charging aliens. Riku's chain gun thumped in a steady rhythm.

A pair of Lumar knelt in the dirt as their four-armed cohorts charged. One held a rocket launcher while the other reloaded. Jackie shouldered her P90, but they were too far away. Instead of firing, she activated her weapon's targeting laser. "Enemy rocket launcher on my mark!"

The Lumar shouldered his rocket launcher and aimed. A rifle shot rang out, and his head snapped back, blood spraying from the exit wound. The dying Lumar jerked the trigger as the muzzle dipped toward the ground. Both he and his buddy disappeared in the blast.

Sayra had scrambled up onto a narrow tower close to Jackie's position. Her rifle's long barrel peeked out from between decorative stone merlons on the round rooftop. "Nice shot!" Jackie said.

"Please, that wasn't even five hundred yards." Sayra fired again, the muzzle flash bright in the darkness.

The Lumar continued to advance, firing a steady stream of beams and bullets into the pillar field. Marcus circled the ruined tower, his MAC popping out slow, precise shots. But for every Lumar he took down, another took its place.

A laser beam skimmed along Riku's shield and burned a line across his chest armor. *"Damn, they keep coming!"*

"Light 'em up!" Double-T called to Ed, and a moment later the *Bunker Hill's* guns opened fire, raking the approaching Lumar with a withering barrage.

A rocket flew from the forest and slammed into the *Bunker Hill's* left side, disabling a machine gun turret. *"More rockets!"* Marcus warned.

"Take off, Double-T!" Jackie ordered. "Give us overwatch!"

"Roger! With all that weight gone, my baby's ready to turn some tricks!"

The *Bunker Hill's* engines roared to life, drowning out the cacophony of battle. It rose vertically at first, and then at an angle as it gained altitude.

Then the number one engine erupted in flames, and the dropship started to list. *"Heat seekers! Trying to compensate! Ed, pop the flares and chaff!"*

"On it, boss!"

Bright orange flares shot out from the *Bunker Hill's* underbelly, followed by a cloud of reflective filament. The night sky turned to day as thousands of twinkling "stars" appeared. The rockets that chased after the limping dropship flew wildly off course, their guidance systems blinded.

"Sorry, JC!" Double-T radioed. *"We're going to land a few miles to the east and start on repairs. Make your way to us for extract!"*

"Understood! Stay safe!"

"Here's a parting gift!"

Canisters fell from the *Bunker Hill* and detonated about thirty feet up. Thick yellow smoke covered the field of broken pillars, obscuring her vision. She studied the *Bunker Hill's* camera feed through her pinplants, noting enemy positions, as more smoke grenades burst. They were surrounded by at least a company of Lumar.

A missile streaked past and blew up nearby. Big Al screamed over the comms, and she heard more than saw his CASPer collapse. She scrambled toward him and found his stricken mecha on its back, side armor dented. She tried to pop the hatch, but it wouldn't open more than an inch.

Lieutenant Eckland and Sayra joined her a moment later. "I'll cover you!" Sayra said as Eckland ran over to help Jackie with the canopy. Together they tried to force it open with their bare hands, but the resistance was too great. Eckland scooped up a laser rifle from a dead Lumar and jammed the barrel into the gap. Jackie held it in place while he stamped on the stock with all his weight. On the third stomp, the canopy popped free with a hiss.

Big Al lay unconscious, his face bloody from a cut along his forehead. They pulled him free and hefted his weight between them. Jackie slipped a hand around his waist but recoiled when something sharp pricked her. Eckland studied the man's side. "Shrapnel wound. Bleeding, but not spurting. He'll make it, if we hurry."

That was assuming any of them made it. She couldn't see more than a few feet in the yellow fog. Where were they going to go?

The ground in front of Jackie suddenly lifted, revealing a narrow hole. A female Caroon with a headlamp strapped to her yellow helmet appeared, long snout sniffing at the air. She looked directly at Jackie and motioned with her digging claws. "This way!"

Jackie glanced at Eckland. "One of the dig team?"

"I think so? They all look alike to me."

"I heard that, Lieutenant Eckland!" the Caroon snapped. "I'm Feesha, *leader* of the dig team! Now, hurry! One of my subordinates will lead your CASPers to a bigger tunnel!"

Jackie looked at where she thought the cargo containers were. Even if she could get to them, there was no way they could carry them to the Philippians' base camp, not with Big Al's CASPer disabled, and Riku and Marcus hard-pressed.

A stray bullet zipped past her head. She ducked. "Retreat!" she said into her pinplants. "Follow the Caroon! Into the tunnels!"

"*What tunnels?*" Marcus snapped. "*What are you—Riku, look out!*"

Jackie and Eckland carried Big Al to the hole. Feesha helped pull the stocky, red-bearded man into the darkness. Eckland hopped down next, followed by Sayra, at Jackie's urging. Jackie took one last look around, her teeth clenched in frustration. The cargo containers would have to wait.

The first order was to survive.

* * *

They walked along a narrow tunnel so fresh the soil was still damp. Dirt rained down on their heads as muffled explosions shook the earth. Marcus's and Riku's voices continued to echo through her pinplants as the two fought against an overwhelming number of Lumar. She silently prayed for their safety.

They stopped long enough for Feesha to backtrack. A loud rumble resounded from the darkness, then she reappeared, her fur covered in dirt. "No one's going to follow us now," she reported, her floppy ears twitching happily.

Feesha led the way, with Sayra taking up rear security and Eckland in the middle. He carried Big Al in a fireman's carry, an impressive feat for a man of average build. If Eckland struggled under Al's bulk, he made no complaint. "Best if you stay on point," he grunted at Jackie, "in case the enemy gets ahead of us somehow."

Jackie joined Feesha at the front of the short line. Before she could say anything, the Caroon pressed a claw to her earpiece. She muttered something in her language, then glanced at Jackie. "Your armored suits are with Yulien. They will join us at the mercenary camp."

Jackie nodded her thanks. She had been aware of the others' situation through her pinplants, but there was no sense in being rude. No one liked a know-it-all, no matter the species.

The transition from freshly dug tunnel to ancient corridor was stark. One moment Jackie's boots pressed into soft dirt, the next they clicked noisily on tile. She looked this way and that, her weapon-mounted light illuminating frescoes and sculptures that hadn't seen the sun in thousands of years. Her gaze lingered on a faded painting of two aliens—one reptilian, the other avian—dueling with primitive weapons. The dinosaur creature wielded a glowing sword, the bird a scythe of ridiculous proportions.

"Beautiful, isn't it?" the Caroon said. "This whole structure is filled with such finds."

As much as Jackie appreciated good art, she wouldn't exactly consider this a good find. Certainly not worth dying for. What were the Lumar really after? What was the Science Guild after?

Not your problem, Jackie. Her goal was still the same: resupply the Philippians so they could continue protecting the dig site. As long as they completed their mission and she got paid, she didn't care if they unearthed a nest of Canavar.

The corridor turned sharply, and they saw light ahead. "Lieutenant Eckland!" a man called out, his voice echoing strangely through the ancient tunnel. "So nice of you to join us again! And you brought guests!"

"We've got an injured man!" Eckland shouted back.

Jackie and Feesha let Eckland lead the way into a round chamber dimly lit with emergency lanterns. Several mercs crouched behind a sandbag fortification in the center of the room, weapons ready. A medic and his orderly ran from an adjoining tunnel. The orderly pulled Big Al from Eckland's shoulders. The medic tried to examine Eckland's bandaged head, but he shook him off. "See to this man first. He saved my life. They all did."

"What about Corporal Rienard and the others?" one of the mercs asked.

"Dead." Eckland helped the orderly carry Big Al down the adjoining corridor. "Along with our comms system."

Marcus and Riku entered moments later, stepping carefully to avoid cracking the ancient tiles. The Justin Timers' CASPers were scarred and scorched, but neither looked badly damaged. They opened their canopies and climbed out. Both were sweaty. Marcus immediately grabbed his pack of Luckiest Strikes.

One of the mercs rounded the sandbag barrier. "I'm Sergeant Hector of the Philippians. Thank you for saving the lieutenant."

"No, thank you," Jackie said, stepping into the dim light. "We'd have been in a tight spot had Feesha not rescued us. I'm sorry we couldn't save the others."

"These things happen in—Wait, that voice." Sergeant Hector squinted. "Candy the Gun Bunny?"

"In the flesh!" Jackie said with a theatrical bow. She glanced up, then over her shoulder. "Minus the ears and tail, anyway."

"What're you doing here?"

Marcus lit a cigarette. "I ask that same question every single mission."

"Quiet, you."

By now the other Philippians had gathered close. As most of the mercs were men, their attention was focused first on Jackie for the "Woah, what a bombshell!" factor, then on Marcus for the "Hey, he looks like he might know a way out of this mess!" vibe his cool confidence gave off, then on Jackie and Sayra because, "Woah, *two* bombshells!"

Sayra sighed. "*Homens...*"

Jackie smiled and waved, though worry gnawed at her gut. The mercs were banged up, low on ammo, and very outnumbered. All they'd managed to do so far was save one man at the cost of one of their own, and their dropship.

She turned to Hector. "Take us to Captain Philips. It's vital we plan our next move."

* * *

"So, let me get this straight," Philips said, rubbing his temples. "Not only was I screwed out of a shipment once, but now my second shipment is in the hands of the enemy?"

"Yes," Jackie said, "but I believe it's worse than that."

Jackie sat on a wide stone bench, elbows resting on the empty crate being used as a table. Marcus sat on her right, Sayra on her left. Riku leaned against the wall, close to the open portal leading into the corridor connecting the various chambers the Philippians occupied. Across from them sat Captain Philips, Feesha, and a freshly bandaged Eckland.

"Worse than that," Philips muttered. "Not what I wanted to hear but go on."

Jackie pointed at the laser rifle leaning against the wall behind Eckland. "That's a J-9a, built in Jackson, Mississippi. Where did you get it?"

"From one of the Lumar your group killed."

"And where did he get it from?"

"One of my men he killed?" Eckland shrugged, then froze. "Wait...None of my men at the LZ had laser rifles."

"I thought as much." Lasers were great anti-personnel weapons, but a stray shot in the right spot could wreak all sorts of havoc on a dropship. Small arms were less likely to damage an armored vehicle, save for 20mm MAC rifles and crew-served .50s. She turned to Philips. "Are all your weapons accounted for?"

"Mostly," he said. "We've been keeping a tight handle on all munitions, since our supplies are so low. Over the last few weeks we've lost a couple of rifles and a few pistols. Oh, and one crew-served weapon. But that's it."

"And was the order you placed with Nuchols similar to what you placed with my company? Ammunition, but also replacement small arms? Rifles, SMGs, the like?"

"Yes. Why do you—" His brow furrowed. "Are you implying that *both* my shipments wound up in enemy hands?"

"Technically my goods aren't yet in enemy hands, but we'll get back to that." She tapped into her pinplants. "Do you have a Tri-V I can jack into?"

A moment later, someone set a Tri-V projector on the crate between them. Jackie removed a pinlink cable from a pouch, inserted one end into the pinplant behind her ear and the other into the Tri-V. "This image was taken from a camera on one of the crates half an hour ago."

The three-dimensional image of a dark-furred Zuparti appeared over the projector. The Zuparti was frozen, its mouth open slightly as it spoke to someone off-camera.

Philips gasped. "Nuchols!"

"No." Feesha flicked her long tongue in the Caroon gesture of exasperation. "You Humans think all aliens look alike. Nuchols is female. That is a male Zuparti. Likely Greshet, her mate."

"You know this Nuchols?" Sayra asked.

"Caroon aren't classified as a mercenary race, but that doesn't mean we don't fight." Feesha patted the pistol on her hip. "Even noncombatants need to defend themselves."

Jackie produced a business datacard and handed it to Feesha. "Our people well understand the defensive needs of civilians. Please consider doing business with us next time."

"I will gladly do so." Feesha pocketed the card, then grunted. "It would seem Nuchols is the one who leaked information about this dig."

"How so?" Philips asked.

Feesha fidgeted. "One of my males has loose lips. He couldn't keep his tongue from wagging about these ruins and the possibility of old technology and weapons. Nuchols and her mate, Greshet, were quite interested." She grunted. "It all makes sense now. Shortly after receiving our sidearms, we were suddenly delayed by station security. They wanted to know everything about us, our mission, the reason a science team had weapons, and so on and so forth. We weren't allowed to leave until the Science Guild sent and then resent our credentials."

"And when you landed, the Lumar were right behind you." Philips struck the crate with his fist. "We were played from the start!"

"Is there any usable tech here?" Marcus asked. "Some sort of weapon we could use?"

"No. That was looted long ago, if any of it ever existed. All that's left are finds of archaeological importance."

So much for finding out how all those pillars got toppled and who set up the towers in their place. "Why not tell Greshet and his Lumar lackeys the site's a dud?"

"We tried," Eckland said, "but the Lumar are out for blood. We've been pummeling them for weeks."

"The only way to convince them would be to give them access to the dig site, and our contract forbids entry by unauthorized personnel." Philips spread his hands. "So, what now?"

"Take a look at this." Jackie loaded up a series of images and combined them into a three-dimensional representation of a base camp complete with buildings, tents, and a low wall made of ferrocrete. "This is where the cargo containers were taken. They haven't been opened, so your munitions are safe."

"Safe in an enemy camp filled with Lumar."

Eckland whistled appreciatively. "Good Lord, how many cameras do you have?"

"Cameras are cheap. Information is not." She smiled. "Don't worry, I won't charge extra for this. Well, maybe a little."

Philips laughed mirthlessly. "So, what do you propose we do with this information?"

"Get to the containers before they're able to defeat my security system, unlock them, arm the Philippians, and win the day. I call it, 'Operation Return to Sender.'"

"Um, Little Miss," Marcus said, "have you noticed the army of very big, very pissed-off Lumar between us and the containers?" He waved a hand at the projection. "I know they're hard to take note of, being very big and very pissed-off and all, but—"

"I'm aware of the enemy army, Marcus, but they can be beaten. They may outnumber us, and they may outgun us." Her smile broadened. "But they won't outsmart us."

Captain Philips looked at Marcus. "She always like this?"

"Only when things are about to go sideways." Marcus took a long pull on his cigarette. "It's enough to drive a man to smoke."

Sayra snatched the cigarette from Marcus's mouth and took a puff. "A woman, too," she added.

* * *

"*There they are,*" Sayra whispered, her voice barely audible even through Jackie's pinplants. "*Three hundred yards north of my position, with*—" She cut off abruptly.

Jackie knelt in the forest floor's detritus alongside Captain Philips and Sergeant Hector. The sergeant motioned for the men behind them to halt. It bothered her that, of them all, she was the most heavily armed. The P90 was only going to be good for a close-in fight against the Lumar. And she'd need a lot of rounds per alien.

Finally, Sayra spoke. *"Four Lumar passed beneath my tree. Scout patrol. Marcus, are you ready? They're heading your way."*

"Almost there. The terrain is more overgrown than we thought. Give us a few."

They had consolidated the fuel and weapons from their CASPers to equip the Philippians' two best units, driven by Corporals Stevens and Hernandez. They had joined Marcus and Riku, raising the number of functional CASPers to four. Only the two Justin Timers had any jump juice left. And two wouldn't be enough for a direct assault against an entrenched enemy, but hopefully it wouldn't come to that.

"I'm still not happy about this, Little Miss," Marcus said. *"We should be protecting you, not running through the woods."*

"If you pull this off, you will be protecting me."

"I'll be watching over our garota from the treetops, Marcus."

"And JC knows how to handle herself in a fight," Riku added. *"You trained her. You trained all of us."*

The night air suddenly erupted with the thumps of chain guns and the chattering of autocannons. *"Contact!"* Marcus barked.

Jackie tapped into the enemy's comms. *"Human armored suits spotted! Engaging!"* a Lumar shouted.

"How many?" Greshet demanded.

"Five. We caught them on patrol."

"That's the majority of their remaining CASPers. Destroy them, and the rest of the Humans will be like puldas to the slaughter! My mate's reputation will be safe!"

"So, that's why they want all of us dead," Jackie murmured. "Interesting."

"Movement in the camp," Sayra reported. *"Lumar platoons advancing on the CASPers. Three, no, four of them."*

There were about twenty left in the camp, if their estimates were correct. Jackie and Philips glanced at each other. He nodded. Time to go.

Philips had broken his group into two platoons of twenty-five men, one led by him, the other by Sergeant Hector. Lieutenant Eckland had stayed behind with the rest of the walking wounded to guard the site and protect the dig team. Big Al had survived thanks to quick nanite treatments, but the merc doctor had forbidden him to join the assault. "I'll hold down the fort," he said. "Kick some ass for me!"

Jackie stayed with Philips as his team cut a straight path through the woods to the outskirts of the camp. "Shame Feesha and her crew couldn't dig a tunnel here," she said in a hushed tone.

"Solid rock under the Lumar position," Philips answered. "Greshet may be a piece of shit, but he's a smart piece of shit."

They stopped when they reached the edge of the woods. Jackie looked through her night vision binoculars at the enemy camp. Four ferrocrete structures had been built in the center of the camp, two to act as barracks for the Lumar troops and one festooned with communications dishes and antennae. The remaining building looked like an armory or a fortified storehouse, with thick walls and positions for machine guns and sniper nests on all four corners of the roof. Only one of those positions was occupied. The three Lumar stationed on top focused on the action to the north. Marcus and the others were doing their jobs well.

The cargo containers sat outside the armory, with a half dozen Lumar standing guard and Greshet hunched over a computer terminal connected to one of the blue containers.

No one was looking their way yet, but they had a couple hundred yards of clearing to run through. "Sergeant," Philips said, "provide covering fire, but only once we're spotted. Make your shots count. We're still in this fight."

"*We're still in this fight!*" Hector replied.

Philips glanced her way. "Ready?"

She tucked the P90 against her shoulder. "Let's do this."

Philips and Jackie led the way, the remaining men close behind in a staggered line. They ran quickly and quietly, their boots all but silent in the tall grass. They covered 50 yards, then 100. At 150 yards, Jackie felt a surge of hope. They could do this. They'd take the camp by surprise and—

A laser beam lanced out. Behind her, one of the Philippians screamed and hit the ground. "Keep moving!" Philips shouted. "Don't stop!"

One of the three Lumar on the roof fired a laser rifle their way. The other two prepped a crew-served machine gun. They'd be sitting ducks if that gun went hot. "Sayra!" she called.

"*I see them.*"

A shot rang out, and the laser sniper fell from the roof. Sayra fired twice more, and the machine gunners went down.

"*Switching positions.*"

Sergeant Hector's platoon opened fire next, placing their shots carefully to conserve ammo. Lumar ducked behind cover and returned fire. The suppressing fire bought Philips and Jackie enough time to reach the perimeter wall at the cost of three troopers.

"We're almost there!" one of the mercs shouted, starting to climb over the fence. "Let's g—"

He spun around and collapsed in the dirt, his face melted off. "Get his ammo!" Philips said, jumping up long enough to fire a quick burst.

"*We're about empty!*" Hector called on the radio. "*Can't provide much more cover fire.*"

Jackie risked a look over the wall. There were more than twenty Lumar. It looked closer to forty. She crouched as a barrage of lasers and bullets peppered the wall. "Can any of the CASPers advance?"

"*Negative,*" Marcus said. "*Too much resistance. Damn, these guys are good.*"

She gritted her teeth. Between a rock and a hard place.

"I'm out!" one of the men shouted. He dropped his rifle on its three-point sling, then drew his laser pistol. He fired several blasts, the pistol emitting a whining crack every time he squeezed the trigger.

Captain Philips' rifle bolt locked back. He cursed. "We have to retreat!"

"Too late for that!" Jackie said, firing a burst from her P90. She ducked, but a laser beam singed several strands of her raven hair. "We can't stop now!"

An explosion echoed from the forest. "*Left arm disabled,*" Riku said. "*Pulling back to reload.*"

"*Stevens, cover Riku,*" Marcus ordered. "*Hernandez, K-Bombs on my mark.*"

"Order your men to pull back," Philips said. "We'll cover you with what little we've got."

"No!" Jackie stared at the containers. They were close, so close!

"Miss Warren, please fall back. You don't have to die here!"

Frustration burned in her chest. "Neither do you!"

"Damn it, woman!" Philips snapped. "You did your job! You delivered the goods. Now go!"

"No!"

"Why are you so hung up on this?"

"Because Papa died this way!" She glared at Philips, unshed tears stinging her eyes. "My father was killed on some nameless rock in the armpit of the galaxy because he needed supplies, and his chickenshit arms dealer wouldn't risk a hot drop." She slapped a hand against her chest armor so hard her palm stung. "I'll be damned if I *ever* let a client of mine die like that, so shut up! We're still in this fight!"

"*Woah,*" Riku said. "*JC's pissed. Reloaded, ready to advance!*"

She risked a look over the wall. Twenty yards to the closest container. So close she could practically touch its metallic, green surface.

Wait, green?

An idea blossomed, and a fierce grin spread across her face. She swapped to a full magazine, then let the gun hang on its sling as she checked her remaining ammo. Fifty-one rounds in the gun, another full magazine on her belt, along with three partials. The P90 would burn through it all quickly, but it would have to do.

"How many still have ammo?" she asked. "Hands!"

Of the fifteen men still with her, only four raised their hands.

Not good. "Grenades?"

In addition to the four, another six.

Better. "All right, on my mark, start hurling grenades. Two per man. Then switch to your weapons and keep their heads down long enough for me to close the distance." She patted her P90. "I'll take care of the rest."

"With that popgun?" Philips demanded.

"*Little Miss, what are you up to?*" Marcus asked, concern in his voice.

"You'll see." She stood, shoulders hunched and head down. She glanced over her shoulder. "Understand this is getting added to your bill."

"What is?" Philips and Marcus said in unison.

"You'll see. Grenades, now! Then one more volley!"

Ten grenades sailed over the wall. Most fell short of their mark, but a couple landed close to the containers. When the first one exploded, Jackie bounded over the wall. She sprinted forward, P90 against her shoulder.

Grenades detonated ahead of her, the blasts blowing Lumar from their feet. The unlucky ones died as shrapnel tore through their armor and shredded their vitals. The lucky ones were knocked to the ground, stunned.

As the "lucky" ones got to their feet, Jackie was on top of them. She used the P90 for snap shots straight into their faces and the gaps in their torso armor. One Lumar fired at her with his laser pistol, the beam barely missing her face. She stamped down on the offending arm, jammed the hot barrel into the creature's neck, and squeezed off a three-shot burst.

She crouched next to the dying Lumar as the second volley of grenades soared overhead. Most of them landed among the shipping containers, the throwers more worried about falling short with her in the middle of it. The grenades blew up as she switched to her last full magazine, the shrapnel pinging off the containers. Her ears rang, but she could still hear the screams of wounded and dying Lumar.

"*Lumar converging on your position, JC!*" Riku called.

"*Mãe de Deus, that's a lot of them! I'll try and thin them out!*"

Jackie could see them: two full platoons of Lumar, charging from the other side of the camp. They must have figured out the CASPers were a feint. She broke into a sprint. *Almost there!*

A trio of bleeding, battered Lumar stumbled out from behind the green shipping container, their weapons slowly tracking her. She filled one full of holes and tried to shift her aim. The remaining two fired. One's laser beam missed, but the other's bullet struck her square in the chest. The armor plate caught it, but it felt like a hammer blow to the ribs. She staggered, her return fire going wild. Cursing, she tried to steady her aim, but knew it was too late.

A bullet zipped past her head, and the Lumar with the laser rifle fell, blood spraying from a ruined eye socket. The other dove for cover as a barrage of bullets pinged against the container.

Jackie ran around the opposite side. She needed to take out that one Lumar before she could risk using the security panel. She needed to—

Something dark and furry slammed into her, knocking her from her feet. The creature landed on top of her and stabbed at her with a knife. She knocked her assailant's paw aside and tried to bring the P90's barrel up.

Greshet dropped the knife, grabbed the P90 with both paws, and crushed it against her aching ribs. "You've ruined everything, you little whelp," he hissed.

Jackie tried to kick him off her, but the Zuparti kept her pinned. His fangs gleamed in the gas giant's yellow light. "I'll kill you, then the Philippians. Then the ancient tech will be mine!"

"There is no tech!" she spat.

"We'll see!" Greshet opened his mouth wide and lunged for her face.

Jackie smashed her forehead into the Zuparti's lower jaw. He threw back his head and howled, a thick piece of his tongue hanging by a thread. Jackie jerked her left hand free and punched him in the face, knocking him aside. She tried to sit up, but she was suddenly pulled toward him as he yanked on her P90's sling, hatred in his beady eyes. Another knife appeared in his paws, and he leaped.

Bang!

Greshet fell against her, body limp, blood pouring from a hole between his eyes. His fetid death rattle washed over her, and then he lay still.

"Keep your filthy paws off my little garota!" Sayra said.

Jackie released the P90 from its sling and shoved the Zuparti corpse off her. She jumped to her feet and ran for the security pad on the green container, her pinlink cable already hanging from her pinplants. She shoved the other end into the terminal's socket and quickly accessed the program. *Come on, come on. There!*

The hard barrel of a pistol pressed against the side of her head. She risked a glance. The third Lumar stood there, a grin on his pale, humanoid face. "Any last words?"

"Yeah." She returned the grin, then spoke the command aloud: "Open!"

The container doors rolled up, and out slid the Camille H5 automated sentry guns, minigun barrels already spinning. One sighted in on the pistol-wielding Lumar.

The Lumar's eyes widened. "Oh, shi—"

His body disappeared in a storm of 7.62 rounds. Jackie threw herself to the side, her hair and armor splattered in blood and gore. They were going to have to hose her armor down after this, and her along with it.

The Lumar reinforcements poured into the encampment at the best possible moment. The Camille H5s had been preprogrammed to target Lumar, and they went at it with as much gusto as their software could muster. In less than a minute, the machines expended thousands of rounds, created mountains of brass, and annihilated nearly a company's worth of aliens.

When the guns finally fell silent, the only ones left alive were cheering Philippians and a weary Jackie. She stood and dusted herself off, grimacing when her hands came back sticky with blood. At least it wasn't her own.

Captain Philips and Sergeant Hector walked through the carnage, eyes wide. They saw her covered in blood and rushed over. "Are you all right?" Philips demanded.

"*What's going on?*" Marcus snapped. "*Little Miss, are you all right?*"

"Better than all right." Jackie wiped blood off her face with the back of her hand and flicked it to the ground. She smiled. "I love it when a plan comes together."

* * *

"**M**iss Warren," Captain Philips said, "pardon my language, but you've got to have the biggest set of brass balls in the Crapti region. That was some damn fine work."

Jackie laughed. "Why, thank you! If I had any balls, I'm sure they'd be pleased with the compliment."

Together they surveyed the damage from their earlier battle. At least thirty Lumar soldiers lay dead, their blood and remains splattered and scattered across the crater-pocked, bullet-riddled field of broken pillars. Combined with the losses at the base camp, more than a hundred and forty aliens had perished in the fight, all for tech that didn't exist.

A handful of Philippians had fallen in the last battle, bringing the total losses of the company to 30 dead and 53 wounded. They were terrible losses, considering they had arrived on Krieben 7-h with 122.

"'The Justin Timers,'" Philips said. He chuckled. "Well, you were on time for us. And that means we owe you quite a bit of dime." He held out his hand. "Dime we're happy to pay."

She took the offered hand in her much smaller one and was pleased at his firm grip. "We're grateful for your business. We do regular deliveries and outfitting, too, so please consider us the next time the Philippians venture into untamed lands." She grinned. "We'll help you tame them."

Philips returned the grin. "Consider it done." His smile faded. "You have my condolences. I didn't know your father was the same Justin Warren who commanded the Wardens. He was a good man."

"Thank you, Captain. He was."

He limped away to see to the fortifications, leaving Jackie alone in the field of dead. In the distance, she could see Sayra assisting the Philippians with camouflaging some newly dug observation posts. If Nuchols returned to avenge Greshet, the mercs would be ready.

Jackie would make sure word got out about Nuchols. Any arms dealer willing to sell out a client didn't deserve to remain in business.

The *Bunker Hill* landed a few minutes later. "*Power's looking good!*" Double-T radioed. "*She'll get us back to the* Justice*!*"

Big Al, Marcus, and Riku waited at the bottom of the ramp, each man puffing away on a last smoke before liftoff. Not that the recycled air would keep Marcus from his Luckiest Strikes. He offered her the pack. "Care for one, Little Miss?"

"Maybe later," she said, crinkling her nose at the acrid stench. "Or never. Thank you, though."

"JC, what's the score?" Riku asked. "We make out big?"

"We will once the Philippians finish their contract. Three more weeks for Feesha to close up the site, then it's bonus time."

"Big Al buys the first round of *cachaça!*" Sayra called. She walked over, her long-barreled rifle cradled in her arms.

"Hey!" Big Al protested as the others laughed. He lifted his shirt to show the bandage on his side. "I'm an injured man!"

"Oh, poor *bebê*."

Jackie's pinplants chirped as a new message arrived from the *Wardens' Justice*. Her face lit up.

"Uh oh," Riku said.

A grin split Big Al's red beard. "That's never a good sign."

"Justin Timers, drinks will have to wait!" Jackie strode up the ramp and spun around, hands on her hips as she studied her troops. "We've got another job!"

Marcus lit another cigarette. "No rest for the weary, eh?"

Sayra thumped him on the shoulder. "*Amigo*, would you have it any other way?"

Puffs of smoke escaped his lips as he chuckled. "Nah, I suppose not." Raising his voice, he yelled, "You heard the Little Miss! Let's go!"

# # # # #

Grunwald
by David Alan Jones

Planet Wandray looked like a blue-green lump from geostationary orbit. Janet Grunwald watched it on the main viewer from the comms station, a smile playing at her lips.

"How's Manny holding up?" she asked.

"*The Pride* is doing just fine, thank you." Simon Price, Janet's business partner and the love of her life, put on a mock tone of exasperation. He insisted on calling their little company's sole CASPer, *The Pride of the Fleet*. Janet called it *Manny* after her favorite uncle, and to take the piss out of Simon.

"How are the bugs treating you?" she asked, turning serious.

"Paying me not a damned bit of attention. Just the way I like it." Simon sounded crisp despite the distance between them. He could have been aboard the *Fiddlehead*, their rented freighter, instead of more than thirty-five thousand klicks away.

"Only five more hours, and you'll be out of that tin can." Janet readjusted the harness holding her in her seat against the *Fiddlehead's* micro gravity environment. She could have held this conversation in her quarters, housed in the ship's spin ring, but she preferred seeing the planet where her lover stood. Silly that. School-girlish.

But true.

"Yeah, this rotation. But we've still got four more to go, so it's not like the contract's over." Simon must have been on the move. Janet could hear the familiar buzz of Manny's actuators through the comm.

"But after that, we get paid," she said.

"My favorite state, paid. Great place to visit, but I never get to stay long."

"But really, the bugs are good?"

"Quit yer fretting, little lady." Simon put on a deep drawl, trying to mimic a cowboy from one of those ridiculous ancient western movies he loved so much. Some were so old they had been shot in flat screen black and white. "Seriously, the bugs aren't doing anything to me. I'm fine."

"Okay. I just worry."

"Don't."

Janet had accepted this guard duty contract on short notice. Like all the jobs handled by Two Guys and a CASP Incorporated, this one amounted to work the real merc companies didn't want. Six days guarding a mine while automated drones prospected for anything to make this little pimple on the ass end of the galaxy worth something. Wandray didn't exactly top the GalNet Getaways list.

The prime company on the contract was a KzSha-owned outfit called Vonlerd Sfard, which roughly translated meant *Armored Star*. It might be small on the scale of merc enterprises—just fifteen mercs on the payroll according to their stats—but Janet thought them too large, too important really, to take on what amounted to standing around for days on end doing nothing.

Though she had never seen one in the flesh/chitin, Janet had studied the KzSha in-depth via GalNet while considering the contract. They looked like those damned cicada killer wasps that scared her as a child. Janet prided herself on avoiding, as much as possible, the general xenophobia that seemed endemic to humans, but creatures like that made egalitarianism tough.

The KzSha didn't make it any easier. Their race had a reputation for despising mammalian species, yet they had taken on TG&C as a sub-contractor anyway.

Of course, they might have had financial ulterior motives for that. Recent Mercenary Guild laws had eased charter fees for larger companies willing to share contracts with smaller ones—a bootstrap program meant to foster growth across the board. Likely, Armored Star was taking advantage of that offer by giving TG&C a piece of the action, which was fine. Janet would take what she could get. Her company needed the credits—badly.

Then there was the KzSha's other reputation, one for outstanding performance in battle and near maniacal bloodlust against an enemy. Should anything go wrong down there, she could at least know her allies would keep Simon safe.

A clangor of metal on metal made Janet spin around. Bill Klimek, TG&C's troubleshooter, programmer, and multitalented fix-it guy, bumbled his way into the *Fiddlehead's* command suite.

"Sorry, Colonel!" he called, as he sailed past Janet on a collision course for the aft bulkhead, the wrench affixed to his belt pinging off a side wall.

Bill persisted in calling Janet by the title of *Colonel* as a way to tweak her nose like a big brother teasing his sister. In point of fact, she had been a cadet colonel at Bruins Academy on Earth when they met three years earlier, but Janet lost that rank when she elected to resign her impending commission in the famed merc company

Bjorn's Berserkers during her junior year. She traded all of that potential fame and glory for managing TG&C's command and control (C2) during missions, as well as its business affairs.

Janet had considered telling Bill to stow the colonel bit. Sometimes it hurt to remember all she had given up and the price she had paid—was paying—for her life now, but Bill meant nothing by it. He could have been pissed off when his best friend decided to bring a girlfriend on as a business partner and overwatch commander. Janet figured most friends would balk at that kind of move, but not Bill. He had treated Janet like a little sister from day one, and she loved him for it. She didn't like to think where TG&C would be without him.

"I hear the unmistakable crash-bang of my oldest friend up there," Simon said. "Hey Billy, you itching to take over?"

Bill, who had brought himself to a stable stop and now clung to a handhold across the room from Janet, rolled his eyes. "Hell no. I'm not getting back in that smelly CASPer till the minute my shift begins."

Daylight lasted just about seventeen hours on Wandray this time of year. In order to fulfill their contracted six-day obligation, Simon and Bill had divvyed up the days into sixteen hour rotations so that each got at least a few daylight hours. Wandray's white dwarf wasn't much to look at—a little yellow ball through the planet's atmosphere—and neither was Wandray for that matter, but any exposure to a dirtside environment was a welcome change after weeks aboard ship.

Not that Janet would know much about that. The contract made no provisions for her or their hired pilot, Iggy, to set foot on the *claim*, as their client's called Wandray in contract-ese. Just who those clients might be, Janet didn't know, just some out-system mining concern. As a subcontractor, TG&C worked for Armored Star, not the actual paying customer. She would find out soon enough, though, as a representative was due to arrive in the next eighteen hours for an inspection of the operation. She hoped it was an Athal. She had never seen one of the kingpins of the F11 futures market.

"Hope you got some sleep while you were up there," Simon said.

"A working man never gets enough sleep." Bill put on a self-important air even though he knew Simon couldn't see him. He pushed off lightly from the bulkhead and managed a semi-graceful free float across the room only to ruin it by colliding with Janet's command chair. His loose wrench bonked her on the head.

"Ow!"

"Sorry, Colonel. Seriously, sorry." Bill set about retying the wrench with the strap on his belt like he should have done in the spin ring garage.

"You know, this is a fairly mundane mission, Bill. It'd suck if I went home with a concussion." Janet slapped his shoulder playfully, careful not to send him winging back across the command suite.

He grinned and made a rude gesture at her. "Iggy's making lasagna. Thought you might want to join us for lunch before rotation."

Janet's mouth watered at the thought. Sometimes, she wondered if they hired Iggy less for his piloting skills and more for his cooking. "Do you even have to ask?"

"Hey, what about me?" Simon protested. "I'm the one busting my coccyx down here...standing around doing nothing all day."

"He's keeping yours warm 'till you get here."

Janet rubbed the spot where the wrench had hit her. Goofy Bill and his stupid tools. This was not the sort of thing that happened aboard a professional merc ship. She gave him side-eye for a second. She knew how to get revenge.

"Hey, honey?" she said, letting a sultry tone round out her words.

"Yeah, baby?" Simon matched her inflection. He knew her well.

"Oh, god." Bill wrinkled his nose.

"Tell me why you love me." Janet enjoyed the look of disgust on Bill's face.

"Well, mostly, it's your ass." Maybe Simon knew her too well—the jerk.

Bill guffawed and attempted to point at Janet, signaling her backfired play at embarrassing him with lovey-dovey talk, except he must have forgotten he was weightless. The sudden movement flipped him up and back to bang his skull against the top bulkhead.

Good enough. Janet laughed before turning back to the comm. "My ass better not be the only thing you're in love with, cradle robber!" Simon was all of two years older than Janet.

"Gold digger," he fired back.

"That's me, enjoying this lap of luxury you provide—riding on rented freighters while we scramble to make CASPer payments."

Simon went quiet. Despite the distance between them, and the fact that they were talking via comm, Janet recognized his hesitation—or thought she did. The man could be prideful at times, and she hadn't meant to make him angry.

"Hey." She leaned forward against her restraints. "I was just talking. I'm happy with what we've got."

"It's not that, hon." More silence on Simon's end. She waited. "I—uh, well, it's like this. Remember a few weeks ago we visited Peepo's?"

"Yeah."

Peepo's Pit was one of the most famous—notorious—mercenary pits in the Union. Mercs frequented it to get lines on upcoming lucrative contracts and make deals for everything from foodstuffs to spacecraft.

"I sort of spent our reserve money."

"You did what?" Now Janet leaned forward for a completely different reason. The reserve was meant to keep them afloat during dry spells between contracts—and there were always dry spells.

"I forgot I left a pot of tea on in the garage," Bill said, scrambling to orient himself toward the adjacent corridor. "Better go check on that."

Janet stayed him with a look. "Both of you spill. Now."

"I'll tell you everything, but it's sort of involved." By the sound of things, Simon had stopped moving. "I've really got to piss. Give me two minutes. I'll be right back."

"Simon Price, you do not get to drop a warhead like this and then bail."

"I'll be right back, hon."

The sound of hissing air told Janet he had popped the canopy and was busily unhooking himself from the CASPer's haptic receptors. That stole some of the heat from Janet's outrage. It was, after all, partially her fault Simon had to leave the suit to relieve himself. Not that he would ever say so, or probably even think it, knowing him. He was too sweet.

The bastard.

Though waste reclamation usually held little concern for a CASPer pilot, Manny's system was broken, and Bill lacked the parts to fix it. Janet kicked herself every time one of them had to leave the suit to relieve himself.

502 | KENNEDY & WANDREY

With such a small company, picking up crumbs left over once their betters had already feasted, money would have been tight no matter what. However, with Janet's wage garnishment eating up twenty-two percent of their take-home, new parts for the CASPer came at a premium. Sure, they needed a toilet. Working without one hampered prolonged hazardous environment duty, the bread-and-butter of any small merc company. Nonetheless, something else always seemed more important, like replacing Manny's right knee when the entire unit blew out three months ago or refurbishing its hydrogen battery units to keep the thing running long-term.

"Be right back," Simon said. "Well, let's make this official. TG&C actual, this is *The Pride*, over."

Janet grinned despite herself. Simon knew good radio discipline was her thing. "This is TG&C actual to *Manny*. Go ahead."

"TG&C actual, permission to offload hazardous bio waste per company standard operating procedures from *The Pride*, over."

"Permission granted, Manny. You have ten minutes per our current statement of work. Will that be sufficient? Over."

"Won't need more than one, TG&C actual. And his name's *The Pride*, over."

From the sound of scrabbling limbs, Janet knew Simon had climbed down from the cockpit before she could answer. The jerk. She grinned at the comm and waited for his return. Staying angry with Simon wasn't easy—it never had been. She turned her gaze to Bill.

"Hey, don't look at me. I didn't spend the money."

"But you know what Simon bought."

"Maybe. But I'm no—"

A familiar sound cut through the silence over the comm to interrupt Bill. Janet had heard it a thousand times during field exercises at Bruins Academy. It was the crackle-hiss of high-intensity laser fire followed by an unmistakably Human scream that could belong to no other living being than the man she loved.

"Simon?" She strained against her harness, her throat suddenly tight.

"Oh, God." From his expression, Bill too recognized that sound. That scream.

"Simon!" Janet unclipped her gravity belt and bound from her command chair to grasp the console. Only a distant hiss of static, probably the wind soughing over the suit's comm inputs, resonated from dirtside.

She stared at Bill. He shook his head, whether to indicate his lack of knowledge or his certainty that something horrible had befallen Simon, Janet didn't know. She keyed the comm for ship-to-ship broadcast. Technically, it wasn't her place to do that. As the *Fiddlehead's* captain and owner, Iggy had that right.

To hell with protocol.

"Vonlerd Sfard command ship, this is TG&C actual." Janet waited while the brown-green orb of Wandray floated in the screen before her. No answer came. She repeated her hail.

"Where are they right now?" Bill asked. "Maybe they're not geosynched. Could be outta comms range."

Janet switched the monitor to show the KzSha ship floating some three hundred klicks off their starboard bow in a synchronous orbit with the *Fiddlehead*. "They hear us." She called again. And again. And a fifth time.

Finally, the line buzzed, and a computer-translated message issued into the silent command suite.

"Humans. Contract done. Leave."

"What just happened planet-side? Was there an accident? What's happened to our man down there?" Cold clarity ran through Janet's blood like frozen methane. She knew the answer. Deny it all she liked, she knew.

More silence. The bugs were done with them.

Bill's face had gone pasty white. He swallowed convulsively, his Adam's apple bobbing. "You—you think they killed him?"

Janet had never lost anyone. Sure, they had simulated casualties at the academy—men and women killed on the frontlines as a result of their commanders' decisions, good and bad—but those hadn't been real. Dead on the game field today, back in class tomorrow. That's how it had been. Yes, she knew death could come any second for mercs on contract. But not like this. Not at the hands of supposed allies.

She switched back to Simon's channel and leaned over the comm as if bringing herself that infinitesimal distance closer would somehow make her voice reach him. "Simon? Can you hear me? If you can hear me, and you're injured, just slap Manny's leg. The comm will pick it up."

More nothing.

"It had to be an accident." Bill clutched the command chair, struggling to hold his body still despite his shaking hands.

"If it was an accident, then why aren't the KzSha answering?" Janet speared Bill with a fiery look that made him frown, though to his credit, he didn't cringe.

He shook his head. "Maybe it's a cultural misunderstanding. Could be when one of theirs gets hurt, they leave them, so they don't think much of telling us to do the same."

The *Fiddlehead's* elevator dinged, and Ignatius Freely floated into the command suite, a sour expression on his face. "The hell's going on down here? I got a message says you tried contacting the other ship. Do I have to remind you—" Iggy stopped short, probably from the look on Janet's face.

"They killed Simon." The words spilled from her lips like poison, making a hollow thing of her heart.

"Oh, Jesus. I'm sorry. How?"

"We don't know he's dead!" Bill spun back and forth, taking in Janet and Iggy by turns. "Could be he's just hurt. We didn't see anything, so even if he is, that doesn't mean the KzSha did it. Hell, I bet he comes back on the comm any second now."

The hollowness that had begun in Janet's heart spread like termites, making a shell of her. Despite Bill's optimism, she knew Simon would never come back to the comm. But why? What reason could Armored Star have for turning on the man they had hired to share the contract?

Janet's eyes went round. "We're their cover."

"What?" Bill asked.

"The KzSha. It would have looked too suspicious for a company their size to take on this contract. They sponsored us as subcontractors to make it look like they were helping us out."

"You're jumping to conclusions." Bill's face had lost all color. He looked ill. "Why in the galaxy's name would they do that?"

"They want whatever's in that mine." Janet's confidence in her words grew as she spoke. "With no representative from the client around, they'll face no resistance in stealing whatever it is. We're in a dead system. There's nobody to stop them from doing whatever they like."

"If that's true, then why haven't they charbroiled us?" Iggy had moved to float next to Bill, holding the command chair lightly with one dark hand where Bill gripped it for life with both.

"Simple," Janet said, "they're afraid of bringing Peacemakers down on their insectoid heads. Sure, they killed a Human on some lifeless planet nobody cares about, but Simon's not rich or famous. He doesn't rate on the GalNet. The Peacemakers don't have time to investigate his death. The Mercenary Guild might care a little more, but it's not worth their while either. And we sure as hell don't have enough credits to hire bounty hunters. The bugs are free and clear on this."

"You're just proving Iggy's point," Bill said. "If all that's true, they have no reason to let us live. We're witnesses."

"No, you don't get it." Janet shook her head at them, trying to muster the wherewithal to explain despite her grief. "The KzSha are smart. They realize murdering a Human is far more forgivable than shooting down a freighter like the *Fiddlehead*. One merc command wiping out another from space without provocation would be bad news for the guild. They wouldn't be able to let that stand. It would set a precedent. One the Mercenary Guild can't allow. They steal some minerals or precious metals, even some F11, and the Peacemakers are as likely to ignore it as help unless the quantities are huge. Wandray is nowhere. It's got no people, no government. Our clients will complain, but I'm thinking the bugs have an escape plan that will see them long gone even before we can get home to bring charges against them."

Iggy looked thoughtful. "You might have a point there. The Shipping Alliance's got some sway within the Peacemakers. They don't like seeing members like me get fried without provocation."

"This still doesn't make any sense." Bill looked flummoxed, like a steer who has taken too high a jolt from an electric fence. "Nobody's crazy enough to burn a contract for some metals. Are they?"

"Shit." Iggy watched Wandray in the viewer though Janet thought he might not be seeing the planet at all. "Of course they would, kid. It's a big galaxy. Steal something in Peco, sell it in Jesc, then disperse wherever you like and regroup when the heat's off. I don't know what's down there worth a man's life, but I'm thinking the colonel might be right."

"I'm going down there." Janet started toward the corridor, but Bill caught her arm, sending them both into an awkward spin.

"Sorry! I'm sorry." Bill clutched her with one hand while scrabbling for a handle to stop them with the other. "I can't let you do that. If you're right about all this, they'll kill you too."

Janet snagged a handhold before they could collide with the aft bulkhead, arresting their momentum. The thought of punching Bill's dopy face blasted through her mind, but she shut that down quick. He meant well. Like her, he had lost Simon already. He didn't want to lose another friend today. She understood that, but it wasn't going to stop her.

"Bill, you need to let go of me. Now." She kept her voice calm and her eyes on his. He got the message. Bill let go.

"If they really killed Simon, they could—"

Janet put a reassuring hand on the mechanic's shoulder just above the TG&C patch sewn to his coveralls. It bore a silhouette of Manny—*The Pride*—facing the observer. "You can stand in my way, maybe delay me by a few minutes, but I'm going dirtside for Simon. So either start swinging or go prepare the dropship."

* * *

"We're going out of comms range." Bill said over the dropship's main channel. "There's still time to change your mind."

"No." Buffeting winds, superheated by reentry, shook Janet in her seat. The rumble of it sounded like continual thunder beating against the ship's hull. Gravity reasserted itself as she plummeted toward Wandray's south pole. Only .75G, but enough to make her limbs feel like ninety kilo bricks after the hours she had just spent on float.

Bill said no more, either because the *Fiddlehead's* escape trajectory had exceeded comms geometry or because he had no arguments left. Either way, Janet felt relieved. She had enough of her own doubts about her plan without piling on more.

Iggy hadn't complained, or even second-guessed her, when Janet ordered him to break geosynchronous orbit for a sling shot out of the system toward the local stargate. Good man. But then again, perhaps he just didn't much care about Janet. After all, she had already paid him for the lift.

He hadn't liked leaving his dropship behind, especially when he knew the KzSha might take offense if they detected it heading for Wandray. However, an immediate blockchain transfer of double his original fee persuaded him.

That money represented every credit TG&C owned. This time next month, Manny would be repossessed—so would Janet for that matter. She could only hope her indentured servitude would last less than ten years. Maybe she'd get a nice assignment, something at one of Bjorn's Berserkers' off-world academies. She sure as hell didn't want to go home to face her family as what amounted to a slave after the arguments they'd had over her leaving school in the first place.

A frozen wasteland expanded beneath the dropship. Janet programmed the computer to take her in low and fast. Wandray might be on the small side, but a transcontinental flight, even at high mach, would take hours. Assuming Iggy was right, and his dropship's transponder could mask the approach, she would still need to land several miles from her target to avoid being seen by the KzSha sentries on the ground. Perhaps, if luck traveled with her, they would all be inside the mine when she arrived.

Janet adjusted her silver and black haptic suit meant to help her interface with Manny. She hadn't worn one of these things in three years, preferring to leave the hands-on portion of TG&C's missions to Simon and Bill. Would that mean she had lost her skill at piloting a CASPer? Worry put a knot in her stomach. Maybe Bill had been right. He had pleaded with her to get Simon's body—he had finally conceded his childhood friend was most likely dead—and come home. They'd double back for her. The offer felt more tempting with atmosphere kissing the dropship.

But no.

Janet shook her head as she adjusted the ship's cockpit chair to its fully reclined position. Doubtful she could sleep, she closed her eyes anyway and fell almost instantly into fitful, horrifying dreams that, nonetheless, paled next to reality.

* * *

"Janet." The dropship's soothing male voice had spoken her name several times already, Janet realized.

"I'm awake." She sat up, wiping sleep from her eyes. Apparently, she had cried while she slept. No more of that. She stared at the forward display. Nothing but gray rocky crags covered with blue-green fungus and intermittent violet scrub brush. "Where are we?"

"Exactly three miles from the mine site, as you designated. If the mine is your ultimate destination, I could take you there in under a minute."

"No. No, don't move. Were we detected?"

"No, Janet. Neither the Armored Star ship in orbit nor the KzSha planet-side have shown any awareness of our presence."

Janet relaxed, but only fractionally. The dropship's computer, while intuitive to the point of appearing sentient, lacked the capacity for true strategic engagement. It could be wrong. She would have to take her chances.

Janet stepped off the dropship's loading ramp and got her first whiff of Wandray. The place smelled like shit. She considered turning up the oxygen-nitrogen mixture in her facemask to eliminate the stench, but just as quickly nixed that idea. Her haptic suit could provide only a short-term supply of the gases her body needed. Wandray's thin air, though suffused with oxygen provided by its high algae populations, would nevertheless kill her within thirty minutes without the boost her suit could supply. She needed that air for the hike ahead.

Janet set off at a slow pace, about five minutes per kilometer. All those hours clocking steps in the *Fiddlehead's* spin ring were finally paying off. Despite her self-imposed role of company intel puke, she had continued academy fitness standards wherever TG&C took her. Well, mostly. It wasn't as if she had a drillmaster dogging her heels aboard ship, pushing her to her limits, but she could run. Bruins Academy had instilled that much discipline in her anyway.

Loping along, careful to keep her gas mixtures in check, she ate up the miles. It felt good to give herself over to the pace, the staccato tap-tap-tap of her footfalls punctuated by her breathing. She put the horror that lay ahead out of her mind.

At one point in its history, Wandray had been a prosperous planet—the home to a race called the Leir. Unfortunately for them, maybe a little too prosperous. Although Janet hadn't looked too deeply into the major causes, someone had unleashed a Canavar on Wandray—or, from the ravaged look of the place, several. The mountain-sized behemoths caused an extinction-level event on the population. Well, the Canavar and an aggressive bombardment of atomics and meteors slung from orbit. Much of Wandray looked made of glass, because it was. Janet wouldn't have wished that sort of attack on anyone or anything, but she had to admit it made the run a little easier since much of the terrain, while craggy, was flat, aside from ancient hills and ridges likely as old as the planet itself.

In a little less than twenty-five minutes, the mine site came into view. Janet slowed to a walk, her eyes darting this way and that, taking in the tactical landscape as rapidly as she could manage while her breathing and pulse slowed.

A KzSha lander—squat, bulbous, and ugly—stood before her in a mining cut so wide it made the ship look like a child's toy. Eight meters below the surrounding land level and a good kilometer across, the depression could have been an impact crater, but its edges were too uniform, its incline too gradual. A central roadway led into it from the eastern side to a perfectly round, perfectly dark hole hewn into the western wall like a gaping mouth. Just five meters from that opening—

Janet's knees gave way beneath her. She collapsed behind a rock outcropping, trying for all her worth to unsee what her eyes had found. She stared at the loose stones piled about her, at her hands, at the slick surface of her haptic suit, but nothing could push the images from her mind. At last, she swallowed and rose enough to peer again into the cut.

Manny stood just five meters from the mine. Forlorn and as still as death, its steel alloy frame cast a long shadow that spread into the entrance like dark water. Its cockpit stood open.

Simon lay on his side just outside Manny's shadow. An unexpected whine escaped Janet's lips upon seeing him. His slim figure appeared reposed, as if he had decided to have a nap in front of the mine. But this was no nap. He lay too still. No irritable fidgets or unexpected yawns—the little idiosyncrasies of his slumber she had come to recognize—disturbed this sleep.

He was gone. Janet had known this before, but in an abstract way. Seeing his body abandoned like this made that knowledge concrete. A knife point of rage stabbed into her breast, and she ground her teeth behind her mask.

Seeing no sign of the KzSha either at the mine entrance or anywhere near their ship, Janet eased her way down the sloping depression to Simon's body. Her heart beat hollow once again as she knelt beside him. She might have been watching this tableau on a Tri-V, and yet she knew it for reality.

Gently, she tugged at his shoulder so that he rolled onto his back to face Wandray's pale blue sky. His green eyes stared upward, cold and lifeless. She pressed them closed with a trembling glove. A burnt hole the size of Janet's fist stood out above Simon's heart where a laser blast had melted through his haptic suit.

She remained that way for a long moment, cradling Simon's limp form with her eyes closed in mimicry of his, fighting the sobs assailing her throat. She would not let them pass. Finally, she eased him to the stony ground and stood.

Janet Grunwald never made the conscious decision to don Manny like a suit of armor. She had climbed aboard and keyed the cockpit by rote before thought even entered the equation. And when it did, that thought was tactical.

She removed her breathing mask and donned the pilot's helmet. Manny's airtight cabin would handle the mix from here. She tried not to think how it smelled of Simon.

Feeling about herself, she fastened her haptic connectors one after another, letting the familiar practice purge her mind. Manny's power indicator switched from blue to yellow, signaling startup. Janet nodded her approval. Good boy. She pinched her right hand thumb and index finger together. The suit rumbled to life as its hydrogen generator kicked on. The power indicator changed again, this time from yellow to green.

Flawless startup. Perfect.

Despite its age—being four generations from cutting edge—the Mark IV CASPer was in good repair, mostly owing to Bill's mechanical and computer genius. He had upgraded Manny's tech whenever TG&C could afford the parts and improvised when they couldn't, which was most of the time.

Janet took a moment to reacquaint herself with the controls and the limited available weapons systems. Simon and Bill had bought

Manny secondhand from a dealer when they started TG&C. Already cannibalized for most of its spare parts, they had gotten what amounted to a third block steel-alloy shell. Scrounging where they could and working whatever jobs didn't require firepower, they eventually managed to buy a shoulder-mounted 50mm cannon with a twenty round magazine. Besides that, Janet had only one steel-alloy blade magnetically mounted on Manny's left arm, one of the few pieces of offensive tech the wholesaler had left in place, likely because no one needed the thing.

Armament hadn't mattered much before now. TG&C had always worked contracts that involved heavy lifting or standing around looking tough. That's what the shoulder cannon was good for—scaring off potential crooks. Janet wasn't even certain it would fire. They had never tested the thing. The rounds cost too damn much.

Sneaking in a Mark IV Shovelhead like Manny wasn't a thing. It weighed nearly 720 kilograms and stood over 2.5 meters tall. Still, Janet managed to keep her pace slow, essentially creeping toward the mine, the sound of Manny's actuators like thunder to her ears, but probably not too loud on the outside.

Recessed lights ran along the top of the main mine shaft, providing ample illumination with Manny's Tri-V display making up for any lack. Laser-smooth walls wound their way into the ground with a blemish here and there where mining robots had found something interesting enough to pry from the rocks. Janet saw no sign of the KzSha. They must have gone deeper inside. She proceeded slowly, her heart racing.

The more Janet walked, the more innate the armor felt. The mine's smooth walls eventually gave way to a more natural look. Raw stone, slick with condensation and some sort of gray-green lichen, jutted out as the way narrowed. More and more gouges opened up in it, exposing veins of lighter material than the surrounding rock.

"Manny, what's this? Can you analyze the mineral content?"

"Spectral analysis indicates xenon salt residue surrounded by sedimentary rock deposits."

Xenon. That couldn't be why the KzSha killed Simon. While xenon certainly had its uses on the galactic market, it wasn't in high demand. However, xenon often accompanied the ultra-rare, ultra-precious compound known as F11, the fuel used to power the known galaxy. If a deposit lay in this mine—even a small one—it may have been enough to compel the KzSha to murder. This was the wrong type of planet for it, but it was a big galaxy and stranger things had happened.

Janet had just turned to inspect a line of xenon residue running deeper along the concourse, when an intricate display of lights caught her eye. She brought Manny to a complete stop, her Tri-V focused down the shaft, and switched off all of Manny's external lights.

A couple of KzSha mercs, black and silver armor layered over their already-tough chitin bodies, rounded the corner ahead of her. They looked small, especially from Janet's vantage aboard Manny. The one on the right stood maybe 1.5 meters, and his comrade was even shorter. But Janet wasn't about to let their size fool her. KzSha were notoriously tough in battle, and reportedly clever as well.

The armor they wore made room for two long antennae to drape forward from their wasp-like heads. The colors Janet had seen emanated from those, flashing up and down their length in multitudinous hues and patterns. Their form of speech? Stunted insectile wings buzzed intermittently on their backs, punctuating the light show.

Janet's mind raced as her breathing increased. A quick glance at Manny's sensors told her the aliens' armor, while formidable, wasn't rated for full-scale combat. She could hear her old drillmaster, Sergeant Major Drakes, screaming in her ear, "Assessments are like assholes! They all stink, and you can't live without them, but you only need one! Make a plan to control the order of battle and stick to it. No second guessing when the engagement is hot. Plan and execute."

Janet envisioned her plan. Simple, inelegant, and useful—like any asshole.

The KzSha mercs were almost upon her in the gloom before the taller one looked up suddenly, its antennae flashing a glowing gold in alarm. Its buddy just had time to pick up the urgent color change before Janet slammed Manny's blade through the tall one's skull, splitting it almost in half. Simultaneously, she caught the shorter one with her free hand in a grip tight enough to crush boulders. Spinning, she slammed it into the stone wall behind her, crushing its upper torso with a thrumming CRACK!

It was all over inside five seconds. Janet flicked green blood from Manny's gauntlet-like hands and continued on her way, her jaw set.

She had never killed another sentient before. Though the hollowness inside her seemed to swallow the encroaching horror of the moment, she knew the impact of her actions would one day catch up to her—but not now. Not while Simon's murderers roamed this darkened tomb.

The C2 maven inside Janet didn't concern herself with such trivialities. Death was a goal, a payment made for a plan well executed. Even now, that inner Janet calculated how far the sound of her previous attack might have traveled through the mine's walls—too far for certain. She had to assume at least some of the others were headed her way.

Five KzSha guards made up their original compliment of mercs. Janet hadn't seen their ship launch more. She had already taken out two, and that left just three to deal with. Assuming she could sneak up on the others the way she had—

"Bitch, female!" The buzzing voice crackled over Manny's comm at such volume it made Janet jerk in surprise so that she stumbled and almost lost her footing.

Two more KzSha spilled into the corridor in front of Janet, some form of assault guns pressed to their armored shoulders with their uppermost limbs. Chemically-propelled bullets pinged off Manny's armor as if someone were striking it with a thousand hammers at once.

Her Tri-V indicators showed no real damage done, but the attack set Janet's teeth on edge. Uttering a command, she engaged the 50mm cannon. Its servo whined like a dying cat when it moved into place, but its indicator glowed green.

An X-shaped reticle appeared before Janet's eyes. She pasted it across one of her attackers in the display, locking in Manny's targeting computer. "Fire!"

A stupendous explosion rocked the mine shaft. The concussion sent a bewildered Janet off balance and stumbling into the stone wall. Rock crumbled under Manny's weight as the Tri-V lit up with red indicators and warnings of system malfunctions.

Janet stared at them in disbelief. The 50mm gun had exploded. Smoke, sparks, and even some flames jetted from the wreckage. Luckily, none leaked into the cockpit. It seemed to have kept its seal despite the damage, although the arm was now dead.

"Die, human!" screamed the voice over Janet's comm link.

One of the KzSha leapt at Manny, all eight of its limbs extended and its wings buzzing. Janet expected it to land on the suit's head or chest and prepared to spear it with her magnetic blade, but the bug surprised her. Forgoing the obvious targets, the merc landed on Manny's right leg and proceeded to saw away at the actuator housing using two serrated limbs like tooth-covered swords. Janet's haptic suit sent a shock through her flesh, alerting her to the severity of the damage.

A new alarm joined those already blaring inside Manny's cockpit, and a series of images pushed their way up the priority list on the Tri-V. The topmost caught Janet's attention.

WARNING: SEVERE JOINT DAMAGE TO RIGHT KNEE SERVO. DISCONTINUE ENGAGEMENT AND SEEK REPAIR ASSISTANCE IMMEDIATELY.

Who wrote these error messages? When the hell could a merc simply leave an engagement to seek out a mech doc?

Manny stumbled, and Janet just had time to keep the CASPer from tipping over by throwing out an arm.

Growling, Janet attempted to backhand the KzSha on her knee. Nothing happened.

"Shit!" She had forgotten about the faulty cannon. She had about as much chance of moving her right arm as she had of swimming back to Earth.

She tried adjusting her stance, but her damaged knee was already compromised. The bastard alien was still sawing away at it.

The other two KzSha mercs had stopped firing. Janet could see them in a popup rear display. One stood fiddling with his rifle while the other watched Manny struggle to remain upright, its antennae glowing a solid blue—probably the KzSha equivalent of a smug expression.

The first finished whatever he had been doing and lifted his gun. A solid beam of white laser light crackled from it to strike Manny in the back.

Heat warnings joined the mechanical sort already plastered all over Manny's Tri-V display. Janet searched her surroundings for any sort of improvised weapon to use, but came up empty. She had been a fool. She should have taken Simon's body and run.

Sergeant Major Drakes returned to her mind's eye. She could see the gray-haired man screaming in her face, flecks of spit flying from his mouth.

"Speaking of assholes! You do not want to be that asshole who holds onto a plan when every indication shows it's failed. Yes, I know what I'm saying countermands the lesson I just imparted to you green as grass recruits, but isn't that the very best sort of lesson, cadets? Here I am proving my mettle, by changing my plan on the fly!"

Sergeant Major had the right of it. Assholes didn't change, but assessments should, at least under the right circumstances.

Janet let go of the wall, and Manny tipped in the opposite direction as she brought her damaged knee forward. The servo felt sluggish, but it rose at her command, cutting the attacking KzSha's escape time by maybe half a second.

It was enough.

Intent on his act of sabotage, the KzSha seemed oblivious to his peril until the last second. He tried to scramble free, but it was too late. More than a ton of mech armor came down on the bug with a thunderous BOOM, crushing its lower half into a green-tinged pulp.

Unfortunately, Manny's blade struck the stone floor at an odd angle that dislodged the weapon. Still attached, but pointing almost straight up, the alloy sword had become as effective as a rear spoiler on a space yacht.

"Dammit," Janet hissed between her teeth. That wasn't part of the plan. At least Manny's damaged knee still functioned— somewhat. Janet kept it flexed, and the smoking actuator obediently held, providing just enough room for her to manipulate Manny's remaining good arm. She would have to work fast if she had any hope of winning this fight.

The KzSha who had been firing the laser bound into a low arc, its antennae flashing from green, to red, to gold nearly faster than Janet could follow. The insectoid merc's leap would have landed it on Manny's back, had Janet remained in place.

Timing the oncoming impact through her rear monitors, Janet shoved against the stony floor at the last possible second to flip Manny onto its back.

The merc, no doubt surprised by the sudden move, nonetheless adjusted his trajectory using his wings so that he landed on Manny's upper torso.

Good move—just what Janet wanted.

Wasting not a second, Janet rammed the serrated forelimb she had ripped from the KzSha beneath her through the attacking merc's neck armor. Its wings buzzed momentarily then stuttered to a stop as its antennae went fitfully dead. She cast it, and her improvised weapon, aside.

Warning lights told Janet that Manny would not rise again without major repairs. With her sole gun gone, and her blade rendered unusable, she had no weapons left at her disposal.

"Red blood, female!" The last KzSha merc's voice cut through the quiet inside Manny's cockpit like a buzz saw.

Janet looked up to the ceiling, the Tri-V dutifully showing her an image of the corridor where her enemy stood, its own laser gun pointed at Manny. Blue-white light spilled from it, instantly overwhelming the sensors so that the image became an insensible white mass.

Janet didn't need to see the KzSha to understand its goal. It meant to cut through Manny's cockpit to reach her or maybe fry her from the outside in, whichever came first. She doubted the bug cared. She had no hope of reaching him with her one functioning arm.

Janet felt frozen in place—like a hunted animal whose burrow had been found by a predator. She had nowhere to go. No escape. She only hoped she had managed to kill whichever bastard had actually shot poor Simon.

With a resigned sigh, she rested her head back against Manny's seat and waited for death to find her. Already, the suit's internal temperature gauge had begun to rise.

"Plans and picnics, infants!" Sergeant Major Drakes screamed in Janet's head, the voice so real, so tangible, she could have sworn he was on the comm. "Neither one survives a thunderstorm unless you're clever. Don't got a backup plan? Fucking make one! Now! Clever is as clever does, which is just a highfalutin way of saying whatever works—whatever sees you and yours through a fight—that was your true plan all along."

Janet stared around Manny's cockpit, her mind racing. She wasn't dead yet. She wasn't even hurt physically. Was she really going to lie down and let some insect burn her to death inside her own suit? She might not have graduated, but she had made it most of the way through Bruins Academy. She had almost become one of Bjorn's Berserkers, and a goddamned Berserker wouldn't lie around waiting to die.

Hell no.

She scanned through the system inventory once. Then a second time. Nothing. No guns of course. No ammo even if she had them. One functional leg and one arm, but the KzSha merc-cum-welder-cum-long pork chef seemed disinclined to move within reach. Manny's comm still functioned, but even if its signal could leave the mine—highly unlikely—she would only alert the KzSha in orbit to her presence. The *Fiddlehead* wouldn't return for two days, assuming they followed Janet's orders—and they would.

This left her with nothing to use as even a makeshift weapon, despite all her frantic searching. She could open the cockpit and attempt to slither out, but to what end? She had no personal weapon. The KzSha merc would just cut her down with that laser. Even without it, she would not stand a chance going flesh-against-chitin with the bug. With its eight limbs, two of which it used like serrated swords, and that natural body armor, the thing would kill her in seconds. Not to mention its wings. The monster could fucking fly.

Fly.

Janet's gaze lit upon the jump juice indicator, and it sprang to the fore in the Tri-V display. It showed a quarter of a tank.

Tears sprang to her eyes. In her hurry to reach the mine, she had never checked the tanks. They had always been empty before. "Simon, you beautiful fool."

This is what he had spent their savings to buy—jump juice. Aside from the hydrogen batteries that powered a CASPer's generator, jump juice was one of its main propellants. It allowed for the use of jumpjets, powerful rockets built into the suit. With credits always so tight, Simon had never gotten the chance to fly. Because of the KzSha, he never would.

A bitter smile spread across Janet's lips. She would fly for him.

"This one's for you, lover." Janet moved her eyes in an old familiar pattern, and Manny's jumpjet fuel injectors whined as if in anticipation.

"It is inadvisable to use jumpjets while operating in an enclosed environment," said Manny's computer.

"Override and engage at full power. Now!"

A sudden skirling that outstripped the sizzle of the laser by at least thirty decibels filled the mine, shaking dust and loose rocks from the walls and pitted ceiling. Fire blossomed beneath Manny's frame in dual cones, melting the floor in a long furrow that grew even longer as the CASPer shot forward.

Manny's shovel-headed cockpit rammed into the offending merc with a titanic scream of metal followed by the crisp shattering of carapace on stone. The concussion rocked Janet painfully against her harness. It felt like getting slapped with an orbital freighter.

"Shut off jumpjets! Power them down!" She shouted over the tumult.

The jets ceased firing. Manny's Tri-V flickered several times as the CASPer rolled onto its side, head pointed down the main shaft. Janet keyed open the cockpit and unbuttoned herself to inspect the damage. Even through her breathing mask, the air smelled of ozone, spent jump juice, and something tangy like barbeque sauce. God, she hoped that wasn't KzSha blood.

Manny had turned the final merc into nothing but a pulpy green smear on the floor. And wall. And ceiling.

Janet pulled a mobile comm unit from Manny's cockpit and headed for the mine's entrance. The barest edge of Wandray's dull sun balanced on the horizon as she stepped into open air. The first stars had appeared in the darkening sky.

The KzSha lander stood where it had been, no mercs around it. If any came out, she was dead, but Janet had a feeling that wouldn't happen. No doubt, Armored Star had sent only a skeleton crew dirtside so as to leave as much room as possible for whatever they planned to steal from the mine. It wasn't like they had expected resistance.

"Armored Star, this is TG&C actual. Your people on Wandray are dead." Janet waited, but not for long.

"Human female. What has happened?"

"Your mercs killed one of mine. I killed all of them. Whatever it is you intended to steal is now out of your reach. You could try to send more people down here to load your ship, but I doubt you'd get much before our clients show up. I'm thinking that's something you wish to avoid."

A long pause. Janet could almost hear the agitated KzSha arguing what they should do. She said nothing.

"Why not we turning you to slag from space?" came the buzzing voice, full of menace.

"You could do that," Janet said, holding the comm close to her lips. "But if you do, you'd better drop to within ten miles, or you'll have Peacemakers on your ass inside a month. You won't be able to transition anywhere in the galaxy without finding one of those bastards waiting for you. And you know, I don't think you've got enough time to climb down from geosynch to just ten miles. Do you?"

"We could send mercs for you."

"Yeah, that's an option. How'd that work out so far? Send 'em. I'd like nothing better than to rip you bugs apart piecemeal." Janet gazed up at the stars as if she might glimpse the KzSha floating amongst them. They could call her bluff. If they did, she would die. No question there.

"We will not forget this insult."

Janet waited until she was certain her voice wouldn't crack or falter before keying the comm to broadcast one last time. "Then remember this name—Grunwald. And know that I won't forget either."

#####

The Quiet Was Fine
by Jake Bible

The ship's debris filled Wesco's Tri-V display. He tried to search for other survivors, but the scan console shorted out almost immediately, and his HUD flickered, then went dark. Wesco struggled for a few minutes, then managed to manually activate his comms despite his disorientation.

Something had happened. Something bad. His mind reached for the something…

An attack. The ship was attacked.

So much noise, then so much quiet.

Wesco started to call out, but his throat was raw and dry. He let the saliva build in his mouth before swallowing hard, hoping to coat his throat enough to speak.

"Hey…Hey. Hey! Wesco here. Who's on the comms? Someone give me a sitrep."

Not quite silence. A crackling. But no answer.

Wesco swallowed again.

"Ramirez! Lawrence! Stokes! Marga! Purvis! Anyone out there?"

Still no answer. Wesco waited. A louder crackle. The distant sound of a voice.

"Who's that?" the voice croaked, barely more than a static-filled burst.

"Stokes? That you, pal?" Wesco asked. "Where you at, buddy?"

More crackling. The voice faded.

"What...What happened?" a second voice chimed in, brutally loud in Wesco's ears.

"Ramirez! Glad to hear you're alive and kicking!" Wesco exclaimed. He adjusted the volume and smiled.

"Alive…yeah. Kicking? Not so much, man," Ramirez replied.

"What's that mean?" Wesco asked. "Ramirez? Are you wounded?"

"How can I not be in this mess?" Ramirez replied. "Do you see this shit?"

"HUD is down. I got no visuals."

"Lucky you. The ship's gone. It ain't pretty."

"Ramirez? What's wrong? You're wounded, I can hear it in your voice. How bad?"

"Not good."

"Talk to me."

"I think I'm missing my legs."

Wesco took that in. Blind and helpless were not his defaults; they were not acceptable. Wesco tried every manual option before him but couldn't get his HUD to return. The system was down.

Something heavy thumped Wesco in the back and sent him slowly spinning upside down. Another thump, and his momentum was halted.

No alarms, no warnings. His CASPer was solid. Blind, but solid.

"Ramirez? What's your status?" Wesco asked.

"Breathing," Ramirez replied with a harsh laugh. "I got that going for me. You took a tumble there, Wesco. Best watch out for that debris."

"Funny," Wesco replied. "You in pain?"

"Not at the moment. Riding the pharmaceutical horse."

"Your seal, over? How's your CASPer's structural integrity?"

"Where's the ship?" Stokes asked, his voice bursting into the conversation with a loud squawk.

"Stokes! That was you!" Wesco exclaimed.

"Yeah. It's me," Stokes replied. "Where's the ship? What happened to the ship?"

Panic wasn't in his voice, Wesco noted, but panic's cousin was paying a visit. Wesco noted that as well.

"Hold on, Stokes," Wesco said. "Ramirez? Your CASPer's structural integrity? How bad?"

"Legs gone, but sealed. Medkit bound my wounds, and nanites are working overtime, for now. Gonna need a little surgical help with this shit when we get back to the ship," Ramirez replied.

Ramirez sighed. "I mean, when I get to a ship," he added.

"What does that mean?" Stokes snapped. "What is all this shit? What happened?"

"Ship's gone, man," Ramirez announced. "Been trying for an hour to raise someone, anyone, but no response until Wesco woke up."

"Could just be comms are out," Stokes said, panic's cousin getting bolder. "They'll come get us. Send a shuttle or—"

"Ship's gone, Stokes," Ramirez snapped. "Sorry. I watched it rip apart just before the drop-pods launched. Gone. Like my goddamn legs."

"You sure because I'm...Oh..." Stokes gulped. "All systems are back now. Tri-V is up. I see."

"Did any launch?" Wesco asked. He closed his eyes. It was better than staring at the red glow of the interior of his CASPer.

"Any what?" Stokes replied.

"Drop-pods, numbnuts," Ramirez snapped. "What else was launching when this went down?"

"Did anyone make it?" Wesco asked.

"Not that I know of," Ramirez said. "All I saw was a bright light just as seating protocol started. Then it was all topsy turvy, helter skelter, ass over tea kettle."

"Ass over what? Stop saying stupid shit, man," Stokes said, then gasped.

"You good?" Wesco asked. "Stokes? Are you wounded too?"

"No. I mean, I'm good, not wounded. Just replaying my CAS-Per's vids. The ship, man…"

"Yeah, yeah, the ship," Ramirez snarled. "Forget about the god-damn ship!"

"Ramirez? Those nanites doing their jobs? You feeling okay?" Wesco asked.

"Great, just great. Having two stumps instead of full legs is awe-some, man," Ramirez growled. "Feeling fine to the nines, brother."

"Sorry," Wesco said.

"What ya gonna do?" Ramirez asked, then laughed. "At least we have a great view from up here in orbit. We are in orbit, yeah?"

"Yeah," Wesco confirmed. "We're in orbit. I saw that before my Tri-V fritzed out."

"In orbit?" Stokes said. "Wesco, you're not in orbit."

Wesco's guts clenched. "What do you mean I'm not in orbit, Stokes?"

"I can see you," Stokes said. "You're moving away from the planet. You're almost clear of the debris field."

"Yeah, but we ain't," Ramirez said. "I'm getting bumped and thumped every few seconds by what's left of the ship. Feeling great on my stumps."

"Moving?" Wesco asked, his empathy for Ramirez lost. "How fast? It can't be too fast. I'm not feeling momentum."

"It's space, man," Ramirez said. "You don't feel shit out here."

"You know what I mean, asshole," Wesco stated. "I'd feel it if I was tumbling."

"You're not tumbling," Ramirez said. "But Stokes is right. You're moving away from us."

"At a steady clip," Stokes added. "Probably a good thing. We'll eventually drop from orbit and burn up as we enter the planet's atmosphere."

"Jesus…" Ramirez muttered.

"And I'll asphyxiate as my air gives out," Wesco said.

"We'll probably asphyxiate, too," Ramirez said. "Dropping from orbit could take days. We don't have days."

Wesco tried every trick in the book to get his tri-v back up. Or every trick in the book he knew from years of fighting as a merc. Problem was those tricks were planet-based or ship-based. Gravity was on his side on a planet, and support techs were on his side on a ship.

On a planet, he could always bail from his CASPer if things didn't go his way. Nowhere to bail when floating in open space.

He gave up on the tri-v and brought up his life support readings manually. That he could manage.

"I have ten hours of air," Wesco said. "How are you two looking?"

"Eight here," Ramirez said. "Nope. Seven and three quarters." Ramirez went silent for a few seconds. "Seven and a half. Shit, I was right. No way I'll survive to fall out of orbit. I'm leaking. Like no legs wasn't bad enough."

"Can you redirect the repairs to seal your CASPer instead of working on your legs?" Stokes asked.

"Do what now?" Ramirez snapped. "You have any idea what has happened to my CASPer? Can you see this shit?"

"I see it," Stokes replied. "But why repair your legs if you're going to asphyxiate? It's logic."

"Come over here and say that logic to my face, Stokes," Ramirez snarled. "Come on. Jet your way over here and let's hash this out."

"Calm the hell down," Stokes replied.

"Calm down? Calm down!"

"Both of you, shut up!" Wesco shouted. "Seriously. We have problems. Big problems. Let's work on those instead of going after each other."

"I ain't going after anyone," Ramirez said.

"Can't you maneuver?" Wesco asked.

"No legs, no jumpjets," Ramirez replied.

"How about pushing off some of the debris?" Wesco asked. "Move from hunk to hunk."

"Maybe," Ramirez said. "But why? One hunk is as bad as the next."

"It'll get you to me so we can share air," Wesco said. "You can patch in and give me your tri-v access so I have a HUD again. If I can see where I am, maybe I can get us out of this mess."

"How, Wesco?" Ramirez asked, bitterness filling his voice. "You a miracle worker all of a sudden?"

"Listen to him, Ramirez," Stokes interrupted, hope in his voice. "What ya thinking, Wesco?"

"Doesn't matter," Ramirez said. "None of us have drop-pods. We can't go to the planet, and there's no ship left up here."

"What exactly happened?" Stokes asked. "I was in my CASPer, then about to be seated in the drop-pod. Next thing I know Wesco is talking over comms."

"I thought you saw the feed," Wesco said.

"All it shows is us in the ship, then everything tearing apart," Stokes said. "My view gets blocked by a chunk of the hull. Then I blacked out."

"Blacked out?" Wesco asked. "You sure you're okay?"

"I don't feel injured," Stokes said. "Systems are running smoothly, considering. Not that it does me any good. I'm surrounded by a few thousand tons of space trash. I try to use my jumpjets, and I'll slam into two tons of heat shielding that's on my eight. About five tons of scaffolding on my two. I think what's left of the mess is about thirty meters under my feet. Might pop down and look for some beer."

Stokes laughed hard and loud. Panic's cousin was settling in and about to let Aunt Hysteria take hold.

"Take some breaths, Stokes," Wesco said. "Ramirez? Can you bring up your feeds? Track back and see if your CASPer caught what happened."

"Sure. Why not? Sounds like a good use of my time. Got nothing better to—"

"Ramirez!" Wesco roared. "You are not helping!"

Several seconds of silence.

"I'll try," Ramirez said. "Give me a few minutes."

"Stokes? Sounds like you have a good view," Wesco said. "Can you see a course for Ramirez? Can he get to me?"

"Maybe," Stokes replied.

"I'm serious, Stokes," Wesco said. "If Ramirez can get to me, we can patch in together. My CASPer is intact."

"Again, so what?" Ramirez said. "Where are we going to go?"

"To find more air, man," Wesco said. "The ship was outfitted for a full campaign. There have to be tanks floating here somewhere. We find them and maybe we buy some time for the cavalry to arrive."

"You know that's not going to happen," Ramirez said in a tone that made Wesco's blood go cold.

"The company won't leave us to—" Stokes began.

"Yeah, they will," Ramirez snapped. "Zuparti hired us. The campaign is off-books, as far as I know."

"Hey, I know the Zuparti are shady bastards, but they know the rules," Wesco said. "The guild will blacklist them if they get caught hiring mercs for an off-books campaign. And what about the company? Getting caught taking an off-books job would mean expulsion from the guild and fines so big they'll still be paying the debt six generations down the line."

"Yep to all of that," Ramirez said. "Just saying what I heard, man. Zuparti are shady bastards, but they're high-paying shady bastards. If they dangle enough credits in front of the company's face, the risk is worth it."

"Got it!" Stokes announced. "Ha! I got full visuals here! Beat you to it, Ramirez! In your legless face!"

"Christ, Stokes," Wesco said. "That's harsh."

"Legless face," Ramirez chuckled. "Nice one."

Wesco shook his head. "Okay. So what you got, Stokes?"

"Laser, for sure," Stokes said. "Sliced straight through the ship. God..."

"What?" Ramirez asked, then started coughing heavily.

"You okay, pal?" Wesco asked.

"No," Ramirez replied bluntly.

"I have the feed from after the attack," Stokes said. "Three ships. Zuparti, from the markings. They dismantled us, then left."

"Crap. I see it too," Ramirez confirmed. "It was Zuparti."

"Wait, what?" Wesco asked. "Zuparti attacked us? They hired us!"

"And bingo was his name-o," Ramirez said. "Shady bastards. Someone paid them to set us up, then take us down. The company can't say anything, because they can't talk about this job."

"This is a mess," Wesco said. He sighed and closed his eyes, tired of staring at dim lights and dead interfaces. "It doesn't make sense."

"No reason it should," Ramirez said. "Probably part of some multi-tiered plan that is way above our pay grades. We're casualties of a corporate war, which is the worst kind of war, in my opinion. It's waged by greedy cowards looking out for their short-term assets. I'd love to see one of those guys face off with me in a CASPer for just three minutes. See how he likes real warfare."

Ramirez began coughing heavily again. It was a wet, racking cough that quickly devolved into hoarse grunts, moans, and wheezing.

"That's a lot of blood," Ramirez whispered, barely audible over the comms. "Wesco?"

"Yeah?"

"You really think we can connect the CASPers?"

"You get to me, and I know we can," Wesco replied. "Remember that time on Karma when Needles and I got drunk and took our CASPers out for a spin to see who was the faster runner?"

"Can't forget that disaster," Ramirez replied around coughs.

"I had to patch in to his CASPer because I broke the hell out of mine after falling off that cliff," Wesco said. "I tethered to him, and he walked us both in."

"That was on planet."

"You got a better idea? Stokes is boxed in by debris, and I'm floating farther and farther away from you. You're legless and coughing up blood. Come get me, and we'll use my suit to navigate the debris field and try to find some part of the ship that's still intact."

"Starboard decks thirty-one through forty-eight are still together," Stokes said. "That's Med!"

"See, Ramirez? Now you have a goal," Wesco said.

No response. Wesco waited. Then he checked his comms. Active.

"Ramirez?" Wesco called. "You hear me, man? Now you have a goal."

"I've always had a goal, man," Ramirez said. "To stay living. What I have now is a chance."

"So, you're on your way?"

"Sure. Gonna pop on over."

"I can direct you there," Stokes said. "I'm boxed in, but I have a clear view of both of you. I can plot the best course, Ramirez. I'll tell you which hunks and chunks of ship to use to get to Wesco."

"Okay, okay, great. You two do know I'm the guy missing the lower halves of his legs, right? Yet I get to go rescue Wesco?"

Ramirez laughed. "We survive this, you two owe me more beers than exist in the galaxy, right now."

"Deal, brother," Wesco said. "Just stay alive and come get my ass, so I can get your legless ass into Med."

"There's a lot that has to happen first," Ramirez said. "Don't get ahead of yourself."

"Stokes? You got that route plotted?" Wesco asked.

"Working on it now. Give me a minute," Stokes replied.

"He ain't got a minute, Stokes," Ramirez said. "Look at him go. I'm gonna lose the window soon."

"How soon?" Wesco asked. "How far out am I?"

"You ain't close," Ramirez said.

"Got it. Route sent to you, Ramirez," Stokes said.

"Received," Ramirez said. "What are you going to do while I save Wesco's ass?"

"You're saving both of our asses," Wesco said.

"Keep telling yourself that, man," Ramirez said, but there was a smile in his voice.

"I'm staying put," Stokes said. "I might be able to get around the twenty-meter slice of hull on my five, but if I hit it, it'll go flying right at you, Ramirez."

"Don't do that," Ramirez responded.

"If I try my seven, then maybe I can hook up under the exhaust port," Stokes said. "Climb my way around that, then push off for the part of the ship that's still intact."

"Do that," Ramirez said.

"But the exhaust port may shift into a cluster of shattered drop-pods. Those could go in any direction, like a bad break in pool."

"Okay. Then don't do that, either," Wesco said. "Maybe staying put, for now, is best."

"Yeah. Stay put," Ramirez said. "Enjoy that option. Me? I'm now on my way to Wesco. Whee…"

"I can wait for it all to shift," Stokes said. "Might be more maneuverability in a few minutes. None of this crap is staying put."

"No shit," Ramirez said. "I'm heading your way now, Wesco."

"Stokes? Study and adjust his route, if needed," Wesco said. "If debris is shifting fast enough, he might have a quicker way to get to me."

"Yeah…I'll do that," Stokes said.

Ice filled Wesco's veins. He wanted to ask. He wanted to know what Stokes' hesitation was. But at the same time he didn't want to know. The fear was real, which made him laugh to himself.

He'd fought on a dozen planets and been attacked by aliens of all sizes and races. He'd once had a giant crab almost crack him open like a tin can before he blasted the damn thing's guts wide open with a well-placed RPG. Wesco knew combat. He knew how to fight and how to dive into a situation without regard for life or limb.

But stuck out in open space, blind, with zero control of his CASPer was almost too much. At no point in his career had he ever felt the slightest bit claustrophobic. Not once. Yet as he studied the inside of his CASPer, he could have sworn the space was shrinking, that perhaps that crab was back, trying to crush him all over again.

"You alright, Wesco?" Ramirez asked. "You're breathing kinda hard there, man."

"What? Yeah. Yeah, I'm fine," Wesco replied. "How far out are you?"

"Ten minutes," Ramirez said. "Gotta make it past this—SHIT!"

The comms crackled, and static filled Wesco's ears.

"Ramirez? What's going on?" Wesco asked. No answer. "Stokes?"

"I lost sight of him behind some blast shielding," Stokes said. "Ramirez! You copy? Ramirez!"

"Hold your horses," Ramirez said, panting. "I'm here, I'm here."

"What happened?" Wesco asked.

"I hit what's left of a bulkhead at the wrong angle, and it flipped on me," Ramirez said. "I need to crawl back over the top to get on track. I push off from here, and I'll be heading straight for the planet."

"I see you," Stokes said. "Be careful with that hunk. You push it wrong, and it'll mess up your entire route."

"You hear me about heading straight for the planet or not, Stokes?" Ramirez snapped. "I'm gonna be careful because of that."

"Still, watch how you move that—"

"Stokes! Shut the hell up!" Ramirez shouted. "Just shut up. Give me some space to make this work. I know what I need to do. Let me do it without your yapping!"

"You got it," Stokes replied, pissed. "If you have this handled, then I'll let you handle it."

No one spoke for a few minutes. Wesco struggled to remain silent. The claustrophobia wasn't helping.

"Ramirez? How close now?" Wesco asked, keeping his voice calm and even.

"I've adjusted my route," Ramirez said. "You catch that, Stokes?"

"I see you," Stokes said, still pissed. "You do what you have to, Ramirez."

"Do not let me drift out into this system forever because you two are being pissy with each other," Wesco said. "Cooperate now, fight later, preferably when we are in Med and out of our CASPers."

"Calm down, Wesco," Ramirez said. "I'm back on track and heading your way."

"Okay. Good," Wesco said. "ETA?"

"Before chow time," Ramirez said. "That work for you?"

Wesco laughed. "Perfect. Thanks."

"No problem," Ramirez replied. "Hang tight, man."

"Huh," Stokes said.

"Don't push me, Stokes," Ramirez warned.

"What? Oh…No, I wasn't huh-ing you," Stokes said. "I was…You know what? Never mind."

"Out with it, Stokes," Wesco said. "You noticed something. What is it?"

"It's nothing," Stokes said. "Nothing to do with you two, so don't worry."

"Ramirez? Can you see Stokes? What's going on?" Wesco asked.

"I said it's nothing for you two to worry about," Stokes stated. "All good."

"I see him, but there's no change in his…Wait. Stokes? Has the debris field shifted?" Ramirez asked. "Is all that shit closing in on you?"

"All good," Stokes stated again. "I'll use jets to adjust my position and get through the gap over…Okay, that gap is gone. No real worries. There's space…"

Stokes sighed.

"Yes, Ramirez, the debris field has shifted and is closing in on me," Stokes admitted.

"Then get out of there," Wesco said.

"You're not seeing what we're seeing, Wesco," Ramirez said. "He's between a lot of rocks and a lot of hard places."

"I got this," Stokes said. "There's a panel moving my way. I'll grab onto that, and it'll keep me from colliding with those twisted beams."

"That should do it," Ramirez said. "Dammit!"

"Ramirez?" Wesco asked.

"Missed my grab," Ramirez said. "Drifting to a new position. Stay put. Don't go anywhere while I adjust course."

"You're hilarious," Wesco said.

"That's what my mama always said," Ramirez replied.

"Really? She never mentioned that once to me when we were in bed together," Wesco replied.

"You want me to get you or what?" Ramirez replied, the smirk obvious in his voice.

"Just trying to keep things light," Wesco said. "Getting stuffy in here."

"Uh oh, sounds like Wesco has finally found his limit in the can," Ramirez said. "Hear that, Stokes? Wesco's getting claustrophobic."

No response.

"Stokes?" Ramirez asked.

"You there, Stokes?" Wesco asked.

"I'm busy," Stokes replied, his breathing labored. "You guys joke alone for a bit, alright?"

"What's wrong?" Wesco asked. "Ramirez? You see him?"

"No," Ramirez answered. "My view of him is blocked. Stokes? What's wrong?"

"Nothing," Stokes responded.

"Bullshit," Ramirez snapped. "Never mind. I'm rotating and will see him in about…"

"What? What's wrong?" Wesco asked.

"Stokes? Push off and rotate forty-five degrees," Ramirez said urgently. "Do whatever you need to do to get out of that shit."

"There's nowhere to go, Ramirez," Stokes replied. "I've been plotting escape routes since the debris shifted. I'm in a no-win here, guys."

"Bullshit," Ramirez said again. "Look up. You have a strut coming right at you. Grab on and roll around it. Let that hit the panel beneath you, then shove off and you're free."

"Listen to him Stokes," Wesco said, blind to all that was happening. "The guy is moving around without legs. He knows a thing or two."

"Yeah. Sure," Stokes replied.

There was a low squelch of static.

"Stokes?" Wesco called.

"He cut the comms," Ramirez said.

"Why the hell would he do that?" Wesco asked. Ramirez was silent. "Ramirez! Why did he cut his comms?"

"So we wouldn't hear," Ramirez said quietly. "He's gone, man."

"What? No way! He had outs, right?" Wesco demanded. "I'm the one drifting, and you're the one without legs! Stokes was safe!"

"It all shifted too fast, man," Ramirez said, his voice husky with emotion. "He couldn't get out. It…crushed him."

"How do you know? Your view could be blocked."

"My view isn't blocked."

"Then how—"

"Because I can see the blood, man!" Ramirez shouted. "He was pressed between several hunks of debris, and his CASPer was flattened! There was nothing he could do! Pull yourself together, Wesco! Everyone else died! Stokes is one more casualty of this mess! You need your head in the game, man! I need your head in the game!"

"You're right," Wesco said after a few deep breaths. "Sorry."

"Nothing to be sorry about," Ramirez replied. "We're the meat in a shit sandwich. It all sucks."

"Wouldn't shit be the meat in a shit sandwich?" Wesco asked.

"Screw you, Wesco."

A flicker.

"Hey!" Wesco shouted.

"Jesus Christ! Turn the volume down, will ya?" Ramirez complained.

"No, my HUD is flickering! I might be able to get control of my CASPer again!" Wesco responded.

"That'd be great," Ramirez said. "Because without Stokes, I'm not sure how to get to you. It's all moving faster than I thought. Chunks of the ship are pin balling off each. Might be better to sit tight and let it sort itself out."

"You got enough air to sit tight?" Wesco asked.

"No."

"Have I stopped drifting off into the rest of the system?"

"No."

"Then get your ass over here," Wesco said as he studied his controls. Lights were slowly coming back on. "If I get control again, we can talk about waiting the shift out."

Wesco flipped switches, but nothing happened. He returned the switches back to their original positions. His eyes moved to a switch away from the others. Isolated for a reason, that switch was a last resort.

"Ramirez? What if I do a hard reboot?" Wesco asked.

"You haven't tried that yet?" Ramirez responded.

"No. I like life support to be on when I'm in open space," Wesco said. "I also like knowing that life support will stay on if I do nothing. If I hard reboot the system, maybe it doesn't work. Maybe my reboot doesn't boot."

"I think that's a chance worth taking!" Ramirez shouted. "Jesus, Wesco! You could have rebooted and gone to save Stokes!"

"Or I could have rebooted and shut down everything instead of most of everything!" Wesco shouted back. "Hard reboots are last resort!"

"This is last resort, man! The ship's destroyed, and there are only two of us left alive! How many more resorts do you need? Huh? How many...How many more..."

Ramirez coughed hard. It was wet, phlegmy. He coughed again and again, and the wetness grew worse. Then he didn't stop coughing.

"Ramirez. Hey, Ramirez," Wesco called. "Take some deep breaths. You probably burst a few capillaries in your lungs. Nothing to get excited about. Best thing is to calm down and relax."

The coughing took a turn where it almost sounded sarcastic.

"Okay, okay, maybe not relax, but you know what I mean," Wesco said.

The coughing increased in intensity, then Ramirez let out a long gasp and went silent.

Wesco waited.

And waited.

"Ramirez?"

A wheeze.

"I hoarked everywhere," Ramirez said, his voice not much louder than a whisper. "There's blood and snot all over."

"At least you're alive," Wesco said with relief. "Uh…Not wanting to be a pain…"

"I'm on my way," Ramirez said. "How's that HUD coming? Any more flickers?"

"I'm not doing a hard reboot," Wesco stated. "My gut says it won't come back on. Better to wait until you get here for backup."

"I'm not much backup, man," Ramirez said.

"You're all I got, Ramirez," Wesco said.

"Ah, I'm touched, man," Ramirez said and laughed. Then coughed. And coughed. "Dammit…"

The coughing grew worse and worse before Ramirez let out a small yelp.

It wasn't much of a sound. A slight expression of pain and discomfort. As if he'd stubbed his toe, but not too hard.

"You good, Ramirez?" Wesco asked. He could hear the static of the comms channel wide open. "Ramirez? Grunt if you can hear me."

There was no grunt.

"Ramirez! Breathe, man! Do whatever you have to and breathe!"

"Huh…?" Gasping. "What…?"

"Ramirez! There you are!"

Gasp. "Wes…" Gasp. Choke. Cough. "Sorry…"

The comms went dead. No static. The channel was no longer open.

Wesco screamed.

He screamed his throat raw.

The screaming didn't help.

Wesco sucked in shallow breaths, five seconds from a full on panic attack. He'd been thirteen the last time he had a panic attack. Part of why he joined the military, then became a merc, was to conquer that fear, to crush the panic that had ruled him for years during his youth.

The shallow breaths became deep breaths, their rate slowing, slowing, slowing, until Wesco could control himself. The panic wasn't gone, but it was subdued.

"Okay," Wesco said to himself. "What are you going to do now?"

He knew what he was going to do.

Stokes was dead. Ramirez was probably dead. Wesco was all alone.

There was no choice.

Wesco was vacationing on the last resort, and he knew it.

"Fine," he said and reached for the switch.

He drew his hand back then reached again, drew his hand back once more, then reached and flipped the switch. It wasn't that simple. There were a couple more steps he needed to take to authorize a full, hard reboot. Soft reboots in the field were one thing, but an entire system shutdown and restart was a whole other monster. Most CASPers weren't even able to do hard reboots, but theirs had been modified to allow it.

The last step completed, Wesco took a deep breath and held it as his CASPer powered completely down.

The darkness was utterly complete. Wesco couldn't have seen his hand in front of his face if he wanted to. He didn't want to. His hands were busy balling into fists as he mentally counted off the seconds.

Twenty-three. Twenty-four. Twenty-five.

Thirty seconds for a hard reboot to begin.

Twenty-eight. Twenty-nine. Thirty.

The darkness remained.

Wesco wanted to shout, but he didn't dare use the air in his lungs. The inside of the CASPer had enough air to keep him alive for a few minutes, but he needed those minutes. It had become painfully obvious he needed those minutes.

Forty-one. Forty-two. Forty-three. Forty-four.

Wesco could hold his breath for three minutes and change. Any merc worth their weight had to be able to hold their breath at least that long. You didn't go into space with weak lungs.

Fifty. Fifty-one. Fifty-two.

A clank. A hum. Another clank.

Lights!

One by one, the systems came back on until Wesco's HUD was up and glowing before his eyes.

"Yes!" he shouted.

Wesco didn't waste any time. He skipped the systems checklist and aimed his CASPer for the field of debris laid out before him.

A long way before him.

"What...?" he whispered.

Wesco checked and rechecked his display. He'd drifted two full klicks from the debris field. Ramirez was never actually going to get to him. Wesco had drifted too far.

"Lock on Ramirez," Wesco ordered. "Lock on Stokes."

Two blips flashed on his HUD, locking onto Ramirez's and Stokes' transponders. Wesco zoomed in and sighed as he stared at Ramirez.

The man's legs were gone, yes, but it was the steady stream of globs of blood drifting around his CASPer that told the true tale. His nanites must have failed. Running out of air was never the real threat. Ramirez had been trying to get to Wesco because Wesco was his only option to get to what remained of the ship, to get to Med.

The ship.

Wesco shook off the shock of realization and focused on the intact part of the ship. Stokes had been right. Med was there. Wesco had no idea if any of the decks were viable, but it was his only chance to get his ass out of the mess he was in.

"I got this," he said to himself as he engaged his jumpjets.

He was off and speeding toward the debris field. Then his jets sputtered and died.

"Dammit!" Wesco yelled as he saw the fuel gauge hit zero.

The tanks had been damaged and emptied at some point. All Wesco did was burn the fuel left in the lines, sending his CASPer speeding straight at a debris field that had already killed one of his teammates.

"Stupid! Stupid, stupid, stupid!" Wesco shouted, pissed off that he'd been in too much of a hurry to check the fuel levels. "STU-PID!"

He raged as he flew toward a slowly rotating panel. He hit the panel at a bad angle and bounced off, unable to grab hold. The CASPer tumbled backward, the feet lifting upward so Wesco was upside down from his previous orientation, facing out toward the system.

Wesco's raging and thrashing and intense cursing slowed then stopped.

He dialed in his display and zoomed in on an object that was out in the system, but coming in fast.

A ship.

Not one of the company's; that was for sure. Didn't look Zuparti, either.

Salvage.

"That was fast," Wesco said, knowing it wasn't fast at all. That ship had to have been waiting close by.

Wesco checked all the comms channels. No one was calling to check if there were survivors, as was standard procedure. The salvage ship knew where it was, and what it was looking at.

"Shit," Wesco mumbled as he tumbled.

A beam about five meters long was within grabbing distance. Wesco reached out and snagged it, stopping his tumbling. He clung hard to the beam as he and the piece of debris twisted and turned toward a length of broken corridor from one of the ship's decks.

Only about four meters in length, and missing an entire wall, the corridor swallowed Wesco up as he tucked his legs and tried not to collide with the walls that remained. The beam snagged at the corridor's opening and Wesco hung tight, knowing he'd only shoot out the other side of the corridor if he let go.

He had a choice to make.

The salvage ship would eventually come for the debris surrounding him, hopefully taking in the length of corridor he was inside. That would be ideal.

Except Wesco was certain the salvage ship was in on the double cross. Maybe not in on it, but aware that survivors couldn't be tolerated. The ship was there to clean up, and the cleanup would not be complete if mercs were left alive.

Wesco's choices were to keep his CASPer systems up and running, risking detection from the ship, or to shut down to minimal systems once more and risk not being able to reboot again. The thought of a failed reboot made Wesco's skin itch. The thought of being blasted into a million pieces made his skin itch worse.

He made his choice.

The first step was to double-check his power supplies. The CASPer was at fifty percent, so rebooting wouldn't be an issue as long as the systems held out.

The second step was to quickly, very quickly, go over a shutdown checklist. Wesco had to make sure he didn't miss anything that was crucial to the CASPer's booting back up.

The third step was to wait as the slice of corridor rotated slowly so the end faced the salvage ship. Wesco wanted one last look to orient himself to the location of his new enemy.

All steps fell away. Wesco tossed his plan out the window and gaped at the scene on his HUD.

He watched in stunned fascination as the salvage ship's prow split open to draw massive chunks of the merc ship into its processing hold. It was a normal sight for a salvage ship, but what wasn't normal was the small shape clinging to one of the chunks being swallowed.

Wesco zoomed in and gasped as he saw a CASPer clamber over the edge of the chunk, then leap off, into the salvage ship's hold.

"Wesco to unidentified CASPer," he called over the comms. "Do you copy?"

He played back the CASPer's jump, but couldn't see any distinguishing marks from that distance. He had no idea who was diving into the belly of the beast.

"Wesco calling unidentified CASPer," Wesco tried again. "Do you copy? Hello? Come on, man, talk to me!"

There were flashes of light from inside the salvage ship's hold, and the prow began to close. But before it could close all the way, several chunks of salvage ship came exploding back out into the debris field. He saw more flashes, then the prow shut and sealed.

Wesco watched in amazement as the salvage ship turned to starboard and slowly moved away from the debris field. Then it picked up speed and the aft engines glowed brightly with the ship's obvious intent to vacate the area.

It was a smart move, Wesco thought. That ship had no idea how many more mercs in CASPers were still alive. A couple could do some serious damage if they got inside.

A hole was ripped open in the side of the salvage ship. It wasn't a large hole, maybe four times the size of a CASPer, but in open space, a hull breach of any kind was potentially catastrophic.

The unidentified CASPer came crawling out of the hull breach and scrambled up across the ship until it was facing what Wesco assumed was the bridge. RPGs flew from the CASPer and impacted the salvage ship's bridge. There were more brief flashes and pieces of the salvage ship exploded outward toward the CASPer.

Whoever the merc was, he was good. The CASPer dodged the pieces of the ship and climbed back through the hull breach.

Wesco waited. He counted off the seconds, the minutes, his eyes locked onto the scene before him.

One last flash filled his HUD. It was not a small flash. It was the flash of an entire ship being demolished from the inside out. Wesco whooped with joy as more and more hull breaches appeared until the salvage ship broke in two.

One half of the salvage ship went rolling into the debris field, sending hunks of the merc ship flying in every direction like massive pieces of shrapnel. Shrapnel that was colliding with more shrapnel, turning the debris into an exponentially more deadly field to be anywhere near.

Which Wesco still was.

"Shit," he muttered as he ditched the idea of shutting down and scrambled to the end of the corridor.

He grabbed the edges with his huge metal fists, crouched low, diverted a good amount of power to his legs, and jumped, pushing off with his legs and steering with his fists in order to get away from the incoming tsunami of murderous debris heading straight for him.

Five meters. Ten meters. Twenty meters. Wesco's CASPer floated quickly away. But not quickly enough.

Bits of the merc ship, and possibly the salvage ship, sped past Wesco. His HUD filled with warnings and alerts of projectiles coming for him, coming at him, surrounding him. He had no fuel for his jumpjets, so trying to outmaneuver the projectiles was impossible. Wesco could empty some of his air and use that for propulsion, but losing air meant a slow death later instead of sudden death if any of the debris damaged his CASPer.

Wesco kept his eyes forward and ignored the constant alarms and warnings. There was truly nothing he could do.

Something hit him in the back. Hard. Wesco spun out of control. His HUD was nothing but a swirling, streaming mess of images and data.

"Shit, shit, shit," Wesco swore as he tried to gain control of his CASPer.

Everything he tried was useless. Whatever hit him had hit him so hard the momentum was impossible to overcome. Wesco was in a spinning free float. Until he hit something that would slow his momentum, he would continue to spin.

Wesco shut off his HUD. He couldn't look at the swirling mess any longer.

But there was still the spinning. Wesco wasn't feeling anything close to a full G, but that didn't mean the force of the spin wasn't trying. It was like subtle unease had settled in his stomach and chest, and it refused to leave. He knew he was spinning—he could feel it—but the feeling was almost dreamlike.

"Like falling and flying and floating at the same time," Wesco called over the comms.

He doubted anyone could hear him. The mystery CASPer must have lost comms, or whoever it was would have been talking to him and Ramirez and Stokes.

Ramirez and Stokes.

All the arguing and bickering and fear. All the planning and plotting to survive.

All for nothing.

What were they going to do? Somehow get themselves onto that piece of ship still intact? Get into Med and do what? Fix Ramirez? If the nanites couldn't handle the trauma, there wasn't anything the equipment could have done, if that equipment still worked.

And they were in zero G. The nanites were good, but not good enough to keep every single clot from forming in those severed legs. Clots that were eventually going to travel to Ramirez's lungs, killing him instantly.

What had they been thinking?

"Hello…?"

Wesco shook his head. They had been doomed as soon as their ship was attacked. They hadn't died right away, but death was inevitable.

"Hello? Can anyone read me?"

Wesco went rigid.

"Hello?" he asked over the comms.

"Oh, thank God!" a voice replied. "I thought I was the only one left. Who is this?"

"Wesco," Wesco replied.

"Marga," the voice said.

"Sweet Hell, Marga," Wesco said and laughed. "Glad to hear you. Where have you been?"

"What?"

"Where have you been? Ramirez and Stokes were alive, but they're gone now. We were on open channels. We were talking and planning. Why didn't you join in?"

"I…I just woke up," Marga replied. "Something hit my drop-pod and woke me up. What happened?"

Wesco opened his mouth, then closed it. He closed his eyes and thought hard.

"Wesco? You still there?" Marga asked.

"Yeah, I'm still here," Wesco responded. "Did you say you're in a drop-pod? We didn't see any intact in the debris."

"I…I can't see any debris. I'm not sure where I am," Marga said. "Wesco, what happened?"

"We were double-crossed," Wesco said. "Ramirez, Stokes, and I tried to get to a portion of the ship that is still intact. That plan went to shit. Then someone, not sure who, attacked the salvage ship that came to clean up. Whoever it was tore that ship open from stem to stern. I got hit by the resulting shrapnel, and now I'm spinning out into the system."

Silence.

"Marga?"

"Yeah. I heard…"

"Where are you? You said you don't see debris?"

"I'm nowhere close to the planet. There's no debris field near me. All I see is a bright circle that is the planet we were supposed to land on. I have to be at least a couple thousand clicks away. At least. Probably closer to twenty thousand or so."

"You're moving away?"

"I'm moving away."

"Have you activated your drop-pod's SOS?"

"Not yet. Probably won't help much, will it?"

"Probably not. Even if the SOS brings us a friendly, that could take days or even weeks. I don't have that kind of air. Neither does your drop-pod."

Silence.

"I can die on an alien beach or while storming a bulkhead, but dying in a drop-pod out in open space? This death sucks, Wesco. I didn't sign up for this."

"Me neither, Marga."

More silence.

"How much air do you have left?" Marga asked.

"At this point?" Wesco brought up his HUD, ignored the swirling images, and checked his air levels. "Jack shit. I have maybe three games of Twenty Questions left."

"I hate Twenty Questions," Marga said with a sad laugh. "Pick a different game."

"Yeah. Sure…" Wesco couldn't think of a different game.

Long silence.

"Wesco? You still there?"

"Right here."

"You think of a different game?"

"No."

"Okay."

"I think…I think I'm going to be quiet. Just quiet as I wait. We live loud lives, Marga. So loud we forget what the quiet is like. Do you mind?"

"I…No. Quiet is fine."

"Cool. Thanks."

Wesco shut down his HUD once more, then slowly shut down the rest of his systems.

All of his systems.

Without life support, the interior of the HUD became deathly cold within minutes.

His teeth chattered, but he barely noticed. Black motes filled his vision as the air thinned, then was gone.

Wesco laughed, expelling the last of his air. He laughed at his end and how quiet it was. True quiet after a life of noise and violence.

Wesco found, in his last moments, he enjoyed the quiet.

The quiet was fine.

# # # # #

A Mother's Favor
by Kacey Ezell

Choking Deluge stepped out into the fetid air and took a deep breath. His Clan Dama, who had once been his sister-kita, Death, hadn't lied. Houston was an ugly town. Worse, it reeked of noxious industrial fumes that were enough to make his eyes water behind his sun-tinted lenses. He blinked rapidly to clear his vision and drifted into the flow of pedestrian traffic leaving the spaceport terminal.

The traffic was mostly Human, of course, here, on their home world. But Houston was a busy spaceport; there were enough other beings that he didn't particularly stand out. For ease of blending in, he wore a non-descript traveler's cloak over his harness and kept his hood up. He could have pulled quintessence, but sometimes it was fun to try and flow with the crowd.

The late afternoon sun slanted down through the broken silhouettes of buildings around him and warmed the pavement beneath his pads. Del kept walking along the curving path that fronted the terminal building while the noise from a departing shuttle split the thick, cloying air.

Up ahead, a group of four XenSha hailed a ground cab with a wave of one of their tentacles. These beings also wore cloaks to hide their long, furry ears and sensory tentacles. Like him, they probably didn't want to draw too much attention to themselves. As he had reason to know, these particular XenSha were mercenaries.

Deluge eased behind a large refuse container and wrapped himself in quintessence. Though he'd never be as smooth as his sister-kita Flame, he had gotten better over the years, until his stealth was complete enough to pull such a trick in a crowded area like this. Once hidden, he removed his cloak and stowed it in the pouch he wore on his back, then leapt back out into the harsh light of the Earthen sun.

The ground cab was a large one, with a door that slid back toward the rear of the vehicle. As Del approached, he heard the XenSha haggling with the cabbie through their translators. While they continued to grouse at one another over the rate, Deluge slipped between the lead XenSha and the vehicle and leapt up into the cab. A few moments later, the XenSha followed, giggling to themselves about the outrageously low price of a tenth of a credit.

Irritation flashed through Deluge. Maybe it was a character flaw, or maybe it was that he'd been raised by a Human, but whatever the reason, Del found the prevailing view of humanity to be grossly unfair. Sure, they were new to the galactic stage, and yes, their economy was underdeveloped in so many ways…but as a species they were interesting and adaptable and fun. He hated to see them treated as the butt of a joke.

Which is why, though he was no thief, Del eased up between the seats and lifted the lead XenSha's UACC from his cloak. While the cab wound its way through the labyrinthine streets of Houston, Del took the UACC up to the payment slate mounted on the center console and scanned it for five hundred credits.

Expensive, perhaps, for a thirty-minute cab ride, but Deluge figured the long-suffering driver deserved a tip for dealing with these ill-mannered tentacle bunnies.

He managed to stow the UACC back in the leader's cloak without being noticed just before the cab slowed to a stop. The driver opened the rear door of the cab with the push of a button, then froze as he looked at his payment display. Deluge leapt up onto the console beside him and spoke quietly in English.

"Do not ask questions. The money is legitimate. Simply drive away and consider this a day's work well done."

The Human reacted well to what must have seemed like a voice coming from nowhere. His pale face reddened. His eyes went wide, and he glanced back toward the departing XenSha more than once.

But he didn't say anything. His finger trembled as he pushed the button to accept the payment and turned off his "for hire" sign. Deluge slowly blinked and leapt from the open window just as the cab pulled away from the curb.

Well. That had gone well, Del reflected as he turned to see where the XenSha had taken him.

It didn't look like much, honestly. The setting sun poured reddish light over a long building with a sagging awning that ran the length of what had apparently once been shops and businesses. Most of the glass in the storefront windows and doors looked like it had long-since been busted out and replaced with wood or cardboard. At the south end, a few panes of glass remained, but they were papered over on the inside, making the buildings look just as abandoned as the rest.

The XenSha headed that way and stopped in front of a door covered in faded blue, with a barely legible yellow symbol. As Deluge got closer, he could see the symbol looked like one of the native Earth species of big cat: a lion.

The XenSha stood in a group, packed together, talking and laughing. They didn't approach the door, though. Instead, they stood with their backs to it and stared up at the corner of the awning where it bent toward one of the thin metal poles holding it up. Something clicked, and to Del's surprise, the blue-papered door swung inward.

"Go!" the lead XenSha said, shoving one of his companions forward. "It only stays open for thirty seconds!"

Good to know, Deluge thought as he sprinted through the opening ahead of the tentacle bunnies. The door swung heavily shut behind them with a finality that belied its innocuous appearance. Ahead, a hallway curved down and to the left, making him wonder what sort of ambush lay ahead. Deep in his heart of hearts, where the elder Del was still a rambunctious kit, he hoped it would be a good one.

Sadly, it was not to be. Though a pair of Lumar could have made an admirable ambush, the two that awaited them weren't interested in fighting. Not right away, it seemed.

"Welcome to the Lyon's Den," the larger of the two said. He spoke in perfect English, sounding like a Human born. Deluge wondered how long he'd been practicing that line. "Do you understand the rules?"

"Yeah, yeah," the XenSha leader said. "Be nice to the staff, draw down, and everyone draws down on you. Got it, Four Arms. You going to let us in?"

"Have a nice time," the Lumar said and moved to the side to let the party pass. Deluge looked closely at the two Lumar, but as he didn't want to lose his quarry, he followed them through the blue curtain into the establishment known as the Lyon's Den.

Del had heard of it, of course. Anyone with any connection to merc circles, had. He had never known where it was located, though, or how to get inside. He certainly hadn't been expecting it to have the run-down and nondescript exterior he'd encountered.

The interior, on the other hand, was a different story. Everywhere he looked, he saw luxury in all its forms. From the brightly colored gas tanks of various off-world atmosphere samplers to the huge octagonal bar and the deliciously scented dishes coming from the kitchen, the Lyon's Den felt like a place where you could get just about anything you wanted.

Which was good. Because what Deluge wanted was to finish this contract and get paid.

The XenSha moved toward a table midway across the cavernous space. As a race, the tentacle bunnies weren't much taller than Hunters, so the table they chose was low to the ground. They arranged themselves on the cushions, and a young man in a server's uniform stepped forward.

"Good evening, gentle beings," the juvenile Human said. "My name is Mark, and I'll be your server. What can the Lyon provide for you tonight?"

"Gut Ripper," the lead XenSha barked. Deluge couldn't help twitching his tail in a silent snarl. What an unpleasant character. No wonder he had a contract on his life.

"Of course. Anything else?" the young man asked.

"Just bring it out," the XenSha snapped. "We don't want to wait all night."

"You got it," Mark said. "If you think of anything else, feel free to place your order on the order slates. I'll be right back with those Gut Rippers."

"I'll be back," the leader said as Mark walked away. "Gotta empty the second gut."

Up until that moment, Deluge's plan had been to slip a slow-acting poison into the XenSha's food or drink. The client had requested something quiet, and the poison was known to be thorough and gentle. Victims went to sleep and simply didn't wake up. Plus, it metabolized quickly in most physiologies and was difficult to detect unless you were specifically looking for it.

But the fact was this guy was *rude*. And Deluge disliked rudeness. Intensely. So when the XenSha stood up and began to make his way back toward the rooms reserved for body waste elimination, Del followed.

The XenSha selected a room and let himself in, then turned and locked the door behind him. Before he could do much else, Del struck.

His first slash took out the XenSha's vocal apparatus, rendering the rude merc unable to scream. The XenSha let out a gurgling cough as his bright blue blood began to run in a thin rivulet down the front of his body, staining his cloak. He staggered backward and fell over the elimination stool. He splayed his hands and tentacles to catch himself against the walls of the narrow room as his eyes and mouth worked furiously.

"You are a cheat," Deluge said. He let his quintessence drop and stood on his hind legs, looking down at the half-supine tentacle bunny. "You are a cheat and you are incompetent. You lied about the results of your latest merc contract, and the client was not pleased. More importantly, though, you are rude. I cannot abide rudeness. It is unspeakably ugly to me."

The XenSha struggled to speak, but Deluge caught sight of one tentacle creeping toward the small holster tucked into the XenSha's pocket. The Hunter laughed and struck out again with his bare claws, this time severing the nerves in the tentacle so that it flopped, useless, into the elimination stool.

"You are sneaky, though," Del said. "I will give you that. I would say that you should be better in the future, but you won't have a future to speak of. Good bye, rude XenSha."

The XenSha's tentacles writhed in front of his face in a vain attempt to block Deluge's next strike, but it was no use. Another slash of Del's claws opened up the main artery in the creature's throat, and within one more heartbeat, he was dead.

Deluge took a breath and looked around, pleased at the economy of the scene. He hadn't made much of a mess, as the majority of the XenSha's blood had fountained into the elimination stool. Del pushed the button to clear the stool and considered his next move. The client had asked for quiet, so it wouldn't do to leave the body there, much as he might enjoy the consternation that would cause.

He unlocked the door and peeked out, careful to stay hidden. The hallway through which they'd come was empty, and there was a door at the far end with a lit "EXIT" sign above it. Del spared a moment of thanks to his Human molly for teaching him to read English and ducked back inside the room.

The exsanguinated XenSha lay sprawled over the elimination stool, tentacles splayed in all directions. With a sigh, Del immediately began to regret his decision to fulfil the contract here…but there was no help for it. The client wanted quiet, so quiet he would be.

Luckily, the dead XenSha wasn't terribly heavy. They weren't a dense species, though the tentacles made them awkward to maneuver. Del considered his options for a moment, then slowly blinked as an idea manifested.

He reached into his pack where, along with his cloak, he carried a length of monofilament cord. Strong and tough, it could double as a garrote if need be, but it was long enough to use as a climbing aid, should one be required. It should do to keep the XenSha's tentacles contained long enough to get him down the hall and out the door. A place like this would doubtless have some kind of bio-waste receptacle in the back. Del just hoped it was big enough to put the XenSha into.

It should be. This was a large restaurant, after all. They always had a lot of bio-waste.

Del pulled out the cord and began wrapping it around the XenSha's body, from his furry ears down. Almost immediately, he could see he had another problem.

"Fuck," Del whispered, borrowing one of the Human expletives his molly used when she thought no one was listening. The razor-edged cord was cutting smoothly into the XenSha's dead flesh. He'd have to balance the tension on it well, or else he'd have bits of the creature falling behind him, like a trail of crumbs left by a kit with a cookie.

With more whispered curses, in English as well as the twelve other languages he knew, Del shifted and wrapped the damned XenSha into a neat little package he could hoist on his back. He concentrated, stretching his quintessence cloak larger to encompass the alien's body as well as his own...which ended up giving him a headache.

Despite his growing frustration, Deluge forced himself to be a professional and carefully opened the door into the hallway. Finally, a little luck: the hallway was still empty. He hitched the cord-bound body up higher onto his back and stepped out of the little room.

Luck continued to smile on him. No one appeared while he bolted for the exit door. The opening mechanism appeared to be a bar stretching across the width of the door right at his eye level. He considered putting the XenSha down in order to open it, but in the end, he just closed his eyes and pressed on the bar with his forehead.

Immediately, an ear-stabbing ringing split the air. Del growled and shoved his way through the door. Of course it was alarmed! This was a business wasn't it? He was too damned old and experienced to be making stupid kit mistakes like this! He never should have indulged his impulse to kill this one separately for his rudeness. What had he been thinking?

With these recriminations echoing in his head, Deluge felt the door slam heavily behind him as he ducked into the nearest shadowed space, that of a large and very smelly trash container.

Within a few moments, someone came. The door he'd used opened, and a Human male stuck his head out and looked around. His eyes swept right over Del and his burden, of course, as he peered deeply into the shadows in the alley.

A noise came from behind a pile of wooden pallets across the alleyway from Del's hiding place. The Human man's eyes narrowed, and he stepped out through the door. He carried a Human weapon Del had only seen in pictures: a shotgun, unless he misremembered the name.

Because he was curious, Del eased his burden to the ground and stepped out from behind the trash container to follow the Human. The man wasn't young. His weathered face and hands said he'd seen several years' worth of Earthen sun. But he moved smoothly, placing his feet carefully to move nearly as silently as Del, himself. He glanced around as he walked, taking in the surrounding area as he approached the pile of pallets.

Del watched as the man peered around the pile to the left and right. He looked as if he were considering lifting them up and looking underneath when the door from the bar opened again.

"Lyon," a female voice said from inside. Del was at the wrong angle to see her. "Alarm is reset, cameras saw nothing."

"Huh," the man replied. "I got nothing out here, either. Musta been a glitch."

"That's what the alarm company said. They're sending out a technician in the morning."

"Perfect, Katie," Lyon said, turning his back on the pallets and walking toward the door. "Thank you."

Deluge stayed where he was and watched as the Lyon walked back into his Den. The door clanged shut once again, and the alleyway went silent.

Too silent. Something was here.

Deluge lifted his face to the air and sniffed. The heavy, greasy scent of bar garbage permeated the small space, but under that, Del got a whiff of something else. Something with an iron tang to it...blood?

He eased toward the pallet pile and stepped carefully on the lowest layer, then bent to test the air again. This close, the hot, irony scent of blood was stronger, and Del could nearly taste the fear that went along with it. The Lyon had been right. Something was hiding under these pallets, and it was hurting and afraid.

Del followed the scent around the back of the pile, toward the cinderblock wall opposite. One of the pallet boards had cracked in the middle and bowed down, leaving a slightly wider space between it and the next layer piled up on top of it. Del bent and sniffed, then crouched flat on his belly over the broken board.

In truth, he probably wasn't quite as stealthy as he should have been. The cracked wood creaked beneath his weight, and he was bulky enough that someone listening could have heard him pushing through. But he was reasonably confident he could get himself out of this situation if necessary. Worst case scenario, he'd draw his energy-pistol and burn a hole in the pallets and just walk out.

Though that would be embarrassing.

Thankfully, torching the pallets wasn't necessary. Once he squeezed through the opening, the interior opened up, thanks to a pallet that had fallen on its side and created a slanted kind of roof in the middle of the pile. And under this roof...

A cat. An Earth cat, obviously in pain and obviously very pregnant. As he watched, her belly contorted with the movement of the kittens inside.

"I greet you, Earth Damita," Del said in his own language, letting his quintessence drop away and standing on all four of his feet. He hoped his translator would transmit the gist of his message to the animal before him. "You smell of hurt. Do you need help?"

"You can help?" the occupant of the pallet pile said softly. Although "said" wasn't entirely accurate. Like a Hunter, she conveyed her message in multiple ways: her scarred ears twitched in interest, and her tired eyes rolled up to meet his. And she spoke like an adult Hunter, vocalizing in a tone inaudible to kits and Humans—and most other beings. But he understood. He understood even before the translator articulated the words.

"I think so, little sister," Del said, pushing aside the wonder he felt. Now was not the time. "Have you a name?"

"No. I have no Human. Humans give names."

"I shall call you Damita, then, if it pleases you. This is what we Hunters call our young mothers."

She let out a mewl of pain that the translator echoed as a laugh.

"I do not think I shall live long enough to be a mother," she said, her tone matter of fact. "The young Humans have hurt me badly. I think I shall die, and my kittens with me."

"Not if I can help it, little sister," Del said, steel in his voice. "May I look at your hurts?"

"If you want," she said. "It makes no difference, I suppose."

Her voice drifted, but she was in so much pain that Del decided not to chide her for giving up. He stepped closer and peered at the network of bloody streaks that crisscrossed her flanks. Her tail was burnt at the tip, as if something hot had been tied to it at one point. There were bruises around her neck, too, as if she'd been strangled or hung.

"Humans did this? How did you survive?" he asked, awe threading through his voice.

"I fought," she said. "They had a rope tied around my neck and a crackling hot thing tied to my tail. I thrashed until the rope nearly broke. They laughed and cut me down, then cut up my sides. Then the alarm went off and startled them. I bolted and hid here. This is a nice place to die. They can't reach me here."

"You won't die," Deluge said. "You will live and have your kittens, I promise. I will bring help."

"Help?" the cat asked, slowly blinking a laugh, even while her blood seeped from her myriad wounds. "There is no help."

"There will be. Just stay here, little sister, and trust me."

"I cannot go anywhere anyway," she said and laid her head down. "My strength is gone."

Del swallowed a string of curse words as icy fury erupted inside him. He shoved it back down as he turned to worm his way back out of the stack of pallets. In his haste, he let a large splinter of wood gouge his side enough to break the skin. It stung, but he ignored it and kept moving. He didn't know how long she had, but unless he missed his guess, she was in active labor. With their mother so badly hurt and weakened, the kittens would struggle to be born.

He pulled himself free of the pallet pile and leapt toward the door he'd used before, only to have bitter disappointment crash in, amping up his sense of urgency. The door was smooth and featureless on this side, with no way to re-enter the bar. Frustration rumbled forth in the form of a growl as he craned his neck, looking around the alley for another door, a window, something…

There! A window fitted with an antiquated cooling unit that some Humans still used. The top half of the window was papered over, but Del could see a thin seam of light next to the unit. It might do.

He leapt up on top of the trash container next to the rude XenSha's cooling body, and from there onto the rickety wooden shelf that supported the cooling unit. It sagged under Del's weight, and the seam he'd noticed widened. Perfect.

Deluge jumped, making the shelf creak and the window groan. He did it again, and again, targeting his impacts to weaken the wooden support brace where it was screwed into the brick. Dust began to trickle down the wall, growing into a stream as Del's exertions ground away at the brick.

One more leap, he thought. *The screw will strip totally out, and I can pull the brace free. The cooler should fall away, and I'll be able to leap into the window and go from there—*

He realized he'd miscalculated right about the time the wooden support splintered and buckled, sending the whole thing—and him—crashing down toward the garbage piled in the box below.

Deluge twisted, reaching with his hands to catch the slimy metal rim of the trash container. The metal stung his pads, but he pivoted around and dropped to the ground as the cooling unit clanged into the mostly empty trash container.

He crouched, knife in hand, and pulled quintessence tight around himself as the alarm shrilled out again, and the metal door slammed open. The Lyon stepped out, a Human-style shotgun in his hands.

"Who's out here?" he shouted. "You're going to pay for that air conditioner!"

"Gladly," Deluge called out in English as the alarm noise abruptly cut off. "But I wish to speak to you first!"

The Lyon pumped the slide on his shotgun.

Deluge sighed and let his knife fly so it would impact—and embed into—the brick behind the Lyon's head. Then Deluge jumped up, angling his body so that he could bounce off the stinking garbage container and land with one foot on either of the Lyon's shoulders.

While the Human froze beneath him, Del dropped his quintessence and bent to whisper in the man's ear.

"I, Choking Deluge of the Night Wind Clan, greet you, Lyon. Welcome to our negotiation."

"You're a Depik?" Tension threaded through the Lyon's voice.

"Many call us that," Deluge said.

"There's a contract on me?"

"Not that I know of," Deluge said, slowly blinking. "If you were my target, I wouldn't bother greeting you with the niceties. I apologize for damaging your cooling unit, but I needed to get back inside to speak with you. It is a matter of life and death, and I didn't know if your Lumar would let me in the front door."

He felt the Lyon shift slightly. "What is the matter?"

"A mother lies dying in your alley, not two meters away. She is very close to giving birth. I believe you can save her, or if not her, at least her kittens. Will you help?"

"Kittens?"

"She is one of your Earth felines. Cats, I think you call them."

"You're not going to cut me or shoot me or whatever?"

"Not if you help her," Deluge said, slowly blinking again, though the Lyon probably couldn't see him, crouched as he was behind the man's head.

"I'd help her anyway, just so you know," the Lyon said. He cleared out the shotgun, then bent carefully to set it down, leaning it against the brick wall.

Deluge launched from the Human's shoulders and twisted himself all the way around in the air before landing on his back feet and giving the man a Human-style smile.

"I am glad to hear it. She is this way." He turned back to the pallet pile and bounded up to the top of it.

"Underneath?" the Lyon asked.

"Yes. There is an opening. You will have to move the pallets to get to her."

"Sure. One minute," the Lyon said. He pressed a button on the time piece he wore on his wrist, and a few moments later the door opened again. The two Lumar from the front walked out.

"There is a mother in distress inside that pile," the Lyon said. "Please move the pallets, quickly but carefully."

"Boss," the taller Lumar said, and he and his partner went to work.

Deluge had seen the Lumar in action before, but their strength and quickness never ceased to impress him. They weren't known for being the galaxy's deepest thinkers, perhaps, but when one wanted to apply brute force to a problem, one could hardly do better than a Lumar.

About halfway through, they uncovered the pallet that had tilted and created the space Damita occupied.

"Boss," the Lumar said, straightening and pointing with one of his lower hands while his upper ones tossed a pallet out of the way. "Cat."

Deluge leapt forward, not missing the way the two Lumar glanced at each other and stepped back as he did so. Apparently they'd met Hunters before. Curiosity about these two raged within him, but he pushed it aside for the moment.

He had other things to worry about.

"Damita," he said softly. She opened one eye to look at him, but didn't raise her head. He could see her belly contorting as her kittens fought to be born. "I have come, with help."

"Katie," the Lyon said, his voice sounding sick. Del looked up to see the Human speaking into a personal communication device of some kind. "Get the veterinarian here, now. It's an emergency. Show him to my office."

"I did not think you would return," the Damita said. Her voice was terrifyingly weak. For the first time, worry that she might not make it crossed Del's mind. He pushed that thought aside and focused on her words.

"I said that I would. This Human is the Lyon. He will care for you."

"He will not hurt me?"

"I would eviscerate him if he did, but no. He is not that kind of Human."

Deluge hadn't noticed before, but she was very young; really just a kita. An aching sorrow tangled with the horror and rage that anyone would have dared to treat her thus…and while she carried young!

"Can the Lyon lift you out, Damita? I think he wants to take you inside, where a Healer will help your kittens be born."

Her skin rippled in a shudder. "Can you?" she asked. "Human hands…"

Del looked up and met the eyes of the larger Lumar.

"I greet you, Lumar warrior," he said quickly. "Will you please lift the Damita gently out? She fears the touch of Human hands, and I am not strong enough to move her without hurting her further."

"Hunter," the Lumar said, confirming Del's suspicions that the warrior was familiar with his race. Del desperately wanted to ask if he'd ever served with the Proud Fist mercenary company—a Lumar company he'd known a long time ago—but it really wasn't important.

The Damita let out a mewl as the big warrior leaned down. He used his top hands to brace the remaining pallets out of the way while he reached in with his bottom pair and gently, slowly, gathered the Damita's battered body into his grasp.

"Excellent," the Lyon said. He tapped out a code on his communication device and the metal door popped open again. "Ruorn, take her to my office. Jhot, the vet should be arriving any minute. Go meet him out front and bring him in through the staff entrance, it'll be quicker."

"Boss," Ruorn said, nodding once to the Lyon. Deluge took the liberty of leaping up to the Lumar's wide shoulder as he turned to carry his precious burden inside. The little Damita closed her eyes, and her belly writhed with the movements of the kittens inside her.

"Quickly and smoothly, if you can, Warrior Ruorn," Deluge said. "Her children struggle to be born."

The route to the Lyon's office was surprisingly direct. Del noticed the passageway he took was not the one through the elimination rooms. Instead, Ruorn turned just inside and opened an inner door to reveal a staircase heading down to a lower level.

"Staff workspaces and guest sleeping rooms are on this level," the Lyon said quietly, from behind Ruorn. "Though I don't know if I should be telling you that."

Deluge turned around and slowly blinked at the Human.

"I know what you are," the Lyon continued. "And I'd just as soon not have you murdering patrons willy-nilly in my bar."

"Understandable," Deluge said. "Once my current contract is fulfilled, I will be happy to avoid conducting future business on the premises."

"You're here on a contract?" the Lyon said, eyes widening.

"Of course," Del said, with a small smile. "Why else would I be in Houston?"

"Because it's a nice city," the Lyon said, his voice going gruff.

"Is it?" Deluge asked. "I hadn't noticed."

The Lyon looked as if he would say something else, but they arrived at their destination. Ruorn opened the door to a moderately sized, comfortably furnished office.

"Ruorn, you can put her on the sofa," the Lyon said, pointing as he followed the big Lumar inside. "Put that blanket down first for her comfort."

Deluge leapt down and grabbed the indicated blanket. He arranged it in a sort of circular nest-like configuration he figured would give the Damita the most comfort. When he was done, he waved Ruorn forward.

The big Lumar moved slowly, his hands gently sliding out from beneath the Damita. She let out a sigh and slowly blinked her thanks before putting her head down and closing her eyes. Her belly continued to ripple.

"Boss."

Deluge, Ruorn, and the Lyon looked up as Jhot stepped into the office. Behind him, a woman of indeterminate age entered, concern on her face, and a backpack slung over her shoulder.

"Thank you, Jhot," the Lyon said. "You must be the vet?"

"Dr. Naomi Faolain, DVM, at your service," she said, holding out one hand to shake the Lyon's. "I was told you had an emergency?"

"Yes, this kitty has been badly treated," the Lyon said. He took her hand and guided her over to the sofa, where Del sat stroking the Damita's head.

"Oh…yes she has," Dr. Faolain said softly. Del heard an edge of steely anger underneath her words. His chest rumbled in a purr of agreement that had the Human healer pausing to give him a thoughtful look before she dropped her backpack and began removing the tools of her trade.

"Does the kitty have a name?" the healer asked.

"I've called her Damita," Deluge said, speaking English. "It means young mother in my language."

"Good enough," the healer said. She bent down and looked at her patient's face. "Damita, if you can hear me, I'm going to help you, all right? Your kittens are trying to be born, and you're too weak to do it on your own. So I'm going to give you something to make you sleep, and we'll get them out. Then I'll fix up your other hurts with nanites, all right?"

The vet looked up at the Lyon with an odd expression: something between defiance and self-consciousness.

"I always talk to my patients," she said. "I swear they understand more than we give them credit for."

"She understands you," Deluge said. "Please just help her."

"Of course," Dr. Faolain said. She reached into her bag and removed a syringe, which she uncapped and gently inserted beneath the injured cat's fur. Damita let out another sigh, and her body sagged limply.

Dr. Faolain waited a moment and used her stethoscope to listen to Damita's heart before nodding.

"Good," she said. "Now, let's get these kittens out. Lyon, or whatever your name is, I'm going to need more blankets, and if you could have one of your big boys bring in a heat lamp from the kitchen, that would be great…"

* * *

T here were five of them, but only two made it through the night.

"It's the way of things when they're so young," Dr. Faolain said, her voice sad as she wrapped the tiny, still form up in tissue before putting it into a plastic bio-waste bag. "And with her being a stray, it's likely she didn't get proper nutrition during gestation…honestly, we're lucky any of the kittens survived. Especially after what mama's been through."

After surgically removing the kittens, the doctor had given the unconscious Damita several nanite treatments for the burns and abrasions she'd suffered during her captivity. Then she'd stitched the Damita up and settled in to wait for the nanites to finish and the anesthesia to wear off.

Deluge waited with her and found himself the subject of curious scrutiny.

"You're an alien, aren't you?" the doctor asked. The two of them sat alone with the sleeping Damita, as Lyon had returned to his business for the time being.

"That depends on your context, I suppose," Deluge said, slowly blinking at her from his perch on one of the Lyon's many bookshelves that towered over the couch. "But as we're on your home planet, the correct answer is probably yes."

"When you blink slowly like that…what does that mean?" she asked.

"It is akin to your smile," Del said. "Though without the aggressive overtones of showing one's teeth."

"But you do that, as well," the doctor pointed out. "I saw it earlier when you spoke."

"Well, yes. But I was raised by a Human, so I have always been a bit odd. And aggression is inherently part of my nature. I am a Hunter, you see."

"Hmm…" the doctor said, looking closely at him before turning and stroking the fur of her patient's head. "So is she."

"Indeed," Deluge said. "I was surprised when she understood me without the aid of a translator. She doesn't speak as such, but she expresses herself through her body language in a way that makes her meaning unmistakable. Elegant, really."

The doctor looked as if she wished to say more, but the Lyon chose that moment to return to his office, effectively ending their conversation.

"How is she?" he asked, concern threading through his voice.

"Her vitals have stabilized, and from what I can tell, the nanites are doing their job. We'll know more when she wakes."

"And the kittens?" he said, stepping all the way into the office and closing the door behind him.

"As we thought, the small tabby didn't make it," the doctor said. "But the two largest remain in the warmer your associates set up. I think they've both got a fighting chance."

"I swear to you, when I find out who did this—"

"Leave that to me, Lyon," Deluge said smoothly, rising up and arching his back in a stretch. "I will ensure they are never in a position to hurt anyone again."

The Lyon went very still, then pursed his lips and turned to meet Deluge's eyes.

"I should tell you, Hunter," he said slowly. "I think I know who it was. And they're…kids. Not fully grown adults. No excuse, but…"

"But they're young," Del finished for him. "I see."

"It's no excuse," Lyon said again.

"No. But it is a factor," Deluge said. "I will probably not kill them. I will, however, ensure that they never torture another being like this. Damita deserves that much."

"I suppose I can't stop you," Lyon said.

"No," Del said, slowly blinking. "I suppose you cannot."

"Just like I suppose I can't stop you from murdering my clientele," the Lyon went on, his voice getting gruffer. A thread of anger wove through the words, and Deluge leapt down from the bookshelf to approach the man.

"Probably not," Deluge said, "But as I promised before, I will not fulfil contracts in your establishment anymore. This was my first visit, and I can easily work elsewhere if you prefer."

"I very much do prefer it."

"Done, then," Deluge said. "But I have something else to say."

"Oh?" Lyon asked, edging backward toward the door.

"Relax, Lyon," Del said, smiling in the Human manner. "We have a contract, you and I. You don't shoot at me, and I don't murder you. But we never agreed on a price for helping the Damita."

"I would have done that anyway," Lyon said.

"I know," Del said. "Which is why I want to give you this."

He reached into a pouch on his harness and withdrew a flat metal disc. It gleamed in the light from the warming lamp as he flipped it through the air toward the man. Lyon reached out and caught it, then ran his thumb over the paw print stamped on one side.

"It's beautiful," he said softly. "Is this what I think it is?"

"I owe you a favor, Human Lyon," Del said. "For your compassion and quick thinking. Without you, I wouldn't have been able to save the Damita or her kits."

"She'll always have a place, here, in my bar," the Lyon said. "Damita and her babies. Cats are good for a bar, truth be told. They keep the rodents and other creepy crawlies away."

"And that is why I acknowledge my debt to you," Del said. "You're a good Human, Lyon. I would be pleased to call you friend."

The Lyon looked down at the token in his hand then over at the sleeping Damita.

"Long as you don't kill anyone else in my place, Hunter, you've got a deal. Ain't nobody too rich to turn down friends."

The doctor snorted a little, then turned her smile on Damita as the new mother stirred from her sleep and opened her eyes. She blinked twice, then began to look around.

"Your babies are well, Damita," Deluge said, stepping toward her on his back feet. "Two yet live. The other three were too small and took their last breaths in comfort and love. How do you feel?"

Damita ignored him and pushed herself slowly to her feet. Del glanced up at the doctor, but the woman didn't protest, so he held his own peace.

"Where are my kittens?" Damita asked with the line of her body and the questing of her seeking nose.

"They're here," Del said, stepping toward the warming apparatus the Lumar had rigged from a warming lamp and a pan lined with towels.

"Give them to me," Damita demanded, as was her right as a mother. Deluge dropped to all fours and leapt toward the pan, gathering the two sleeping kittens in his hands. He jumped from the pan to the end table, then onto the couch itself, where he deposited his precious burdens next to the warm bulk of their mother.

Instantly, the kittens began to squirm. Their little, open mouths reached for the sweet warmth of her milk, and their little paws kneaded desperately at her belly as they sought the nourishment they needed.

Damita let out a sigh of pure pleasure and used her paws to guide the greedy mouths home. Dr. Faolain murmured her approval as the kittens began to nurse with enthusiasm.

"I heard the man speak," Damita said then, looking up at Deluge. "He was kind when we needed him. I will stay with him, if he wants."

"I think he would like that very much, Damita," Deluge said. "I could also bring you home with me across the stars, if you wished."

"No, my kittens need to stay here," she said. "But I thank you for your help, Hunter. I would not have lived without it."

"It was my honor to serve you, Damita."

"I think I'm just about finished here," Dr. Faolain said, standing up. "Lyon, you'll want to bring all three of them to my clinic in a day or two for a follow up. They'll all need vaccinations, and I'll neuter the kittens when they're old enough."

"Thank you, Doctor," Lyon said, gripping the woman by the hand. "I can't tell you how much I appreciate it."

"Thank you for rescuing her," she said. "And please call me anytime you find a stray in distress. I know a fantastic rescue organization. I would offer to enroll Damita and her kittens, but it looks like they've found a home, here, with you."

"Yes," Lyon said. "It looks like they have. I'm thrilled to have them."

"He wants to love you," Deluge said quietly. "Can you let him?"

584 | KENNEDY & WANDREY

"He saved my kittens," Damita replied. "How can I not? Tell him, with your clever words, that he alone may touch me. I would share his scent."

"Lyon," Del said, awe at the Damita's courage in his voice. "She says...she says you, and you alone, may touch her. She is willing to trust you."

"Oh sweetling," the Lyon breathed. He took two steps and went down on one knee beside the couch where the kittens still nursed. His big, scarred hand shook as he reached out to gently stroke the top of Damita's head and scratch lightly behind her ears.

She lifted her chin, closed her eyes and pressed into his touch, letting out a satisfied "mewl."

"Yes," the Lyon said, his face splitting into a mile-wide grin. "You are quite the queen, aren't you? Welcome, Damita. Welcome home."

# # # # #

About the Editors

A bestselling Science Fiction/Fantasy author, speaker, and publisher, Chris Kennedy is a former naval aviator and elementary school principal. Chris' stories include the "Theogony" and "Codex Regius" science fiction trilogies and stories in the "Four Horsemen" military scifi series. Get his free book, "Shattered Crucible," at his website, https://chriskennedypublishing.com.

Chris is the author of the award-winning #1 bestseller, "Self-Publishing for Profit: How to Get Your Book Out of Your Head and Into the Stores." Called "fantastic" and "a great speaker," he has coached hundreds of beginning authors and budding novelists on how to self-publish their stories at a variety of conferences, conventions, and writing guild presentations, and he is publishing fifteen authors under five imprints of his Chris Kennedy Publishing small press.

Chris lives in Virginia Beach, Virginia, and is the holder of a doctorate in educational leadership and master's degrees in both business and public administration.

Located in rural Tennessee, Mark Wandrey has been creating new worlds since he was old enough to write. After penning countless short stories, he realized novels were his real calling and hasn't looked back since. A lifetime of diverse jobs, extensive travels, and living in most areas of the country have uniquely equipped him with experiences to color his stories in ways many find engaging and thought provoking.

Find out more about Mark Wandrey and get the free prequel, "Gateway to Union," at http://www.worldmaker.us/news-flash-sign-up-page/

* * * * *

Four Horsemen Titles

Cartwright's Cavaliers

Asbaran Solutions

Winged Hussars

The Golden Horde

A Fistful of Credits

Peacemaker

For a Few Credits More

The Good, the Bad, and the Merc

CASPer Alamo

Alpha Contracts

Assassin

Honor The Threat

A Fiery Sunset

The Midnight Sun

Dark Moon Arisen

Stand or Fall

Sinclair's Scorpions

Legend

Weaver

The Colchis Job

* * * * *

The following is an
Excerpt from Book One of the Revelations Cycle:

Cartwright's Cavaliers

Mark Wandrey

Available from Seventh Seal Press

eBook, Paperback, and Audio Book

Excerpt from "Cartwright's Cavaliers:"

The last two operational tanks were trapped on their chosen path. Faced with destroyed vehicles front and back, they cut sideways to the edge of the dry river bed they'd been moving along and found several large boulders to maneuver around that allowed them to present a hull-down defensive position. Their troopers rallied on that position. It was starting to look like they'd dig in when *Phoenix 1* screamed over and strafed them with dual streams of railgun rounds. A split second later, *Phoenix 2* followed on a parallel path. Jim was just cheering the air attack when he saw it. The sixth damned tank, and it was a heavy.

"I got that last tank," Jim said over the command net.

"Observe and stand by," Murdock said.

"We'll have these in hand shortly," Buddha agreed, his transmission interspersed with the thudding of his CASPer firing its magnet accelerator. "We can be there in a few minutes."

Jim examined his battlespace. The tank was massive. It had to be one of the fusion-powered beasts he'd read about. Which meant shields and energy weapons. It was heading down the same gap the APC had taken; the tank was heading toward Second Squad, and fast.

"Shit," he said. He had to stop them.

"Jim," Hargrave said, "we're in position. What are you doing?"

"Leading the charge," Jim said as he jumped out from the rock wall.

* * * * *

Find out more about Mark Wandrey and "Cartwright's Cavaliers" at: http://chriskennedypublishing.com/imprints-authors/mark-wandrey/.

* * * * *

Made in the USA
Columbia, SC
13 October 2018